The FLEDGLING

C. K. Osborne

AuthorHouse™ UK Ltd.
500 Avebury Boulevard
Central Milton Keynes, MK9 2BE
www.authorhouse.co.uk
Phone: 08001974150

1663 Liberty Drive
Bloomington, IN 47403 USA
www.authorhouse.co.uk
Phone: 0800.197.4150

This is a work of fiction. All of the characters, names, incidents, organizations, and dialogue in this novel are either the products of the author's imagination or are used fictitiously.

© 2013 C. K. Osborne. All rights reserved.

No part of this book may be reproduced, stored in a retrieval system, or transmitted by any means without the written permission of the author.

Published by AuthorHouse 09/10/2013

ISBN: 978-1-4817-9301-8 (sc)
ISBN: 978-1-4817-9302-5 (hc)
ISBN: 978-1-4817-9303-2 (e)

Any people depicted in stock imagery provided by Thinkstock are models, and such images are being used for illustrative purposes only.
Certain stock imagery © Thinkstock.

Because of the dynamic nature of the Internet, any web addresses or links contained in this book may have changed since publication and may no longer be valid.

The views expressed in this work are solely those of the author and do not necessarily reflect the views of the publisher, and the publisher hereby disclaims any responsibility for them.

*To all those friends who have helped
me to bring this book into publication.
Their support has been invaluable.*

ACKNOWLEDGMENTS

Historical research for the early Han period in China came from:

'Everyday Life in Early Imperial China' by Michael Loewe.
Text copyright Michael Loewe 1968
Originally published in Great Britain by B T Batsford Ltd.
Carousel edition published 1973 by Transworld Publishers London.

Chinese names taken from the dictionary pages of 'Chinese' a complete course for beginners (teach yourself range of books) by Elizabeth Scurfield copyright 1991 by Hodder and Stoughton Ltd. UK. Published in US by NTC Publishing Group in 1992

CONTENTS

CHAPTER 1	The Honour	1
CHAPTER 2	Governor Choi's Domain	8
CHAPTER 3	Preparations	24
CHAPTER 4	The Temple Beckons All	42
CHAPTER 5	A Night to Remember	59
CHAPTER 6	Times of Change	70
CHAPTER 7	A New Awakening	86
CHAPTER 8	Lessons in Humility	99
CHAPTER 9	The Fellowship is Formed	113
CHAPTER 10	The Ways of the World	132
CHAPTER 11	The Heart of the Matter	150
CHAPTER 12	Lost and Found	180
CHAPTER 13	Destiny	204
CHAPTER 14	Testing Times	223
CHAPTER 15	Joint Ownership	263
CHAPTER 16	Before and After	293
CHAPTER 17	Farewell to a Great Warrior	303
CHAPTER 18	The Reckoning	328
CHAPTER 19	Home	337

CHAPTER 1

The Honour

'It was morning when they came for me. In my fist I clasped the small glass bird which had been fashioned by an old man's hand. This was to be the only possession I would be allowed to take with me. I had little else of my own'

THERE WAS LITTLE ROOM FOR sentiment in such a structured and disciplined society as the one that existed in imperial China at the time of my birth. Our family consisted of my father, my mother, my three older brothers (who were, of course, as male children given a higher place of importance in the family structure), my sister, Lái, a little older than myself, and Ha Chang, my little sister, still a babe in arms. My given name was Su Ling, and my departure was viewed as a golden opportunity and an 'honour' for a child of ten years to receive. Feelings of love towards one's family had to become secondary to doing what was regarded as the best thing at the time. The stark reality of our lives was that survival was a priority.

Females were considered to be of no importance in imperial China. The chance to work in the Temple of the Heavenly Bird should have been taken up by the eldest female child. For some reason, however, my older sister, Lái, found a place nearer to my parents' hearts. Who is to say why, even in a land where a female child was as nothing, a little girl's shining nature melted the hearts of her parents? My father and mother must have been torn between giving the 'honour' to a favoured one, knowing that she would be protected in the temple buildings, or keeping my sister at home with the family in poverty while I lived in greater comfort. They were unable to let her go. My mother and father, I am sure, felt that they had no choice but to send me instead. My departure offered recompense: there was one fewer mouth to feed when I was taken away.

During my early childhood, we came under the rule of the Liu House, imperial successors to Liu Pang, who bore the title first of king and later of emperor until his death many years before my own birth. Those were times of much change, and there was continued fighting for control of the remaining provinces by factions from within other kingdoms. Within four years of my leaving home, Wang Mang established his own dynasty in AD 9. This, however, proved to be a short-lived reign of just fourteen years before the Liu House was restored once more to a position of power.

The Temple of the Heavenly Bird stood in a complex of buildings which surrounded our Regional Governor and Grand

Administrator's commandery and residence. The opportunity to work at the domain of Governor Choi Yen-Shù came because of family connections to servants of some standing who had worked there for many years. As relatives, they were able to pass on a favourable report on behalf of our family. It was decided that I should be given the opportunity to go, and of course the decision was seen as improving my chances of survival, as I would be well clothed and fed.

It was understood that if a new employee let her relatives down in some way, even as an innocent child, she would pay dearly. Such were the times. We were expected to be very grateful indeed to come within the protective walls of the temple. I, like other children of the emperor (a broad term for many), was set to work as soon as I was able. Mostly, we were very serious children, but even so, there was sometimes within us a shining, an inkling of a free spirit which emerged as a little mischief and fun.

This is my story. It was morning when they came for me. In my fist I clasped a small glass bird which had been fashioned by a wise old man's hand. This was to be the only possession I would be allowed to take with me. I had little else of my own.

My older brothers had left earlier to work in the fields without a single glance towards me. My father, Hseng Fù, bade me a quiet farewell as he prepared to follow them. Our eyes met briefly, and I thought I saw a flicker of regret in his gaze. The emotional stirrings between a parent and child were buried so deeply then that neither of us could fully understand at the time how they found a way of coming to the surface.

"There must be no foolishness to hold us back" were the words spoken by my mother, Sòngqi, the day before. This morning, however, she was silent. Holding Ha Chang in one arm, she opened the other to me in a hurried embrace and spoke a few words of comfort and encouragement: "All will be well, Su Ling." There were no words that could comfort a little girl leaving her home and her family. I waited quietly in our humble home for my escorts. I could hear the sound of a horse outside and after a while turned to watch the first person enter.

For reasons of grandeur, Li Jing, a male servant of the temple household, though not of the sacred area, entered. It seemed then that he was considerably older than me because of his height. He was dressed in a loose wrap-over tunic, which was beige with black edging, and had motifs on his trousers. He bowed and announced the entrance of the junior master of the household, Master Noih Chen. Master Noih entered into our presence with just the hint of a bowed head that befitted his position. He was taller than anyone I had seen in my own village and wore a long robe of the most striking colours; it was wine red and embroidered with green and gold dragons and birds. To my small eyes, he looked very grand indeed, yet even the sight of this grand-looking master would not compare with what I was to see later.

We bowed to our honoured guest. Daringly, I returned his gaze. As he studied me carefully, my heart fluttered in fear of the man who was to play such an important part in my life. I did not know it then, but there would come a time when Master Noih himself would become my teacher and enable me to fulfil my obligation to the temple. After I said a sad, yet discreet good-bye to my mother, Li Jing took my hand firmly and led me outside to where a canopied carriage and horse was being steadied by the driver. I sat silently behind, and slightly beneath, the seat of the master. His servant Li Jing sat beside me on the boxes, which provided makeshift seats. He watched me closely as if to observe every part of my being. I knew little about the workings of the male mind, and the little I knew was from observing my own father and brothers. Master Noih sat next to the driver, who handled the horse and carriage with great care in order not to upset his passenger, whom he evidently held in high esteem. I was told later that the drivers also acted as bodyguards to their masters.

I turned my head to try to catch a glimpse of the familiar landscape. Our village, Laopíe, was small, but it occupied a strategic place close to the fields and was not very far from the governor's commandery and the temple. Our farmers and traders took their wares there to sell at the appointed times and to gossip; news and many other stories reached our ears while we were struggling to survive. The great city of Peking stretched to the left of our village on the far horizon.

The groups of dwellings which made up the villages were often given names to signify an order or structure that formed part of the province as a whole and also for the purpose of record-keeping and administration. Our small shacks allowed families and sometimes friends to shelter together, and often those with the least shared the most. The dwellings themselves were very meagre and made from layers of wood, leaves, grasses, mud, and sometimes stone, which were all taken from the surrounding countryside.

We spun fibre for rough cloth on small handheld looms, shaped fleeces, and made use of animal hair for our clothing. Our farmers raised hemp for use in textiles and kept mulberry orchards for silk worms to spin their threads. These went into more luxurious garments for wealthier members of Chinese society who were of higher standing in the community.

I saw my sister Lái hard at work in the fields; this work formed part of her duties. At home she would weave, help my mother care for Ha Chang, and assist with the preparation of food. As I watched her, I sensed that somehow she knew I was passing by. My heart felt heavy; it would be some time before we would meet again, if we ever did. The previous night we had said very little to each other before we slept. I had shown her the small glass bird given to me by the old man from the village. Usually she would have shown much interest in such a prized possession, but she did not question that I should have been the one to receive such a gift. She smiled sadly, knowing why such a gift had been given to me and not her.

We continued on down the hill, passing fields that made up the farmer's co-operative. I watched my father speaking with another member while they examined part of the crop which had just been harvested. Our carriage passed by seemingly unnoticed as more important matters were being discussed. In the village we passed some of the other shacks; one or two women glanced up from their work, and an old lady even slightly raised her hand to me, as if to say, "Be brave, little one." Traders going about their business passed us coming from the other direction, and one or two stole discreet glances at our carriage. We travelled on until gradually the fields gave way to hilly ground with scattered dwellings here and there.

The track appeared to widen ahead of us, and I could just about see it winding its way up a gentle, sloping hill towards the largest walls I had ever seen. As the huge outer courtyard gates loomed over us, I could see soldiers high up on watchtowers on each side of the entrance studying us on our approach. I entered my new home full of fear and with a heavy heart.

CHAPTER 2

Governor Choi's Domain

NOTHING HAD PREPARED ME FOR the sights and sounds I encountered as we passed into the first courtyard. I glimpsed the hustle and bustle of the many servants and tradesmen attending to the business of selling products needed for the inhabitants of the vast complex of buildings before me. Agog with excitement and fear of the new surroundings, I was aware of the presence of men selling coloured paper windmills for children. In my innocence, I thought one might be for me, as a welcome gift to my new home. I was wrong, of course. In this 'home from home', only those of a higher status would be spoilt with such a gift. I was soon to learn that my own glass bird would be coveted by many, and it would take all my ingenuity to hide it and keep it safe. Later, it would be taken from me temporarily. After it was returned, I would pretend my innocence as to its whereabouts, so that all presumed it stolen by another child who had no wish to share.

For the moment, I watched people going in and out of the buildings around the edge of the first courtyard. I could see in the distance another set of these large and highly ornate doors. I could only imagine what was beyond them. The buildings in the courtyard seemed to be holding houses for all kinds of dried goods. On the other side of the yard, I learned later, some of the buildings were for officials whose work was to itemise all such deliveries on large scrolls of manuscript and to deal with payments. There was much bargaining and sometimes arguments from poor peasant traders who felt they had been cheated, but had no redress against such a mighty force as the soldier-guards of the commandery.

When our carriage reached the other end of this first and most interesting courtyard, we were confronted by a second doorway as ornate as the first, with colourful and decorative emblems engraved and painted around its perimeter. As we passed through, I caught sight of shapes similar to my little bird amongst the engravings there. Again, there were the watchful eyes of guards, so I lowered my eyes for fear of offending them. The new world of abundance before my eyes made me forget for a moment the pain of leaving my own home, family, and poverty. My mother had told me that all would be well, and my new home seemed to fulfil all my dreams. The other side to this perfect picture was not at that moment apparent to me: greed and cruelty, too, were a reality in my new home.

I noticed to one side of the second courtyard a smaller gateway. This, I was told, led to the temple gardens and the offices of Administrator Choi, who governed our region. Here also were the living quarters of all who were felt to be of sufficient stature to live there. These were for the family of our governor and for servants of a higher status.

There were many other rooms, some of which I would be able to explore in the future. I looked around in awe at the second courtyard where our carriage finally stopped, for I could smell the beautiful fragrance of the white-blossomed trees that were scattered here and there. Li Jing assisted Master Noih from the carriage and then instructed me to step down. There were large buildings here, too, and buildings on one side of the courtyard which appeared to house many soldiers and guards. My attention shifted to the large building before me. Master Noih explained to me that my new home would be in one of the rooms in this very large house. I was to sleep and eat there and be taken to work in the part of the building which dealt primarily with the cleaning and repairing of clothing and a variety of other materials used in Governor Choi's household. These would only be some of my tasks. Later I would get the opportunity to acquire other skills under the watchful eye of the master himself.

A tall woman, the overseer to the children of the house, came down the steps of the house to greet and study me. I couldn't see her clearly at first; she seemed so high up, though she was only standing on the lower steps. She was in a shadow. As she moved a little nearer, I looked up into her eyes, but they showed little emotion. She turned and bowed to the junior master of the household, and as she returned her gaze to me, Li Jing spoke. "The child from the family Hseng – the one we have spoken of."

Turning to me, he said, "Su Ling, this is your new mother, Madam Shu. You will honour her at all times with complete obedience. If you work hard and fulfil your duties here well, you will not incur her displeasure."

I noticed how Madam Shu's clothing was of a finer quality than my mother's plain garments, or indeed my own. The colours were quite beautiful, but her manner did not reflect their beauty. Madam beckoned to me and took me firmly by the hand, and we climbed the steps of the towering house. Its splendid roof curled upward at each corner. Before I had even reached the top, I could hear the carriage move off behind me. I did not dare turn around.

I was taken silently through a doorway into a large room where there were many children occupied with various tasks. There were women teaching different groups, and all appeared to be concentrating on their work; they hardly glanced at the new girl entering the workroom. We passed by doorways where children of all ages were working; all seemed to have their duties set out for them, and the atmosphere seemed most solemn. I was used to working outside and inside our small home, but there was no such atmosphere there, poor though we were. Here, there seemed to be an underlying sense of anxiety and fear hidden in the silence.

We passed by many more rooms, and I tried my best to keep up with Madam Shu, for she had a very firm grip on my hand. We turned into a section of the building with a long, narrow corridor which had screens forming a wall on one side and what looked like an outer wall on the other. The screens were slightly opaque and decorated with beautiful patterns and scenes of the surrounding countryside. There were patterns and pictures everywhere, it seemed. My heart lifted a little, and again I felt that

I should try to be a little braver and not quite so fearful of my new surroundings.

Madam stopped at last and pulled back a screen that became a doorway into a long, narrow room unlike the workrooms I had seen. Along each side of the room were many bedrolls similar to the bedding I had at home, which would be pulled out when it was time for us to sleep. There seemed to be nothing to distinguish one bedroll in the seemingly endless rows from the next. A tall cupboard stood at one end of the room. Madam Shu opened its doors to show me the contents, which were layers and layers of clothing and footwear. She informed me which articles of clothing I would be wearing, when I was to change them, and where to take my soiled clothes. This proved to be a room leading off from our sleeping quarters, where each day we were to perform our ablutions. On the ceiling of the room where I was to sleep, I saw that two large lanterns of red, green, and gold were situated at each end of the room. There were no windows, so that even during the daytime the room was not bright but adequately lit.

The demeanour of Madam Shu was quite unlike that of my own mother, and the strangeness of so many children living together made me feel miserable. My fears were returning, even through the abundance of colours, smells, and sounds which surrounded me. I was led back to where the other girls were hard at work, but just as we entered a gong sounded. Everyone stopped in silence and waited for instruction. Each tutor led her charges towards the room for ablutions. Madam followed with me and ordered me to have spotlessly clean hands before I was to be allowed to eat. After all the children from the workroom had completed this task, each tutor examined her children's hands and fingernails closely.

Having done this, we all returned to the large workroom and waited for a command from the overseer herself. After a moment's silence, Madam Shu gave her command loudly and clearly so that no-one could possibly miss her cue. My heart gave a leap at the unexpected noise. In perfect order, we all left the room and filed into another vast area where large containers of food stood, guarded by the kitchen staff. I was given to one of the younger-looking tutors, Tutor Chéng. I sensed somehow that she was a little more approachable. As we waited in turn to receive our meal, I slipped the small glass bird, my one and only treasure, into the folds of my tunic while I observed the other girls in my group. Some seemed oblivious to me; others were curious, and one or two looked suspicious and harsh in my eyes.

When the order was given for us to collect our food, we first assembled in a line to collect a bowl and chopsticks. We then went forward for the meal, which was a slightly larger portion than I had been used to and consisted of rice and a little minced fish. We ate in silence, cross-legged on the floor on top of coloured matting, and had to be very careful for fear of dropping any grains of rice onto the floor; our food was very precious to us, and waste would have been viewed as a crime.

I did not notice my small bird drop from my tunic as I stood up at the end of my meal. As I handed in my bowl, one of the older girls caught my attention momentarily to show me a glimpse of what she held in her hand. My little bird! To have picked up the bird without catching the tutor's eye, she must have moved swiftly. To my horror, I was several girls behind the thief who had stolen my bird. How would I get it back? I felt a steely strength grow within me. I would get it back! I would come to rely on those early stirrings of strength to get me through the early days in my new home.

We were put into small working groups by Tutor Chéng; some girls were sent to various rooms in the house, and the others, including myself, were led back to the large workroom. I was given my first task, which was to clean a beautiful pair of silk slippers a little larger than my own footwear and very different indeed. At home we would sometimes go barefoot; in other climates, our footwear would consist of a stiff leather base, to which simple strips of animal carcasses were attached to form a secure grip for the foot. However, before leaving home, I was provided with a special pair of shoes. I had never worn such shoes before; they had a wooden base like a clog, and the tops were woven strips of animal skins, which still retained some of the fur. I did not have very long to accustom myself to such strange footwear, for these were soon exchanged for simple slippers taken from the collection in the tall cupboard in the sleeping area.

The cleaning of those padded silken slippers had to be undertaken with the greatest of care. Tutor Chéng instructed me several times in the art of dabbing minute traces of cleaning substances onto soiled areas of the material. The many and varied cleaning substances were kept in colourful pots of different sizes which stood on low tables in the workroom. Before I was to be allowed to handle the precious footwear, for they belonged to a favourite servant in the governor's house, I was to practice on a small piece of silk. During this time I was still struggling to come to terms with the loss of my little bird, but I was disciplined enough to concentrate on what was required of me by my tutor. All children of that time were able to do this, for fear of what might befall them. I found that concentrating hard on my work made me very tired at first, as all was new to me; later, this work was to become second nature.

At certain periods of the day, we would often be led through vast areas of the house for the purpose of exercise and to see some of the other activities which were taking place. There were many colours to be seen on the ceilings and walls, in patterns and designs I had never encountered before. We were told that even this did not compare with the beauty of the temple and Governor Choi's private residence. I found that I was able to relax a little on these short journeys, though my mind was never far away from the thief who had stolen my treasured bird. At night I was never placed near enough to speak to her, and I sensed that my efforts to convince her to give the bird back would be futile. We were watched most carefully at all times, so I had to think of a plan for my bird's safe return.

My thoughts drifted to the relatives whose recommendation had led to my being placed in my new home. I thought that I had glimpsed one of them hard at work as we passed by one of the textile rooms on our daily excursions. Time went by, and I waited for a chance to speak to her. One day I saw my chance; more vegetable fibre was needed for the padding of a ceremonial robe. I bowed to Tutor Chéng and quietly asked if I might fetch some in a basket for her. My adversary the thief glanced up briefly and eyed me suspiciously; I ignored her. Tutor looked at me curiously and said, "You may, Su Ling, but be quick."

Walking as fast as I dared, for we would not have been allowed to run, I hurried to the textile room, where I hoped to find my cousin. I had only met her briefly, but I needed to enlist her help to find my bird. My heart sank at first, because I could not see her among the vast array of workers and materials. I headed towards the fabric used for padding of garments and was relieved to see her pass by. Chuntian turned and half-smiled at me while sorting through the piles of filling and fibre. I crept as close to her as I dared and whispered quickly to her my plight in between words relating to the material I was required to fetch. She replied in the same fashion but promised nothing except to keep her eyes and ears open to gossip concerning the younger members of the household. This brief communication was carried out at some speed, and I was soon on my way back with the basket full of vegetable fibre.

The early days were hard, and it was difficult to get close to people, especially my peers, many of whom were trying to come to terms with the enormous changes in their own lives. There were some children who appeared quite at one with their surroundings; I wondered at night-time whether their new home was preferable to those they had left behind. Many days passed after my meeting with Chuntian, and I was beginning to fear that she had forgotten me or that she had just been trying to pacify a newcomer and had no intention of helping me. These days were spent in rigorous order and routine, from the moment we were awoken in the morning to exercise in a small yard at the back of the building. The slow movements we performed were ancient and brought a certain discipline into our lives as well as being beneficial to our bodies. Often when we were exercising in the courtyard, we would hear the shouts of soldiers on the other side of the courtyard as they practised their own exercises. Theirs were similar movements to ours but much faster, transforming them into a fighting art. This exercise was compulsory for the young warriors who served their emperor, and every one would have been willing to lay their lives down for him should the occasion arise.

Everything was done to order, whether we were queuing to collect our clothing, performing our ablutions, working at our tasks, eating, or collecting extra covers for sleeping. The list was endless. I patiently waited for news of my little fledgling. I guessed it was not too far away, as my enemy had little choice but to hide it nearby; she could not escape to other forbidden areas. I studied her as I prepared for sleep, and I felt that she was fully aware of my watching eyes. She seemed oblivious to my plight and was enjoying her clever achievement, smiling at two other girls who obviously adored her.

One evening as we were preparing our bedding for the night, I saw Madame Shu in the lantern light at the top of the room, gesturing and snapping her fingers to Chuntian, who was carrying provisions for the wash room. This was most unusual; Chuntian did not normally perform this task. While my heart leapt to see her, I dared not stare as she hurried by, and I knew she would keep her own eyes lowered until she reached the room and was out of sight. Madam Shu walked along our ranks to make sure we were all lying quite still with our eyes firmly shut, ready for sleep.

There was no question that sleep would quickly claim all of us, as we worked so hard. I soon began to feel drowsy, but I was aware of Chuntian's return journey and wondered what was happening. I slept soundly and experienced dreams filled with flying birds, some of which were real and some like my glass bird. They were all circling around my home in Laopíe. I hoped it was a good sign.

The next day held a surprise for us all: there was to be a pronouncement from my former travelling companion, Master Noih Chen. Master Noih spent much of his time working from the offices in Governor Choi's residence, which were housed in the temple gardens. The order was given for all household staff to assemble in the second courtyard at midday. A proclamation from the governor and most loyal servant to Emperor Liu, grandson to Liu Pang himself, was to be read to us all.

There were whispers and excitement mixed with fear. As children, our minds were full of more fear than excitement at what was to come, especially as we gauged the reaction of Tutor Chéng, who herself looked worried. She could never quite manage the blank, hard expression which Madam Shu had. My young mind couldn't quite take in the fact that for a short while everyone in the household workrooms would be neglecting their tasks and everything would be behind schedule. How could this be, that the ordered way of living we were used to would be disrupted in this way? I later learned the simple truth: we would all have to work that much harder to make up for lost time. The workrooms, particularly where I worked, were usually quiet, but the total silence that morning as we awaited instructions to assemble in the courtyard gave even more of an air of oppression in the house. At the appointed time, we silently took our positions in line and followed our tutors out of the workroom and through the passageways to the front of the house.

When we stepped out into the courtyard, there were already many servants assembled there. We were to stand in an area next to those who worked in the textile rooms, and as I caught sight of my cousin Chuntian once again, I felt very excited. I stood very still and hoped my appearance was acceptable for what seemed through my young eyes to be such a serious and grand occasion. I swiftly tugged at the folds of my tunic and promptly froze as Madam Shu's gaze swept in the direction of our group. Ahead on an elevated platform, I could see Li Jing along with four other male servants who had been given the honour of standing at either side of Master Noih's splendid chair. It was very ornate and appeared to be covered in an embroidered fabric of red, blue, and yellow flowers on a black background. For some reason, the sight of Li Jing there brought to my mind a slimy snake with watchful eyes. After a while, there were no more sounds of scurrying movements from either side of me, and I saw Master Noih mount the platform.

Li Jing stepped forward with a large scroll, which he proceeded to unfurl and hold before the master to read out to the crowd. Master Noih momentarily paused to search the faces of the servants before him and then proceeded to read the proclamation. "We are to be honoured here, at Governor Choi Yen-Shù's commandery, by a visit from Most Illustrious Emperor Lui. This visit will be of a special nature and will coincide with the anniversary of his ascension to the position of superior authority, son of heaven, and governor of our land. His most worthy servants, the grand administrators from across the regions, are to be called before him with a view to achieving a closer and more harmonious way of working together. As a combined force, they will be able to demonstrate their ability to work together against outside warring factions across the kingdom and to teach their humble servants valuable lessons through their actions. We can only strive to emulate their actions as they forge tighter links between the regions.

We, as loyal servants, must respond by ensuring the smooth running of the complex at this time. We must be most vigilant with regard to our duties. There must be no room for error, which could dishonour our own Governor Choi and his administration. There will, of necessity, be many preparations before the arrival of our grand visitors; every effort must be made on their arrival to fulfil their every need and comfort. All of our commandery staff will be given additional duties to be carried out before, during, and after this visitation. We are most honoured to be chosen. Dismiss." Li Jing took the scroll from Master Noih's hands as he rose from his chair. He took one more searching look at the assembled crowd and then left the platform with his servants.

The crowd began to file out of the courtyard; some, like Chuntian's group, waited for their order to leave. Madam Shu and Tutor Chéng led away the first line from our workroom as each tutor in turn led their own charges back to work. There seemed to be a lot of movement around the steps to the house. Chuntian's group came very close to ours. I saw a flash of red as her tunic sleeve brushed mine, and I nearly froze as I realised that she was trying to thrust something into my hand. I felt the shape of my own glass bird once again. I had thought of a name for my little colleague, Tóngshí, and I recognised the feel of it immediately; it had no sharp edges, just gentle curves, as if it were made to be held and not just adored from afar. There was no time to express my gratitude for now, and there were other matters of importance on my mind, but I vowed never again to let anyone take my treasure, my little fledgling, away. It had come to mean so much to me because it was part of who I was. It was the only thing to identify me as different from all the other girls. I did not know if they had any treasured possessions; if they did, they kept them well hidden, and I had to find a place of safety for my own. I wondered where or how Chuntian had discovered my little Tóngshí. I would try to find out whenever I could.

I dared tell no-one of this, as I did not yet have a special friend and had only managed brief conversations with those who slept nearest to me. I had learned a lesson the hard way, and the thief from my room dared not tell others that it was missing again, especially the house mother. I kept Tóngshí with me at all times for a while, difficult though it was with all the extra work and preparation for our beloved emperor's visit.

During one morning's activities, several of us were carrying costumes along the corridor outside our workroom when Chuntian came scurrying by with materials for other rooms. At the pretence of nearly dropping some, she took the opportunity to whisper the former whereabouts of my little bird, which had been concealed by my adversary in the washroom at the end of our sleeping quarters.

Before sleep each night, I would try to think of a plan to find a hiding place nearby where my Tóngshí would be safe and easily retrievable should I wish to hold it. After examining my surroundings closely, I noticed an area on the outside wall of the house along our corridor, near the partition which slid back as an entrance and exit to our sleeping area. This part of the outside wall required some repair and restoration, as the once-bright colours were worn and fading, revealing the clay and wattle underneath. There were tall wooden beams in the walls which supported the sections in between. One of these had caught my attention, and I toyed with the idea of placing my bird inside the fragile, damaged wall. However, I was aware that if restoration work began without my knowledge, I would never be able to retrieve it. I desperately tried to think of a way to overcome my problem. Perhaps the wooden beams themselves could provide an answer. They were tall and strong and never moved. If there was a way, I would try to find it, but it could not be an obvious hiding place, and it must not be at eye level – mine or Madam Shu's!

On my daily visits to the workroom, I studied the area around the beams. They seemed well set into the floor, for the house was constructed onto platforms and built into the hill. At the end of one particular day's work of frantic preparation, I returned with my peers to the resting area feeling very drained and tired, frequently checking that I had my little bird about my person. As I was about to pass through the doorway, I glanced again at the spot on the outside wall which had need of repair. I hadn't noticed before that a little further along the corridor, the floor against the outer wall was uneven and sloped down very gradually; one would hardly notice. Suddenly my eyes became sharper, and my tiredness left me. I thought for a moment I had glimpsed a space between one of the beams and the flooring as it began to slope downwards. It was not wide enough to endanger a person as they walked there; a shoe would cover the small gap easily. This was certainly worth investigating further. I found inner strength from my discovery; thoughts were circling round and round in my head as to how I would be able to get a closer look without being seen. Eventually sleep overcame me, which was fortunate there was still much hard work to do in order not to dishonour Governor Choi.

My chance came sooner than I could have dreamt of. The next day in the workroom, I was asked to fetch an ordinary article of clothing from one of the tall cupboards in the room where we slept; the material was to be incorporated into the lining of a robe being prepared for one of the governor's children. Glancing quickly along the corridor, I crouched down close to the gap I had been studying between the beam and the floor. My fingers explored just inside, and I was able to find what appeared to be a strong ledge; this was part of the support structure for the flooring. I guessed there would be few, if any, opportunities to hide Tóngshí, so I placed it on the ledge just under the floor and prayed that it would not be seen. I hurried as fast as I dared to collect the article of clothing from the cupboard and all the way back to the workroom.

CHAPTER 3

Preparations

WEEKS OF INTENSE ACTIVITY FOLLOWED, and garments were scrutinised far more than usual. I was tutored in the preparation of materials from different types of weave. Fine taffeta, gauzes, and crepes were fashioned into festive garments. Even gold leaf was skilfully introduced into some cloth by the weavers.

Like many others who were in a perpetual state of anxiety, I was also fearful lest I should fail to retrieve my little bird for a while; but just knowing it was hidden and safe comforted me. I sometimes caught sight of my enemy giving me a curious glance; she was not sure whether to believe those who had passed on my conversation regarding the lost treasure and my continued search for it. Apart from the one thief I was aware of, I had cautiously spoken to several of my peers, though not appearing too anxious to retain their friendship. I, like many others, covered my own loneliness well; I endeavoured to build a mental wall of strength around myself so as not to appear too weak and therefore vulnerable to others' plots against me. Mostly, I believed children's cruelty arose from their own sense of fear and loneliness and from imitation of some of those who taught them.

I still hadn't been able to snatch a brief conversation with Chuntian to thank her and enquire how she had found my bird. I did not know her well, and the fact that she had taken the trouble to help me in my time of need meant much to me. Often actions spoke louder than words. I would wait for the right time, a safe time, to speak to her.

As I worked hard, my thoughts would briefly break through my concentration, first regarding the emperor and then my own father and brothers. Men seemed remote to me even within my own family, but I knew they had been a quiet support to me. This was especially true of my father, whom I looked upon with awe. Perhaps this was because I wasn't allowed to get too close to him or view him as I did my mother and sisters. I often thought of them too as I lay my head down to sleep at night, and I found the thoughts hard to endure, particularly if I dwelt on thoughts of my baby sister lying in Mother's arms.

The nights went too quickly; I was still tired on waking. Tutor Chéng had to shout to waken us these mornings leading up to the grand visit. She dare not let us lie in, for fear of displeasing Madam Shu herself. Though our tutor appeared stern, I never really felt the deep fear around her which came so easily to me at times when in the presence of our house mother.

The work was hard, but the variety of work I was now being given compensated for much. I would never have had access to such beautiful materials at home in Laopíe. I felt that it was a privilege to be given the opportunity to acquire skills in the care of such fabrics. We heard tales of the governor's private residence being turned upside down to accommodate our illustrious emperor's own needs and those of his entourage. Vast rooms leading off from the temple were to be made even more hospitable for the other governor-administrators from far-off provinces.

A moment came when I was given an order to return to the textile room to fetch some material trimmings. My heart beat faster as I approached the room; I was desperately hoping to see Chuntian. The room was a hive of frenzied activity, and I saw Li Jing lurking at the back of the room speaking rapidly and with some agitation to one poor soul already under much pressure. I dare not spend too long there, so I went straight to where the trimmings were kept. Suddenly, I felt a swift tap on my shoulder: it was Chuntian! She bent down, pretending to sort through a basket of fabric. "My bird, thank you." I whispered

"I can't stop now" she replied. You will soon see the temple."

With that, she was gone. I hastily pulled my basket away and hurried back to my workroom tutor. Soon to see the temple – what could she mean? How would I or any of my peers be granted such an honour?

When I returned, I saw Madam Shu deep in conversation with Tutor Chéng. I left my basket of trimmings and returned to my tasks. From time to time I dared to glance up at the two women deep in conversation; as I did, I saw many pairs of eyes doing the same. As I sensed the conversation was coming to a close, I quickly reverted to my task. The rest of the morning's work was carried out in silence. The gong sounded at the usual time for food and refreshment. On command we were led to the washroom to perform our bodily needs and wash our hands for inspection.

On this particular day, as we were waiting to receive our food, Madam Shu briefly appeared, nodded to Tutor Chéng, and left. Tutor Chéng then informed us that as part of the entertainment for our emperor and honoured guests, our group were to form part of the background in a theatrical tableau to be performed on the first night of the historical visit. Because there were such high hopes for the conference with the administrators, a sacred ceremony would be performed in the Temple of The Heavenly Bird on the first and last evening of the visit. This would be followed by the evening's entertainment of dance and drama in which we were to play a small part. A gasp went out from the group, half in fear in case something would go amiss and half in awe because none of us had been allowed into the temple gardens before or seen the magnificence of the temple itself.

The dramatisation was to take the form of the enactment of an ancient tale, which had been passed down from generation to generation in the form of poetry. Most Chinese children were familiar with the tale, as the grandparents of even the poorest felt it their duty to pass on what, to them, was part of an illustrious heritage, but only the fortunate could clearly identify with the story. The tale spoke of an ancient and very brave warrior, King Lao Chu, who lived under the Shang dynasty (1600–1100 BC). There were many legends from this and earlier times, and perhaps the telling of the tale became a little distorted over the years by the many who enjoyed embellishing it to their own satisfaction. We knew it as 'The Journey'.

The poet's expertise at catching the imagination of old and young alike brought a little colour into the often hard and drab lives of the lower classes. 'The Journey' referred to was taken by King Lao Chu and his entourage as the king strove to bring two warring kingdoms together for the sake of prosperity for both their peoples'. We could see how aptly the dramatisation of this fitted in with such an important visit of today; it provided a link from the past to the present. Lao Chu had sent word into a neighbouring kingdom that he wished for hostilities between the two to cease. He was prepared to go into the unsafe territory of his rival, leading a limited number of warriors and servants to show his honourable intentions, and meet his enemy at a half-way point which had been mutually agreed to.

The neighbouring kingdom was bare of certain minerals which were plentiful in King Chu's land. It was, however, abundant in forests of Lac trees, which were tapped for their juices and transformed into lacquer ware. Lao Chu felt an exchange of commodities would be beneficial to both kingdoms and its peoples.

The neighbouring kingdom was ruled over by a strong-willed individual by the name of King Tóngxian, who distrusted all, as did many warrior kings of that age. But he especially mistrusted any opponent who would so foolishly try to 'barter' for his people. He felt that this showed weakness in a leader. Why did he not just do battle in order to take what he wished? Tóngxian's father had been born inside what was now Lao Chu's territory, and he wished to conquer and rule over this to enlarge his own kingdom.

Tóngxian spoke in contemptuous tones to his men. "This man Lao Chu is weak; he may fool others into believing that he is a worthy king, but I will have none of it. Let him come; we will make plans, my generals. We will surround the meeting place with many more men than my opponent will bring with him."

Such a plan, of course, should be fool proof, so why did Tóngxian feel uneasy as he lay down that night, and before sleep overtook him? Why did one man's apparent weakness cause him such concern?

Our dramatisation explored the myths and legends of the times, in which animals took the form of spirits to be either admired and worshipped or feared greatly. It showed Tòngxian's undoing and subsequent surrender to his opponent. What could have become a prosperous union with King Lao and an opportunity to lead his people correctly, showing the way for aeons to come, led ultimately to his death as he tried, after the act of surrender, to murder his opponent, even though a treaty between the two had been signed.

As Lao Chu led only part of his army and his servants into the neighbouring kingdom, he also took along his priests and carried certain symbolic emblems which could attest to the beliefs of the time. It was rare for the chief priest to ride directly behind the king; in times of war, the generals were placed closest to him. However, for Lao this was to be a peaceful visit. Still, he was no fool; he needed extra protection from the spirits, and this is where Mr Rooster came in. In Chinese philosophy, horoscopes were constructed along serious lines and thought to be somewhat scientific in their approach. Years and even months were given individual animals to characterize each. The Rooster was tenth in order of the year; it represented the West and was associated with the month of September. Among its characteristic traits was the trait of dignity. There were, of course, some which would be viewed as negative traits, but the one the king wished to convey on this journey was the one of dignity.

His enemies would later laugh when they heard that the rooster emblem, in a pale blue silk, adorned the cloak of Lao's chief priest. Tóngxian joked with his personal general that the rooster represented one who was rarely successful when unaided. This was indeed believed to be another representation of one born under the sign of the rooster, but King Lao Chu was not unaided; he was aided by priests who were practised in interpreting the religion of the time, a religion which also embraced aspects of the occult. Lao set out on his journey with high hopes of a peaceful outcome – this is to say, an eventual peaceful outcome. He trusted that benevolent spirit guides would aid him along his path towards peace, which, because of Tóngxian's opposition, inevitably would contain dangers at some point.

As the king and his companions crossed the border between the two kingdoms, there was at first a lull in the proceedings. Some would call this the calm before the storm as the procession continued on its way unhindered. By nightfall they had travelled far and hoped they would make good time the following day and reach Tóngxian's palace by dusk. The whole entourage circled around a makeshift encampment where extra protection surrounded the king's tent. Then fires were lit all around the circle of tents, horses, and carts, which were full of provisions and gifts to bring to their unwilling host as a goodwill gesture.

Lao Chu sat that evening with his generals and most trusted warriors and servants. There was much discussion regarding the journey. Later his priests, the most prominent among them being Chief Priest Liáng, were called into the meeting in order to contact honourable spirits to advise the king.

Priest Liáng, who had formerly warned of Tóngxian's treachery, advised caution to his king. "There will be small skirmishes, but specifically, the danger will come after midday tomorrow at the resting point, after food has been taken. I see another, larger circle than ours, not encamped, but surrounding our own and waiting to destroy you! They will not wait for dusk; they do not wish you to reach any farther than that point. Tóngxian hovers in the background waiting for your capture, my king; he then plans to strike you down himself. This we know."

King Lao listened with a mixture of sadness and anger. "So, it is a trap! My enemy does not take the hand of friendship when it is offered to him, even for the sake of his people as well as my own. Plans are in place for tonight. I wish all my entourage to be protected, not just myself. We were wise to prepare our special traps in the dark; they will not be detected, but by sound and by vibration, they will tell us when our enemy approaches!" Lao picked up the pieces of minerals which lay at his feet. Some were like colours of the rainbow; others glistened like glass but were, in fact, finer crystalline pieces. These had been taken from the ground in his kingdom and cut like jewels by craftsmen. They were special because they had magical properties; when laid at strategic points around their encampment, they would warn when danger was near. The priests and the enlightened ones in the camp would instinctively hear the vibrations from the minerals, but those with treachery in their hearts would not.

Priest Liáng nodded and bowed to his king, but he knew that for the main battle something else was needed if they were to occupy the hearts and minds of Tóngxian's people, whom Lao Chu had no wish to harm. *This is where we call upon the magic of the rooster*, thought the priest. Liáng knew much thought would be given to tactics by his king and generals when they planned how to fend off the attack. However, during his own meditations with his spirit guides, Liáng was told that where there was an imbalance in manpower, something else was needed for a successful outcome. The spirit guides knew what was in the heart of King Lao Chu and that his motives were for the good of all, so they were prepared to help him.

The chief priest advised his king there and then to take part in a magical and sacred ceremony. His closest general and his political advisers were to join him, and the battle plan would be incorporated into the ceremony in which the symbol of the rooster would play its part!

Leaving the other priests and soldiers to guard the camp, the royal party adjourned to the king's tent. In an honoured position and held high was the embroidered emblem of the red rooster, surrounded by pale blue silk in an intricate design. The king, his general, and his advisers stood around the chief priest, who bowed and said, "Most Illustrious One, you have already taken the positive influence of dignity from the rooster in your plan. Here we combine the influence with its negative traits, to bring about a positive outcome and redress an imbalance. Just before midday tomorrow, we make our temporary camp before taking food; we know we will be watched, so we take advantage of this. Here we use the first negative trait attributed to the rooster, moodiness. There must appear to be discord among the ranks of your soldiers and servants. A mood of apprehension must illustrate to our watchers under cover that all are not concentrating on the journey and task ahead; rather, they must appear to *want* to return home! Lulling Tóngxian into a false sense of security is essential. As the servants proceed to fetch water from outside the encampment, they must become very talkative on the subject of returning home: that is another trait attributed to the rooster. All will play its part in giving a false impression of an army that is unprepared. However, even your servants must be trusted with short swords to hide in their garments, as Tóngxian's men are sure to attack! Your slaves and servants are very loyal to you, my king. You treat them well, and they would lay down their lives for you. Traps must be set, but they must be clever devices of such magnitude as to be able to cut the enemy army down to size as they surround us."

King Lao listened again very carefully to his chief priest. "You are a very wise man, Liáng, but with such odds stacked against us, even I can only wonder what kind of traps would have such a widespread effect on Tóngxian's army."

"This is where the rooster's trait of vanity comes in to help us," replied the priest. "You see, vanity in a king or an emperor will often filter down to those of the lower ranks, and *overconfidence,* the last trait of the rooster, serves to show us the way here. The people in our camp must be heard to be discussing King Tóngxian himself, praising him and comparing him to their own king in a favourable manner. They must be heard repeating tales of courage and strength while stressing the weaker points of their own King Lao. Tóngxian's army will need the cover of the hills, and the traps which I speak of must be prepared beforehand as there will be little time as we appear to take food before completing the rest of our journey. We are carrying many medicinal wines, some meant as gifts which you were hoping to present in a spirit of peace to your adversary. We know how potent they can be, and only small amounts can be taken with care. Your physicians have plants and herbs which, when combined with some of the wines, will cause weakness and a temporary paralysis. We need to get as many of their soldiers as we can to drink the wine; giving us the chance of victory over the rest."

"How can this be done?" Lao looked searchingly at his chief priest.

Liáng slightly bowed to his master. "We need warriors who will make up the leading party tomorrow, to play an exceedingly clever game. They must be men who are skilled in their ability to act out a part well. They need to be verbally gifted in order to mislead the enemy, who will undoubtedly confront them in order to pick them off one by one. One of your highest-ranking officers, my king, with the skill to manipulate the truth while staring his enemy in the face, should lead this group of men to add authenticity. Your men will appear to be weak and beg for their lives when approached. Then they will speak of something they have to bargain with, something which will give any army advantage over their enemies. They will promise this magical solution to them in return for their lives and permission to leave their own king and join Tóngxian's army. Of course, they will have a sample of this special wine with them to bargain with, a wine usually reserved for King Lao, his top generals, and priests because of its magical properties. This trickery, if delivered in the proper manner, will have its effect. The leading party will offer to 'liberate' some of the tincture before the rest of their army and servants make camp at midday.

"Ego and greed will play their part here, for Tóngxian's generals, I feel, may wish to keep this information to themselves for two purposes: they will want to kill us and then overthrow their king in order to seize power. If, as I guess, your search party are allowed to return, followed closely by some of Tóngxian's warriors, the wine we prepare this night must be available to moody, undisciplined soldiers, some of whom are wishing to return home. The danger for your soldiers in the search party will come at the point of the hand-over of the wine. So your men must be very clever again here, hinting at more magic presently at the disposal of King Lao, which explains why he felt so confident entering enemy territory with a smaller entourage than was wise. Much then depends on the first group of Tóngxian's soldiers and their attitude to the seeming good fortune which has been placed at their feet. Some may feel uneasy in their plan to tell no-one of the precious cargo which lies hidden in King Lao Chu's camp. Their leader warrior, who like many has had a taste of authority, will wish to rise further in the ranks, perhaps to the very top. He will be thinking that this will be his one and only chance of success. I believe this will sway him, and he will take many of those with him who are afraid. The rest he will dispose of.

"This then, will become a pattern for your own soldiers, as each group of the enemy is led into the traps and disposed of; for some must die, my king, for the highest good of all. Yet we know our earthly bodies are only part of what makes us whole, the part we shed while we are here: there is no real death, and we continue on a journey of glory. When those warriors who unwittingly give up their lives so that others may live in peace look back to their lives here, they will be proud of the part they played in this. On with our plan! Small groups are to be enticed to the edges of our encampment by our search parties to confront apparently helpless servants in search of more water. There will be no food taken by many of our own camp tomorrow, so they must eat well this night. There must just be the appearance of people eating and resting before the next part of their journey. Again, I say, so much depends on your apparently disgruntled search parties, their cunning and persuasive manner, and your servants' idle talk and ability to act the part. By these means we hope to redress a balance against the number of soldiers you will come up against. All must be done discreetly, so that the odds are not only balanced but in our favour.

"Tóngxian's own men, who are to be given the knowledge of the magical wine in the early stages of the plan, must play *their* part in fooling their own comrades, keeping them away from the places where the wines are kept. All is up to the gods, our spirit guides, and providence, my king. Your ability to instruct your generals,

Illustrious One, will be the key to success! Let us now proceed to the sacred ceremony, to call upon our spiritual ancestors and gods in whom we put our faith and trust for an honourable victory and for the highest good of the peoples of the two kingdoms."

And so it was. On that night, ceremonial chants and prayers were given up to the spirit gods, and some of the medicinal wine was treated with the special herbs. Around the camp, skirmishes broke out as small parties of the enemy soldiers attempted to steal in quietly, taking the guards by surprise. The wise ones heard the warning sounds vibrating from the crystals and were able to give advice to Lao Chu's soldier warriors as to where they would strike next. The next day, the men trusted with the task of showing how accomplished they were as actors were given their orders and informed of the overall plan. The priests, under the leadership of Liáng, went around the camp talking to people as if giving them blessings for the day's journey. They were, of course, telling everyone of the plan and advising, sometimes with great difficulty, how to pretend to be disloyal to their king. However, they were left in no doubt as to the importance of this deceit in order to protect their king and themselves. As the whole camp set off for the day, fully prepared to obey their king, the search parties left with samples of the tainted wine.

In spite of everything, Lao Chu's entourage rode through the enemy territory still with hope in their hearts for a good and positive outcome for both kingdoms. At first nothing untoward happened; this was just as Priest Liáng had predicted. However, a little while before the middle of the day, the first search party had already been confronted by Tóngxian's men in the hills. Some fast talking was called for by Lao's captain, with the full backing of his soldiers. Following orders, they begged to be listened to, hinting at a secret which could bring more wealth to their captors than they could ever imagine. The captain, knowing that their lives were in peril, spoke of their frustration at being beholden to such a weak king. Greed, as expected and spoken of by Liáng, saved the day. They were listened to, and the captain's eloquence of speech persuaded their captors that here, indeed, was a once-in-a-lifetime chance to seize power for themselves. They whispered amongst themselves that these weak fools from King Lao's army could be disposed of later when the magical wine was in their possession and more, much more, of the magical secrets would be theirs.

By this time the signal to make camp was given. Lao Chu dismounted and prepared to look as if he were tired and about to take food. The whole camp followed, but there would be no food taken that day; it was prepared, yes, for all had to appear as normal. The servants sent to collect water played their part in bemoaning their lives under King Lao and telling each other tales they had heard of Tóngxian's bravery and exploits. Hidden beneath their garments were short swords tipped with a substance similar to the mixture of herbs and wine on which so much was at stake. They were prepared to lose their lives if necessary for their king, but all their efforts were to be concentrated on survival if attacked. As the enemy listened to the lies of the water collectors, there were indeed confrontations between the two warring parties. There were those among Lao's servants who did forfeit their lives, but many of Tóngxian's men succumbed to paralysis after a brush with the treated swords.

Each search party led their enemies towards their encampment to steal the special wine, and all Tóngxian's men fell under its peculiar spell of sleep and paralysis, enabling Lao's men to tie them up and guard them as they slept. King Lao, along with the main body of his army, then prepared to confront Tóngxian and his men face to face. By now the odds were firmly in Lao Chu's favour, yet he took no pleasure in the possibility of further loss of life to anyone.

As Tóngxian led his army down from behind a low range of hills, Lao was ready for him. Tóngxian charged forward, but to his horror as he gave the order to those hidden in the surrounding hills to join in the strike, they were nowhere to be seen. As he rode towards Lao's army, he could see that he was now outnumbered. He couldn't understand how this could possibly be: how could such a weak fool outwit him? His anger knew no bounds.

Face to face, the two kings and their armies battled, and victory was eventually Lao's. The two kings survived the fighting, and Tóngxian was taken into custody. Legal representatives from both sides were called to draw up a document of surrender to King Lao and for him to rule over both lands, thus combining their resources for the benefit of both their peoples.

"You could have saved your people who have now been taken up into the spirit realm," Lao said to his enemy. "You could have kept your kingdom and befriended me to help our people to prosper. Instead, greed and warfare have brought you to this."

"But my friend," said Tóngxian slyly, "of course I see the error of my ways now. How foolish I was to underestimate you, the wisest of kings. Come; let us sign a declaration of peace. If you will graciously grant me the return of my kingdom, I promise to work together with you for the enhancement of our peoples' lives."

Lao Chu doubted the other king's words, but he felt that he could not seem ungracious. Priest Liáng gave his king a warning glance, but Lao was not looking. "If this man is willing to change and sign a treaty of peace, we can do business together. I am uneasy, but I will take a chance."

So a peace treaty was drawn up by scribes there and then. With great ceremony, each king made his mark, his sacred and binding word to uphold the points of the treaty. Lao Chu was pleased and turned towards his priest to praise him for the help he had given him. But as he turned his back on Tóngxian, like lightening his enemy produced a dagger hidden behind his belt and thrust forward towards Lao's neck. If it hadn't been for Priest Liáng's awareness of the danger, Lao Chu's life may have been lost there and then. The priest threw a quartz crystal wand so sharp in its form that it flew past his king and into Tóngxian's heart, striking him dead!

Lao Chu, full of sadness for the stupidity of mankind and the whole ethos of killing and maiming for the sake of greed, looked down with despair at the stricken man while speaking to his priest. "I see you have come to my aid again, Liáng. Perhaps I am not worthy of the title of king; my weakness nearly ruined everything."

"As I am meant to be a priest, you are meant to be a king, oh Illustrious One," Liáng replied. "Your kind of strength and your view of what humanity can become are much needed now. There are times to be ruthless, as in the formation of our plan, but that was to fight against deceit. You are right about the futility of war, but your voice is a lone one. Where you lead, others must follow."

And so it was. The tale of 'The Journey' had been told to generations of children, and now we had the honour to re-enact it for our emperor at the Temple of the Heavenly Bird. We were to form part of the backdrop of the tableau for this tale and were told to stand very still for some length of time. The disciplined life of the workroom had prepared us to some degree for this exciting opportunity. Any task which took us away from our routine for a short time was to be treasured.

As the exhausting schedule of rehearsals, fitting costumes, and day-to-day tasks began to take its toll on us, we were very relieved indeed to be told one morning that the very next day our illustrious emperor would be arriving. We were to expect the regional governors early in the morning so that all would be ready to greet Emperor Liu on his arrival.

CHAPTER 4

The Temple Beckons All

WE WERE AWAKENED ALL TOO soon by Madam Shu, who had been flitting between the tutors and their charges, checking that everyone was awake and ready for the day's events. The overall effect was to make us all even more apprehensive as we went through our morning rituals. We prepared ourselves in the new clothing we had been given to wear; this was for the sole purpose of greeting our emperor. I felt proud to be able to wear a garment so very beautiful, and so unlike the tunic I wore on a daily basis. The garment was of a delicate green and pink silk fabric, decorated with tiny flowers and birds just like my little Tóngshí. I thought longingly of him and hoped he was still safe outside in the wall, for I hadn't had the opportunity to check on him because of all the extra work I had to do.

After a brief meal, Tutor Chéng informed us once more of our itinerary for the day. We were to assemble in the courtyard with many of the servants and soldiers in order to greet our grand guests from the other regions as they arrived. Governor Choi himself would be present to greet each regional administrator on his arrival amid some ceremony and musical entertainment. Later, the governor and his guests would retire to their quarters to rest themselves so that they were fully prepared to greet Grand Emperor Liu.

Our own Father of the Household, Choi Yen-Shù, emerged from his quarters in the splendid attire of a long golden robe decorated with large red dragons. On his head he wore a tall, soft hat with a single, gold and black shiny accessory at the front and a long, black tassel at the back. We watched silently as this somewhat forbidding figure came out to greet his guests. One by one they came, each with his own entourage following on behind. They rode through each courtyard lined with a throng of people who were bowing to them as they passed. Some greeted Governor Choi as an old friend. Some were much more wary. I watched this strange display of human behaviour play out before me. The arrival of the other governors seemed to take a very long time to me and to my companions; but we dared not move or there would be trouble indeed. At last, after the final guests had retired to their quarters, we were led away to continue with our tasks until our emperor's arrival. Tutor Chéng sat us down and said, "Let us be calm for a moment. Your own tasks will be fewer today, children. You will be allowed to rest in order to do your duty in welcoming our Beloved Emperor Liu and to prepare for the roles which we will all be playing this evening for our honoured guests. All must go well. I have every faith in you."

So spoke our tutor and teacher, trying to lessen our anxiety by opening her heart to us a little. Appreciating this remark, I beamed at my tutor, only to see my little enemy, the thief, glance at me with a look of contempt. I studied her from time to time; I came to know her by her given name of Kùai and wondered why she was so sour and unpleasant.

Children in China were brought up to know their place and would rarely disobey an order or risk a 'crime' because of the consequences! What was it about me that Kùai hated so? Did my arrival mean that she transferred her acrimony from some other unfortunate child to me? I felt that her circle of friends worshipped her out of fear rather than love. Perhaps one day I would find out; in the meantime, I would need all my strength to stand up to her. Kùai must have been most perplexed at the disappearance of her stolen trophy, especially knowing that I was in her sight for most of the time!

My thoughts returned to the task in hand. Our class were called to gather around another tutor who had come to show us how to make attractive arrangements with some of the flora from the surrounding countryside. She proceeded to create the most beautiful floral displays; moving her delicate hands slowly and surely, taking us through each step until she was satisfied. Her completed creations were to be sent to the temple to form part of the décor. These were for the pleasure of guests primarily, but of course even the humble players and servants would see and enjoy the beauty which added to the splendour of the occasion. We were allowed to help with some of the basic designs, and for a short while smiles found their way through the nervousness we felt as we glanced at each other's progress.

The time eventually came for us to finish our work and stand in line, ready to be led out into the courtyard again to take our place with the many already assembled there. My eyes, and those of my companions, I'm sure, were agog at the colours, sights, and sounds which greeted us. Musicians were playing; jugglers were performing with an assortment of clubs, plates, dishes, and balls; and many brightly coloured flags displaying emblems were floating in the breeze. Members of the administration staff stood grandly in robes which illustrated their status as clerics and scribes. A straight and wide clearing had been made in the courtyard in order to greet our illustrious emperor. Rows of soldiers in ceremonial garb were mounted on horseback along either side. Their tunics and trousers were beige and red in colour, and each carried a staff decorated with a small tasselled flag in the colours of his regiment. Many people were dressed in new garments which reflected a shade of every colour I had ever seen. We stood alongside all the other children there, each in their own group, silent and still. I caught sight of my cousin Chuntian and the other servants from her workroom; they all looked splendid in matching tunics.

After a while, Master Noih Chen emerged from the inner courtyard, a place we had not yet been allowed to see. He was followed closely by Li Jing and another favoured servant, Ennin, who stood silently behind him while he addressed the crowd. "Welcome again, our governor and grand administrator, Choi Yen Shù, who honours us all with his protection from within the strong walls of the commandery." The entire retinue of the commandery bowed low as the Governor entered the second courtyard and stood before them. He was followed by servants from his private residence, which stood in the grounds of the inner courtyard, and priests from the temple who wore mystical robes of deep blue, embroidered with silver emblems. There were a group of grandly dressed children standing near to Governor Choi; I presumed them to be members of his own family. One or two looked of a similar age to me, but how different our lives were.

The other governors from the regions filed out one by one, each taking a seat adorned in coloured silks. The musicians resumed playing, the jugglers juggled, and the dancers and acrobats performed their arts spectacularly while we all waited with bated breath for the descendant of Emperor Liu Pang, grandfather of us all, who lived and reigned over his people over two hundred years before. The Emperor Liu of my own time had never visited Governor Choi's household before, but he had an important task to perform there for the sake of all his people. Such an historical meeting would only happen once in a lifetime.

The signal was given from watchtower to watchtower: the emperor, his staff, and his warriors were approaching the first courtyard. We could hear the sound of the horses' hooves as they entered through the main gates, but everyone inside would be bowed and silent in awe of their illustrious leader! With permission from Emperor Liu himself, the greeting as he entered the second courtyard was to be full of ceremonial music and entertainment. The rest of the crowd would continue to bow our heads until our illustrious guest arrived at the place where Governor Choi waited to welcome him.

We stood motionless and silent in the warm sun, and as the royal procession reached the gate of the second courtyard, on cue, musicians, dancers, and jugglers performed, flags were waved, and we bowed low in subjugation to our father, king and emperor, Liu Seng, as he entered with his entourage.

I felt my heartbeat quicken; I was so overawed at the arrival of this man whom we looked upon as a god. We could see the legs of the horses and people pass by in a seemingly endless procession until the music and welcoming sounds suddenly ceased. At this point, we were allowed to raise our heads and survey the sight before us. There could be no confusion of status as we saw our emperor mounted on horseback in a splendour which befitted him and the occasion. His clothes were of the most expensive and exquisite ice white silk that Tutor Chéng had often spoken to us of. On his head he wore the tallest and most magnificent headdress I had ever seen, or indeed been given to clean or repair. It seemed to be adorned with precious lapis lazuli, garnets, rubies, and other stones of deeper hues, which shone in the sun. These were surrounded by embroidered figures in subtler shades of soft pinks, greens, and ivory. Golden strips of the finest silks framed each side of the headdress, and were edged with golden tassels which hung down just below the rim. Similarly, his ice white silken robe was a wonder to behold. There were golden silk tie cords around the neck of the garment. The sleeves and hem were edged with what looked like small dragons in various colours; although I was in the crowd quite near to the front, I had to strain my eyes to see the detail. On the back of Emperor Liu's robe was a large circular illustration in silks of the deity which the emperor himself worshipped.

He was escorted by two of his top generals. Behind them, the exquisite Imperial carriage which had carried him for most of the long journey was pulled by four of the finest horses. Following behind came line after line of soldiers on horseback wearing the regiment's ceremonial colours and horses pulling small carriages that bore elderly and infirm administrative staff who were essential to oversee the proceedings and ensure that documents of the meeting were properly recorded. Behind these stood a very beautiful carriage bedecked in drapes of the finest materials, which were covering the windows so that those inside could travel unobserved. I learned later that this carriage contained young women from Emperor Liu's palace chosen to serve his needs. The covered windows were essential to guard them from prying eyes. The empress, I was told, would not travel on occasions when business regarding the regional governors was to be dealt with. There were many, many servants and horses pulling covered carts laden with objects we could only guess were necessary for our illustrious emperor's visit.

Governor Choi stepped forward, bowing low to his eminent guest as he welcomed him to his humble domain. *This must be the proudest moment of his life,* I thought, and for a moment I felt my head swim. Panic overtook me as I feared I would faint and disgrace him and everyone else. I found the inner strength to stay upright largely because of the strict discipline I had become accustomed to. Our emperor sat before us on a special throne that had been carried all the way from an area northwest of Ch'ang-an, where he had established his new palace. For a while, he watched a display of dancing from some of Governor Choi's most skilled dancers. I studied him a little, trying not to look too obvious. He looked quite warrior-like and strong, yet somehow I sensed that he was a fair man.

As the dancers finished, Governor Choi stepped forward to address the people assembled there. "Our Illustrious Emperor and Son of Heaven Emperor Liu Seng will honour us with his wise words."

Emperor Liu paused for a moment beneath the draped canopy which was held above his throne by four servants, each holding an ornately carved wooden pole. As the emperor stood and stepped forward to address us, they followed. This was to protect their master and his exquisite silk garments from the sun. We bowed again to our illustrious father. His eyes searched the crowd as he began his speech.

"We must all remember this time, this place, and the coming conference with awe and contentment. Awe, because of the enormity of the problems we must resolve; make no mistake of this, and do not underestimate them, my people. We have our enemies to conquer amongst the other kingdoms, but we are hindered by in-fighting amongst our own people. This has continued for too long. This visit must also be remembered with contentment by our people when we look back at what we must and will achieve in the short time we have together! It is not a time for us to weaken under our own pettiness of greed, jealousy, and an unwillingness to work together as one people. That way, we become too vulnerable, too easily taken in by our own enemies, for there are still many across the lands who wish to invade this kingdom!

"My own illustrious grandfather, founder of the Liu dynasty and your emperor, Liu Pang, was a man who achieved greatness. Coming from humble origins, he achieved his great position through his ability as a courageous warrior on the field of battle. There have been many wars, and the victor accepts the spoils of war by embracing his opponent's resources as his own. This is how great kingdoms are born and continue to grow. He may well have been a target for some of his own people, who wanted to succeed to imperial greatness, but his abilities to rule are legendary: he has shown us how great dynasties are created. I am your emperor now, and I shall not allow dissension amongst those servants of higher rank who come under my protection. I have faith that our conference will prove fruitful and illuminating, especially to those who have not heeded my words in the past!"

Turning to Governor Choi, he said, "I am most pleased with my reception and welcome here today. Please continue." With this, our emperor returned to his throne, and there was a momentary silence throughout the crowd as they stood in awe at his great words. This was followed by loud applause throughout the courtyards and voices calling out, "Hail our beloved emperor".

My own thoughts at this time were confused; part of me stood in fear of such a great man, and another part was struck by a side of the male character I had not encountered before in my young life. Our emperor was a strong man, yet a peacemaker, and adept at setting a good example to his people. I could only come to terms with this in my innocence by presuming that I was indeed, in the presence of a god!

As our magnificent guests left the courtyard to return to Governor Choi's residence, we were led silently back to the room where we slept, to change into our everyday clothes, and then on to the section where we had our meals. Looking around at my little colleagues, I saw that most of them found it difficult to take even a mouthful of food. But of course wasting food would not have been allowed, so we all dutifully cleared our bowls before being led back to the washroom for our ablutions. One girl who wasn't part of Kùai's group caught my eye. She was looking at me with fear in her eyes, as if the whole proceedings were proving too much for her. Before we were about to be led out to the Temple of the Heavenly Bird, I managed to stand near her and silently reached out to her with my eyes and heart.

We were led by Tutor Chéng through unfamiliar rooms and passageways until we reached an outer door which led directly to a walled courtyard where beautiful large stones and boulders had been placed in various positions. They led an air of calm to a garden which, though lacking in many plants included a number of small trees strategically placed to create an overall appearance of balance and beauty.

Having been told that our costumes for the tableau were waiting for us in one of the temple rooms, I was anxious to see what treasures the temple and its gardens held. Having passed through the courtyard of the stones, we could see at the end two large ornately carved doors from which precious stones gleamed from the myriad of designs illustrated on them. Two guards stepped forward as we approached, and Tutor Chéng spoke with them briefly. I stood in awe, gazing at the beauty of the doors, and wondered what lay beyond. My frightened little companion seized the opportunity as our tutor's back was to turn and mouth her name, Wèi Wèi, to me. She followed with a whisper so that I would be left in no doubt of it. There was no time to reply, as a shout went out from one of the guards to those on the other side of the doors, to let us through.

The great doors swung open, and we walked through in procession into a haze of colour and lantern lights shining brightly, as it was now dusk. A heady mixture of perfume from the flowers filled the air as we surveyed a garden full of wonder! The coloured lights from the lanterns added a mystical sense to the flowers and exotic plants, which were quite unlike the flora that surrounded the area in which we lived. I could hear little streams of running water nearby and wondered if any of these splendid species would ever be picked for decoration. Tutor Chéng paused to explain one or two horticultural facts about the garden, pointing out a plant with long, red spiky leaves that, though it looked ominous, had a special quality all of its own.

"These, children, originally came from India; that is a land not very far from our own, I'm told, but the journey would be long to reach there. They were brought to China by an envoy of our beloved emperor. One or two of the varieties of these plants from the temple garden will adorn Emperor Liu Seng's throne as he is entertained this evening. Members of the emperor's staff are, as we speak, preparing items for the conference agenda, which will be distributed among the advisers to all the governors in attendance. This means no part of the official conference will begin this evening, leaving our illustrious emperor free to relax and enjoy the drama and dance." There was an audible sigh of relief amongst us that our emperor should at least be in a pleasant frame of mind while we performed to the best of our ability before him and the other honoured guests.

We carried on through the temple gardens, passing by one or two cages occupied by tiny little birds which were trilling their messages to us as we passed. I thought the cages very pretty, but hoped the birds were free to fly around as often as they wished, for they reminded me again of Tóngshì. Though he was not a real bird, I valued him just as much as one and I still had not had the time or the opportunity to check that he was still safe. We were then led up a long flight of steps leading to more ornate doors, which were a side entrance to the temple itself. The limited view I had of the large building's grandeur surpassed all of my expectations. I glanced at Wèi Wèi. Again, she looked more frightened than I felt at the time. If anything, her face was becoming paler. I jostled a little closer to her to give her what little strength I possessed. We were now nearly to the top of the steps, and Tutor Chéng was watching us closely.

The doors were opened to us, and my initial reaction was to gulp at the spectacle of golden hues mixed with very bright colours, all of which attacked my senses. At every new sighting, I found it hard to fully take in the richness and beauty which I was totally unaccustomed to. The floor, the columns which supported the ceiling and the ceiling itself were covered in colourful pictures which told stories and motifs which took one's breath away. Wèi

Wèi swayed a little; Tutor Chéng immediately took her to the front of the line and held her hand firmly as we were led into the room for our preparations. A bowl of water was quickly brought out by a servant, who seated Wèi Wèi and proceeded to bathe her face and brow. We watched as this lady prepared a reddish potion for her to drink. Poor Wèi Wèi spluttered a little as she bravely tried to keep the medicine down, and with her own determination and my secret prayers; she managed to do so. Kùai and her followers smirked contemptuously, of course, as befitted a little thief who led others in her own ways. My own usual indifference took on more of a warrior's glare, which seemed to take her aback. For some reason, my own strength always emerged when trying to protect others.

When Wèi Wèi had fully recovered, Tutor Chéng gathered us all around her. Her voice was strict but always exuded a hint of warmth, no matter how hard she tried to conceal it. "We are to prepare now with help from Governor Choi's personal servants, who are helping here today. You all have your instructions, and I expect the highest standards from you. I want you first to bathe, as there is a large bathing area provided here which we can use. The servants will help you, and when you are dry your costumes will be brought to you, and your hair will be arranged by them." It was all we could do to stop our mouths from dropping wide open. The idea that we were to be prepared in this fashion, as Master Choi's children would have been on a daily basis, was almost too much to comprehend!

His servants led us into an adjoining room with beautiful patterned tiles on the floor. In the centre were three large bathing areas which could easily accommodated our group. The baths were sunk into the floor; and around each one stood servants carrying soft cloths for drying purposes and robes for us to wear after we had bathed and were clean enough to perform before our Beloved Emperor. We all looked slightly aghast at the steam coming from the water, but the sweet smell of perfumed lotions drifting from it was most enticing. Tutor Chéng spoke briefly to the servants who were left in charge of us, and then she went into another room to prepare herself for the tableau.

An elderly woman who seemed to be in charge clapped her hands once, and the servants immediately helped us out of our clothes and put us into the steaming baths. The temperature of the water came as a shock, and I felt it would be too hot to bear, but the servant who proceeded to scrub me seemed quite unaware of this! I could see Wèi Wèi over on the other side of the bath, shutting her eyes as if to trying to block out the experience. The longer we were immersed in the water, the more we became accustomed to the temperature, though I was secretly glad that this would not be an experience I would have to endure on a daily basis. When I felt that every inch of my skin had been scrubbed raw, we were all helped out of the baths to be thoroughly dried and dressed in the robes provided for us. Each of us had a glow to our complexions and smelt of a delicate perfume: the tortuous operation seemed to have magically revived us. I noticed with surprise that my adversary, Kùai, usually so sure of herself, was now showing signs of nervousness. It seemed strange that one who always seemed so strong and powerful was apparently more nervous than I.

We were told to line up and then led into yet another large and beautiful room, which was cooler than the last. Different servants waited to attend us here. First our hair was dried and brushed as we sat on large cushions on the floor. Then strange potions were painted onto our faces; when the process was finished, we all resembled characters quite unlike who we really were. I studied my reflection in a shiny glass which was held in front of me. My painted face appeared as a mask to hide behind as I prepared to do my duty. We were waiting patiently for our costumes to appear when the woman in charge once again called all to attention. To me, she seemed very imperious in her manner and very like our own Madam Shu.

"I am Madam Shì Hei. The performance you are about to take part in is, as you know, a dramatic play about the kings of warring territories and has a moral to the tale. Like many dramatisations of this kind which have been performed before masters of high standing, the idea was to re-enact ancient tales which originated along with ancient funereal and other sacred ceremonies. At one time these were only known amongst a certain level of society. Therefore you are highly honoured to be given this task, especially as it is before our Most Illustrious Emperor Liu, Governor Choi, and their guests.

"Before the drama begins, we are all required to be present at the opening sacred ceremony of welcome and good fortune. This will be presided over by Emperor Liu's chief priest. I will lead you to your positions on the left-hand side of the main temple hall, where you will have the opportunity to observe the ceremony. When this is over, you will be led back here to await instructions. You will be in your costumes for the ceremony, and this is perfectly in order as long as they are kept clean. You are about to see even more of the grandeur of Governor Choi's temple as I lead you through. For your own interest and education, I will inform you that the most sacred part of the Temple of The Heavenly Bird is behind the large area in which we will be performing this evening. It is hidden away and only seen by Governor Choi himself, chosen family members, his priests, honoured officials, and visiting dignitaries."

As we stood before her with eyes and, very nearly, mouths wide open, listening spell-bound, Madam Shì Hei clapped her hands once more. Our costumes were brought out and laid before us. We noticed that special care was taken by each servant as we were dressed in order that no face paint should touch the fabrics.

I, like many of my class, was to portray a child servant to King Lao Chu. His servants would have been trained from a very young age. However, there the similarity ended, for these special young servants would have spent their whole lifetime serving their king at close hand. The rest of my class were to portray servants of a lower standing whose parents were also in service to the King. I watched Wèi Wèi closely for signs of strain; she just looked blankly around but seemed awake enough to obey instructions given to her. I tried to catch her eye as we were being dressed in our costumes. Wèi Wèi and I were playing similar roles, but our costumes were of different colours. She wasn't looking my way, but I noticed her splendid robe of blue and silver, which had beautifully embroidered pockets on each side. My own was of a slightly heavier silk but just as lovely in a bright, but softer shade of orange. It had decorative panels on either side at the front of the costume in a floral design of small blue flowers and deep green leaves. This was finished off with a matching panel down the back of my robe. Wearing it made me feel important. Tutor Chéng returned to our room dressed in her costume as one of King Lao Chu's priests. She, along with others, would place the magic crystals around the king's campsite. We all gasped at how wonderful she looked; we had never seen Tutor wearing anything so grand before, and we all broke into spontaneous applause. Her hair was pulled back tightly under her cap because she was to play a man, of course, but her costume sparkled as little beads had been sewn on all around the magic symbols on her purple cloak. She surveyed us all and smiled a little. Then, checking that Wèi Wèi was not going to let us all down and deciding that she was fit to join us, she called us all to assemble by the door. There we stood, by now in a trance-like state, waiting to be led out into the main area of the temple. Wéi Wèi stood at the front, closely supervised by our magnificent-looking Tutor Chéng!

CHAPTER 5

A Night to Remember

THERE WAS A TENSION IN the air as we were led through two more large rooms where other performers and actors were completing their preparations. The overall appearance of these rooms was simpler, but very beautiful: less seemed more, as we could pick out and study the details more easily. There was more dark wood in evidence on the supporting columns and ceiling, so that the shiny colours of the pictures and motifs stood out more starkly. We saw many lacquered cupboards and boxes, exquisitely decorated in colour and design. Some of the boxes were open, and we glanced at more lotions and other mysterious potions as we passed by. Everyone looked most serious and very busy. I wondered if they, too, were overwhelmed by this special occasion.

We could hear the sound of gongs being struck before we had even reached the magnificent doors of the main hall. The doors towered over us as we approached. They were large and ornate, with a backdrop of the brightest red beneath gilded herons. There were flowers, fish, and warriors, all making a golden contrast.

Everything seemed slightly blurred to me at first, as people were marching here and there to take their places. Madam Shì met us just inside the doorway and led us over to the left-hand side of the hall. I was most fortunate to be standing on the edge of the crowd assembled there against a tall pillar, just behind Wèi Wèi and a few others at the front. We faced an elevated platform at the end of the hall where breathtaking statues of the gods sat, each on their own throne. There were three, and each had a differently coloured and styled robe. They wore headdresses which were, surprisingly, smaller than the large hats our emperor wore, but their golden foreheads were encrusted with jewels. Each carried a different object, but I could only make out one god clearly. He looked as if he carried a giant peach in his left hand and a staff made from a tree branch in the other. The statues nearly reached the ceiling of the hall. I had only learned of a few legends attached to these magnificent beings in my time working for Governor Choi, but just to gaze at them brought a lump to my throat. I tried to focus on their faces a little more; the eyes of each god were of a striking lapis blue below high, arched eyebrows, suggesting that they were indeed the all-seeing gods.

Leading up to the platform, and stretching the whole length of it, were eight steps. Beneath the gods in the centre of the platform stood what was very clearly our beloved emperor's throne. I recognised this from his arrival in the courtyard, but this time it was not covered by a canopy. Along either side, a row of ornate chairs had been placed; they were splendid enough in their own right. As we stood patiently in our positions, I allowed my eyes to wander a little further, which was difficult because I was trying not to move my head. Magnificent lanterns hung on the ceiling high above us. When I thought no-one was watching, I slightly moved my head to the centre of the hall, still looking upwards. Among the embellished paintings on the ceiling hung the largest lantern I had ever seen, casting a beautiful glow over the proceedings.

The more I looked, the more wonder I beheld. It was quite a task, for I wanted to see as much as I could. I only had a clear view of the wall on my side of the hall; I guessed all were the same. At intervals along the wall, there stood tall red and gold candle holders with their creamy candles casting a softer glow among the shadows. The markings on the floor were unlike any I had seen before either; I was curious as to what they were.

Another gong sounded, and Governor Choi appeared from behind the statues to announce the arrival of His Imperial Highness Emperor Lui, who entered the hall followed by his entire entourage.

All of us assembled in the Great Hall bowed low to honour him as he entered and took his seat. This time, his robes shone golden yellow like the sun, a colour often reserved for imperial use. The same exquisite golden threads adorning the robe he had worn earlier in the day were woven into intricate patterns here and there. In the centre of his headdress for the evening shone a huge gem of lapis lazuli, dazzling us all with its beauty.

The chief priest was seated nearest the emperor on his left, and Governor Choi sat on the other side of the imperial throne. Master Noih, our junior master of the household, came onto the platform with his counterpart, for two held the post. I was not familiar with this other master, and Madam Shu had only spoken briefly of him. Each was accompanied by four of his own servants, and all took their place behind the chairs. I could clearly see Li Jing among them with something of a superior expression, standing as he was in a place of such importance. All the visiting governors followed in turn, taking their appointed seats with their own servants standing behind them. I studied the deep blue robes of the chief priest with its strange motifs. It reminded me a little of Tutor Chéng's costume, but hers, of course, was modest against the elegance of the robes I saw before me.

All of the governors on the platform displayed a multi-coloured splendour in their choice of fine garments for this occasion. None, however, outshone the magnificence of our beloved emperor. Never had I seen so many illustrious people gathered in one place, nor would I again.

After everyone had taken their places on the platform, Governor Choi rose from his chair. "We open this memorable occasion with the first of the evening's two sacred ceremonies, followed by entertainment to welcome our beloved Emperor Liu Seng to our humble Temple of the Heavenly Bird. The second ceremony will mark the last evening of his visit and the closing of the forthcoming conference, which he will oversee."

Turning to bow to his emperor, Governor Choi continued, "We trust our beloved father will enjoy this evening's proceedings." Turning again towards the chief priest and nodding slightly, as etiquette required, he said, "I call upon your honourable servant,

Priest Mou Ling, to lead representative priests from both temples in the sacred ceremony of She (the snake)."

Priest Mou rose from his chair and stepped to the front of the platform. The priests from the emperor's palace at Chàng-an joined our own temple priests, coming down the eight steps to stand in a half circle in front of the emperor on the area of the floor covered with strange markings. All held candles and faced Priest Mou on the platform. My eyes wandered to a table which had been set before the chief priest. After studying the items which lay there, he raised both arms out wide to the level of his chin and chanted a deep sound while his eyes remained closed. We were later informed that this was a secret incantation to the gods and to the spirits of our dead ancestors. The priests on the floor below joined in with the incantation as the sound the chief priest made appeared to take on an even lower note and vibration.

I kept my eyes very firmly open, as I had not been instructed to close them, but I noticed that the elders around me had all shut their eyes in reverence. The sound reverberated around the Great Hall and, strangely, had a calming effect on me. When all was silent once more, I could just make out the chief priest's hands flowing from side to side. He held a strange ornament that smoked slightly and seemed to be emitting a heavy perfume. In a clear voice he called upon the gods to bless our temple, Governor Choi's whole complex of buildings, and its inhabitants. He made a special mention of Choi Yen Shù and his family, asking for a blessing on them all. Governor Choi had been the instrument which enabled the grand proceedings to be held there, in truth, of course, he had little choice in the matter.

Silently servants appeared, each carrying a precious crystal. The largest and most spectacular was a clear quartz crystal shaped rather like a mountain of smaller peaks leading up to a summit. It gleamed and reflected all the colours from the temple among its prisms. This one was presented to Priest Mou, and as he placed it on the table I could see its colour change to blue, refracting light from his robe. I noticed that each priest in the half circle had a special crystal placed at his feet as they stood silently, holding their candles. At this point each of the regional governors came down the steps in turn to place his ceremonial sword within the half circle of crystals. This was explained to us as a way of bringing honour and glory in fighting for our beloved emperor against enemies. The manner and position in which they were placed signified a willingness to unite and destroy any discord that might arise amongst them.

As the governors returned to their seats, a prayer was offered up by Priest Mou to ask for protection during battle for our emperor. There was a moment of silence, and then the sound of an instrument I had never heard before emitted soft music, which made the crystals dance and sing in the candlelight. It was such a rare moment for me that it brought a tear to my eyes. Priest Mou had spoken of the sacred ceremony of She, and my thoughts went back to the lessons we were given on what the snake emblem represented. Its personality was proud, determined, and wise. It was talented in many arenas, almost always successful, courageous when necessary, cool headed, and charming. At once I understood why such a fearsome creature was honoured to name such a sacred ceremony.

When all fell silent again, one of the priests, carrying a crystal with beautiful fire sparks within it, began to weave in, out, and between his colleagues in much the same fashion that a snake would move. When he had completed the half circle, he stood at the front facing Priest Mou and offered up the crystal to him with an incantation. He then climbed the steps and presented it to the chief priest, who carefully placed it beside the large quartz crystal already before him on the table. Gracefully stepping backwards, the priest of humble status bowed low to his emperor and the chief priest; he never once took his eyes off the platform before returning to his place. Once again Priest Mou Ling raised his hands high above his head, and a strange atmosphere filled the hall. Each candle suddenly dimmed, shrinking to a small flame barely perceivable to the naked eye, and then just as suddenly flickered back to life, illuminating the Great Hall as before! I held my breath and wondered what on earth could happen next. I glanced at Tutor Chéng. She was still holding on to Wèi Wèi, whose expression I couldn't see; I could only see the back of her head. Another gong sounded, and the emperor left the platform followed by Priest Mou Ling and the other dignitaries. Servants hurried to pick up the ceremonial swords from the floor to return each one to the regional governors. People began to file silently out of the hall.

I noticed that scenery was being brought in at the other end of the Great Hall, where there was another, slightly lower platform. When we reached the doorway, Madam Shì informed us that this was where the tableau would be performed; this was to be *our platform*. Perhaps it was the ceremony itself, I'm not sure, but most of the fear I had felt earlier had disappeared. It wasn't just relief I felt but a sense of calm that I had not experienced since leaving home. We were then led to another area of the temple by Madam Shi and Tutor Chéng and could hear chanting nearby. There were many priests opening and closing doors to the left of us. We finally reached a smaller hall where everyone who was to perform that evening was waiting and checking their costumes. There were dancers and jugglers there, and I could see many actors who would be performing 'The Journey' with us. Our group just stood quietly to one side of the room, taking in all the hustle and bustle before us. The actors who were to play the main characters of King Lao Chu and his enemy, Tóngxian, looked very fierce and proud, and the actor playing Chief Priest Liáng was practising looking very knowing and very cool headed.

Tutor Chéng gathered us all around her and quietly said, "The stage is nearly set for our tableau tonight; remember all you have been taught and all will be well. The jugglers have left the room, and they will perform first. When we see them return and the dancers leave to take their turn, we will assemble near the far door with the other actors. Behind that door will be a curtained area beside the platform itself. We will have a clear view of the actors performing, but the audience will not be able to see us. We have practised our entry often, and we all know our positions on the platform. We are very, very, privileged this night, and all we can do now is wait." I thought Tutor Cheng looked rather wide-eyed and a little breathless. It made me feel a little uneasy again, and I hoped that we didn't have to wait too long to be called.

Wèi Wèi by this time seemed unconcerned, which puzzled me a

little as I remembered her former state of confusion. She reminded me a little of a boy from my home village: he seemed to have had some kind of accident of which no-one would speak. He too had the same expression on his face, rarely spoke, and just obeyed instructions and commands given to him. I put this concern out of my mind and watched carefully as the jugglers began to return amid sounds of applause. The dancers, in traditional Chinese costumes, left the room silently to perform their skills for their emperor. At once, Tutor Chéng led us to the far side of the room over by the door. There were actors in front of us and actors behind us, all waiting to be called on cue. After a while the sound of the music stopped, and the familiar sound of applause was heard. The door flew open, and the dancers returned, having done their duty.

We went through to the curtained area and saw that screens had been placed at the front of the platform, to enable us to take our places partially unobserved. Through the gaps I could see musicians immediately below the platform but not much else. Then as we were all prepared, and with my heart beating faster, the screens were removed!

There were many lanterns and candles placed all around, which lit up every part of the platform. Emperor Liu and the other dignitaries were now placed in chairs just behind the musicians, not above us as before, and in semidarkness, for which I was grateful. As the re-enactment of 'The Journey' began, I found myself caught up in the wonder of the proceedings. My imagination seemed to take me away from the hall itself and into the open air, as if we really were part of the old tale travelling into King Tóngxian's territory.

All went smoothly. No-one disgraced Governor Choi Yen-Shù; much to our relief, for our fear of punishment from him was great. We finished our performance, brought the tale to its conclusion, and, stepping forward a pace, bowed before our emperor. For a moment there was total silence. Then suddenly, we were aware of a movement from Emperor Liu himself as he stood and applauded! Everyone followed, loudly clapping in appreciation of the performance; even the jugglers and the dancers standing at the side of the platform joined in! For the first time since leaving home, I felt a surge of happiness. Perhaps the relief of completing such an onerous task made me feel slightly euphoric. I didn't know if I would ever experience such a feeling again, but at that moment I felt very proud for everyone who had performed that night.

Governor Choi, in a controlled and serious manner, brought the evening's entertainment to an end by thanking Emperor Liu profusely for honouring his household in this way. At this, he led the imperial entourage away as we bowed in respect to our leader.

Madam Shì and Tutor Chéng led us back through the rooms we had entered earlier to the room where servants had prepared us for the performance. Madam Shì said nothing to us regarding this; she just clapped her hands, and servants hurried to help us out of our costumes. We bowed in respect to her, as instructed by our tutor, but I saw this purely as a duty and nothing more. I glanced around at my colleagues, who all looked tired but flushed with excitement. Kùai was showing off, as I had expected, and pretending she had felt no fear at all. My contempt for her was growing; it made me feel strong but also uneasy, in spite of the fact that she was a thief. I decided to examine my feelings towards her, for my contempt also seemed to take away my energy. I felt indifference would be a better attitude to cultivate. This might prove annoying to her, but it would be less trouble for me.

Our painted faces were cleaned with cloths dipped in sweet-smelling potions, which worked like magic in restoring our natural appearance once more. It felt a little strange to have no mask to hide any longer. Yet the performance made me feel stronger, and I made up my mind to help Wèi Wèi help herself so that she, too, would become stronger.

First, however, I had to find an opportunity to make sure that my little bird, Tóngshì, was safe. Tired and ready to return to our sleeping quarters, we were led out of the temple with all its splendour, out of the side entrance, and through the lantern-lit gardens with the little caged birds hanging here and there. The large doors decked with precious stones swung open for us, and we stepped back into the small walled courtyard with its natural stones and miniature trees. It was very dark now, and once back in our familiar surroundings, we walked through the passageways in a sleepy state until we stood before the welcome sight of our own small bedrolls. If I had dreams that night, I forgot them by the morning, for I slept very soundly.

CHAPTER 6

Times of Change

IT SEEMED ONLY A FEW fleeting moments before morning arrived. I struggled to wake up at the very moment Madam Shu shouted for everyone to put away their bedrolls and assemble in line by the washroom door. "Hurry, hurry, there is still much work to do!" her voice boomed at us. She clapped her hands sharply, and all the magic of the night before seemed a long way away. We obeyed instantly as always, but the speed with which we moved was slower than usual.

After Madame had left, Tutor Chéng pulled back the heavy screen doors to the washroom. The small outer door on the other side of the room was ajar, and we could hear the bubbling of the nearby stream as it flowed down the hillside. It was from there that the servants fetched the water each day for our ablutions. There were deep wells in various courtyards around the buildings, but the water from the stream was seen as a precious commodity. On occasions, we were led out to a safe and level part of the stream to bathe in the warm sunshine, for lower down the hillside was seen as far too dangerous and lacked the privacy of the higher ground.

The servants would collect the water in vessels which proved to be a heavy burden to carry, especially for the weakest amongst them. They would bring them back to the washrooms to fill the large molten metal troughs which were fixtures all along one wall of each room. These would then be covered with large bamboo lids until we were nearly ready to bathe. First, however, we would all go to the top of the room, where small moveable screens cordoned off an area where rows of pots were provided for us to perform our toilet each morning. When we had finished, these would be solemnly carried to the furthest trough at the top of the room and emptied there. A large metal plate on the wall outside would regularly be removed to reveal a hole which ran along a cavity into the trough itself. Our waste ran through the trough down the hillside and into the ever-flowing stream.

Along the centre of the room stood three long wooden tables on which earthenware basins were placed. When the order was given, the bamboo lids were removed, and jugs were filled with water to pour into the basins for our use. Several girls stood sharing each basin, which seemed very large to us at the time. The coldness of the water and the rough cloths we were given to remove any grime from our bodies were enough to awaken even the drowsiest amongst us. We performed our ablutions twice daily in addition to other calls of nature when absolutely necessary. This, of course, was a far cry from the hot baths of the temple rooms.

As we sat silently eating our meal that morning, my thoughts strayed to my Tóngshì and its secret place. I glanced over at Wèi Wèi, who sat nonchalantly picking at her food as if she were hardly hungry. The expression on her face from the night before of a frightened rabbit had gone, yet far from seeming relieved she appeared somewhat strange to me. She gave the impression of being almost indifferent to everything going on around her, as if she wasn't part of the surroundings. After our meal, we began to file out of the room, and I caught Wèi Wei's attention.

"Are you well, Wèi Wèi? There is still extra work to do for the guests." She blinked and nodded to me with a half-hearted gesture. I couldn't imagine Tutor Chéng or Madam Shu getting any extra work out of her that day and hoped she wouldn't get into trouble. It wasn't possible for me to take on the extra burden of her workload, as I could only just manage to cope with my own.

Once back in the workroom I was given the task of repairing the hem of Priest Mou Ling's robe. This sort of repair was nothing new to me; I seemed to have an aptitude for it and was able to pick up new skills quickly. It did not seem so remarkable to me that I had been trusted with such an important person's garment. However, some months earlier I would have been overawed at such a responsibility. I concentrated hard whilst working on the beautiful robe and was not aware of time passing. Suddenly I felt someone rush past me: it was Wèi Wèi carrying some textiles. I watched her for a moment as she went about her task in a fast, and far more regimented, manner than even I was used to. The blank expression on her face had returned. This change of mood and behaviour puzzled me: I wasn't sure what to make of it. Earlier she had seemed vulnerable to bullying from others, but there was much about her I couldn't understand. Kùai and her friends were all watching her movements closely, but the contempt usually shown was replaced by wariness as to what Wèi Wèi would do next. "Continue!" Tutor Cheng shouted, and everyone settled down again to work.

It was another long day of hard work, and at the end of the day we were set more tasks before retiring for the night. These were by nature occupations which others would normally carry out, but because the normal servants had been called to serve the guests in some special way, their tasks were carried out by others from among the various workhouses.

Four of us were given bowls of coloured powders, each of which had a different aromatic fragrance. These we poured into beautiful jars with matching ornate lids. If we hadn't been so tired by then, I'm sure we would have enjoyed this unfamiliar, but pleasant task much more. We were told that some powders were to be mixed with medicinal potions and others used for cosmetic purposes. In fact, some of these powders and potions were to play an important part in my life, but I was unaware of it at that time. My eyelids became heavier and heavier until the timely, and welcome, order to stop work came at last. Wearily we prepared for sleep, and my dreams were filled that night with Wèi Wèi spinning around in clouds of coloured powders, which finally vanished along with her into a huge jar.

The days which followed were filled with the hustle and bustle we had come to expect during Emperor Liu's visit. We were not to be allowed to attend the closing ceremony, nor did we have any knowledge of the serious matters relating to the grand meeting itself. All, however, were to be allowed to stay up to witness the firework display on the last evening from the top of the steps of our house. There was an excitement in the air on the day leading up to the display, and we felt much silent relief that our work would be a little easier to cope with. At the appointed time, and in a somewhat sleepy state, we all assembled in line with Tutor Chéng on the steps and waited expectantly. At first there was a period of silence, and I started to wonder if the display would ever start. Then a huge bang, the loudest bang imaginable, made us all jump! The most spectacular display of colour, movement, and noise I had ever witnessed in my short life began. It was as if a giant with a huge bow were shooting his arrows up higher and higher into the heavens, where they burst into brightly coloured clouds. Some were flame red, sending sparks everywhere. Others whizzed and twirled in hues of blues, yellows, purples, and greens. The accompanying noises were met by gasps and "Ooh's!" from each and every one of us. We were now fully awake, gasping and smiling at such a treat to the eye.

The following morning after ablutions, we dressed once again in the splendid clothes we had worn to greet our emperor on his arrival. I was happy to be wearing them again to bid him farewell. I looked across at Wèi Wèi, who seemed a little solemn: I thought perhaps she would be feeling a little relieved and happier, as I did. We were not supposed to waste time on idle chatter, but I went over to her as if to straighten her tunic and whispered, "What's the matter, Wèi Wèi? It will all be over with soon."

"It's nearly time," was all she would say, over and over again. I saw Tutor Chéng eyeing us and so quickly returned to my place.

We all assembled once more in the courtyard for the final farewell to our beloved emperor, waiting expectantly for his closing speech from the platform. In front of us stood the whole of his entourage, preparing to set off on their journey home to Chàng-an. One half of the attachment of Emperor Liu's army stood at the front of the procession, and the other half guarded the back. Between them stood the emperor's own imperial carriage and the smaller carriages which had brought members of his family, his priests, and his servants. The regional administrators and their servants were to be the last to leave, following their emperor's party for a way before each set off back to their own commandery.

No jugglers or dancers were to perform this day, and the mood seemed much more solemn to me. This was reflected in the emperor's speech, which was about the need to carry out in unity decisions which had been reached and spoken of at the meeting with his governors. He spoke of how much determination would be called for from his people to help to overcome the enemy. This was expected of his warriors, but everyone was included here, down to the most humble of his servants, to ensure the smooth running of every governor's household during times of war.

As he descended from the platform, all eyes were on him in his splendour, for he wore the most brilliant turquoise robes, and the large ruby set into the matching headdress shone in the sun. I thought perhaps our emperor would leave in the imperial carriage, but his horse was brought forward for him to mount; he had chosen to leave the complex in the same manner that he had arrived. This way every one of his subjects would have a better view of him. Later on in his journey, he would take to his carriage. And so, for the last time, we bade farewell to our beloved Emperor Lui Seng. The procession moved out of our sight through the large gates and beyond the walls of Governor Choi's own small kingdom.

Deep in thought, Governor Choi left the platform with his own priests and servants following behind. I wondered why all looked so serious. I hoped that their meeting had gone well, but I felt concerned.

Later in the day when we had changed back into our working clothes, I was sent once again to the textile room where my cousin Chuntian worked. As I filled my basket with materials, Chuntian whispered to me of gossip she had heard from servants who delivered to the governor's private residence. It appeared that Chief Priest Mou Ling had studied the regional governors carefully and did not believe some of the promises they had made to their emperor stating that they were willing to work together in unity against their common enemy. The emperor's old priest was never wrong in these matters, and Emperor Lui had been forced to issue a warning to all the governors before they set off home. This information I dared not repeat for fear of trouble, which is why I guessed Chuntian trusted me enough to tell me.

The following few years brought much change throughout my country. Priest Mou Ling's prophecy proved correct, and the unity promised by the governors was not to last. Territories continued to be fought over, and during my fourth year of service to Governor Choi Yen–Shu, the power moved from the Lui family to Emperor Wang Mang's dynasty. Emperor Wang did not know at the time that his rule would prove to be a short one, for his predecessor's family would be restored to power fourteen years later. I understood later that Priest Mou Ling would have foreseen this and counselled members of the Lui family to take heart and wait their chance.

I also felt that there was a somewhat unexpected little prophet amongst us in the form of Wèi Wèi because of her strange declaration, that it was 'nearly time'. I decided to keep such thoughts to myself, as she would never explain what she meant.

Soon all kinds of prophecies would reunite the land in an unexpected way: through fear, the great unifier. The animals and birds which had come to symbolise many things to us were carefully reconstructed in the art work of the temples, buildings, and dwellings of the eminent classes to favour their own particular cause. These were seen as symbols of power and magic, bringing good fortune to those who displayed them.

During such times of change, when whole dynasties could be overthrown, there were inevitably changes in and around Governor Choi's household. There seemed to be more tension than usual in the air and orders given one day to servants and soldiers alike might be altered the next. As things began to settle and the new ways began to be accomplished with ease, Governor Choi decided on a new course of action: to enlarge his own private army. More young, poor men from the surrounding countryside were recruited and trained as soldiers for his commandery. There was no choice in the matter, of course, but most of the young men felt that it was an honour to be chosen. Their families however, had to work harder to compensate for the loss of labour in their fields and workshops. My colleagues and I had never had contact with soldiers before, and there were very few male servants. The only time we had seen so many men was during Emperor Liu's visit, but that seemed a long time in the past.

During the years of change I spent quite some time with Wèi Wèi, mainly during working hours but also during the other times in which we were allowed to speak with one another. We were trusted then, because we were a little older and knew what was expected of us. Wèi Wèi was a girl of few words; she spoke only when she was most calm and relaxed. Mostly she just listened to others. Her long silences, when she would stare at people wide-eyed, were punctuated with vague sentences that appeared to relate to matters which would surface at some later date. To my surprise, she was still able to carry out instructions in the regimented fashion we had all become familiar with. I became curious at the close attention Wèi Wèi received from Tutor Chéng and Madam Shu, who appeared to listen intently to what she had to say while pretending not to hear the vague, fragmented remarks she would make. "Concentrate on your work, Wèi Wèi," was all Madame Shu would say before hurrying off. I too seemed to have an instinct for being aware of people's sometimes strange way of saying one thing and meaning another. It made me even more conscious of the atmosphere around me.

My feelings as I came into womanhood were a confusing mixture. Sometimes I would feel light-hearted for no particular reason and sometimes very sad. Tutor Chéng taught us about our bodies and the changes taking place within them. At times, my anxiety to see my little fledgling bird became unbearable, as if my whole life depended on touching it again and making sure it was safe in its hiding place. I would think up the most elaborate plans to find a reason to make my escape and go to check that Tóngshì was still there. I told no-one and trusted no-one. Kùai, the thief and my adversary, had taught me this when I first arrived. Looking back, I can see how my mood swings affected how I felt about my little gift, but I always felt that there was something deeper inside me that drove me to such lengths to keep it safe. I came to understand that it was not so much the material object as what my little bird represented to me.

My enthusiasm for my little bird wasn't for reasons of power or out of any fear of others. It represented my very survival after leaving home and was a symbol of freedom: a bird can fly higher to escape those who would try to cage and confine it. I was soon to discover that there were those watching me who would wish to transfer me from one area of confinement to another within the walls of the temple itself.

Of all the skills I had acquired during my early years in the workroom, the one that seemed the simplest, mixing the powders for medicine and cosmetics, was the most fascinating to me. I did not understand why at the time, as I had also become accomplished with my needlework, which took far more concentrated effort. From time to time, if the temple staff were otherwise engaged, the jars of powder would be brought to me, weighed, and carefully mixed together for the final stages of a process which I knew nothing of. It was on one such occasion that a familiar face entered the workroom, accompanied by Madam Shu: it was Li Jing! I hadn't seen him for some time, and I felt a little tense when he approached.

"You are to leave this for now, Su Ling; Master Noih Chen

wishes to see you in his office. Li Jing will take you there." With this, Madam left us together and me to ponder my fate!

Li Jing studied me for a moment with a blank look upon his face. He saw before him a taller Su Ling now, with a hint of steel in her eyes, and I was prepared to face his stare. "Come quickly," he ordered, trying to remain superior. I followed him at once. He led me out through the other workrooms under the gaze of many watchful eyes and into the courtyard.

Crossing the yard, we passed by the small trees and made our way towards the small gateway which led into the Temple gardens. I began to feel anxious, fearing that I had displeased Tutor Chéng or Madam Shu in some way. Li Jing shouted something out loud, and the gate swung open immediately, as if we were expected! Even before we took a step through the gateway, the sweet smell of the flowers, shrubs, and trees from the other side filled my nostrils and had a calming effect on me. *Whatever crime I have committed*, I thought, *this must be the recompense for what is to come: to walk once more among the beauty of the temple gardens.* However, catching sight of the real-life heavenly birds in their cages again made me view my recompense in a very different way.

I was led away from the front of the temple along another path towards the back of the gardens into an area where an ornate, one-story building nestled among bushes and trees full of blossom. The red and black doors were already wide open, and as we approached I could just make out in the distance the figure of Master Noih Chen seated behind a huge desk. Li Jing entered ahead of me, bowed low before his master, and then stepped aside to bring me forward into the master's presence!

"This is Su Ling, who is from the Hseng family, Master." With my heart beating faster, I also approached the desk, bowing to Master Noih with respect and very much in awe of him.

"Come closer," he said seriously, but with no aggression in his tone. He studied me silently for a while, but I dared not return his gaze. "We feel you have carried out your duties adequately and noted the level of your various skills, Su Ling. But we have to take you on farther now in respect to one specific task you have performed for us. I'm referring to the mixing of the powders, which you may have felt was a simple task, perhaps even insignificant. However, we study our workers closely and are always aware of those who have an aptitude for certain tasks. It appears to us that such workers pick up skills fairly quickly, especially if they enjoy their work, though this is not necessarily a requirement. There is a certain art in measuring and mixing even basic ingredients, I can assure you.

"You appear to be competent, and I shall be instructing you myself in the full process of potion-making as well as the application of them and their uses." I lifted my eyes then in amazement and met Master Noih's gaze. He looked splendid as always. He wore a tunic in many shades of blue and a tall hat which was black with blue silk edging and curved to fit his head. I hadn't envisaged anything such as this happening to me, and I wondered if I would upset anyone by stealing their occupation.

"Is there something wrong?" Master Noih said gravely. "You have no choice in the matter, child." I stumbled and stuttered over words relating to the task and my fear of taking another's occupation. I immediately wished I hadn't! Instead of anger,

I thought I glimpsed a spark of humour in Master Noih's expression.

"There are those," he replied, "who, once having reached a certain aptitude in their work, move upwards in status of their occupation. You understand me. They move to a higher position in Governor Choi's employment. Today your advancement comes in the manner I have stated, within the temple walls."

Li Jing stepped closer to the master's chair and bent forward slightly to listen to his instructions, which were given in a whisper. With this, we were gestured away. Li Jing gave me a sharp nudge and ordered me to follow him. He bowed again to Master Noih before leaving, and I copied him as I had always been taught. The doors closed behind us, as if by magic.

While I was busy wondering who had closed them, Li Jing's sharp voice brought my attention back to him. "Listen, we are going to return to the workroom and sleeping area. You are to fetch just one set of clothes; new clothing will be given to you tomorrow. I will speak to Madam Shu, as she has not been informed. She will not like it, but that's not my fault!" he barked.

I felt my old, steely self returning and observed him coldly. "Is there anything else?" I said.

"Yes, I am also to escort one of your colleagues; do not ask me why."

I followed him out of the garden, still trying to take in what had happened to me. Instead of a reprimand, I was to be honoured. It was the second honour bestowed upon me! I felt strangely light-headed, and as we hurried along I suddenly thought of my Tóngshí. I gasped.

Li Jing swivelled around. "What is it? Speak up!"

Feigning weakness, I whispered, "So sorry, it's just the magnitude of my new appointment."

He looked cautiously at me, as if he couldn't work out whether I was genuinely overcome. I was a little, of course, but would never betray my little bird's hiding place! I didn't know how I would be able to retrieve him in so little time. We left the temple gardens in great haste. I tried frantically to think of a way to collect Tóngshí along with my clothes. I knew that this could only be done if there was no-one in or near the sleeping area. My heart was pounding at the thought of leaving my treasure behind, for I feared that he would be discovered and stolen again. I could not let that happen; he was my gift, given in the spirit of love by the old man.

As we reached the passageway to my sleeping quarters, I was aghast to discover Madame Shu coming through the screen door. Li Jing hurried up to her and explained Master Noih's orders concerning me. She eyed me strangely and yet somehow not so coldly this time. She listened carefully to him and then sent me to fetch some clothing from the tall cupboard. Searching through the cupboard, I had the greatest difficulty concealing the tears which stung my eyes. Finding an inner strength, I managed to brush them away quickly before turning back to face Madame Shu and Li Jing in the corridor. To my amazement, Madam Shu said, "Wait here a moment, Su Ling."

I was almost frozen to the spot, not understanding what had happened. My eyes fell to the floor and to the place near the beam where my Tóngshí was hidden. I lunged forward to feel into the gap along the slope in the floor. Fumbling around desperately, I finally took hold of my precious bird! I could hear voices along the corridor and stood up quickly, still feeling shaken. I couldn't believe the gods had given me this opportunity, just in time.

To my amazement, Madam and Li Jing had Wèi Wèi held very firmly between them and were pulling her along the passageway. Of course! It then dawned on me that she too had been chosen to work in the temple, perhaps because of her strange prophecies. I was pleased and reassured that I would not be going alone. Wèi Wèi collected her clothes and then stood staring around, uncomprehending. Li Jing barked another order at us to hurry, and we left following him, this time at a more sedate pace under the watchful eyes of Madam Shu.

Just before we reached the outer door, the same door we had passed through on the night of the performance for our emperor, a screen door was pulled back from an unfamiliar room. Emerging from the doorway, Tutor Chéng stood before us. Li Jing was annoyed at this interruption to our journey, but Tutor lifted up her hand to silence him. She spoke seriously and with dignity but also with a slight tremor to her voice. Speaking quickly, so that we should not get into trouble, she said, "Always remember your lessons here; you have both worked well as my students. There are those here who will not forget you. Farewell." With that, she disappeared as quickly as she had come.

Wèi Wèi and I were both mortified and realised how much we would miss her. Li Jing, however, quickly brought us back to our senses. "Hurry, we have already stayed too long." I felt a strong urge to kick him, but we just continued on.

Soon we were outside in the small courtyard with its stone

artwork and tiny trees. I could hear Wèi Wèi catch her breath, and felt sorry for her because she still had not been told the full nature of her employment – but then, neither had I! We went back into the temple gardens and entered through the jewelled doors, still guarded as before by the soldiers with the watchful eyes. Li Jing led us along a narrow path around the side of the temple until we reached a small, plain door. Inside it was quite dark, and we found ourselves in a small space at the bottom of a flight of stairs, which Li Jing proceeded to climb two steps at a time. We did our best to keep up with him and only managed to do so as he paused in front of another small door at the top. This door seemed to be much heavier, and we watched him put his whole weight into pushing the door open. Breathlessly, we all stepped through to the other side.

CHAPTER 7
A New Awakening

WE STOOD ONCE MORE INSIDE one of the vast rooms of the Temple of the Heavenly Bird. Wèi Wèi and I exchanged glances again as we witnessed many masters and scribes moving around in small groups, whispering to one another. They all seemed to be going about their business in an orderly fashion, but I couldn't make out the nature of their work. I glanced up at Li Jing and followed his eyes as he scanned the room, searching for something or someone. Suddenly, in the distance, I could see who he was searching for: it was Master Noih himself!

Our escort poked us both sharply in the back. "Do not keep the master waiting, come on!" I had a strong urge once more to retaliate, but Wèi Wèi seemed completely accepting of this treatment.

We came before Master Noih just as he finished instructing a group of elders who had been listening intently to what he had

THE FLEDGLING

to say. He turned and fixed us with his eyes for a moment. "In this room, many discussions take place between the eminent men you see before you. They talk together of things of a political nature and of matters concerning Governor Choi-Yen-Shù's whole territory here. They confer, they bring their ideas to me; and I in turn bring their ideas, if acceptable, to the governor's attention. My work, which concerns the running of the entire household, I share with Master Fu Chàng; he is my counterpart in this role. However, I also have duties here, in the temple itself."

He moved his gaze over to Wèi Wèi. "I spoke to your colleague earlier about the process of 'moving on' in terms of a servant's employment. This only happens if a person is deemed suitable," he said seriously.

Wèi Wèi gulped but seemed to have her gaze fixed very firmly on Master Noih's long white beard, as if not daring to meet his eyes. "I myself will be moving on. I have been given the honour of a change in status by our dear governor. Master Fu Chàng is to take over some of my duties concerning the day-to-day running of the household, while I am to be given the overall charge of it." Gazing around the room, he continued, "Much more of my time will be spent in the temple, overseeing work here. I will not be in the most sacred area, you understand; that is the priest's domain. You will never be allowed to see it; very few guests are invited there. Emperor Lui's visit was an exception."

His voice lowered to a whisper at this point, as if some might see his words as a betrayal to our new imperial emperor, Wang Mang. "Li Jing, and my three other most trusted servants, I take with me in my new occupation. Amongst others, you have been chosen as my pupils. I will be your tutor, and you will work directly under me. You will also obey Li Jing, as he is instructed by me. Come." We walked off with Master Noih in front of us and Li Jing behind. I began to feel like a little caged bird myself, with no way out. Looking around at the beautiful decor of the temple, now somewhat changed under our new emperor's influence, I silenced my fearful thoughts. We walked through halls where many were occupied to ensure their smooth running. It was too much for me to fully comprehend at the time, and my senses told me that it was the same for Wèi Wèi, who was still recovering from the revelation that Master Noih was to be her new tutor!

We passed through to a large room where many women lay. All appeared to be in various stages of confinement, awaiting the birth of their babies. There was much noise from the sound of many of the new born, already expressing alarm at their arrival into a strange, new world! Wèi Wèi and I stood wide-eyed as Master Noih came to a halt here.

He took us to a corner of the room where many potions were arranged on low, lacquered tables and shelves. Amongst them were some of the coloured powders I had become familiar with in the workroom. Tall jars of little creatures, long since dead, stood at one end of a long shelf. Master Noih, noticing our curiosity, called us closer. "Here we have many lizards, small snakes, scorpions, and parts of other creatures we use in our medicines."

He watched our faces closely. I tried to keep a blank, but interested expression on my face while studying the jars. "Many of the coloured powders, Su Ling, came from dried herbs, plants, and flowers from the surrounding hillside. Many of these ingredients are also used for artwork, of course, but when combined in a certain way; they are also used by the priests. However, all that must be left until later. Some of the potions are of great benefit to the women patients you see before you as they give birth."

Listening to the sounds which some of the women were making, I was not sure if they were beneficial at all. I kept such thoughts to myself. "This is where you will begin your studies, Su Ling; this will occupy some of your time. Wèi Wèi will be occupied elsewhere, but will join you when you both come before me to learn the special skills which I will take you through step by step."

Master Noih paused as if in deep thought. Then, a little more gravely, he said, "In time, as you both become adept in your new skills, there will be much work for you both. Working in the Temple of the Heavenly Bird is both an honour and a privilege; do not let me down, either of you! Li Jing will take you to your living quarters now, and I will see you both this evening for a short introduction to the kind of work you will be doing." With this we were ushered out of the birthing room by Li Jing.

He led us through another large room, and yet another, until we finally came to the large wooden doors of our living quarters. We noted with relief a beautiful plaque of a turquoise bird on the wall next to the doors, which would help us to find our way home in the early days. The fear was always that we would get lost and displease someone! Li Jing rapped on the doors to announce our arrival and ushered us in. So this was to be our new home. It was quite unlike our old, dimly lit living room with its sparse furnishings. The wonderful decor of the Temple seemed to extend to every room, including this one. On first glance the rows of bedrolls seemed to be absent, until Li Jing pointed to small screens around the magnificent room. He pulled one aside to reveal neatly stacked bedrolls hidden away until they were needed. Our own allocated bedrolls were behind the screen nearest the door, and we noted that small embroidered patches identified the temporary ownership of each one.

I wanted to reach out and touch the material; I recognised a superior fabric when I saw it. I started to move my hand towards them, but Li Jing pulled it away. "There is no time now! This is to all intents and purposes the sleeping area. However, the cushions and rugs around the floor are for social purposes; servants are sometimes allowed to study together and share their knowledge. This will not occur very often, as there is much work to do for Master Noih."

He had his superior voice on again, so I tried to remain interested but indifferent. I would not show undue deference to someone I did not respect, but my expression never showed as much. Wèi Wèi was paying particular attention to the room as a whole, as if listening for something. I had come to understand a little of how things can be mentally 'picked up' from a room, even if it was empty. This was especially true of very old buildings.

We were shown slightly smaller rooms off of the main area; though smaller, they were still large enough to my eyes. The ablutions room was of similar style to our last one, but the large bowls for washing were, again, of a superior material to those we had been accustomed to. On one side of the room stood a collection of large tubs which had been provided for deeper bathing. They reminded me of the hot sunken baths in one of the other vast rooms of the temple; I hoped that these would be a little more comfortable! A girl not much older than us came to take over from Li Jing, much to my satisfaction. She was slightly reserved in her manner; I sensed no obvious animosity and not hint of a warmer welcome, either. She was very beautiful, and I felt sure that she would be taken as a bride soon or become a special servant to Governor Choi himself.

"I am Meirén; I also live in this area. There are always procedures, as you know, which everyone will follow. There is a strict protocol to abide by here; always the oldest comes first. It is a matter of priority. This means that although you take your orders outside the main room from Master Noih and Li Jing, inside is quite different. You have freedom of movement, such as it is, within your daily schedule, but you will also give deference to the older girls, as befits their position here. So there are rules to follow concerning this, and you will both need to be very aware of the way things are done in order to fit in here.

"There are three older girls who have served here in the Temple the longest; they all arrived together and are very close, so all are to be treated equally with respect. They are Niang, Héshi, and Ci, and they occupy a particular place in the living room area. At night-time, they retire to the far end of the room in the centre, in front of the most ornate wall panelling. No-one *ever* approaches them in their area during the evening unless invited to do so. During social and study periods they occupy the very centre of the room. They sit on their own special cushions with their backs to their sleeping area, facing the doors. No-one *ever* takes their place! If called, you bow to them courteously with a small nod of the head and *listen*. It would never do to cross them, for they can make your life very hard here."

Wèi Wèi and I looked at each other but again said nothing. Meirén paused to let this information sink very firmly into our minds before continuing. "You will, of course, respect the rest of your colleagues, including myself." We both nodded. "In the first few months in your new home, you will always ask permission, even to leave the room. This, of course, is usually frowned on, as there are adequate times for ablutions and such. If Li Jing comes to collect you, there is no need to ask permission; you will simply leave at once. The longer you are here, the more you can assume that permission will be automatically given without asking. You will be told when this is true so that this is perfectly clear to all concerned. As the older girls leave to take up new positions and new girls arrive, your own status will alter accordingly. This, then, is the way."

Meirén proceeded to give us a long list of do's and don'ts in matters of protocol for our new living quarters. My head began to swim, and I felt that I was a ten-year-old again. Feelings of panic swept over me; it was not unlike my first meeting with Madame Shu! Wèi Wèi looked nervous but didn't appear to be about to faint, as she would have done several years earlier.

Although the old anxiety had returned to me, I was much stronger now and able to conceal my innermost feelings. I could hold a gaze without as much as a flinch. I was to discover later, however, that one man could always see through this mask: Master Noih Chen!

"We shall eat now," Meirén instructed. "We take our food in one of the halls with the other servants, this way." Meirén led us back along one familiar corridor, and I counted five other girls walking ahead of us who seemed to have come from our own room. We followed silently until our procession came to a halt. Meirén left us and went to the three girls at the front to inform them that we had arrived. I turned to Wèi Wèi, who was leaning to one side, trying to study them intently. She straightened up, turned back to me, and put a hand to her lips as if to say, "Say nothing."

Our new colleague returned, and we began to walk on. We soon found ourselves in a large hall where many were already eating. I saw line after line of people. Some were seated on matting, having their meals, while others seemed to have low tables placed before them. The tables stretched the whole length of the hall. There were various bowls placed on them, from which the more fortunate, and worthy servants of Governor Choi could pick. I could see why people would always be anxious to rise in rank according to their occupation: there were always more privileges to enjoy! I was also aware that there was a price to be paid for those privileges. While holding that thought, I became aware of three pairs of eyes watching me. I took my bowl of rice and fish and, passing Niang, Héshi, and Ci, sat where I had been told to, next to Wèi Wèi.

We were later to learn from Meirén that the three most important girls from our room did everything together. Meirén seemed under the impression that this was because they were such close friends; my awareness of them was a little different. I'd observed from my days in the workroom that it was often those servants who were fearful deep down who would stick closely together, as it was harder for them to function alone. This may not have been apparent to some observers, but of course there were many in the temple whose awareness and perception went beyond what was on the surface: a carefully constructed mask. Because of this, I vowed to treat them with respect. During whispered conversations with Wèi Wèi, we spoke of how such people can turn nasty, if and when the mask begins to slip! However, on this first day, which was rapidly turning to dusk, we returned our bowls and, after a nod of permission from Niang, followed our colleagues out along the passageway and back to our room, with its plaque of the turquoise bird on the wall outside.

We kept our heads down and averted our eyes from the gaze of all the other girls in the room while we waited to be collected and taken to Master Noih. After a short time which seemed like an age, a knock came at the door, and Meirén brought Li Jing to see us. Before he could bark an order at us, we immediately stood and stared straight at him with what we hoped would be a neutral look. We could feel his irritation as he led us along the passageway and through new areas as yet unexplored. We turned a corner and found ourselves in a very small area indeed: there were just two doors here, one on each side of opposite walls. Something told me that the two small doors hid much more than a casual observer might think! Li Jing rapped on the plain door to our left, ushered us in, and left, closing the door behind him.

Master Noih stood silently with his back to us in a robe of scarlet red with an open eye in its centre. The motif was quite large and embroidered in gold silk with a lapis iris. It was most striking, as if the master's own eyes could follow us everywhere. I felt a tinge of fear, yet the feeling was combined with something else: a kind of knowing which was not quite so fearful. I sensed that the eye represented something important, and I was later to discover just how right I was.

After a moment, he turned around to look at us, smiling quite warmly. We were both quite taken back by this; it was a new side of the master. I had been a little fearful of him since the moment he had entered my home in Laopíe, but this did not compare with the heart-stopping fear I had felt for Madame Shu and when observing Governor Choi for the first time.

"You may look around and take note of everything you see," he said quietly. Without a moment's hesitation, Wèi Wèi and I slowly walked to opposite ends of the room to survey all before us. By allowing us a moment to ourselves, Master Noih Chen was able to watch and observe us closely. We were not really aware of this, as our minds were full of interest at the beautiful and unusual things we could see. On my end of the room were intricately woven rugs of vivid colours and design. These were not unlike the strange motifs I had seen on Priest Mou Ling's robe during the opening ceremony of Emperor Liu's visit.

My thoughts drifted. *These must be of some importance too; I wonder what their significance can be. I feel a link to Priest Mou Ling here – or perhaps the magic he performs.* My eyes skimmed over the large embroidered silk cushion on one of the rugs and a few smaller ones scattered here and there. Suddenly, my attention was caught by a sparkle of light. On an ornate plinth a little taller than me stood a large ball made of crystal. It was large enough,

I guessed, to fit into both palms of the master's hands. My mind wandered back to the opening ceremony again and the ceremony of She with its sparkling crystals. My thoughts returned to the present as I stood transfixed in front of this wonderful clear ball. I observed swirls within it, and beyond them I seemed to detect the movement of hazy figures. "Carry on," Master Noih said again quietly. I reluctantly pried my eyes away. Against the wall stood rows of shelves full of manuscripts, some of which looked very old indeed. Along the bottom shelves stood many ornate jars. There were so many treasures to be seen. A tall cupboard stood there which, when opened, appeared to be completely empty. Master chuckled softly behind me.

Walking on, I found myself near the centre of the room, where Wèi Wèi stood studying the master's large desk. It was even larger and more ornate than the one I had seen at his house in the grounds of the temple. I caught Wèi Wèi's eye, and we allowed ourselves a small smile of satisfaction. We didn't need to speak; we knew we had come home. Momentarily we forgot that there would always be difficulties to overcome, no matter how splendid our new surroundings.

We continued to study the desk together. There were little ornate lacquered boxes placed here and there, but our senses told us not to open them and pry. "Good," came the observation from behind. A long scroll of manuscript lay in the centre; it must be of some great importance, I imagined: I would have been disappointed to learn that it was only on general matters relating to housekeeping! Wèi Wèi sniffed at a little pot of sweet-smelling herbs. I recognised the blend in the aroma and felt sure we had picked some of those herbs from the hillside. I pointed to a long, narrow tray which held the very fine brushes needed for calligraphy. I ran my finger along one of the brushes, itching to pick it up, but would not dare to, of course. Nearby was a little statuette of one of the gods; it was the one who carried a giant peach in one hand and a staff in the other.

"Lao Zi" came from the master's voice in the background to explain its meaning. "He holds the Peach of Immortality in his hand. His work is the 'Tao Te Ching', which means 'Classic of the Way and Power of Virtue and Nature.' We will be studying this together in the future. Some scholars disagree with his philosophy, but all who study Tao Te Ching come to recognise some of its truths."

We both nodded silently to Master Noih and proceeded to explore the rest of the room. I crossed over to where Wèi Wèi had already been and noticed a tall screen made up of four sections. Each section had two hinges, one near the top and the other near the bottom, which joined together with the next section, making it possible to bend the whole screen into various angles. It was very beautiful, and full of the flowers and birds I had come to recognise. As I looked a little more closely, I could see ladies depicted on the two inside sections who were pouring something into a little pond. The pond had a small bridge across it, and as they poured, clouds of coloured steam rose up over the bridge. I could see several miniature figures there. One figure looked like a great warrior; there was another, a priest who appeared to be waving his hand towards the ladies and had his mouth open as if he were speaking to them. The third looked to be a very poor and humble fisherman who was holding out his fish to offer to the ladies. I dared not question the Master but looked at him hopefully, desiring an explanation of the illustration.

"Later, all in good time," was all he would say. So I carried on around the other end of the room, looking at large vases here and there, until I came across a very large black lacquered box with a red dragon painted on the lid. I did not even bother to look towards the Master; my instinct told me this was not for me to open.

"You are wise, child; some things are better kept locked away until such time as they are needed. Hurry now, both of you; you must retire to your room!" I turned, preparing to leave, and just had time to notice something small in the top corner of the room. I wasn't completely sure what it was; I just knew it was long and narrow in shape and made of bronze, and it stood on a low contraption which appeared to be made for it. We bowed to Master Noih and were ushered out to find Li Jing waiting on the other side of the door.

CHAPTER 8

Lessons in Humility

ONCE WE WERE BACK IN our room, Li Jing called Meirén to take charge and left. It was late by this time. "Collect your bedrolls and wait," she said, motioning towards the screen. We pulled it aside and picked out our own bedding. We watched and waited as Meirén collected her own bedroll and lay it down nearby. We were shown an area just along the wall from her bedroll: this was to be our own sleeping space. As I was preparing my own bedding, I was concentrating hard on what Meirén had told us regarding matters of protocol of the washroom. It seemed like an age that we stood by our bedding waiting for something to happen. Nobody seemed to move until Niang rose to leave, followed by Héshi and Ci. They walked in procession to the washroom with the rest of us following silently behind them. We were, of course, the last to go in.

I noticed that our three superiors had each taken a tub to bathe in; the tubs had already been prepared by some of the other girls in the room. A delicate aroma from the perfumed oils in the water wafted around the room. Wèi Wèi closed her eyes and breathed deeply to take in the fragrance. This was a treat for us all, but for now we were resigned to using the bowls provided for our own ablutions. By the end of the evening we had understood much, if not all, of the new routine and what was expected of us. We also knew we would be expected to learn the rest very quickly. Standing again by our bedrolls as we had done so many times for Tutor Chéng and Madame Shu, we waited as the three at the top of the room prepared for sleep. Only after everyone followed suit did we lie down to sleep.

We were awakened by the sound of tinkling bells ringing throughout the temple. It was still quite dark, and for a moment I was confused as to where I was. Then the memory of the previous day's events came flooding back to me. Wèi Wèi whispered in my ear, "What will today bring, I wonder?"

"More to learn and remember" I replied, with a sinking feeling. I was not sure I would be able to remember everything. We all proceeded to go through a similar ritual to that of the previous evening before walking along the passageway to our first meal of the day.

Throughout all this time I had managed to conceal Tóngshì in my clothing or bedding. This sometimes proved difficult, especially when bathing. I still needed a safer place to keep it. I could never trust others to guard it, for I looked upon my fledgling bird almost as if it were real and my responsibility. It had come to symbolise all that I held precious. Although I instinctively felt that Wèi Wèi knew about my treasure, nothing was ever mentioned between us: some things were silently understood without the need for words.

After we had eaten, I saw Li Jing approaching from across the hall. He was stopped by Niang, who gestured to him humbly and bowed slightly, for in matters of status she was still below him. She spoke in whispers to him while glancing sideways at us and questioning him; I guessed this was regarding us. Wèi Wèi felt the same. "The one who wishes to know all things," Wèi Wèi said softly while she pretended to look the other way, "even things which do not concern her!"

"We must play a very careful game here," I said. I kept an unconcerned expression on my face as I said this, but my thoughts were already racing.

Li Jing left Niang and signalled for us to follow him; at such times we did not have to wait for the haughty Niang to leave first. He led us back to the birthing area, once again with its significant sounds from the mothers and babes. One of the servants approached us and, after hearing instructions from Li Jing, looked me up and down in a noncommittal way. Turning back to me, Li Jing said, "You will work here for the first part of the day, Su Ling. This person will instruct you, and I will fetch you later." With this he hurried Wèi Wèi off to another part of the temple.

I was led past women sweating heavily in their labour; some looked hardly older than me. We came to the shelves of plants and small creatures which had caught my eye the day before. "There are potions to be prepared here; you must pay attention! When the physicians and the old birthing mothers come, they will expect you to have the necessary potions already prepared, and you will be required to fetch them quickly and quietly. None will have time to wait for you." The old servant spoke to me severely. "Some births are quick, and they will require nothing from us. Others take longer and are more difficult; this is when we will be needed. There are potions to be mixed which, when taken by mouth, dull the birth pains to hurry things along, but the correct proportions of ingredients are vital. Too much, and the women will fall into a stupor and be unable to push their babies forward. They can also become poisonous to both mother and babe; we try not to lose them. I remember one who made that mistake; it proved fatal for her. The woman in labour was the wife of an important servant here. Be warned!"

I didn't need to be told twice that mistakes here were not tolerated. I felt the old anxiety I'd come to know so well, and my heart missed a beat as she told me the story. I felt sure that many mistakes must have gone unnoticed or been covered up over the years by some who were sympathetic, for it is the nature of people, when learning their skills, to make errors of judgement sometimes. While trying to understand the different ways of people, I found that even in a structured and disciplined society, people gave themselves or their feelings away. It could be a change of expression, a nervous twitch, or a small movement which was almost indiscernible unless you were keen-eyed.

I was taught how to mix many potions that day. Remembering them didn't seem so hard, as I was very interested in my subject. I was taught how to cut up the bodies of the little creatures that had already joined their counterparts in the spirit realms. When I was expected to do the same to those freshly caught and very much alive, I hid my distaste and shame, silently apologising to the souls of the small creatures. This was to become a daily chore which I would have to adapt to very quickly! They were crushed together with roots, plants, and sometimes aromatic flowers. A little prepared liquid would be added to form a soft paste, and these would be used on the foreheads of feverish women, before or after the births.

The time seemed to fly by so quickly that I was surprised when Li Jing returned to collect me. "This will be part of your daily duties; every morning you will come here." He had put his aloof voice on again. "For the next part of the day, you will join Wèi Wèi for lessons with Master Noih in his rooms. I will come for you each morning for seven days more; after that, you will be expected to make your own way here. Leave at the appointed time, with your instructor's permission, and find your way to Master Noih's teaching rooms for the latter part of the day's work. Remember the way well; you cannot afford to be late." I bowed to my instructor, and we left.

The way was exactly as I remembered it from the night before. There were one or two particularly striking murals on the walls, which I used as my markers along the passageways. We passed by them and continued on until we arrived once more in the small area with the two doors on opposite sides. Li Jing knocked at the door opposite to the one we had passed through the evening before, and I was ushered into a room of similar size to the other. However, this one appeared quite sparse and plain. The surrounding walls with their many designs provided most of the colour and detail, a closer examination of which showed small pictures of ancient tales woven in and out of a repeated pattern: I did not dare to dwell on these, as Master Noih was waiting for me. He stood at one end of the room, tall in stature and very powerful. Wèi Wèi sat cross-legged before him on the floor.

"Quickly now!" He was stern and formal in his manner of speech now, which brought me to a new alertness and apprehension.

I bowed low and took my place beside Wèi Wèi on the floor. She did not move or turn to acknowledge me but kept her eyes fixed firmly on the master. He moved aside from his position to reveal a low, lacquered table which had been hidden behind his considerable frame and his purple and ivory robes. He stepped back and, in one graceful movement, lowered himself onto a large silk cushion with as much grace and ease as one might expect from a man of much smaller stature. Shorter people, of course, were the standard size in our society. Tall people were looked upon with awe; as if their very presence was somehow very special.

Master Noih looked at us both searchingly again. His eyes transfixed me, as if I were looking into deep, mysterious pools. "I come down to your level across this small table to illustrate an important point," he said, "and one which must always be remembered! When we seek to obtain a certain status through our studies, as we progress we have to contain an ego which, when it sees itself as powerful for the first time, must be taught a valuable lesson in humility. This is as vital as the breath of life itself. The more powerful we become through our accomplishments, the more tightly we rein in this illusion of our self – or delusion, I should say."

Wèi Wèi and I sat in silence. I was at a loss to see how I could possibly see myself as powerful when it had always been my duty to be a humble and obedient servant to our beloved emperor: *powerlessness* was a feeling I lived with daily.

"Not *all* manage to contain the beast; I refer to the negative ego, of course," he continued, still watching us closely. "Eventually, however, they become devoured by the very beast they have created. All are tempted; it is the very nature of mankind. Only certain students have the strength to take on this work and learn the skill of balancing their newfound power with humility and a return to The Way. I spoke of this earlier in regard to the work of Lao Zi, also known as Lao-tse or Lao-tzu. This great man was sometimes misunderstood because of his view on life. His idea of Wei Wu Wei (doing nothing) was seen as passivity. This was an incorrect observation. Students can enter a state of bodily awareness in which the right stroke or movement happens by itself, effortlessly, with no interference from the conscious will. What is seen as a pattern for non-action becomes the most effective form of *pure* action. So we have two sides to our work here. Lessons in the mysterious, ancient arts of magic passed down by our ancestors are balanced, in part, by the observations of Lao Zi regarding passivity and humility in all we do and by the very essence of our spirituality. Emperor Lui from the Lui dynasty was a prime example of this, attaining great power but never forgetting his status before the great gods. We feel his presence still! This is kept as a great secret, as we feel all is not lost concerning the great Lui dynasty."

Looking directly at me, Master said, "While you have begun your work in an area of the most basic of healing skills using natural ingredients in your preparations, your colleague Wèi Wèi has been given instruction in understanding her own natural gift and skill as an oracle of sorts. After blurting out prophecies, she has not yet been able to understand or even acknowledge her actions. These gifts have to be handled carefully to protect the physical body and prevent harm to the conscious mind. Wèi Wèi has been learning to recognise when these special moments are about to overtake her. There are certain breathing techniques to adhere to, and there is a skill of taking control to block the flow of information if the time is not right. Above all, only that which Wèi Wèi is able to comfortably accept is the way forward for her. Too many prophecies in one day will do her harm. We have many in the temple like Wèi Wèi; she will not be put under any pressure to 'perform' her skills, as we value them highly. However, and mark my words, in the wrong hands – that is, of those who would not wish to protect her but to extract as much information as possible – she would be in great danger."

Wèi Wèi and I both gulped. *What a price for the honour to work in the temple now*, I thought. As if he could read my mind, the master looked at me again.

"There are different ways of receiving the kind of information which flows from Wèi Wèi so easily – too easily at times, Su Ling. This is why she has to learn to perfect her particular art. There are others here who began such work in many different ways. Some have a very developed intuition, for instance, sensing things about people or situations before they are given any information about them. This skill often takes the form of sensing an outcome before it actually happens. Like you, they have an awareness of people and what mask they show to the world. Others hear whispers while drifting off to sleep or in that state of semi-slumber as they awaken each morning. You will begin to remember your dreams and to understand their meaning, learning much about the self by sometimes dreaming of events of the past, present, and future.

"Many oracles have been tragically put to death due to the fear and ignorance of their murderers. People feared what they did not understand. Much *has* been understood since by those intelligent enough to nurture such skills and value them. However, not all can bear the discipline which is needed to grow and develop in this way; and there will still be those who would wish to harm us through their own fears and shortcomings.

"When we combine these skills with the magic of old, there will be a force for much power. We can use this power to help our own cause against our enemies, but be warned! There is a difference between using this power for honourable battles and using it for pure evil. We do not intend or seek evil, because this power has such force that it will return the very evil that we use against others." There was a brief pause, and the master's voice seemed to take on a different tone. "Our mainstay is the knowledge I now give, to be clearly understood and written on our souls. The circle of judgement then goes against us if evil is combined with the power, but we receive recompense for good and honourable actions also – the circle works both ways. We must do everything in our power to prevent the use of evil against us while trying to balance our own judgement. We do not wish to anger the gods too much by becoming perpetrators ourselves. There is a cause of something, and there is the effect of it. The thing to remember is that all are affected by this process. Where we help or harm others then we can expect at some point in the future to be helped or harmed ourselves. If someone attacks you with anger the temptation is to mirror their action back to them. This seems analogous to man fighting man fairly on the battlefield, each man fighting for his own cause, but it is not. Evil goes beyond this; it can come with great strength or with such subtlety that many would not see it for what it is. So if we were on the receiving end of such circumstances and retaliated in kind, we would feel its full force! Before you ask, we find a way around the problem. We use our intelligence; we use our magical skills to protect us along with the wise words of Lao Zi. We look to our ancestors to help find solutions before we jump in too quickly."

I stared in awe at the master and could hardly believe that I had become a part of this momentous work. Indeed, I wondered why I should have been chosen. A servant broke the following silence, bringing a tray with bowls of rice water. We sat in silence, all three, drinking until we had finished and were refreshed. Then Master Noih spoke. "You will learn the ways I have spoken of together. The rest of the time, you both have your separate arts to learn. Discipline is essential! You will learn much about the Self, as mentioned before. For what you see in the physical is only a small part of the whole of what you refer to as 'yourself'. We are going to begin today by learning about this thing we call the self and its many levels of existence. Before we begin, I wish to say that we always acknowledge other people's beliefs and customs regarding who they worship, but we keep our silence at such times, for we have been chosen as a branch of mankind who know the true ways. For this reason, we only speak among ourselves about such matters, until a time comes when we are instructed to teach our skills to others on a wider scale. You saw a little of this on the occasion of Emperor Liu's visit, when Chief Priest Mou performed the ceremony of She. Such powerful ceremonies depend on the genuine wishes of those concerned working in unison with their Higher Will to bring about a powerful, positive magic. As we observed, some of those present manipulated the power for selfish, negative reasons; thus, valuable skills relayed by the priests from the Temple were to no avail. Those soldiers and administrators were put on their trust to accomplish what all others sought: unity in the land.

"Now we turn to what constitutes the Self. It is seen and understood by many but unseen or acknowledged by most. What we term the self is much more than the physical or material body which all can consciously see. There are also subtle energy bodies invisible to the naked eye. These energy bodies are within and without the physical. They are of the aura, part of the energy field that surrounds each and every one of us and every living thing. They combine and interpenetrate the whole of the self, while each inhabits its own level of existence. In turn, they are the Etheric body (nearest to the physical body, and supporting it with its very fine, web-like structure); the emotional energy body, and the mental body. These are followed by other levels of form, some of which constitute the spiritual levels of the self. We say 'level' here, but we could just as easily say 'area', 'field', or 'dimension'. Even the lower ones, nearest the physical body, vibrate at a faster speed than the physical body. All have their associated colours, which many have the skills to see or have been trained to see.

"Darker hues in the emotional field, for instance, suggest turmoil and dis-ease, which can eventually manifest as disease in the physical body unless counteracted in some way. Each body has its associated energy centres; in the physical they are close to important organs of the body. You have both heard of the meridian channels of the body and the acupuncture points; these too are part of the invisibility and the hidden magic of the human body. Soul or self is attached to others, constituting a universal energy which is too powerful for us to even imagine. It may appear as if we are separated here, in this world of matter, but our invisible energy fields are constantly reacting with the fields of others. We can learn later how the energy centres of the bodies spoken of before draw life force in and out of the body; without them we could not exist."

I was overawed by the knowledge I was being given, which was so unlike anything I had heard before. I had a question in my mind, and as always Master was aware of it. He fixed me again with his penetrating gaze. "I know this is difficult to take in, Su Ling, and at this level of existence does not *appear* to be the case. Always remember: you must not judge or form an opinion simply by what you see with your physical eyes, though it's natural to do so. Rather, concentrate on your invisible third eye. The celestial part of the self vibrates in a much faster, rarer, and purer atmosphere than this one, and it sees in a much wider and more enlightened way. You will say to me, 'I can't see it'; nevertheless, it is there. Our work requires that we utilise all of our senses, including that extra ingredient, trust. We do not trust blindly; we trust intelligently and with our hearts, too. We acquire the appropriate knowledge in order to trust. To access those hidden parts of ourselves, we need to follow a disciplined technique which makes for much work. However, you will never again think of life in such a narrow, confined way as you are used to; your whole spiritual outlook will now change."

We studied for some time with Master Noih, taking our first tentative steps into the mysteries of life and the afterlife. There seemed so much to learn; by the time Li Jing came to collect us, my mind was swimming around and around with this newfound knowledge. As we followed him out along the corridor, I could see from the window at one end that it was growing dark. Wèi Wèi signalled to me that she was hungry, and I nodded without speaking a word. Fortune seemed to smile on us, for we were led directly back to the hall where everyone took their food. Li Jing turned to us and said, "You must find your own way back after you have eaten. Do not take too long over this, and be back in your room by the appointed time!"

We knew that servants came to check each room at the end of the day, making sure everyone was in their place, and now people had begun to leave the hall, so there was little time to eat. We made as much haste as we comfortably could over our small meal and found our way back through the temple to the familiar door with its turquoise bird plaque. I could already hear doors opening and closing as the servants made their rounds along the passageway.

We went quietly into our living quarters and noticed that all of our colleagues were sitting in the social area reading various scrolls – all, that is, except for Niang, Héshi, and Ci. They were playing some sort of game with what looked like small discs. No-one looked in our direction as we entered; it was as if we didn't exist. Wèi Wèi cast me one of her warning glances as if to say, 'Wait, and don't do anything yet.' I, too, sensed a potential trap just waiting for us if we were not careful. As we needed permission for most things from our three superiors, we stood absolutely still for a while before Wèi Wèi asked, "May we join you?" This she asked with humility but certainly not fear! Meirén glanced up at us, and we could feel the others in the room follow as the silence in the room continued. Niang, Héshi, and Ci continued with their game, whispering amongst themselves and ignoring us totally. Both Wèi Wèi and I realised that they had been waiting for us to make a wrong move by joining the group without permission. As we were too clever for them in regard to this, they decided to leave us standing! This we did without complaint, staring straight ahead with pride. So they were unable to complain that we had been staring at them. Clearly we were not the weak victims they had hoped for.

CHAPTER 9
The Fellowship is Formed

OVER THE FOLLOWING WEEKS AND months, much was taught to us, and all came as revelations which challenged our way of thinking. I learned that although Master Noih Chen was our tutor here in this world, in a sense we were our own tutors too. We became aware that ultimately, all answers were within ourselves. Master Noih showed us how to access that information but warned us that we needed courage, as we would also discover dark sides to our own souls. This is true for everyone, but many people were unaware of a darker side to their souls unless some traumatic situation in their lives put them to the test. I was not aware of this until I came to meet my True Self; that is, all I had ever been and had become at that moment in time. Until then, I was only aware of the personality of the Su Ling living in imperial China.

Master Noih taught us that through the journey of our

individual souls, we had progressed enough to be given such spiritual knowledge. He taught us how to create a better life for ourselves in the future in whatever dimension we found ourselves and with whatever restrictions would be placed upon us. The art was in knowing and understanding the positive and negative influences within ourselves and trying to balance the two in order to progress spiritually. He showed us that even when negative things happened to us from the *outside,* they could be turned into positive achievements by how we chose to overcome them.

During this time, my work duties in the mornings taught me much about womanhood. My teachers told me that I had a 'magical' way with potions! I did not reveal to them the extra ingredients I placed in each, for they would not have understood. These additions were simply my positive thoughts put into each potion in a way which had to remain secret because of my work with Master Noih. This was my offering. Some of the others working with the women in their labours had their own special offerings in the way they were able to empathise with their patients and calm them in ways I myself viewed as magical. These particular servants were not of the majority, and most went about their profession in a detached way. I had learned as a younger child how some people's apparent hardness was used as a form of protection; often, this was a habit acquired from a childhood during which affection or love was never shown.

As a young woman working in the temple and helping to deliver infants into the world, I never had the slightest inclination to become a mother myself. I also realised that women in my country had little or no choice in the matter and believed this to be true for all women.

One particular girl about to give birth seemed very much taken with me, and I was mystified as to why this should be. Her name was Hanàn. She appeared to be very young – not much older than me, I guessed. We were comforted by the fact that she was strong and healthy, being the daughter of a general in the service of Governor Choi. This meant that her chances of an unhindered delivery were so much the greater. Her cries of woe as she experienced her labour in fear and confusion, not knowing what was expected of her, made me feel uncomfortable inside and stirred up old feelings of when I cried out for my own mother. I did not experience these feelings with other patients, for we had been taught only to focus on bringing the new babes into the world.

Hanàn broke through the detachment I had endeavoured to create for myself, making me feel vulnerable. Later I was to understand a little more about the unseen forces which can draw people together. This was to form part of our exploration into mysteries to be disclosed to us at some other time by the master.

I busied myself around Hanàn, giving her instructions on how to breathe and generally trying to calm her. There was a moment when the old servant I had been helping left us. Hanàn whispered, "Please, Su Ling, help me. Will you do something for me?" I replied cautiously that I wasn't sure.

"They are going to take my baby away from me. It is to go to an older sister and her husband, for my sister cannot carry a child for the full term. They believe I will be able to have many more children; they do not understand my wish to cherish my firstborn.

I know they think that I am selfish and should put my sister and her husband first. You must help me!"

Hanàn began to cry out, becoming more distressed by every moment. Her cries brought the old woman over, and she looked at me sharply. I shrugged my shoulders and told her that everything appeared to be going well. I asked if something unusual had occurred, appealing to her superiority. The woman examined the girl and was satisfied that all appeared to be going well. She spoke sharply to her and told her not to make so much fuss, as she was a healthy young woman! I was ushered away to prepare a potion to calm Hanàn while the birthing mother took charge.

I had the greatest difficulty in hiding my own distress and felt that my predicament was almost too much to bear. What could I do for Hanàn? I could not appeal to my instructor's better nature, for she would have feared for her own life and mine! To go against the wishes of servants who were superior to her was unheard of. My mind raced. I had thoughts of hiding the child away somewhere until Hanàn came for her; but a baby was not my little Tóngshí, which I had enough trouble hiding each day. As I combined the ingredients of the potion, I felt as if I should burst with frustration! I summoned up all the courage I had and, whilst appealing silently to the gods, put very strong thoughts of my own into the potion in the manner I had been shown by Master Noih. This poor girl was, in many ways, far more fortunate than the peasant girls, yet she had to pay such a terrible price because of the family she had been born into. I felt a little faint; I was not sure I should be using my skills in this way. I felt angry and confused that I should let my feelings outweigh my judgement, which told me to stay detached from my patients. *What if something bad should befall me now?* My mind raced with the question.

Hurrying back to Hanàn with the potion, I could see her pleading eyes as I handed it over to my instructor. I averted my eyes as the woman insisted Hanàn drink it while assuring her that all would be well. Within a short time, Hanàn became calmer, albeit in a rather sad, resigned way. I cannot begin to describe my mixed emotions while tending her as she entered her final stage of labour. Thankfully, we were not left alone; after her earlier outburst, the old woman watched over her, anxious that all should go well for Hanàn's family.

Suddenly, the moment arrived! Hanàn gave birth to a beautiful little girl. This would be a disappointment for the family, of course, as a boy child would have been preferable. Something in the old woman's expression alarmed me. The babe did not cry out loudly as the others around her. I watched as the old servant examined her and cleared out her mouth, nose, and ears. The babe gave out a pathetic cry, and I nearly collapsed with fear that I might have done this awful thing.

"They will not want *this* for the older daughter. The family are most unfortunate," the old woman snapped.

With this, Hanàn held out her arms and said, "Give her to me!" The servant thrust the child into her mother's waiting arms and hurried away to inform the family of their bad luck.

Hanàn, however, was as proud as she could be. "I will make her strong, whatever my family say. I will not let them destroy her or put her aside. Thank you, Su Ling; it must have been you who brought me this good fortune!" I could not speak; I just patted the baby's head, hoping I had not done too much damage. I knew it was nearly time for my lesson with Master Noih, so with heavy heart I made my way to his room. I decided to confess and await my fate.

I approached Master Noih's door and found that it was half open; thinking that a visitor had just entered, I went in very quietly and, without glancing around, closed the door behind me.

"Come in, Su Ling; we have been waiting for you." I looked up and to my surprise saw just the master standing there with Wèi Wèi in her usual place. "You are not late, but you have much to tell me before today's *planned* lesson."

As he sat down, he motioned me to come forward: I approached and solemnly bowed low. Somewhat shakily, but with a clear voice, I told my tale. I described how I felt I had abused my position as his pupil by using my powers in the wrong way, which resulted in the poor health of Hanàn's babe. As I finished speaking, I felt myself sway a little:

"Sit down, child," Master Noih ordered.

Wèi Wèi put out her hand to steady me while looking at the master as if she wasn't sure if she was allowed to do so.

"Pass your friend some water." Wèi Wèi instantly fetched a bowl of water from the corner of the room and encouraged me to drink before she sat down. I gave her a weak smile of acknowledgement.

"So we have an additional lesson today; it was learnt primarily by Su Ling but is useful for you too, Wèi Wèi, as an observer in this case. Firstly, I would say this is a very opportune lesson to be learning at such an early stage in the development of your art. In our work you could say we come up against certain anomalies from time to time while going about our other duties, which we call our 'mundane' work. Not to belittle it, you understand, just to emphasise it as part of our day-to-day life here at the physical level of existence. We have spoken before about walking a path 'between two worlds'; that is, one foot in the spiritual world and the other in the material one. The dilemma you found yourself in, Su Ling encompassed both; that is not to say that one should not have intruded on the other at all. " I felt myself sway a little again as Master Noih's eyes fixed me with a stare as only he could. "Before you faint away completely, Su Ling, I will say to you that this time, no actual harm was done." My spirits lifted a little, but I was still in total confusion.

"As much as we would wish to sort out everybody's problems, we have to stand back from them and protect ourselves in the way I have taught you. You must pay particular attention to the mental and emotional levels. Easier said than done! Especially in the earlier stages of our development, and with special reference to your youth, saying no to some is hard – particularly in matters of the heart, as you will find later. Some things are laid down for us before we come into this world. We have actually agreed to go through such things before coming in! This is because we use such situations to further our spiritual development while we are here. You see, our memory is wiped clean as we are born into a physical body, so we are not consciously aware of our choices before we enter our lives. Unconsciously, it is a very different matter; much is known and understood. We know that it is all part of the circle of life. All the situations which cause us sadness and fear are not necessarily 'written in stone,' which means they will not *definitely* happen. We are all given free will, and according to legend, when working with magic, things can sometimes be changed. However, we always remember the teachings of 'The Way' and our eminent friend Lao Zi. Certain spiritual laws have to be abided by." I heard an intake of breath from Wèi Wèi and knew she was struggling to understand the master's words too.

Master Noih Chen closed his eyes and contemplated for a moment. We sat in silence, waiting to hear him speak again. After a few moments, he opened his eyes and looked down at us, first concentrating on me and then on Wèi Wèi. "In this world there are the positive thoughts and actions, and there are the negative ones. We think we can easily spot which is which. The problem is, you see, that perceptions of positive and negative vary from person to person. One person might see a negative act as a very positive one! It is a very complex matter, especially because good can come from a negative act and bad from a good one. This is not necessarily so, of course. Before I speak a little further on this, I want to come back to Su Ling's experience today. Of course, you deviated from the simple instructions you were given in the birthing hall, Su Ling. That does not endear you to any teacher in the temple; it usually means a form of punishment is given."

Master paused as I sat in a trance-like state, desperately trying to focus on his wisdom. "You felt torn today between the mental level of yourself and the feelings and emotions of the heart. They are a powerful combination when they work in harmony but a terrible burden as opposites! This, then, is what we come to expect when we enter the material world. Our beloved country, our imperial China, is torn in several pieces too. You could liken it to the Whole Self, which, as I have said before, is so much more than just the physical. There is fighting between many different factions; tribes within various kingdoms all wish to capture the whole land. To achieve greatness, a whole self or a whole country needs to work together in harmony. I have to tell you here today that though much work can be done in one lifetime to bring about balance and harmony within oneself this cannot totally be done here, this land, like many others, will be torn between the positive and negative forces around us for as long as I can foresee. "

My heart sank. Both of us let out small gasps. I pondered on our fate in the future without taking my eyes off of the master. "Yes, Su Ling, you will have to make choices sometimes, even if it means disobeying a direct order, in which case you would expect to be put to death! In your life lesson today, you were trying to do the impossible. It was not just one whole culture and way of life that you were up against; it was also mysterious forces beyond your comprehension. Your positive thoughts while mixing your potion were intended, and intention is everything. It is the important word here, to solve Hanàn's problem as if by magic. True magic, if it in any way tries to alter a person's true fate – that is, those conditions laid down by the soul itself for this life – is a very serious matter! Unless you had great expertise in the kind of work we are doing now, you would not know whether the person's higher self had agreed to go through a set of circumstances to promote greater enlightenment for itself! Now, this is one of the hardest lessons to learn about the soul's journey.

"There is a free choice here to a small degree, but we, as Chinese citizens, believe in obedience above all in order for our country to flourish and grow. Of course, matters of war upset the balance there. Non-intervention is the key, Su Ling, unless – and I say this cautiously – the gods say differently. So this is where our skills come in; we ask the gods to give us a sign or tell us what is to be.

"Su Ling, you have done well in standing back from too much emotional attachment to patients in your care. This case was different. At a higher level, your soul recognised someone you knew before from another place and time. This is why you had so much trouble keeping a detached stance from Hanàn's suffering. Your thoughts in no way harmed her child, who was already expected by the spirits to be a sickly child. Hanàn will be allowed to keep her, as the family will be concentrating on an unexpected delivery by the eldest daughter of a healthy baby son later this year."

I felt my heart leap with joy again but kept my composure, aware that Master Noih would know my every thought and deed. "Hanàn's daughter will live for a good ten years due primarily to her mother's care. If this had not been possible, the babe would not have lasted the year; of this we are certain. You see, Su Ling, this is a life-changing event for Hanàn, which may well be a situation for all to learn from. Your own interference just put a little more positive influence into the birth itself. You will be even more surprised to know that this action was meant to be."

Master Noih paused and lowered his eyes for a moment. Then he glanced up towards the door just as a soft knock was heard. "Come." The visitor entered, gliding slowly across the floor as only a master can. "Ah, Master Ma Sing, you have not met my new pupils."

I noticed Master Noih spoke with respect to his colleague and with no hint of animosity towards the old man as he approached us. He was obviously advanced in years, much older than Master Noih, I guessed. We were allowed to stay seated as we bowed in respect to the old sage. Master Ma Sing said nothing aloud but whispered a message obviously too important for us to hear. Master Noih sat silently as the old man conveyed his words. Then both nodded, and our visitor left as silently as he came.

After he had left the room, Master spent some time telling us about the venerable old gentleman who had worked in and served the Temple of the Heavenly Bird for most of his adult life. As a young man, he was revered in his village for having special qualities; word of his gifts had reached the governor in power at the time. He was subsequently sent for and had remained forever in service here. We were told, to our surprise, that he was also the tutor to Niang, Héshi, and Ci, and therefore took an interest in anyone who shared a room with them.

"There are just one or two small matters left which need to be dealt with before we move on today." Master looked so deeply into our eyes that I felt he could see into our very souls. "I am pleased, Wèi Wèi, that in your lessons separate from Su Ling you are gradually learning to control your gift. In time, Su Ling, you will develop similar skills, but you will have some fundamental differences in the way you work; this is all in order. Secondly, I feel it is time, Su Ling, for you to let go of the burden of continually having to hide Tóngshì!"

I gasped. The master knew everything I did, including my efforts to conceal my little bird. "You have learned the hard way that others would covet what you have and try to steal it from you, but here in the temple, while you are under my tutelage, they would not dare!"

At once I relaxed my taut body, relieved that Tóngshì and I could at last be ourselves and be out in the open. "You may keep the gift which was given to you – and by a real craftsman, let me say. Each of you will be given a pouch in which you may keep a precious gift – that is, all those who occupy you're living quarters.

"Each will store her pouch away within her own bedroll while sleeping. In the morning, the pouches with their secret possessions will be worn for all to see. This will signal to others in the temple your status as my pupils. What do you say, Su Ling?"

"I cannot say how happy I am, Master. I started today with a terrible dilemma, yet you reward me in this way."

"All will receive a pouch, remember. The lesson you received earlier was a gift in itself." It was as if a mist suddenly cleared as I took in my teacher's words. At last an honour had been bestowed on me that I felt completely comfortable with!

Later, as the lessons ended for the day, Wèi Wèi and I made our way to the Great Hall to stand in line for our meal. We whispered excitedly about the day's events and discussed the pouches we would receive. Already a little more fashion-conscious now, we wondered how they would fit in with our garments.

While eating our meal, we glanced up at our three 'superiors', taking care that they should not see us. They seemed unconcerned about receiving a new gift; we thought perhaps they had not been told. We found out later that they had, but they had taken this information in a matter-of-fact-way. They left the hall before us, neither looking to the left nor the right, but we saw the other girls get up at once to follow them. Meirén hadn't finished eating and carried on, not worrying about the others. Wèi Wèi assessed the situation. "What do you think, Su Ling? Shall we stay and return alone later to our rooms?"

"I think we should finish our meal and follow Meirén; that way we can't get into any trouble." Meirén got up to leave, and we followed soon after.

There were many people coming and going through the passageways and rooms, and sometimes we noticed soldiers of the temple going about their duty. As we approached the large wooden doors to our rooms, we noticed one was slightly ajar. Emerging from it, Master Ma Sing spotted us at once. We stepped aside and bowed, unsure what to do. His old, lined face was very white, as was his beard; he stood in silence for a while before speaking. "So, we have here our two new little fledglings."

For a moment I was quite stunned, His voice was quiet and calm, like tranquil waters, quite unlike my perception of a powerful master. Master Noih did not speak to us loudly, yet there seemed much more strength in his tone. I presumed that this soft voice was as the result of Master Ma Sing's very advanced years. It seemed strange that Wèi Wèi and I should be thought of as fledglings in the way I thought of Tóngshì.

"I am told that you have not disgraced yourselves in matters of protocol here. See that this continues and you continue to offer respect to the senior girls."

"Yes, Master," we said in unison.

He paused again before speaking. "It's often in matters of protocol that we find out who takes their position here seriously and who does not." Still the soft, hypnotic voice seemed to contain no hint of malice or condemnation. "Often, something done to us which appears to us to be unfair and tests us severely is done for a reason, a specific purpose. It strengthens and builds our characters."

I was not sure if I felt that Niang, Héshi, and Ci's sarcastic glances designed to humiliate us came under Master Ma Sing's definition of character building! I was remembering the differences in attitude between Madam Shu and Tutor Chéng. Both were treated with respect by their pupils, both could be severe, and both were instantly obeyed by their charges. Yet the admiration we felt for Tutor Chéng was far greater than that which we felt for Madam Shu. I silently decided that, as with many things we had been taught, there needed to be a balance in how rules were administered.

At that moment, a servant came rushing out of one of the rooms nearby, making much noise in the process. He was obviously late, and on seeing Master Ma Sing he dropped his basketful of clothing. I looked up at the master, and suddenly there it was! His eyes blazed like a fire with strange blue flames that lit up his whole face. We held our breath as we witnessed his obvious displeasure with the servant. Just as quickly, his eyes returned to normal, and he said softly, "My room" to the terrified servant.

We had seen his hidden strength and power. So fast it came and went, but we were left in no doubt of its ferocity. Many must have witnessed his power, even when he was a young man. So our last lesson of the day was never to judge by appearances or what is on the surface.

Master Ma Sing nodded towards the door to our quarters. Bowing again, we slipped quietly back through the doors. This evening, everything appeared to be different. Instead of engaging in quiet activities in the social area, everyone seemed to be preparing for sleep earlier. Most of the other girls were already in the washroom. Before Meirén went through to join them, she said quietly, "Tomorrow is a special day; you must be ready."

We awoke early simultaneously, as was so often the case. We had spent something of a restless night wondering about events of the forthcoming day. There had been neither proclamation from Master Noih nor word from Governor Choi, yet we sensed from Meirén that something was indeed 'special'. There was an air of expectancy in the living quarters, yet no word was spoken. In the washroom, the cleaning and cleansing ritual seemed to take on a special urgency for the other girls, making Wèi Wèi and me respond in the same fashion. There were no instructions to wear any special clothes, but of course in these quarters our clothes were already far superior than those from our pasts.

Our pouches were ready for us that morning. Meirén handed them to us; we were last in the pecking order of the room, of course. I carefully placed my little Tóngshì into my new pouch, which was made of a delicate shade of lilac silk embroidered with deep blue and white flowers and emblems of gold. The pouch had a long silk handle, which I placed over my head. Glancing around the room, I thought everyone would be staring at it, but no, everyone was more interested in their own precious possessions. I couldn't see what the other girls had put into their pouches, but Wèi Wèi showed me her own treasure, a little green silk butterfly she had made herself. It was exquisite, and I could see that she had taken the greatest care in making it. We motioned silently to each other and waited to be given our orders.

Niang, Héshi, and Ci, usually only concerned with themselves, stepped forward to the centre of the room. Then there was a moment's silence. All eyes fell on Niang as she alone took another step forward. "Today we honour our ancestors and our beloved emperor by attending and witnessing a splendid martial arts display of our brave soldiers as they pay tribute to those who have died a valiant death on the battlefield, fighting for their emperor. Here, we pay a special tribute to our own brave warriors, who have also laid down their lives in service to Governor Choi Yen Shù, our master and protector.

"Today we witness many remarkable feats, which will, in turn, encourage us in our own endeavours to approach them with a new vigour. We do this on behalf of all in the living quarters, but most importantly for Master Ma Sing and Master Noih; we will not let them down! We go now to the Great Hall for our first meal of the day. We then proceed to the front entrance of the temple, where our two masters will be waiting for us. We will follow them on from there. The displays will take place in the second courtyard, and all servants will attend."

With this Niang led the way out along the corridor. It felt

strange to me that for once we were in unison; for some reason it had the effect of increasing our feeling of power: I could actually feel this from everyone.

"Have you noticed a change today too?" Wèi Wèi said quietly. She was the first to speak, as we had been eating our meal in silence for some time. The atmosphere we had been aware of in our room seemed to permeate throughout the temple. "Yes, though I'm not sure why. Perhaps it is something to do with wearing our pouches for the first time." I wasn't even sure what I meant by that remark! "I can't help remembering Beloved Emperor Liu," I whispered, afraid that someone might have heard me. "He had hoped that his visit here would bring all the warring tribes together."

"What is to be is to be," Wèi Wèi said with no apparent concern. I was taken aback by this remark. I said nothing to her but began to ponder her words. We had been taught that some things are set out for us in life by our own souls, which in turn are being guided by great teachers in the spirit world; just as Master Noih guides us here. Yet we had also come to discover the power of our conscious minds and how in unity of thought, even wars could be erased from our beloved China. We concentrated again on Niang, Héshi, and Ci as they rose to leave the room. In complete unity, the rest of us rose up and prepared to follow them. I marvelled at the synchronicity of this action.

In line we followed, out along the passageways and halls along with the rest of the temple servants. Here and there we noticed soldiers keeping watch. I realised that the temple was guarded at all times, even times such as this. As we approached the main doors, there seemed to be a little more order, and people assembled into groups. We stopped behind Master Noih and Master Ma Sing, waiting for instructions. I stood wondering how long it would take for all these people to get through the smaller gateway in the garden wall, which I had first noticed on arrival at the work houses. Without any instructions, we followed the two masters through the temple doors and out into a wide courtyard with gardens on either side. We seemed to be at the top of a flight of steps, and we could see Governor Choi up ahead mounted on his horse, surrounded by his generals. They were all facing the temple wall, some way from the doorway I had remembered. I was most perplexed; why did everyone face the wall? Nobody moved or made a sound.

Suddenly, a wide portion of the wall itself seemed to move before our eyes! It appeared to open like a huge door. Meirén whispered to us. "This section of the wall is an illusion to all on the outside. Even if enemy soldiers were able to reach it, it would be seen by them as an ordinary wall of matter; they would try to climb it, but they would still be unable to reach the other side. This, however, could never happen; no enemy would be allowed to get this close!" My mind raced with questions. I looked at Wèi Wèi, and she gave me a rare smile, as if to say, 'Wait and see.'

Master Fu Chàng, Master Noih's counterpart, joined us along with the temple priests and Li Jing, whom I promptly tried to ignore! As one large group we descended the steps of the temple on foot, following immediately behind Governor Choi and his generals as the first group to go through the Wall of Illusion.

The crowd was partially hidden from us by the large podium straight ahead. Governor Choi and his guard of honour were easily able to dismount not far from the top and take their seats on the platform. As our group prepared to climb, we found ourselves facing three smaller platforms, each with its own set of small steps leading up to the next. Wèi Wèi and I looked at each other, surprised; we had not noticed them before. The rest of the group continued to look straight ahead. As we climbed, we were able to get a wider and wider view and were finally able to take our seats at the top.

Our seats were at the back and on the far side of the podium, so that our view was slightly obscured in one corner yet still superior to that of the crowd standing below. This was something that I was quite unaccustomed to, and I felt overwhelmed and unworthy of such an honour. As the other groups were taking their places, I became aware of a small entourage of three mounted soldiers carrying flags and waiting for orders to be given below. Some instinct drew my attention to the soldier in the middle.

There was nothing very remarkable about the young warrior that distinguished him from the rest, yet I was transfixed. I studied him closely. What was this thing I had been taught in Master Noih's class, this strange sense of awareness? I had been taught many things during my studies, yet this was different. I felt a sense of familiarity, as if we had met before at some other time and in some other place. Little did I know then that the young soldier would play such an important role in my life!

CHAPTER 10

The Ways of the World

THE THREE SOLDIERS ON HORSEBACK were the first to be presented to Governor Choi. Each carried a flag depicting the green dragon, guardian of the East. These were lowered in unison and with heads bowed before their governor. With a nod from Governor Choi, three servants of the temple stepped forward to collect the flags, which were then folded and secured. Thus, the ceremonial part of the proceedings began.

I watched along with everyone else the ceremonial opening to the wonderful show. It proved remarkable to watch the soldiers and temple guards performing the skills they had worked so hard to achieve, honouring their emperor and their governor.

The young warrior I had been drawn to disappeared and merged in with the rest of the soldiers on display, who all appeared to be wearing the same tunics. As each display of martial arts was performed, I became aware that there were in fact four teams.

Each had distinctive coloured armbands worn on the left arm. I marvelled at the swiftness and agility of the soldiers as they demonstrated their fighting manoeuvres. There were no weapons used in some of the displays; they used their own hands and arms. A wrong move could prove fatal against an enemy; a correct move could bring victory to a foot soldier on the battlefield. The same weapon-less displays were then performed in slow, flowing movements. I gasped at the change this brought to the vibrations in and around the courtyard. What was felt before as firecrackers in the air now took on a calming, soothing air.

These graceful movements were performed to gentle music, and as I glanced sideways at Wèi Wèi, I saw that her eyes were half closed and she was swaying very slightly to the sound. I could see she was affected by the energies around, too. This transformation of mood suddenly brought to my mind one of Master Noih's lessons. To keep a sense of balance on occasions such as this, or whenever there were great mood changes around, we needed to protect ourselves. In crowds especially we could be easily pulled one way or another unless we learnt the art of closing ourselves off from too dramatic a change. If the change was unexpected, we had to take control nevertheless, placing an invisible barrier between ourselves and the situation. This was always done from within ourselves; those on the outside of our special family who are practised in the Divine Mysteries would be unaware of what we were doing. Such an action was not meant as a barrier to enjoyment, merely a technique to restore a sense of balance and harmony. I nudged Wèi Wèi and whispered "the barrier", but I could sense that she had come to the same realisation as I.

We had been sitting still and observing for a very long time, yet to me it had seemed just a few moments. The victorious team proved to be the yellows. There was loud applause from the crowds in the courtyard and more subdued clapping from the platform as Governor Choi rose to his feet. Surveying all from his commandery, he said, "You have all surpassed yourselves on this historic day; I am pleased." In the same manner, he beckoned forward a representative from the winning team. I was wondering why this particular day was so historic when suddenly my heart stopped! I recognised the young leader of the yellow team; it was my unknown soldier. He was presented with a flag depicting a tiger; this was solely for the use of his own team to be used in any future skirmishes or battles. The leader always followed his captain, of course, but he alone had the privilege of carrying the flag on horseback. If he fell, another in the team would take up the flag and be allowed to carry it. This was understood by the generals watching from the platform; all would know that the flag had been personally given by the governor himself.

Our splendid day was not yet over. As all the teams returned to their places a silent anticipation fell over the courtyard once more. There was some deep contemplation taking place on the platform; in the silence, I could *feel* it. Pictures flooded my mind, and I was aware of some confusion. 'Truth,' that simple word, filled my soul. I symbolically heard, smelt, saw, and even felt it; all of my senses became aligned with the word.

Governor Choi rose again to address us. "Today we mark an historic day for imperial China. Our illustrious emperor, Wang Mang, established his own dynasty on this day two summers and two winters ago." I immediately sensed his dilemma. The founding father of the Liu dynasty was still greatly admired throughout the land, and the temple priest had predicted a return to the Liu dynasty at some point in the not-too-distant future. Emperor Liu's earlier reign would come to be regarded by scholars as the former Western Han dynasty.

Before becoming emperor, Lui Pang had his own kingdom in the west. The expected glorious revival of the Lui dynasty would later become known by scholars as the Later Eastern Han period, and Lo Yang city would act as the capital. This information was only relayed mind to mind by those of us seated on the platform; if word were to spread further and reach the ears of the present emperor, the perpetrators would be identified and killed.

One of the responsibilities and difficulties laid upon us as we progressed in the sacred arts was to uphold truth. So Governor Choi was torn between who he wished to honour and who he was obliged (on pain of death) to honour. Spies everywhere would have been only too willing to bring a wayward governor down if he spoke out of turn. "We are rightly proud of our country and its warriors who lay down their lives for their emperor. There have been many in the past that have performed heroic deeds, and as their special qualities were recognised; they rose through the ranks to take great office. We salute them all here today, our illustrious ancestors."

No-one was left in any doubt that Lui Pang himself had risen through the ranks through his skill on the battlefield, first becoming king and later emperor. By mentioning our ancestors, Governor Choi had cloaked this salutation. Should anyone query this, he hastily returned to honour Emperor Wang Mang by listing his many accomplishments. Thus, he felt his mind could be at peace. Those who wanted to know would understand, and those who were suspicious would find no fault with his speech, no matter how hard they studied it.

The ceremony was brought to an end by the chief priest in his deliberations. Wèi Wèi and I stood to take our place behind the others leaving the platform but were surprised to be ushered alongside Niang, Héshi, and Ci. They didn't acknowledge us, and yet I sensed an acceptance as we descended the platform and went through the Wall of Illusion. The way back was much quicker!

During the next week, Wèi Wèi and I noticed a shift of mood in our living quarters. The order of hierarchy was still in place, of course, but there was a tangible difference in the room. A relaxed atmosphere prevailed. I reminded myself of the lesson of illusion and was wary of becoming complacent, but there was a definite change.

Through the weeks and months which followed, I slowly progressed in my work with the mothers in the birthing room. My potions became more potent as I experimented by adding juices from the small dead creatures, such as insects and small reptiles, from the many jars on the shelves. I would also grind down flowers and shrubs to add to them, which provided pleasant aromas. These potions could not be given by mouth as they would prove to be poisonous. Governor Choi would sometimes send servants for my readymade potions. I sensed that they would sometimes be used for other purposes than healing, but I quickly cleared such thoughts from my mind. As time passed, I gradually became accomplished at helping the elders with the birthing process. In order to be able to do this work to the best of my ability, I closed myself off emotionally; this was important because emergencies would arise where calmness was needed or mothers and babes could be lost. So what may have appeared to be an unfeeling stance to some actually helped the mothers, as there were no heavy demands placed upon me, unlike during my experience with Hanàn. However, I was also sure that I might be faced with this dilemma again if my soul recognised another from the long and distant past.

Being able to cut off emotionally from the situations around me made me feel much stronger, but it was a little strange; it felt almost like becoming a different person. I sensed that balance was needed here too. If one went through life permanently in a detached state, one would become like Madame Shu. I had no wish for this because of the impression she left on all those in her charge. To go to the other extreme, continually becoming overemotional, would drain the energy of those near to me, who would then wish to avoid my company altogether. There was so much to learn. I would often hold Tóngshì during my meditations and gain much comfort from it. Often I thought of the old man who carefully crafted it, realising that he must have put some of his own comforting thoughts into creating it.

I entered Master Noih's room one afternoon to find him whispering something to Wèi Wèi. He turned and motioned to me to follow him to a far corner of the room, where a heavy curtain hung. I'd often thought about this corner, as nothing appeared to be behind the curtain, not even a door. Master Noih flicked it back in one smooth motion. Nothing was said as I studied the bare wall for a moment. Then I remembered the rule of illusion. At once the wall appeared to take on an opalescent quality, which changed again to a clear, transparent space, just as if no wall were there. I found that I was looking at the garden outside as if I stood there in the open air. "Observe the wall and courtyard beyond, Su Ling" I studied the outer wall of the garden as it gradually became transparent. My attention was drawn to a particularly lovely white blossoming tree growing in the courtyard: two figures stood beneath it. I was overjoyed to see my cousin Chuntian there but could not make out the other – a stranger, I thought. They were in conversation for some time before the stranger turned to walk away. I used all my powers of observation to study the small, stooped figure of a peasant. There was a sense of familiarity then, but what was it? My mind tried to block out the truth, yet the area around my solar plexus indicated that something was wrong! Master Noih drew the curtain again and motioned me to sit in my place. Wèi Wèi stared straight ahead, and I sensed coolness about her. Nothing in her manner gave me any sense of empathy or reassurance.

"Your cousin will be here soon, Su Ling." The master spoke firmly but softly. "She brings a message from your home and village."

We sat in silence waiting. I tried to close down emotionally but was not very successful. There came a knock, and Chuntian stood in the doorway. Bowing to the master, she waited to be allowed to speak. "Give your cousin the message, Chuntian." She turned to me in a disciplined and distant manner, but as our eyes met there was a brief moment of recognition and pain which disappeared as quickly as it came. "Your sister, Lái, has brought news; your mother has returned to her ancestors in the spirit world. This happened several weeks ago. The passing-over ceremony was, of course, carried out not long after." I felt the strangest sensation completely enfold me, like a blanket.

After what seemed like an eternity, I collected my thoughts. I hadn't recognised that poor, wretched creature as my sister. It was the earliest Lai Lái would have been allowed to come, of course; she would have much more to do at home now. I mumbled, "I could have tried to save Mother with my potions, if only Father had sent for me earlier."

It was not Lái's fault; she could have done nothing. I felt myself sway. I knew what was happening: my body had gone into a state of shock! Chuntian and Wèi Wèi sat me down as I absorbed the news. There were no condolences. Chuntian was dismissed, and Wèi Wèi seemed oblivious to my pain, as if she didn't understand what was happening.

After a while, Master Noih spoke. "There are only two ways to protect ourselves in such situations as this, where a loved and respected one has passed over. The first comes with much practice and skill. You have already mastered this with your work, Su Ling, but we have a long way to go before we are able to 'hold ourselves in check', shall I say, where families are concerned. The best we can hope for more often than not is a balance between the two extremes, so that our bodies respond by giving away a little, yet we feel that pain inside. This is, of course, if we were close to the deceased." So here I had the lesson of achieving balance before me, and in the most unbearable circumstances!

Master continued, "The second comes naturally to those like Wèi Wèi, who are not close to their family. So the closing down, the distancing from such news is automatic. It would not seem like such a terrible loss to her." I acknowledged this information from Master Noih but pondered to myself that it might just be the opposite for some like Wèi Wèi who would grieve for what might have been.

At that time, all I could think of was my poor mother and Lái, who was almost unrecognisable to me: I had been given the honour that was meant for her. Now, however, I couldn't imagine what had become of her. Dark thoughts started to filter through my mind, but I was not yet ready to confront them, I felt completely inadequate and powerless. Why had someone not sent word sooner? This was too cruel to contemplate. The ways of the world mystified me.

I remembered the words of the master regarding balance and tried to focus hard on my duties and lessons. I kept an emotional distance from Wèi Wèi, who carried on in her usual way, but once or twice I felt her studying me closely. My tears I kept for night-time, and I learnt how to weep silently. I should have known that the other girls would be only too aware of my grief, however strong I appeared to be. Some of my lessons with Master were now being played out in my own life. My mood was having an effect on the other girls in my living quarters, even Niang, Héshi, and Ci. Wèi Wèi, however, seemed oblivious to it. I became aware that living and working alongside people day after day created an invisible bond between them. Even those who, on the surface, seemed oblivious to others could find themselves caught up in

THE FLEDGLING

another's grief and affected by it in some way. This, then, was the mood I seemed to have triggered off in people after the death of my Mother. I was puzzled by Wèi Wèi's stance. I remembered the early days of our first meeting, when she had turned to me for support through pleading eyes. I felt sure that there had to be a reason for this bizarre behaviour now.

I had learned much about the order of things in the heavens and on the Earth plane. Becoming overemotional was not something pupils in our room succumbed to. We were taught by master magicians and priests and were honoured with knowledge of the secret ways, yet there was a discernible difference in the energies around us as we sat quietly working. One evening in the social area of our rooms, as I sat next to Wèi Wèi studying my scroll of Tao Te Ching, I heard the sound of a bell tinkling. Looking up, I saw that it was Niang herself who had rung the bell to catch my attention. She motioned me to draw closer to her; this was something which had never happened before! I sensed the other girls' interest as I stood up and approached the Holy of Holies, the top of the room occupied solely by our three leaders. Héshi and Ci sat motionless nearby and averted their eyes while carrying on with their tasks. "There is something puzzling you," Niang said. This was not so much a question as a statement.

I sat before her in silence for a moment or two with my head slightly bowed. "I sense changes, changes in the energy patterns around me," I whispered with the respect reserved for those of a higher status. With her eyes lowered, she retained the coolness by which I had come to know her, yet as she began speaking there was a distinct change in her tone, bordering on softness toward me. "It is the invisible chords; you must remember the lesson." My mind went back to one of the early lessons in the arts. How could I have forgotten it?

"Master Noih would have spoken to you about the seen and the unseen worlds we inhabit." She spoke in a measured way. "Only those who study the sacred arts would be aware of the Unseen World and its influences. It is stated that people come together at particular moments in time because of the natural laws and that our spirit guides and ancestors come together in order for a process to be worked through to its conclusion. All kinds of pupils, some who may not even like each other, are pulled together by a great, invisible force in order to complete this process, this sequence of events, for the progress of their own spirit bodies."

She paused and lifted her eyes towards mine. "When people live or work closely together, then, the invisible cords, which can appear to some of us at times, grow between people via their solar plexuses and sometimes other areas, according to how close people are – in a spiritual sense, that is. So each person will have a significant effect on the lives of all." Nodding from side to side at Héshi and Ci, Niang spoke of the particularly strong cords between all three. "In the invisible spheres, people who have very little to say to each other here in this world interact with each other in a very different way. This is all part of the great mystery; we are all working in some great plan. The cords, then, are firmly attached. You have not yet become fully aware of them; yet you sense the change in energies, so you are progressing well."

To my astonishment, I was witness to another side of Niang emerging in front of me. Before I had a chance to speak, she said,

"This is why your colleagues in the room are affected by your present mood." Bowing her head again, she went on, "We can close down our emotional selves, but the effects on the spiritual cords which bind us are felt by all. Go now." I bowed to Niang, Héshi, and Ci and slowly walked back across the room to my place.

As I pretended to study, my thoughts were firmly on the new personas I had witnessed from two of my colleagues. I wondered if I had inadvertently shown mine. As I had observed before, the ways of the world were complex. I was about to discover one of its complexities in my own life. I was not aware at the time, but my own grief was matched by another working in the commandery. Within and without Governor Choi Yen Shù's small kingdom, there were, scattered here and there, many small shrines built to honour our beloved ancestors. The governor himself had his own special shrine, of course, in a very private area of the temple gardens. During the first few months of my own grief, I had wondered if I would be allowed to pay my respects to my mother at one of the shrines. The obvious choice would, of course, have been one of the courtyard shrines inside the complex, but in my heart, I had a secret desire to lay some flowers on a small shrine which lay beyond the outer wall, near to the main gates. Being in the surrounding countryside, nearer to my home village, would have made me feel a little closer to her. I would not dare ask for such a favour, which would certainly not be granted to all in such circumstances.

One morning, as we ate our first meal of the day, one of the birthing mothers approached me in the hall to tell me that I was not needed that day. Instead, I was to go directly to Master Noih.

He would be waiting for me at a side entrance of the temple, the very same one through which Wèi Wèi and I had entered earlier. Again a negative thought came to me, and I wondered if I had done something wrong. We had been taught humility, but I found that fear itself caused much negativity in people. When I listened to my heart, I knew that I had done nothing wrong, but at the time I still had a tendency to expect the worst! "I have to go," I said to Wèi Wèi, who expressed no surprise. Our relationship had entered a different phase by then, and we said nothing else.

I walked quietly through the corridors, taking one or two of the short cuts which I had discovered during my time in the temple. Eventually I found myself in the large room I had entered some years before. Just as then, there were many elders and masters standing around discussing important matters. I kept to the very edge of the room, hoping no-one would notice me, and no-one did.

I came at last to the small, heavy door I remembered from before. At that moment, and with perfect timing, the door swung open to reveal Li Jing standing in the doorway before me. I noticed that he had grown even taller, and his expression gave nothing away; he nodded to me and ushered me through quickly. We both descended the steps to the outer door, where Master Noih was waiting for us. "This morning, Su Ling, you will visit a shrine in order to pay your respects to your mother. You will be allowed to collect a few flowers from the garden here, on this side of the temple." I gasped, and quickly closed my mouth as the master held up a hand to stop me from speaking.

"You are to take this dish with a small piece of material which has been dipped in oil. When set alight, it will burn brightly for some time. You will say sacred incantations to your ancestors in the spirit realm and lay it at the foot of the shrine with the flowers – just a few, remember! The shrine I have chosen for you lies just outside the main gates of the temple. Go now!"

With Li Jing as my escort, I hastily picked some small, delicate flowers, as pure and as white as I could find. Sensing the time, I hurried after Li Jing through the garden door into the second courtyard. This was an area where many went about their business, and there was always much activity, but as we passed into the first courtyard I hardly noticed a soul. My mind was on the task ahead of me, and I was curious to know why I, of all Master Noih's pupils, should have my secret wish granted. I knew that this was not a favour given to all! As we approached the main gates, Li Jing signalled to the guards above and on the ground below that all was well. As we both stopped in the huge gateway, he turned to me and said, "I hope you realise the honour given to you?"

"Yes," I said quickly and, I hoped, with some humility, as my feelings towards him had not changed. With that, he turned his back to me and stood talking to one of the guards. This completely took me by surprise; I had thought he would be watching my every move!

A short distance down the slope of the hill, I could see the small shrine with its carvings of the snake and the tortoise, a symbol of the North. I had only gone a few steps when a young man came, it seemed, from nowhere. He had come to pray at the shrine and was completely unaware of my presence. His head was bowed, and I sensed a great deal of pain emanating from him; it seemed to touch my own, and I didn't know what to do! I knew I could only spend a short time here, yet I could not disturb him. Then suddenly he became aware of another close by. He lifted his head, and saw me standing there. My heart leapt as I recognised the young soldier, the victor from the tournament! Still hardly daring to breathe, I turned to Li Jing for advice on what I should do next. Li Jing, however, was still talking to the guard, and both seemed oblivious to my plight. Turning back again to the young soldier, I saw in his eyes a flash of anger at this interruption to his private grief. When his eyes fell onto my own offerings to the shrine in honour of my mother, his expression suddenly changed. He moved sideways and motioned to me to step forward onto the grass verge in front of the small shrine. He had created a space for me so that we could honour our mothers together! Feeling confused, I stepped forward; this was not the usual way of things. A soldier would not usually share such a sacred moment with a servant girl! My mind raced. The same words kept repeating over and over in my mind: "Two honours in one day, two honours in one day." Time seemed to stand still as we both knelt and laid down our small offerings. Two small flames burnt brightly as we whispered our incantations. With bowed heads, we entered the silence, opening our hearts and minds to those we had just lost.

After a while I opened my eyes and stood up to find the soldier already standing, watching me. I felt my cheeks flush and lowered my eyes quickly! "Who do you honour here today?" he said quietly.

"Mother," I said, still staring at the ground.

"My mother too," he said gruffly. "I must go."

He took two steps and turned back to see my eyes watching him there. "I am Wu Fang, and you are?"

I raised myself to my full height and said, "I am Su Ling from the Hseng family." For a moment I thought I saw a flicker of amusement in his eyes. He turned swiftly and ran back through the main gates with what seemed to me a lighter step. At once Li Jing turned away from the guard towards me. He didn't have to speak, I knew I had used up all the allocated time so generously given by Master Noih Chen. I do not remember much of the way back to the master's room; it is well that I was accompanied by Li Jing, who said nothing.

Entering the room earlier than usual, I noticed some bowls of rice and fish laid out on a small table, and I wondered who they were for. Had I mistaken the time? No, Li Jing had brought me there, so there could be no mistake. For the first time, Wèi Wèi entered the room after me; she nodded and stood silently waiting with me. Suddenly the master appeared from behind the curtain in the corner of the room. It was the same curtain that hid a plain wall yet was a window for the initiated to look through.

"Sit," he ordered. "The food is for us; we eat now. You will have your usual meal at the end of the day in the hall with the others; for now, you will eat with me." This day was continuing to be a very strange one for me; I could barely take it all in. Yet as always, I never let my expression give away my feelings. Master Noih, of course, knew everything and saw everything!

After eating in silence, he said, "Today has been as a milestone for you both, a milestone in your respective lives. You do not fully understand my words right now, but you will come to know and understand them." So Wèi Wèi too had experienced something unusual during the morning. I wondered what it could be.

"We are like links in a chain," the master went on. "We link with other minds and souls which inhabit our material world. One door closes and another opens, and all for good reason. What often *appear* to be unexpected circumstances are always unconsciously expected. Much of the mundane is not planned, of course; men have a certain amount of free will. If they are wise, though, they consult their honourable spirit ancestors at the appropriate times for help."

There was silence again in the room while we finished our meal, during which time my mind wandered to Wu Fang. Each time I tried to clear my mind, his face would return, causing me much confusion. This was annoying; I felt I had been making progress with my mental discipline, but I was soon to discover how much more difficult it would become in my new situation!

After the meal we sat in silent contemplation again, as we had been taught. Master Noih rang a small bell, and we prepared to return our thoughts to the mundane world. As I opened my eyes, I was surprised to see Master Ma Sing sitting beside him and observing us closely. We bowed and waited for permission to sit up again. Master Ma gave a slight flick of the head upwards, and we returned to our positions.

"Master Ma Sing is here today to give us the benefit of his considerable knowledge; we consider this a great honour." Master Noih turned and gracefully bowed to his guest.

Master Ma Sing began to speak in the soft, calm voice I recalled from our first meeting. "Today is an introduction to a new form of training, which you will both be taking part in together with other colleagues. The new lessons will take place twice a week, with Master Noih and Master Fu Chang in attendance. The rest of the week, your lessons with Master Noih will continue as usual, as will your morning duties."

I found his voice to have an almost mesmerising effect on me, and time seemed to pass very quickly. Each word he spoke appeared to waft over me half forgotten, yet I was sure that if I needed to recall them in the future, I would have total recall of all that was said!

At the end of the afternoon, as Wèi Wèi and I made our way to the food hall, suddenly she said, "Do you feel more yourself now?"

"Yes," I replied, "and you?"

"I do, and I am wondering which of our colleagues will be joining us. Perhaps it's Meirén and one or two of the other girls. For me, today has been truly different and very strange." As we entered the hall, she was silent again, giving nothing more away of her own experience of the day.

CHAPTER 11

The Heart of the Matter

THE NEW TRAINING DAY STARTED in a most bizarre fashion. We rose and ate with everyone else at the usual hour, though we were not quite sure where to go or what to do. I watched Wèi Wèi, who seemed oblivious to everything again, until I suddenly saw her twitching! Her head nodded slightly, and I was becoming increasingly alarmed, "Wèi Wèi, Wèi Wèi, what is it? Are you ill?"

Others around us looked up but just continued eating, as if the spectacle were a common occurrence. It was not common to me! I had never seen such a thing before, not even in the birthing room or through lessons regarding the human body. Just as suddenly, it stopped! She turned to me and said, "I remember now."

My own head began to swim a little, and it was as if a clearing in my mind had taken place. I remembered Master Ma Sing's lessons of introduction to our new training. I saw his image clearly, just as he was that day, and recalled every word spoken and every instruction given.

We both knew what was required of us; we rose and made our way towards the doorway of the hall. There, already waiting for us, were Niang, Héshi, and Ci. Behind them Meirén stood, but the two other girls from our room were missing. We followed them along the corridor, where we were joined by Master Fu Chang, Master Noih's counterpart, together with the same group of junior priests who had assembled at the temple doorway with us when we went through the Wall of Illusion. A little further along, we were joined by Li Jing. We stopped before a very large doorway, and at that moment I felt as if all of us except Master Fu Chang were surprised to see it! This proved to be true; none of us except Master Fu could recall such a doorway ever being there, only an endless corridor through the temple. The large door before us had the appearance of an abalone shell, with shimmering colours which fluctuated as you ran your eyes across its surface. I could see no handle, and as soon as the thought entered my head, the door vanished. Like the garden wall, it was an illusion. As a group, we entered the space beyond together!

Observers chancing on this room may well have been disappointed. It was not too large, about the same size as Master Noih's room. It was completely bare of any cabinets, curtains, or artefacts. Just three doors broke the plainness of the room. One door appeared opposite us, and there were two more, one on each of the side walls as we approached. We stood silently, taking in the newness of all before us, and this time it was not just Wèi Wèi and I who were unaware of what the room signified.

Presently the small door opposite opened, and out stepped Master Noih and Master Ma Sing. "Before we split you up into groups, there is something we have to reveal to you all." Master Ma spoke again in the fashion which we had come to know him by; this time, however, I felt very wide awake and aware of all that was taking place.

"We have to introduce you all to the Watchers." Each master waved an arm towards the door nearest him, and from either side of the room entered the two missing girls from our living quarters! They bowed to the masters and then briefly to us, the assembled pupils. In the silence which followed, I could just imagine the questions on everyone's minds. Niang, Héshi, and Ci were the leaders, yet even they were not aware of this. I sensed, though, that there was not a sign of confusion from anyone, which was as it should have been.

"It is not often that we have a situation such as this," Master Noih said. Then he paused, watching us all for a moment. "You have been taught that people and situations are not always as they seem. Still, over a period of time we become complacent with the familiar, day-to-day faces and sequences of mundane events. This just shows us how we are not aware of everything. The day-to-day faces and patterns of events that *appear* not to change can lull us into a false sense of security. It is the natural way of human behaviour, and yet—" he paused for a moment. "This is where we learn of things which were always meant to be hidden, until the time was right to divulge them.

"You see, we need those like the Watchers, who in their very ordinariness and anonymity are best placed to do the work which has been set for them. Over time you will see that every so often, Watchers are needed in specific situations which are a little different and special."

"They are called in here to report directly to us," Master Ma Sing added. "When a group such as yours – and I do include all here – come together to be in the same place at the same time, the need for Watchers is not altogether uncommon. Before we go on, I wish to distinguish one amongst us today who is separate in a sense. Master Fu Chang has been brought in more recently as an honorary Watcher or overseer, and of course we offer him the respect which befits his station here."

Master Ma paused to acknowledge Master Fu Chang, and there was a mutual sign of acknowledgement between them. "So we go back now to the nature of this particular group. You would not, for instance, recognise the fact that you were different in any way to many other groups working together in the arts, despite all your training up to now. No, this has been foreseen only by elders whom you are not even aware of. Elders from the unseen world have watched your progress from the very beginning. We brought the Watchers into the female quarters in natural sequence to the rules of the temple. Watchers are well able to play a part of humility and obedience in this material world, yet they have exceptionally high status in all religious and secret arts. They were born to it, you see, and they were sent to us from the elders I have just spoken of."

Master Noih took over again quite naturally, without so much as a glance towards his colleague. It was as if each knew when to come in and speak. "All of you have in common things as yet unknown to you. So to formulate a plan, Master Ma Sing, Master Fu Chang, the Watchers, and I have all met together secretly. We needed to be able to draw you all together with a view eventually to be able to work as one larger group, even including males and females. Even the rules of our society and the rules of the temple are secondary to the great mysteries. This, my friends, is why we have come to meet at a place which is just outside time itself."

He took a moment to search our faces for astonishment but found none. We had been taught many things, among them the lesson not to give away our feelings by outbursts of emotion. "Good", he murmured. "No souls within the Temple of the Heavenly Bird, except the most senior priests, are aware of this place. *No*-one else will see the doorway, only a clear passageway. None will miss us, wonder where we are, or even need us while we are here. Only at the appointed times will we see the doorway. This is where I must convey to you a point of the utmost delicacy. Such will be the unusual nature of our work that even our beloved grand administrator, Choi Yen Shù, is unaware of such circumstances as this."

Master Noih's voice then took on a stern tone so that everyone would understand him well. "Yet still we will serve him and would gladly lay down our lives for him. Our very work is done in his honour." Then quietly, and almost in a whisper, he added, "And in the honour of the Illustrious Others."

At this point, there was only silence in the room. We were given time to adjust to the master's words and to meditate in order to calm our energy fields. This, in turn, made for a peaceful atmosphere around the whole area of the room outside time.

Presently I lifted my head, and I noticed that everyone in the room was doing the same.

Master Ma Sing stepped forward. "I will tell you a little about our friends the Watchers." I glanced over at the two girls I had shared our living quarters with for some time yet knew very little about. They were so quiet; Meirén had taken charge of us when we first arrived, and any further questions we had were directed to her. If I didn't include the exchange I had with Niang, I had hardly conversed with the other two at all! Wèi Wèi and I had concentrated so much on our three room elders and on trying not to break the rules of protocol that we had hardly any dealings with them. They, in turn, seemed to have very little to say to us. The more I thought of it, the more strange it seemed that we had never heard their names mentioned in all that time!

Just as the thought had occurred to me, Master Ma spoke. "The purpose of the Watchers, I believe, is self-evident. They work in a framework of concealment. They have to be able to infiltrate a group so unobtrusively that the rest are not even aware of their names. So clever in the mysterious arts are they that they are able to erase a thought from another's mind! So whenever a naturally occurring thought about them comes to their notice – and yes, they can tell – it is erased from the person's mind without them even being aware of it." At this point I could feel a tension emanating across the room from all of us.

"I must add that our Watchers have not been allowed to replace or put any other thoughts *into* your minds. For that has been the objective: to see how you would react in certain circumstances, not to sway you from one direction or another. The particular forte of our Watchers is in making themselves almost invisible, like objects in the background.

"You have all become aware that as masters we often know your thoughts; this is, of course, through years of studying the sacred arts. The Watchers, then, are an extra aid for us – which is not to belittle their status, because they are very much our equal in some things and are of a higher ability than us in others. A female body was needed by each of them at this time and in this incarnation. So your thoughts and actions, even within the framework of protocol, have been watched closely. As your masters, we have watched you all; we have kept a very close eye on Li Jing, our faithful servant, along with my young priests, who have chosen a life of strict discipline. This work takes us to another level of discipline entirely."

Master Noih stepped forward and addressed my female companions. "Before we leave this place today, we have to explain that there will now be two fewer in your living quarters; this is as it should be. Our Watchers will be housed elsewhere and will join us at the times of our meetings. You will refer to them as Shen and Jing. These names were given to them by our unseen masters and represent the mind or spirit of a person, in the case of Shen, and the essence or underpinning of all organic life, in the case of Jing. They can teach us much. Now your living quarters and the energy within each room will take on a new vibrational quality. This is because now everything is out in the open; our life purpose has been revealed, so there will be no need to 'test the water', as they say, regarding the thoughts and actions of your companions.

"Discipline and respect of status must be adhered to; this is a matter of course. But each will have a new understanding of how progress can be made by coming together to study the mysteries. We will all leave now through the same door you entered earlier. We will go through a small group at a time. When you leave, resume your normal work and timetable for the day. My two eminent master companions and I, together with the Watchers, will be the last to go and to seal up the Door of Illusion as we leave it. No-one in the passageway will be aware of what will be happening. We meet again three days from now; you will instinctively know the time to come. Go now!"

Slowly Wèi Wèi and I made our way back to Master Noih's room; we sat quietly, waiting for him to arrive. We did not look at each other or mutter a sound; we just silently waited, lost in our own thoughts. When the master arrived and sat before us, he announced, "We will meditate in a while, but first I want to speak to you about the physical body or counterpart. I say 'counterpart' because of course we are primarily of the ether, the world of the spirit, and we only inhabit this body of flesh for a while. We have to adjust to the new energies around us now that we are bringing you a little farther into the mysterious art. You have already felt the difference within your bodies; it is like an awakening of the soul. The physical body can take some time to adjust. Balance is the key; we will alter your diet a little, and you will be allowed certain foods which are not available to all. You have a set routine, but this will change, particularly when you are in your rooms. I will give your group certain exercises in order to help with your adjustment and to bring a sense of balance to your bodies. We have already discovered how emotional instability can affect us, so it will be essential at times to work with your group of companions in order to bring in some stability and calm. This work will be a continuation of what I have already taught you about closing yourself off from too much noise and activity."

Master Noih clicked his fingers, and music emanated from the corner of the room, behind the curtain. It was similar to the music of our culture, yet it had a quality and a beauty I had never heard before. Out of the corner of my eye, I could see Wèi Wèi sway a little. The Master said sharply, "Centre yourself, Wèi Wèi!" There we sat, master and pupils, with our eyes closed and our backs straight, drifting off to another place where time seemed to stand still.

Many images came flooding into my mind and my consciousness that day, together with a growing awareness of my own strength. It seemed like a paradox to me, because when I was not developing my skills in this way and going about my normal day-to-day tasks, I felt my usual self. This duality of experience took some getting used to. I knew from past experience that I had to acknowledge and allow myself to feel the many new emotions which were emerging now as I grew into womanhood. Everything had its purpose; therefore it was all part of my life's lessons and work. Leaving all this temporarily behind when going through the doorway of illusion was a very different matter, but it was also an opportunity; all things there became clearer, as if everything was in its place.

We had been following our new routine for two weeks when I began to notice a helpful influence during my working day in the birthing room. I was much calmer and able to act well in a crisis.

This was noted by the older women, who complimented me but stressed that all credit should go to my master, as he was such an excellent teacher. The old birthing mothers would not, of course, put any of my accomplishments down to their own teaching. No-one thought that way; they were simply there to serve their emperor. I knew differently but did not speak of it.

One evening I was studying a scroll on rare herbs and flowers when I became aware of Wèi Wèi's unease. We were all quietly sitting in the social area of our living quarters. Niang, Héshi, and Ci were contemplating in silence at the top of the room, and Meirén sat painting designs onto a plain lacquered box. Wèi Wèi's unease and preoccupation with her robe, first moving it this way and then another, irritated me and finally broke my concentration altogether.

"What is it, Wèi Wèi?" I whispered.

"I don't know if I should tell you."

"Well, you clearly must tell someone, or it will drain your energy field. I can already feel the friction around you!" I was irritable but curious.

"For some reason I wish to tell you first," she said. "Then I must tell Master Noih."

My eyes went heavenward. "He probably knows already," I said, "but you can tell me if you wish."

Wèi Wèi looked up at me, eyes staring widely, and began her story. It was about her unusual day, the same day I was allowed to visit the shrine and the day I met Wu Fang. "I was allowed into the temple gardens that day, Su Ling. I was to study the vibrations of the plants and flowers and to see if I could alter them with my mind. I was studying seriously when I became aware of gentle warmth which had completely surrounded me. I was not afraid; it made me feel secure and relaxed, and I became less anxious in my work. I found that I could make progress much more rapidly, as my anxiety had been a considerable hindrance to me. This, you see, had been a new experience for me, because nothing previously had ever blocked me in my work."

At this point Wèi Wèi stopped again, hesitating about what she was to say next. I said nothing but waited for her, because we had been taught to let others make their own decisions. "After a while I felt drawn to another part of the gardens where there was a pool full of fish and water lilies. My lessons were forgotten for a while as I knelt down, following the movements of the pretty fish; it was very calming. Then a strange thing happened. All at once the pool became crystal clear and appeared to have no bottom, just endless, clear water!" Wèi Wèi had really gotten my attention now, not to mention my curiosity.

"I could hear the trickle of the water through the bamboo pipes at the back of the pond, but the appearance of the pool had changed completely. I have seen many pictures in my mind, but this was different. You see, I was relaxed, and everything appeared real to me. I saw movement on the surface, and when all became calm again, I saw you, Su Ling."

I said nothing because my excitement had faded a little; I just motioned her to carry on. "I saw your face and what you were wearing that day. I turned around expecting to see you, but there was no-one there." Wèi Wèi paused for a moment again. I continued to say nothing and decided that this must be a new aspect to her lessons in the arts. What I wasn't so sure of was why my own face featured so prominently in the pool.

She watched me for a moment and then continued. "Suddenly there was a young man in the pool facing you."

Trying to appear unconcerned, I said "Go on".

"The next part is a little strange," she said quietly. "The young man's face kept altering. At first I could see him clearly; then the picture would change to that of a baby. There were many ripples around your own face, which suddenly turned dark. I did not like the feeling I was experiencing in my solar plexus. A wide ripple crossed the face of the young man. Then he and the baby were covered in blood! I heard a cry like a wounded animal."

There was a deathly silence across the whole room, and we realised that the other four were listening intently. Wèi Wèi sat looking at me expectantly, waiting for my thoughts on what she had seen.

"Is that everything you saw?" I asked. "Yes. There was not time to speak with Master Noih then. I must be truthful: I did not want to."

The feeling of light-headedness which I had become used to enveloped me, and I closed my eyes for a moment to centre myself. As I did this, I became aware that everybody else in the room was doing the same, restoring a balance in the unsettled vibrations in the room.

None of us spoke of Wèi Wèi's experience that evening, and once a sense of harmony had been restored to the room, Niang, Héshi, and Ci led us on the evening ritual in the washroom a little earlier than usual. As I lay my head down to sleep later, a strange and merciful sleepiness came over me. I believe that I had a little extra help from my friends around me and those from the Unseen World.

I named our special group Kou, or 'family members', but I kept this description to myself, though I was not entirely sure why. We were due to meet at the appointed place the following day. I wanted to put Wèi Wèi's vision to the back of my mind as I went about my work preparing potions in the birthing room. There were few births that morning to take my mind completely off of the events of the day before, so I used a technique Master Ma Sing had taught us in order to focus our minds on our work. He showed us how to put whatever was making us anxious into a large, imaginary bubble and float it to the far side of our mind. We were aware of our worries, but they would be contained for a time until we were ready to deal with them later. Our *intention* here was everything. Master told us that the mind often does this delaying action automatically, but sometimes it needs a little help from us.

I was pleased to be able to complete my work that morning before making my way to the corridor where we usually met. I was alone on my journey through the temple and had one or two passageways to travel before I reached my destination. Along one of these that day, there were soldiers guarding doors to all the rooms. This always happened when dignitaries were present for important meetings. The very last door was quite a way from the others, and as I was about to pass the guard, something made me lift my head. There stood Wu Fang! Our eyes met in surprise. We both quickly resumed our composure, and I hurried along to the next corridor, desperately trying to put Wu Fang into a bubble!

Along the final passageway, I met Wèi Wèi and Meirén. We spoke no words, just silently carried on until Niang, Héshi, and Ci joined us. By this time I had gained some control over my emotions and achieved a calmness of spirit. We entered the doorway of illusion.

Together we performed the opening ritual for the day's lessons. We were all there: Master Ma, Master Noih, Master Fu, Li Jing, the young priests, and my fellow colleagues. None ever missed a meeting; it was as if the teachers in spirit cleared away any obstacles. After the ceremony, Master Noih spoke. "Before you divide into your work groups, I wish to say a few words concerning any information you may have received from the unseen world in regard to those close to you."

Of course the master knew of Wèi Wèi's vision! "This kind of information, specifically clairvoyance or prophecy; needs wise consideration. Some things are meant to be passed on. Some are interpreted for the receiver; some are left for the receiver's interpretation. We know that the ways of the unseen world are strange, but there are always reasons why some things are told and some things are held back. These things can be a matter of trial and error; if an error is made, we can deal with it here in this room. Naivety or emotions can sway pupils to make the wrong decision; all is part of a learning experience. Somewhat dramatic visions can be handled by older, more experienced members of the arts. They can look beyond the emotional impact of such a message and prepare their lives accordingly. However, it is never safe for a young, inexperienced pupil to unburden such a message onto a friend. Any of you may come to us if you are concerned about your visions or messages. This will have to be the case for some considerable time, until all here know instinctively how to act without recrimination. Of course, if such information is received and you are easily able to keep it to yourself, then things can be left as they are. You are all aware that *we* are aware of everything that happens. So seeking our counsel would be necessary only if the information became a burden to you.

"As we progress in this room, it will be necessary to hold many things of a controversial nature in our minds as we learn to see things in a wider sense and perceive why things happen. As this is the first time we have spoken of the matter together, the few instances which have occurred recently among you can be dealt with in your ordinary classes in the arts. That is all."

So there were others! Other members of Kou, my name for our new group, had had similar strange thoughts to the ones Wèi Wèi and I had experienced. I knew, too, that Master Noih would be speaking to us about those experiences the very next day. I had mixed feelings about this and wondered what the outcome would be. The main topic of the lesson that day with the female group from Kou, concerned things that would help us to see the very subject of our personal experiences a little more clearly. These things were so secret that they cannot be spoken of here!

The next day, our work took on a new twist. My mind was still reeling from the secrets disclosed the day before during our meeting, which meant that I had to discipline myself in order to stay grounded while I worked in the birthing room. Yet simultaneously,

I found that I had a new perspective on my responsibilities. On the one hand, the knowledge of the previous day had been put aside, but on the other it immediately affected every part of the morning's events.

There were several births that day, and even as I prepared potions, I became aware of the situation of each of the women in labour. I was aware of the future outcome for each patient, of whose babes would survive, and even of the regrets some women had as they struggled to give birth. This awareness even stretched as far as the potential future lives of each babe. I say 'potential future' because, though some things were set by the souls themselves, some things could change unexpectedly. Although it was a personal burden, this awareness proved fortunate in the way I approached each patient. Rules of the birthing room had to be followed, but a small gesture here and a quiet word said at the right time made a significant difference to each woman, sometimes eradicating the need for calming potions.

The other side of the new gift showed itself in demonstrating how much I needed to draw from my inner strength whenever I became aware of the sad or traumatic events about to enter the lives of the mothers or their offspring. This brought the lessons of the day before home to me. It severely tested me at times as I endeavoured mentally and emotionally to stay detached from such challenging knowledge. I had been tested before, many times, and I had realised even then that it was part of my preparation for the next stage of my development. I thought of my female colleagues from Kou, and I knew without doubt that the activities of each one would be affected by the events of the previous day.

The afternoon lesson with Master Noih taught Wèi Wèi and me much about receiving such information at odd times and about how we were to deal with it. Much information flowed through Wèi Wèi all the time, and she had to work hard to switch off such an influx of thought, to know what to do with it, and to learn how and when to use it. This was an acquired skill that she still had to develop, as did we all.

After our evening meal, as we sat together in our living quarters, Niang announced that we would all retire earlier that day. I was glad and saw that the day had taken its toll on everyone. I wondered how my male colleagues had fared.

As I slept that night, I entered a strange dream state. It felt real somehow, though I was aware that I was asleep. I was walking through the corridor in the temple that led to the room of illusion. The doorway became clear to me, and as I entered, the room was empty except for Wu Fang. I asked him what he was doing there and warned him that this was not allowed! He stared at me intently and said, "But you have brought me here, Su Ling. This is *your* dream. I was summoned, and I came."

I was perplexed and confused by this; I felt a flash of movement out of the corner of my right eye. The wall in the room seemed transparent, and I could see a procession of all the masters, Watchers, and members of Kou walking along the corridor; I even saw myself following behind. This was most strange. Suddenly the room disappeared, and I found myself with Wu Fang on a White Mountain top. In front of us stood our two mothers, who were holding hands and smiling so serenely that I thought my heart would break. Wu Fang and I instinctively held hands, and an overwhelming flow of love passed between us. Our love surpassed anything I had experienced before and was all-encompassing. I felt as if we had known each other forever. I became aware of my mother's words, even though her lips never moved. She told me that I must be very brave, because our lives here were just moments in time; everything was for a higher purpose. She told me that the things I was about to experience would be hard to bear, but all would be understood in time.

"We four have stood on this mountaintop many times before; our souls are old friends, my child. You have chosen to walk a difficult path, balanced between the heavens and the Earth. I am proud of you. Remember, in spite of everything, I love you very much!"

I turned to Wu Fang, who seemed to be absorbing a silent conversation with his own mother. Suddenly, both women vanished. I felt a pain and sadness I thought I could not endure. I looked to Wu Fang for strength and saw that he too was experiencing the same emotion. I felt very cold, and then a hand was shaking me to awaken. Niang stood over me with a concerned expression on her face. I came to my senses quickly, amazed at the intimacy of the moment between us.

The atmosphere in our living quarters had settled into calmness and peace interrupted only by moments of disharmony when a colleague was very anxious over a personal matter. Each instance was dealt with alike; moments were taken to collectively breathe deeply and rebalance the energies in the room. This in itself did not erase the problem which surfaced, but it enabled us to cope and to react in a manner which did not cause us more suffering.

The knock-on effect of working together, instead of against each other, meant that relationships which had become strained became bearable. Some, like those among Niang, Héshi, and Ci, were of a closer nature, of course. Where this was not possible for everyone, respect was the order of the day.

As winter began to set in, I was grateful for the sturdy walls of the temple to protect us from the worst of the elements. At times, my thoughts strayed to my home village and how there is little to protect them from the ravages of winter. I could only offer up a prayer for my family and others there; I could not afford to slip into self-pity and worry. Holding my little bird, my Tóngshì, brought my family a little closer, for we both came from the same place.

One day as I approached Master Noih's room, I saw Wèi Wèi suddenly stop for a moment before going in. I was curious to see why. As I entered the room, I saw Master Noih, Shen, Jing, and Wu Fang waiting – for me, I felt!

Master Noih called me. "Come in, Su Ling. There is an important matter to discuss." I averted my eyes from Wu Fang, alarmed that I may have done something wrong. "This concerns your relationship with Wu Fang."

I blushed and my face was a deep red, I felt foolish and uneasy. Ignoring my embarrassment, he continued. "Your dreams should have told you much, Su Ling. In matters concerning both the visible and invisible worlds, people and events come into our lives to help our growth. After much consideration, Wu Fang has asked permission to speak to me on the matter at hand. He wishes to take a wife, Su Ling: you!"

I lifted my eyes to meet the master's and just said, "Yes, Master." I knew there was to be no choice in the matter, but I also knew that this was meant to be, and I wanted it to be. Our meeting at the shrine to honour our mothers was no chance encounter. I had learned enough to know that it was meant to be, and for a purpose – a wider spiritual purpose. I did not know, however, how much Wu Fang knew about such things.

"I have given my permission for this union. Because you are a very special servant to me—" Master fixed me with his eyes, for neither of us was permitted to divulge the existence of Kou. "We are granting you a room to share in the temple servants' quarters nearest my own. This is only granted in very rare circumstances."

Wu Fang bowed low in astonishment at this honour bestowed on him, whispering his thanks over and over again. He did not, and could not, fully understand the situation. I began to understand that I was not fully aware myself. "You will guard the outer temple entrances for the time being, Wu Fang. The union will be sealed in a sacred ceremony seven days from now. That is all. Go now."

As Wu Fang left, we all stood silently for a few moments until Master told us to sit. In unison we sat together. "You have been told about affairs of the heart, Su Ling; we do not usually allow such a match, as Wu Fang comes from a family of a higher status than the family Hseng. The added dimension to your union, of course, is a spiritual one. Wu Fang is not really aware of what this means. He is only aware of the religion and customs of our times. Yet his dream was a reflection of yours, and he will feel stirrings deep within his self that tell him of the underlying importance of what is going on here. Also, I have to say that where the Kou is concerned, such dedicated work usually precludes the need for marriage."

He paused, watching me. Knowing my thoughts, he continued. "In answer to your current thoughts, Su Ling, I have not allowed this union for Wu Fang to join Kou; our group is complete. The Watchers are here to give you a message. You will not be able to hear this, Wèi Wèi. I will put you in a dream state until later, when we resume our lessons for the day."

I lifted my eyes to see the Watchers. They were now standing before me, yet I had heard no movement. Shen spoke first. "What we speak of here today, Su Ling, will be forgotten by your conscious mind, but your awareness will guide you in the future. Of course, your unconscious, or 'hidden', mind is totally aware of everything."

Jing spoke so softly that I almost lost her words. "We are going to show ourselves to you in a different form." I suddenly felt lifted a little and had to adjust my eyes to the brightness of their beings. I saw before me two beautiful and pure spirit forms; I could not tell if they were male or female. Their white and gold robes shone in the gloom of my surroundings, and I bowed my head to the floor, thinking that I was not worthy to see such spiritual energy.

"Lift your head, Su Ling," a male voice said to me – or was it a female one? I could not be sure. "Through your dream state, your mother came to you to tell you a little of your future. You will experience the loss of your loved one Wu Fang soon; this is meant to be. It is important that you have met and will spend a little more time together, however briefly. The connection between the two of you had to be made at this time on the Earth plane, for reasons we will now disclose."

I don't know how long I was in such an altered state with these two magnificent beings. I was even unaware of Master Noih and Wèi Wèi being with me in the room. Very gently, I felt my consciousness being lowered to the floor again, and the brilliance was gone. Shen and Jing stood before me once more, with just a hint of the fading light still shining in their eyes. My only conscious recollection of the message brought to me that day was that it was most important that my union with Wu Fang be consummated before the end of the seventh day and therefore before the appointed time for the sacred ceremony. In spiritual terms, the true sacred contract had been made aeons before; the physical consummation, in this case, was more binding and important than the ceremony itself. I also remember being told that my family at home – my father, brothers, and sisters – would be financially rewarded again as the union took place.

For the next few days I was excused from my duties in the birthing room as preparations were made for my marriage to Wu Fang. Preparations for me consisted of lessons, not only in matters of a physical union with a man but also in the spiritual dimension of such a union. As Wu Fang was consciously unaware of such things, the task would be my responsibility – to set the scene for body, mind, and spirit. I spent most of the day with the governor's chief concubine, who instructed me in the physical arts of bringing pleasure to my future husband with my body. Shen and Jing, in their female guise, explained how a spiritual experience is obtained in such circumstances.

On the third day, my last before joining Wu Fang, I was instructed to collect a rare plant from the temple garden. This was to be placed in the room of our forthcoming union. Shen lent me a warm cloak with a hood to wear, as there was a biting wind outside. I was almost lost in the garment and not easily recognisable. As I approached one of the outer doors, I heard a great commotion! Several guards were busy keeping at bay desperate peasants who were pleading to be let into the temple. With the winter upon us, they would soon be short of food, however hard the co-operatives had worked to provide for everyone during the freezing months. I saw several women obviously heavy with child who needed a warm place for their confinements. I did not cry out or sway then; I had learnt much from my work with Kou. However, I still felt a stirring inside, for I had not yet experienced a union with a man or carried a child inside of me. My path seemed very hard indeed, but perhaps it was not as hard as that of the poor souls at the door. Who can measure one kind of suffering against another? I heard the anger and saw the ruthlessness of the guards as they kicked and pushed the peasants away, for they had been trained and ordered to do. There was an order to everything in China, and no lines were crossed, no rules broken, whatever the circumstances.

As I approached, one guard broke away to allow me through the crowd. I recognised Wu Fang at once, though he did not recognise me under the cloak and his thoughts were still concentrated on keeping the peasants from the door. So there it was: the other side of Wu Fang. It was just as I had seen Master Sing change in a flash. Here was my heart's desire fulfilling his duties as a good soldier to his master governor and his beloved emperor. Fulfilling his duties demanded such ruthlessness! As I stepped outside into the garden, it was not just the cold I shuddered from.

I crossed a small courtyard edged with shrubs and went into another area, as I had been directed. I came upon a group of large, smooth stones near running water. There were two identical plants growing amongst them, and I knew I had found what I was looking for. I picked one as instructed and examined it closely. At first it seemed plain and unremarkable. There were two long, slim, and sturdy dark leaves, with another growing at their base. Looking closely, I could see the tiniest of spores growing outwards all around the edges of each leaf. Some had little dots of colour at their tips, which were the beginnings of the new blooms. I silently promised the masters of the Unseen World that I would tend and protect this very special plant. I held it close to my body to protect it from the wind.

By the time I reached the door, most of the peasants had left. Just one or two still struggled with the guards. As I attempted to pass, Wu Fang prepared to strike me just as my hood fell to my shoulders, revealing who I was. He seemed struck dumb for a moment; then his mood changed as he instructed the others to let me through on Master Ma Sing's orders.

I carried the plant with care along the passageways to a place in the temple where Master Noih's living rooms were and found the room nearby which had been allocated to Wu Fang and myself. This was indeed a great honour in itself, yet I had a sense of unease stirring deep within me. I put this down to the confrontation I had just witnessed at the outer door. As I stepped inside, I felt a warm, calming sensation; there was no fear in this room. I placed the rare plant on a little ledge on the outer wall of the room underneath a small shaft of light coming from a window near the ceiling. The room seemed to be rather ordinary, yet my life would be far from ordinary after the following day. Whatever my thoughts and feelings towards Wu Fang were after witnessing his ruthless side, I could not judge him for obeying orders from on high. In spite of what I had seen, I knew I still loved him, and this emotion was mixed with sadness knowing of the darker side of people. I closed the door and made my way back to my own living quarters. I slept well that night, to my surprise. I believed this to be the result of help from the Watchers, for I knew them to be very special beings indeed.

The next day was my special day! Niang, Héshi, Ci, Wèi Wèi, and Meirén accompanied me to the little room with the rare plant. They helped me to bathe in hot water perfumed with flowers and special oils. It was strange to be pampered so, and it gave me a feeling of deep relaxation. After I was dried, a beautiful robe of the most delicate fabric was placed over me. Sometimes it appeared like pure white gossamer; then again it seemed to change to a delicate shade of shining lilac! There were shoes to match, and even the braids in my hair matched my robe. My colleagues removed the tub of water to swill away and returned with a fresh tub of perfumed water for Wu Fang. We bowed in friendship to one another with eyes cast downwards. Then, silently, they left the room.

A few moments later, Wu Fang came to join me. I bowed to him and began to feel a little embarrassed. I raised my head and saw him cast his eyes over me, studying me closely for a moment before smiling warmly. Looking into his eyes, I saw once more the man I remembered. Gone was the cruelty and pretence; he stood before me as his true self. "You honour me, Su Ling; your beauty lies on the inside as well as the outside. I have chosen wisely."

"The honour is mine," I replied. "Let me help you with your clothes."

I slowly and gently performed the bathing ceremony, as I had been instructed, and felt the softness and contours of his skin for the first time, in contrast to the rougher skin on his hands – the hands of a soldier. In the distance we could hear a musical instrument being played softly for us, a sweet, sad sound. It did not seem familiar to me.

As I helped him from the tub and tried to dry his wet body, he held me closely with eagerness before I could finish. I spoke softly to him. "Wait just a little more time." I led him across to a screen in the wall, which I opened to reveal a sleeping area already prepared for us. All my training with the spirit masters and the governor's chief concubine were meant for this moment. I slowly disrobed, and he pulled me down onto the bedding. So began the consummation of our union, which was more wonderful than my expectations of it. It was like drifting on an endless sea, enveloped in each other's souls with our bodies joined. I knew it was meant to be a moment in time to cherish.

After we lay in each other's arms for some time, a time I was not even aware of, I heard a tap on the screen and went to see who it was. As I pulled it back, I saw that the tub had been removed. In its place had been laid some delicious food to which we were both unaccustomed.

"What is it?" Wu Fang gasped.

"Come and look, husband!" Tidying my clothing, I waited to see if the food pleased him.

He stood for a moment in amazement at the feast laid out before him. "I don't understand. I have never had such food as this." He turned to me, unable to comprehend why we would be allowed such a feast; there were unfamiliar fruits, meats, and even fish laid out along with some food we could not even identify until we studied it carefully. They were tiny little birds, fledglings!

"You must be a very special servant to Master Noih, Su Ling."

I beckoned to Wu Fang to sit while I offered the food and served him first. Carefully avoiding the poor little birds, I took a little of the fruit and fish to eat. I ate in silence as my husband began to talk. I listened quietly as he spoke of his home and family. "You would have liked my mother, Su Ling. To think we met at the shrine when paying our devotion to our mothers!"

He sighed. I had a brief recollection of my dream at the mountaintop but could not remember what was said. I dared not mention this to Wu Fang, as he would have thought me strange, so I began to speak to him of my own village, Laopíe. I told him about the members of my family, especially Lái, my elder sister, who should have taken my place.

"Perhaps our ancestors and the spirit gods decreed it," he said, taking me by surprise. "I know little of such things, Su Ling, but it is unusual for the oldest to be overlooked in such a way?" I felt that even though Wu Fang was a soldier, he had a good insight into such things.

After we had eaten our fill, I showed Wu Fang my little bird, my Tóngshì. He held it for a while and smiled. He could see how precious a gift it was to me. "The man who made your little bird must have been very skilled. You must take great care of it."

The day became the evening, and we returned to our sleeping area, but sleep was a long way off. Wu Fang lay me down, and with his finger he slowly traced every part of my hair and face before kissing my lips. We were lost again in each other's arms until morning came too soon. I woke just in time to see that he was already dressed in his armour. He turned to me and said, "I cannot wait until we next meet my little wife."

His smile told me everything, but with that, he was gone. In the silence of the room, I thought I heard a baby cry from a very far-off place.

I rose and, after my ablutions, tidied the bedroll away. I pulled back the screen and saw that all the dishes from the day before had been quietly removed. Neither of us had noticed. I stood on my toes and carefully checked the small plant on the wall before I left for the hall. I was not particularly hungry; I felt as if my heart were full of love and happiness, with a sense of spiritual uplifting, too. I turned my little Tóngshì over and over in my hand as if it were responsible for my happiness. As I gazed upon it fondly, I seemed to experience, for a moment, a tiny flutter of wings as though my little bird were inside of me as well as on the outside. I put him away just in time to see the other girls arriving. They studied me closely and then lowered their eyes, trying with the greatest difficulty to hide their smiles. Only Niang continued to look seriously at me, and all through her meal, her expression hardly changed.

I ate my meagre meal, which could not compare with the feast of the day before, in silence while wondering when I would get the chance to talk to my colleagues about the wonderful feelings I was experiencing. I prepared to leave and say good-bye with a brief nod of my head, but just then Niang stood up in front of me. "A small wedding gift: this is to wrap your little bird in."

She pressed into my hand a beautiful silk scarf of lilac and white motifs. I gasped. This was entirely unexpected! "Thank you, Niang. I will treasure your gift. Look, I will wrap it around Tóngshì now and keep it in my special pouch."

I spoke softly so that other servants nearby did not hear. I left for the birthing room to catch up on some of my tasks. Immediately, I saw that things were fairly quiet with the expectant mothers, and so I went to work creating my mixtures and potions. Disciplining my mind to concentrate on the work was even more important that morning, or my beloved Wu Fang would have entered my every thought. The extra discipline I used that day stood me in good stead, for many potions were needed.

Towards the middle of the day, I sensed extra movement along the passageways alongside the room. The older birthing mothers glanced up too, as soldiers were hurrying by towards one of the outer doors. I thought of the desperate peasants trying to gain entry to the temple. Trying not to think of any poor pregnant young women in trouble, I had to make a conscious effort to steady and calm myself as I had been taught to do. As I did, I became aware of a continuing stream of soldiers marching by. For a brief moment, I felt strange inside. Wèi Wèi's dream of the pond flashed into my mind, yet in my state of heightened consciousness I continued to feel calm. As things quietened down in the temple, I returned to my normal state and began to finish my task by filling the jars with my preparations. I had been instructed then to go to the master's room to learn about the ceremony to be held on the seventh day. I was surprised, as I expected to be summoned the following day, the day before the ceremony.

Making my way back along the corridor, I looked for signs which might tell me why so many soldiers had been called. Two servants hurried by whispering about an enemy warring party nearby. I realised then the threat to the temple: there was an enemy at the outer gates! Our brave warriors were called out to repel them before they could enter the compound. I was silently glad that Wu Fang was on guard duty at the door, but I also felt a sense of unease, which I tried to put out of my mind as I prepared for my lesson.

CHAPTER 12

Lost and Found

AS WAS OFTEN THE CASE, it was silent in the room, but there was something else. I felt a difference in the vibrations. Wèi Wèi sat as always before Master Noih, and they were both already in deep meditation. I was a little taken aback, as they would always wait for me before a meditation began; I stopped for a moment, wondering what I should do. We had been taught to walk so quietly and skilfully that others would not notice our approach. With this lesson firmly in my mind, I walked across the room and silently took my place beside Wèi Wèi. Placed on the floor in front of Master was an open lantern burning brightly. The most delicate fragrance was emanating from it. I was used to the aromas of many oils and many plants and flowers, but this was totally unfamiliar to me. Breathing in its perfume made me slightly drowsy, but I managed to stay awake long enough to see Master and Wèi Wèi open their eyes.

I bowed my head, and when I looked up again I saw a gleam in Master Noih's eyes that I had only ever seen before in the Hidden Room. "Ah, Su Ling, you have come. Good. First I have to inform you that the next meeting of Kou will be a little sooner than expected: it will be tomorrow." Something must have happened to alter this; everything had its place and time, especially the meetings of Kou! I sat patiently waiting for instructions concerning the ceremony. Though I had been prepared thoroughly for the consummation of our union, as yet I knew very little of the sacred ceremony itself.

"Wèi Wèi," Master Noih said softly. At this Wèi Wèi rose to her feet and kneeled before me, bowing in recognition of our friendship. "I have seen a vision for you, Su Ling, but this vision concerns your life some years into the future. This is the time I have been given it, so this is the time I will give it to you." I returned her gesture with a slight bow and waited to hear the news. "In my vision you are older, Su Ling, a serene and wiser woman. You have gained much strength and skill from your work with our colleagues in Kou by this time, and you are to be honoured or awarded something unusual, which I could not see. Evidently I was not meant to see it. It was a very bright and positive vision, and you were surrounded by your colleagues from Kou and others from the temple. There was a great outpouring of love for you!"

"Is this for me, Wèi Wèi? Are you sure?" I was astonished at the idea and also at my undisciplined outburst! Only people of great eminence were rewarded for their work.

Master stepped in before I could say anything else. "Remember, both of you, sometimes we need to expect the unexpected – the unthinkable. All things come to pass."

Bowing to Master, I then thanked Wèi Wèi, still a little unsure if an error had been made. But I knew at the back of my mind they were both correct; they could not be wrong. With a polite nod, Wèi Wèi sat down again.

Trying to fully take in Wèi Wèi's message and still feeling a little drowsy from the fragrance in the room, I tried to bring my focus back to the ceremony, which I had temporarily forgotten. Master closed his eyes again for a moment, opened them, and rose to his feet. Our eyes followed him as he crossed to the far corner of the room where the curtain hung. Pulling it back, he once again prepared to view the magic window. From where we sat, there seemed to be much movement. I could just make out horses rearing up and soldiers fighting. It was the battle with the enemy! Silently I sent out a request to our ancestors in spirit and to the spirit masters themselves to keep our soldiers and land safe. Things appeared to go hazy then; I could not see the window as clearly as Master Noih obviously could. I thought that perhaps I was overcome with the fragrant incense and it had hindered my view. Master drew the curtain again across the corner of the room and returned to us.

As he sat down, his face took on a strange, rigid expression. There was something in his eyes which I could not clearly recognise. He spoke. "As you may know, there have been skirmishes with the enemy just outside the main gates. A group dressed as priests presented themselves as messengers from a neighbouring kingdom, in the pretence of friendship and peace. Our guards on the watchtowers listened to them but became aware of one man whose eyes gave him away. Their astute observation of this emissary warned them of danger and treachery. Recognising this, they called for reinforcements just as the enemy threw off their disguises and revealed themselves. Others sprung out from bushes on the hillside and tried to gain entry by scaling the walls on special ropes."

He paused for a moment, breathing evenly, while Wèi Wèi and I almost held our breath. "Their bowmen brought down some of our guards from the watchtowers. One of our battalions prepared for battle inside the gates. The gates were opened, and they fought bravely – as we would, of course, expect. Victory is now ours; most of the enemy have either been captured or killed. Two have escaped to tell their sorry tale to their leader; however, along with the watchtower guards, four of our foot soldier warriors have been brought down. We salute their memory and honour them tomorrow when Kou meet again."

Our brave men had protected us again! Wèi Wèi and I sat quietly for a moment, and I was thinking of what Master Noih had said earlier, 'expect the unexpected.' With eyes cast down, Master continued. "The yellow banner of the tiger fell, but it has been taken up by another worthy of the honour and will continue to be carried into battle as before." For a moment I was stunned, but suddenly I knew. I knew! My training kicked into action automatically, and within a second or two I had put into action a motion to protect my heart and solar plexus as much as possible from the shock. Still, it could not protect me completely from the knowledge that my husband, Wu Fang, had been killed and had passed from this material world into spirit! My beloved husband, who had been presented with the banner of the tiger by Governor Choi at the ceremony, was dead! The pictures flashed through my mind. He had been called away from guard duty because, of course, he was the leader. He had been appointed to ride into battle carrying the banner and leading the men because of his considerable skill in the contest.

The room spun around me as my mind tried to take in what had just happened. The honour, the beautiful union, were all for nothing! Yet even as my thoughts touched on these things, I sensed the far-off words the Watchers had spoken when undergoing their transformation. Sometimes we are tested. *This must be mine*, I thought, yet I could not rise to readjust my equilibrium. Everything continued to spin. I was not even aware of Master Noih giving me a potion while Wèi Wèi supported me. Hands had lifted me up and taken me to an area where physicians performed their work. I was informed of all this later and of the fact that Master Noih had ordered them to administer only the most basic of care to me for three hours, after which time servants would return to take me to my living quarters – my *old* living quarters.

During those three hours and for most of the night, I drifted in and out of a hazy sleep. I remember very little but a vague awareness of Niang keeping vigil over me. My other colleagues drifted in and out of my mind now and then.

Morning came, and Niang lifted me into a sitting position and encouraged me to eat a little. Everything still seemed so far away, and as I had no inclination to eat, she slowly fed me – not forcibly, but firmly, as if I were a small child. Meirén laid me back down,

THE FLEDGLING

and I drifted off to sleep again. As I started to come to, I was aware of drifting effortlessly down passageways. It took a few moments for me to realise that I was being carried on a stretcher by some of the young priests from Kou. On either side of me, my colleagues walked in procession with the masters and the Watchers, leading the way at the front. As I glanced up, I could see that Li Jing and the rest of the young priests were following behind. Wondering why I was so ill and being carried, I looked ahead and recognised that we had reached the Doorway of Illusion. In one moment, we all walked through together.

The whole room took on a strange quality. My stretcher was set down on a low couch in the centre of the room, and I could hear whispers before Master Noih spoke. "If this is to be dealt with quickly, the full force of the trauma must be released. Months of grief must be condensed into the time we spend together today. It is the only way for us to be able to continue our work; that is for all, not just for the two little ones." Dazed, I wondered which two little ones the master referred to.

"Before the trauma is released, the foetus must be protected for the sake of both mother and child. The after effects will be reduced but still considerable, as Su Ling's awareness will tell her much. However, this way, with the training we have given her so far, she will be able to function and work with some normality.

"Of course, we will see a new persona at work in the temple, but in this room we recognise the whole spirit. We will all experience the trauma as one! Even your masters and Illustrious Watchers will take this on as Su Ling gives off the full force of emotion. We will prepare to contain this and follow by bringing a calming energy in. First we must put a protective energy field around the unborn child, and then we will surround Su Ling with the same."

For a while my mind found it hard to take in Master Noih's words; I began to, but then I became aware of a white or golden circle of light around me. I felt very warm, loved, and protected. Gradually I became aware, and I began to remember what had happened. I recalled the union and the love, and then from a deep place I could hear a primeval scream emanating. It grew louder and louder, until I realised that it came from me! All my past hurts from childhood and being sent away from home became mixed up with grief at the loss of my beloved. It was a terrible sound, and at that very moment I realised that we were all as one, experiencing my pain, my agony! After a while all became silent, and I began to see the most exquisite colours around the room. They blended and mixed together like so many potions I had created in the past, yet these were no ordinary colours! They shimmered and shone like lights from another world, perhaps the Unseen World. They healed and calmed us, and as they subsided I knew my fellow Kou members felt better and more balanced. I also knew that I was calm but raw inside. Even after such a magnitude of healing energy, I felt the effects of my pain and loss. I felt it because I cared so much for Wu Fang, not just as my husband and lover but as a spirit, too!

A candle was lit in memory of Wu Fang, and the love felt in the room was harnessed and sent out to his soul as it embarked on the next stage of its journey into the unseen world. A weary Kou sat meditating on the flame until it was time to return to the temple in the known world. Once back in my living quarters, I slept soundly until the morning. When I awoke, I knew that it was my responsibility to return to my workplace.

I felt the eyes of everyone in the birthing room on me as I entered. I went about my duties, saying nothing. One young woman looked at me warily as I prepared to help with the birth of her child. "She looks so strange; I don't want her!" I heard her say to the birthing mother. The old woman was sharp with her and told her not to be so foolish. I tried to alter my demeanour towards the young woman, to reassure her, but I could not. It was as if my movements were wooden and my expression stuck in a strange mask, a mask which showed no feeling and no emotion.

The following week passed slowly, it seemed to me. Each day I went about my business as usual. I continued with my work in the birthing room and then my lessons with Master Noih. I was strangely unable to take in his teachings at such a time. I wasn't sure how. On the seventh day, Master informed me that Wu Fang's body had been taken some days before by his family and had been returned to his home village. Although it was not thought wise to allow me to attend his funeral, the rare plant from the temple garden had been given to me as a means of honouring his memory and also our union. *The plant,* I thought *I had forgotten all about it; it was my responsibility to nurture it.* Master Noih nodded to Wèi Wèi, and she turned to face me. "Niang has been looking after it for you, until you were ready to receive it again."

"I see," I murmured. Niang was full of surprises – and so different from the haughty Niang of old.

"Thank you, Wèi Wèi," I said. "I will nurture the plant from now on."

Master Noih came closer to me and said softly, "We did not expect you to remember everything, Su Ling, but tell me how you feel. You are eating very little, I see."

I felt a little guilty and lowered my eyes. "It is hard, Master. I have hardly any appetite."

"You must think of the child now, Su Ling. You have the responsibility to nurture your unborn child as well as the plant." Master Noih fixed me with his eyes that saw everything. As he studied me, I knew that he was aware that I had not fully come to terms with the knowledge that a child was growing inside of me. There had been so little time since the union; others outside of Kou would not even be aware of it. Everything had happened so quickly. It was hard for me to think of the child and my future when I ached so for Wu Fang!

"I feel as if I am lost in a mist, Master; I do not know what to do. The union, the loss, the meeting with Kou – there has been so much to take in."

"We have healed much in you, Su Ling, but some things you can only do alone. There is a small annexe attached to the hall where the priests worship at a private altar. The annexe has a small altar of its own. There is no-one there at the moment, and you have my permission to go there now. You must kneel before the altar, in silence; no-one will bother you. You will know what to do and when to come away. Go now."

I was bemused by Master Noih's instruction but made my way through the corridors until I came to the doors which opened onto the sacred hall where only the priests were admitted. Wondering what to do next, I waited for a few moments until a small door at the end of the corridor opened and two of the young priests from Kou appeared, beckoning me forward. I could see the small room with its little altar through the open door, and after bowing to my colleagues I entered, closing the door behind me.

I had rarely been completely alone. It felt strange, yet it was a relief somehow. As I knelt before the sacred altar, my attention was drawn to the vase of flowers which had been placed there. They were flowers of the same delicate white variety that I had picked from the temple gardens and laid at the shrine to honour my mother. For a moment, my heart felt heavier, but I found the courage to bring my mind to our illustrious ancestors and masters in the spirit world. Opening my heart to them, I asked their forgiveness for anything I might have done to offend them. Then, whispering my request for help through this very difficult time in my life, I continued to worship in silence.

It was calm and peaceful in the little room, and I hardly noticed a slight stirring around me. But when it happened again, I was left in no doubt. I looked up and felt immediately that there was another presence in the room! A glow emanated from all around the altar, and before me on the floor a pair of feet began to appear! Holding my breath, I watched as two legs, a torso, and the rest of the body materialised in front of me. My Wu Fang! My Wu Fang! I thought I would faint with joy.

"Oh please, please, take me with you, my love; I want to be with you," I cried out.

"No, my dear, you cannot yet; you still have much work to do. There is much I understand now, but you, you must take better care of yourself and our child! It is important that it be born; it must touch the Earth plane. "

Not entirely sure what Wu Fang was trying to tell me, I promised nevertheless to eat a little more and to rest where and when I could. With shining eyes he looked down on me. "I cannot protect you from everything, my love. There are reasons beyond our full understanding. We cannot know them until it is time. Remember everything I have said. Go now in peace!"

With that he was gone. I felt as if I had lost him all over again. And yet why? Why did I feel a sense of calm? As I left the room, I realised that this was Wu Fang's gift to me. This feeling of peace and calm was given in order that our unborn child would be protected. At that moment, I opened up my heart to the little foetus growing inside me. One day, unlike my little Tóngshì, it would be able to fly up to the heavens.

The following weeks passed by quickly in the temple; the days went faster than the empty evenings. So at the end of each day I tried to read and absorb as much knowledge as I could in order to pass the time. I watched the small plant begin to grow as my own child began to make its presence felt in my womb. My pregnancy was common knowledge by now among the temple community. I could not understand at the time why there was such interest in the birth of one more babe. As an observer of the past now, I am aware of the fact that however much spiritual knowledge I had gained as a member of Kou, I still hid truths I was not yet ready to see.

Upon waking, I would take some of my own special potions to alleviate the sickness I was experiencing. I felt then that I could identify a little more with the expectant mothers in my care. My colleagues kept a careful eye on me whenever I was sick, but Niang in particular was attentive. Whenever I would go into my own little world, she would speak to me and keep my attention on something. Wèi Wèi was supportive, but emotion was not something she could deal with; she was able to help in a practical and intuitive way.

As the members of Kou gathered one day, it was Master Ma Sing who led the proceedings. He began in the quiet, sure tone of voice we were all familiar with. "Today we enter into another stage of our development by working together as one whole group, male and female members together." We all knew this would happen one day, but the announcement took us by surprise and caused a ripple of disturbance of the energy field in the room. Men and women were never allowed to work together in imperial China. However, as usual all in the room were still and showed no sign of surprise.

"We need the masculine and feminine energies to come together now. We are all aware of Su Ling's child growing inside of her; as we come together today, the rest of us will be, in a sense, concentrating on our own symbolic inner child. As Su Ling sends love and encouragement and begins to link closely with her child, so each of us will link with our own symbolic children, that part of us yet to be born – or should I say 'reborn'. We can obtain much knowledge in this way. This knowledge will come from deep within our beings from the very roots of our being!"

Such a wonderful thing happened that day. I felt a connection, and a blending with my unborn child. I felt as if we were as old friends who had met long ago. It was a similar feeling to that which I experienced in my dream state, when Wu Fang and I met with the spirits of our mothers on the mountaintop. It seemed to me that reality was in the deep, deep places of my consciousness and our day-to-day lives in the physical world were only a passing phase, like a short journey to be discussed with friends on our return.

I met my son – for it was at that meeting with him, soul to soul and mind to mind, that I first became aware of the sex of my unborn child. We spoke of many things, and he showed me pictures and symbols which I would remember at different points in my life. They would emerge in my conscious mind as, and when, they were needed. Much of what we spoke had, of necessity, to be forgotten, but during my work with Kou some of these matters could be retrieved for the benefit of all in the group. I remember very clearly, though, the word 'divine' and the divinity within us all. At the close of that first meeting together as a whole group, where the masculine and the feminine came together, I came away with a warm understanding of what love truly meant in its widest and most powerful sense.

That evening the other girls and I sat in the communal area discussing the day's events. This was far more interesting to me than working in total silence for most of the time, though silent meditation certainly had its place. All, as usual, were aware of each other's thoughts to a degree. When the members of Kou were assembled together, much more was known to all of us; however, for the sake of harmony and our own privacy when returning to physical consciousness, our minds were blocked to some of the private matters relating to our fellow colleagues. This did not apply to the masters and the Watchers, of course, who were aware of all matters regarding Kou.

The value of these discussions became self-evident as each person's perception of the meeting differed a little from the rest. Everyone agreed on how the meeting was structured, the theme, and the knowledge gained from it. It was more a question of the awareness each individual gained from the information and how it related to their own personal journey through life.

Niang spoke first. "I have understood much today about how we can alienate ourselves from others unknowingly. It seems to be a question of how we see others and of how we mistrust people in general. I understand more now about the invisible walls we tend to build around ourselves. I knew this before, of course, but knowing and fully understanding are two different things. Alienating others comes from a fear deep within us, a fear which is hard to understand in one such as I, who has always thought of herself as strong. So the invisible walls we create are a protection of sorts. That is the perception, anyway. Walls serve their purpose, of course; they keep others out, but they can also serve as prisons." Everyone nodded in agreement.

Wèi Wèi spoke. "I have discovered why others can alienate us, laugh at us, or single us out as different in some way. In effect, this comes from fear too; by denigrating us, they divert attention from their insecurities. It makes them feel stronger. There are exceptions; there are those who are not insecure at all when they single others out and alienate others. They do so out of malice and secret enjoyment, and they are more dangerous than the others! We see many of these people in our culture. Changes must come."

Each girl spoke of her own reflections of the meeting and how interesting it had been for her. "What of your thoughts, Su Ling?" Ci asked.

I told them about the blending exercise with my son and how his soul was to help me in the future. "I have also observed issues relating to chaos. All which *appears* to be chaotic can be viewed in a different way. Those things which seem to come suddenly, causing much disturbance, appear chaotic and random in their happening but, in fact, can belie deeper truths. Once wheels are set in motion, mankind's thoughts, words, and actions, create an eventual outcome. A process is put into action that appears to lead to chaos, yet everything is exactly as it should be. Thoughts, words, and deeds, if not addressed carefully, can inevitably lead to complete and utter chaos. Then we ask, 'Why?' We feel we have not taken part in such a process. Yet at some point in time, we have all played our part in creating negativity."

To nods from everyone, we finished our discussion for the evening and prepared for sleep. Before closing my eyes that night, I thought of Wu Fang at the small altar and the prophetic words he spoke, which seemed to fit very closely to my own that evening.

Through the weeks which followed, I began to take much more of an interest in my unborn child. I fantasised that perhaps one day he would follow in my footsteps and work secretly with a group such as Kou, learning the true but secret knowledge. Or perhaps he would gain favour with Governor Choi himself, gaining a greater status in the temple than I? As these thoughts fluttered through my mind, I knew instantly that a fanciful idea would not necessarily be appropriate for him and that his life was not under my control. I could guide him through his childhood within the laws of imperial China and of the Governor's domain, but I knew he would have others in the temple to oversee his upbringing. Above all, I wished for his happiness and a long life; that was my primary concern.

Three months into my pregnancy, I had a question which began to concern me regarding my child. I left the birthing room one day after attending a particularly difficult birth. The young mother was exhausted, and the new-born child needed extra care. The incident made up my mind for me; I would ask Master Noih during the afternoon lesson. As I reached the master's door, I was surprised to see Niang and Ci speaking to Wèi Wèi. They were deep in conversation. What, I wondered, would be so important that they couldn't wait until the evening to discuss it? As they saw me approach, they smiled and nodded in friendship and Niang and Ci intimated that they must hurry off to their own workroom.

"What has happened, Wèi Wèi? Is the master not well?" I already knew the answer but did not wish to appear too inquisitive and impolite. Opening the door, Wèi Wèi cleverly and easily evaded my interest by speaking of the next meeting with Kou. I nodded to Wèi Wèi, as if understanding, but she knew and I knew that I was fully aware that the conversation was not entirely as she had explained it to me. I did not question her again, as we were about to come before Master Noih. My question for him, should I be allowed to ask it, was burning in my mind.

Master looked particularly striking that day wearing a robe the colour of indigo. The small bowls of water placed to his side were also of the same shade. Colour always affected my interest in things; I appreciated the beauty of the various hues, especially when mixed together or as a contrast to each other.

"Today we begin with a question. Wèi Wèi, you have something to ask me?" I patiently waited for my turn to ask a question but made myself listen intently to Wèi Wèi's.

"If you please, Master, I have a question regarding the health of Su Ling's unborn child."

I should not have been surprised by this, as we were both members of Kou, yet I was momentarily taken aback that we both should have exactly the same question. Was this what was being discussed outside in the hallway? She continued, "We have very powerful forces working with us and through us when Kou meet together, Master, and I know these powers have been used to protect Su Ling's child in her grief. As the child continues to grow inside her, is it possible that such powerful work can damage or harm the babe in this way?" My eyes widened a little. Until today I had felt a little foolish in wanting to ask this question, particularly after the blending exercise!

"This is interesting." Master Noih closed his eyes for a while. "As a matter of interest, there are very few occasions when the question would arise. Such groups as ours rarely have pregnant women amongst their members. It is not unheard of, but it is rare! As you mentioned, great universal forces have been used to protect Su Ling and her child after the passing over of Wu Fang."

I lowered my eyes as his words, though spoken quietly, caused a murmur in my heart.

"Those forces were manipulated by our leadership – that is, the other masters and I and, more importantly, the Watchers. The manipulation of such forces was all-important to the success of the exercise. Just the right kind and amount of force was used to ensure the safety not only of Su Ling and child but of all members of Kou. All were felt by that stage to be able to handle such a task, but all still needed protection. Such were the powers in the room! Now, that was an exceptional case. Such forces are not needed all the time, nor should they be used; it's much too dangerous." He paused for a moment of contemplation, which seemed at the time to be a very long moment!

Glancing at me before turning back to Wèi Wèi, he continued. "You must remember this: when we are picked for this type of work, our selection is of course known by our spirit masters long before we are aware ourselves. When you first came before me – both of you, that is – I knew immediately. I was aware of your coming earlier, but the final recognition was left for me to acknowledge, shall we say. No names are given prior to someone's arrival, but I can recognise through someone's force field who is able, or will be able, to do important work such as this, which benefits mankind in general and specifically ourselves. So a pregnant woman would not normally be able to hold such energies, but then she would not normally be allowed to do such work. Su Ling is different. It is perfectly in order for you to ask such a question for your own interest and knowledge. We are, however, acutely aware of this unusual situation, and the energies used for the duration of the pregnancy will be adjusted by our friends in the unseen world themselves. They would not let any harm come to the child through our work with Kou. It must be born!"

There it was again! Wu Fang's words to me were, "It must touch the Earth plane," and here was Master Noih intimating the same. Yet many babes did not survive birth at that time; why was mine so special? Something stirred inside me again, like a memory of long, long ago. I had remembered some things in the blending exercises with my son but had forgotten others. I was pleased to think that my son was protected from such serious work, and that knowledge eased my mind a little. Yet there was still something I could not quite remember that I felt I should know.

The next day, Kou was due to meet. As before, we were going to work as a whole group; each of us was acutely aware of the spiritual significance of working in this way. As we assembled in the room, the Watchers stepped forward, looking like the quiet, unassuming roommates we had come to know. How deceptive those earlier impressions were! They spoke in unison, as was often the case. "We have today an exceptional rarity in the room: a living crystal plant!" They paused to let their words take effect. "Not a crystal fashioned as a plant, you understand, but an organic plant crystallised on the *outside* while still growing as any other plant on the *inside*. Unlike something enclosed in ice or frozen in time, this is a living, growing plant which grows *with* the crystal until it reaches its full height."

A ripple of excitement spread around the room. How many more things could we be amazed by! Many, was the answer, but at that moment we waited patiently for a glimpse of this oddity. The Watchers stood aside to reveal a podium displaying what, at first, seemed to be a multifaceted crystal which had been carefully sculptured from its rough form. "Come closer," they said, beckoning to us, and as we moved forward we all gasped at this strange botanical phenomenon.

"In answer to your unspoken questions, the crystal was *not* hewn from rock and formed again by a man's hand." Master Ma Sing turned to the Watchers. "Tell them how you came across it, my friends."

Regarding the crystal plant with pleasure, they replied, "We have travelled far and wide over aeons of time, as you would speak of it. There are many wonders we cannot speak of here, even in this mystical place. However, this particular little wonder we came across on another plane far from here, a plane which is more beautiful and peaceful than our world. We were travelling invisibly; at other times we would show ourselves in various guises. As we arrived on that plane of existence, we were struck by the skyline. There were shining hues of every colour in that place. Our attention was so taken by the sky that we almost missed something shining far below us. Going to investigate, we noted at first a very precious crystal. Our senses told us that this was something even more than we had anticipated something we were meant to find and to share our knowledge of with others. We cannot keep it; it will be returned to its resting place on a rock in the centre of a large blue lagoon on that beautiful plane. If you look closely, you can see that the plant within is almost identical to Su Ling's rare plant taken from the temple garden."

My eyes widened as I noticed the similarity. The Watchers' eyes twinkled with amusement at my expression. "We also noticed the familiarity of the plant, but the experience of seeing it encased in crystal was new to us, and we have seen many beautiful plants and crystals. As we gathered around it, the crystal plant spoke to us and seemed pleased that we had come, almost as if it were expecting us! It explained how it was unique on that particular plane but not unique in the whole of the hidden world."

Li Jing intimated that he would like to ask a question. The Watchers, as usual, were aware of his question. "We cannot speak now of the other crystal plants or of their whereabouts; that is for another time. You cannot water these plants as others are watered and fed. This little beauty grows by the reflection of light through its crystal from the magnificent display of colours from the sky there. We wanted you all to see it and to understand that it is no coincidence that we have been able to bring it to you here. There has to be a connection, a link. There always is, you see. Despite whatever appears to be going on in our country during times of war or peaceful coexistence, there are still deeper reasons for such things, as there are for such precious plants to exist as they are. We wish you all to take from today's lesson the analogy of the multifaceted crystal and the plant at the centre as the soul's growth through its journey."

Master Ma Sing stepped forward again and in almost a whisper said, "This will be of particular relevance to you, Su Ling, as you care for the plant which was given to you as a gift; you can think at times of this other, special version." I bowed to master with mixed feeling of awe and unease which I had no understanding of then.

The rest of the lesson was taken up with an examination of the lovely specimen. We were mesmerised by it and could hardly speak of anything else that evening when we were back in our living quarters. Even my unborn child was more active, as if it were jumping for joy inside my womb.

As the weeks passed, I began to tire more as I went about my duties. I was expected to carry on as usual in the birthing room, but I wondered how long it would be before I was put onto lighter duties. I was quite content mixing my potions, but there seemed to be a never-ending flow of young women about to give birth. One morning we had an unexpected visitor; Master Fu Chang entered the room and spoke to the servant elder. Her eyes met mine for a moment, but her expression gave nothing away. I sensed surprise and annoyance, even a hint of envy about her. "Su Ling," she called sharply, "Master Fu has come for you; you must follow him." With that, she went back to work.

There was a discernible expression of greeting on Master Fu's face, as one Kou member greets another. No-one noticed this unusual event, and I was completely taken by surprise, as the masters never greeted me in such a way. I bowed low in response, as any servant of the temple would be expected to do. My own expression gave nothing away.

He led me through into an adjoining room which I had never entered before. I noticed the difference at once in the decor and fine furnishings. It was a birthing room for our governor's own household servants and favoured friends. "This, as you can see, Su Ling, is a more accommodating place for the favoured to deliver their babes. Even the concubines have their offspring here.

Governor Choi's own family deliver their children within their private chambers, away from prying eyes. The women in this room are also attended by our beloved governor's own physicians, who in turn instruct the old birthing women."

He paused while I took in the sights and sounds of the room. I was taken by surprise at the opulence and splendour of what was, after all, just a birthing room. Here I noticed there were more people in attendance to every young woman in labour. How different it was from our own. "You are here just to observe today, Su Ling. This is part of your future, for in time you will attend the women here yourself."

I glanced up at the master. Then, lowering my eyes and trying to pick my words carefully, I said, "Why would this honour be given to me, Master?"

"You are always surprised, Su Ling. Well, that is no bad thing. I will leave you here for a while to observe things. You notice that there are no potions prepared here. The physicians bring their own preparations in." Knowing my every thought, he watched my expression for a moment and then left.

As I watched the activities of the room, I pondered on the physicians' own potions and wondered how beneficial they were to the women. I surprised myself with this way of thinking; after all, they were presumably far superior to mine. Nevertheless, I studied them carefully as they went about their duties.

Suddenly a cry rang out from the other side of the room. I edged a little further along, staying close to the wall. I could see two physicians and two servants attending the patient, who cried out in distress. Although I was used to hearing cries in the birthing room, I sensed that the young woman was in some danger. The old birthing mothers looked at each other, acknowledging what was wrong. The physicians, however, insisted that all was going as it should and told the old women to administer their own herbal potion to the young woman. I instinctively knew that the potion was unsuitable for her; I became alarmed and wanted to shout out, but I knew this would be useless. We would never go against the governor's physicians, who thought they knew best. The old women knew it, and I knew it. Then the inevitable happened. With a last cry of anguish, the mother and her unborn child died a painful death! With insight I could see that the potion used would have helped a minor problem but had poisoned them both in this instance. The physicians had killed them!

CHAPTER 13

Destiny

THE WEEKS AND MONTHS PASSED by quickly at first, but then they became laboriously slow. I was deemed 'too slow' to work alongside the birthing mothers, so all of my mornings were assigned to mixing and creating potions, though I tired very easily even doing this work.

Early one evening I sat picking at my meal across the table from Wèi Wèi. She glanced up at me from time to time, but I pretended not to notice. I was not in the best of moods, something which I had expected after observing my patients in the latter stage of their pregnancies. Wèi Wèi broke the silence and spoke in a matter -of -fact way. "It won't be long now, Su Ling. Your transformation will come quickly, and all that is to be will be."

I gave her a furious glance at this vague, unfathomable statement. Even if my own analytical powers of deduction were failing me of late, I was in no mood for this type of message. Of course I would be transformed; I was to be a mother for the first time! At that moment Niang, Héshi, Ci, and Meirén approached the table, having finished eating. Sensing the atmosphere, Meirén said, "Are you finished now? We can all return together." I shrugged and rose from the table, followed by Wèi Wèi. We walked back to our room in silence.

While the others settled down in the communal area with their various activities, I began to feel restless. I couldn't help it! I knew it would disturb the calmness in the room, but I found myself pacing to and fro, unwilling to speak to anyone. This was not a comfortable feeling. I did not have long then to wait for my child to be born, but I was not sure what to do with myself. Reaching down into my pouch, I held my Tóngshì for comfort and remembered all that we had been through together. Then I heard a faint sound coming from somewhere, and I began to tire from my pacing. I sat down and saw my colleagues sitting and swaying slightly as they hummed softly together; they were producing such an exquisite sound that it was as if a group of musicians were playing together. I sat still as an observer, totally calm, and just listened. Before long my eyes began to close, and I fell into a deep sleep. I must have been carried to my bed, because I was awoken in the morning by the sound of my own retching. Niang held out a bowl for me as I continued to feel sicker than I have ever felt before!

"This should not be happening, Niang!" I cried. "My sickness stopped some months ago."

"Do not worry now; we must prepare you for the delivery of your son." Did I detect strong emotion in Niang's voice, perhaps betraying a longing she had for a child of her own? I thought I must be delirious.

"We wanted to keep you here," she whispered. "But Master Noih said that the governor would not understand why you were not with the others." With that, Niang and Ci attended to me, and Wèi Wèi ran to fetch servants to carry me into the birthing room.

The old women were waiting for me there, and I was placed in the corner of the room near the smaller birthing room I had visited earlier. I thought this strange, as there were only three others in the room giving birth and plenty of places in between. As I began to experience contractions, Niang, Ci, and Wèi Wèi left the room. I begged one of my potions from the women to help me in my confinement; this was granted. There was no reason for me to be denied the little comfort I had given to many others.

So there I lay with the roles reversed, experiencing what every woman in our care had experienced. The time seemed to go slowly as I felt never-ending labour pains. I knew just the right time to take a little of my potion to ease the pain. I knew, too, that it was perfectly safe, and for a while it worked its magic, making things feel a little hazy and detaching me from my discomfort. The time then came for me to push my son into the world, and I needed a clear mind and the strength to do it. *Come on, my little one! Why do you not try harder?* My thoughts raged from impatience to *I can't go on*. Why is the journey into this world so hard for babe and mother?

One of the old women spoke sharply then. "Come on, Su Ling, you are not trying hard enough. You have attended enough mothers; you know what you have to do!" I gritted my teeth in anger, giving out a strange sound which muffled my words of contempt for the old one. Then suddenly he arrived! My relief and satisfaction were apparent as I saw my son for the first time. Even as a squalling new-born babe, I recognised him. Yet his crying became weaker, and as they cut the umbilical cord and cleaned him up, I could tell by their expressions that something was wrong! One of the women went through to the smaller birthing room and fetched a physician. I was horrified. It was the very same one who had caused the death of the other young woman as I watched.

"No," I shouted.

"Silence!" He glared angrily at me, unused to being spoken to in such a way. Examining my child, he said, "It is no use; he will not survive. He is not fit enough."

Again I screamed, "No."

At this he bore down on me, eyes alight with fury. "Silence! The only reason I am here is on request from Master Ma Sing and Master Noih Chen. What is so special about a wretch like you, I cannot imagine. If I had known how insolent you were going to be, I would have refused to come! I could have you beheaded for that," he spat at me!

To my surprise, the elder birthing mother said, "Do not concern yourself, Master Physician; she is nothing. She is mad in the head!" This distracted him for a moment, and the two women fawned over him, telling him how gracious he was to even think of attending such a lowly servant.

I lowered my eyes and whispered, "Please let me have my son?" The physician was about to turn on me when one of the old women suggested that we were taking up too much of his valuable time. With that, he left and disappeared through the door.

"You must be favoured by some, Su Ling, for him to spare you like that," the old woman said. With that, she thrust my son into my arms. I didn't care what she or the arrogant physician thought. I only cared about my son!

I could not altogether take in what was happening, though I sensed that he was fading fast. I could feel the life force ebbing away from his tiny body, yet still I deluded myself that this could not be true. There had to have been some terrible mistake! Master Noih himself had said that my child must touch the Earth plane – yes, that was it. This must be a hallucination, an after effect of the potion! My thoughts ran wild for a moment, but then I centred myself long enough to speak softly to my child. "You are most loved, my little one, and most precious to me. I will be the one to name you; you are my Rènshi, which means to know and to recognise."

He opened his eyes as if in recognition of my words, and then his spirit left, leaving behind just the small, physical shell. I looked up at the old women and sensed that behind their hard gaze was a flicker of pity and sympathy, but this would never be shown or spoken of.

After a while, I called out to one of them. "I will not let anyone cast aside my son and have him thrown onto a rubbish heap like the others! He will have a proper burial." To my surprise, she replied, "It is all taken care of, Su Ling; Master Noih has made the arrangements. Tomorrow when you have rested, you will be carried out to the temple gardens for a short service to honour the child. I have never known anything like it during my working life that such an honour should be granted to you and your son."

I gasped. They knew, they knew! It was too much for me. I remember nothing afterwards but sinking into a deep sleep.

In a haze, I became aware of voices and the cry of a new-born babe. Opening my eyes, I puzzled at first as to why I was lying down, but the soreness I felt from the birth brought me back to the terrible truth. I could not cry out; I couldn't do anything. I felt as if I were at the bottom of a very deep pit, a very dark place indeed. Though aware in one sense of what had befallen me, I felt numb, as if I existed in some sort of void.

An old woman fed me herself when I refused food; she was determined that I should take in some kind of nourishment. Then another came and bathed me as I lay motionless. "The masters will be waiting for you, Su Ling; there is little time. We must not keep them waiting." As she moved away another came and helped me to stand up, dressing me in a robe just before two servants appeared to carry me out into the garden on a makeshift bed.

I was hardly aware of the journey through the temple itself. Guards and servants passed by in a blur. Then suddenly I could feel a faint breeze on my face and warmth from the sun. Trying hard to focus, I became aware of a group of people standing in the garden who seemed to be waiting for me.

Hands lifted me up, and cushions were placed behind my back, enabling me to see the group a little more clearly. My sight became a little clearer then as I studied them closely. I followed the line, which was longer than I at first imagined, and realised that I was in the presence of Kou. Everyone was there. My female colleagues stood silently beside the young priests. Li Jing stood in attendance to all three masters and the Watchers. All faced me in silence. I felt no warmth seeing them all there, and I gave no acknowledgement to them, which was unheard of in matters of protocol.

Master Ma Sing stepped forward and stood before a small shrine with familiar-looking white flowers planted around a small hole in the earth. Then the Watchers approached the shrine together; they laid a small bundle wrapped in white swaddling clothes in the freshly dug earth.

They stepped back, and Master Ma Sing began to speak. "Today we come to honour a very old soul whose journey brought him to us for such a short while. This was his choice, but he knew that one day we would all be reunited in the unseen world. We honour his mother, Su Ling, for bringing him into this world, and his father, Wu Fang, who is now in spirit and has come to escort the little one to his spiritual home. There are important reasons why little Rènshi should have touched the Earth plane at this time."

Something stirred in me when his name was mentioned. Did I tell them his name? Did the old woman tell them? As a musician played softly nearby, I glanced at the faces of my friends. I noticed that they were all very pale, even Wèi Wèi. Had they been touched by his presence? I couldn't imagine why.

Master Ma Sing continued to speak for a while in the fashion of a mourning ceremony for the dead. I hardly remembered his words later, but I remembered the young priests, even Li Jing, each in turn coming forward to lay their tokens of respect at the shrine, to honour my son. Master Noih performed a sacred ritual known to Kou members, and a guard began to fill in the small hole as the earth prepared to take the remains of my Rènshi's little body. I weakly felt for my Tóngshì in my personal pouch. At least they had let me keep that. But just as I held it to my heart, it broke into two pieces!

A burning and rumbling sensation began somewhere deep inside of me, from a place I had only visited once or twice before. Like fire rising up from a mountain, I found my voice and my despair. I would not wait to go through the doorway of illusion this time, for it was all a sham! My anger came up and out like a ferocious dragon as I spat out my hatred for them all. "You all knew, you knew, you treacherous deceivers. You have put me through all this pain. You lied and made me feel that my union with Wu Fang and my confinement were both special! You are betrayers of trust to the innocent; you are not worthy of the posts you hold! You look down on others who are made to feel inferior. You, you are the inferior ones! What was it all for, you despicable snakes?" I roared like a lion, showing a side of myself I never knew I possessed, but I meant every word.

"You can kill me if you wish. I welcome death after what you have put me through. I cannot bear being in your presence!" I screamed. The musician bent his head down low and trembled; the guards stood ashen faced, unable to comprehend how a 'nothing' could speak to eminent people in such a way. They stood in silence waiting for my imminent death while the masters, the Watchers, and the other members of Kou stood calmly with their eyes closed. When Master Ma Sing opened his eyes, *all* opened their eyes, and in order of status they filed away, leaving me to grieve. I was inconsolable. I had lost my child, my Wu Fang, and my Tóngshì!

I don't know how long I lay by the shrine. I was aware of darkness falling around me and of hands lifting me up and carrying me through an outer door of the temple garden and into a small room, where I was put down. Exhaustion overcame me, and I sank into a merciful sleep.

I awoke to the sounds of birds singing in the garden, yet their beautiful conversations only brought me more pain. My head felt heavy, and when I tried to move I became dizzy. I lay motionless, waiting for the feelings to go away. I did not concern myself with thoughts of my own potions, which would have eased my symptoms. They seemed irrelevant then. After a while my eyes scanned the small room, which was bare except for bowls for my ablutions and a small enclave in the centre of one wall where candles, flowers, and incense holders had been placed. High on the wall overlooking the garden was a long, narrow window with its shutters closed. No-one was here; I had been left. I could imagine why! Who would wish to listen to more of my ravings and be disturbed by them?

Later, I heard the latch on the door lift. Two female servants entered with food and water. I could not respond warmly to them, or with gratitude; I felt *nothing*. They tended to my dressings, but after spending time trying to encourage me to eat, they left. They were just obediently carrying out their duties. *Poor wretches*, I thought.

Time passed. Every day was the same: the servants would come and go in silence, and I would say nothing. One day they came and started their duties, but there was a difference to their routine. The dressings over my stomach were removed but not replaced, and one girl produced a long pole to pull back the shutters on the window. A shaft of light lit up the area of the room where I lay. I pondered this small act. Once I would have considered it an act of mercy. Now I just observed it with a little curiosity. A sound broke my attention: someone else was coming. Li Jing entered the room.

Gone was the arrogance of old; he stood watching me with an expression of seriousness. I returned his gaze with indifference. "Master Noih," he said. Then he paused. If he had expected a conversation with me, he was to be disappointed!

Master Noih silently entered the room. He fixed me with his eyes, and my own swivelled around to meet his. I would not rise or bow down to one whom I despised. Li Jing left the room and closed the door. Silence fell.

"So, Su Ling," he said, "it is time." I did not reply but kept my eyes firmly on him. He looked every bit as powerful as ever, but I did not care. I did not fear death or torture; I had already been tortured.

"I see you still feel the same towards us, Su Ling."

"Why, Master Noih," I said with scorn, "did you not know this already?"

Turning, he slowly walked across the room and stood by the enclave. For some reason I was compelled to stand to face him, whether by my own volition or his magic. I swayed a little; my body felt weak lying down for so long, but I did not care. I stared into his eyes defiantly, almost willing him to have me executed.

"You have much work to do, Su Ling, in the temple and, more importantly, with your colleagues in Kou."

He still held my gaze, but he did not raise his voice. I was incredulous. He still expected me to continue as if nothing had happened! "You really think that I would have any part in this work after your contemptuous lies? You must have some very dark magic indeed to make others bend to your will and make them believe your lies. A woman who is seen as nothing here *is* very much something to be reckoned with, oh Great Master! When you take everything from me, you expect me to whimper in fear before you!" My anger rose again and again at his matter-of-fact demand that I return to work as his puppet.

"You are not the first to lose a husband and child. There are countless others all across the land." His voice was calm, and his words were measured and firm. He spoke as if what had befallen me was common to many and therefore didn't matter.

"How dare you!" I spat out my words. "Those poor wretches could not have expected anything else; such is their lot, as they have come to know through experience, but this! You tell me that I have been given a great honour, to be chosen to work with Kou. You bring about a union between me and Wu Fang. You tell me it is of the utmost importance that my child should be born into this wretched life, only for him to be taken away from me almost immediately! For what possible purpose could all this suffering and grief serve anyone?"

"For a far greater purpose, Su Ling!" His voice was raised now, but his impatience was quickly checked. "You have been taught as much, have you not?"

This drove me to even more fury. "Oh, for some mysterious grand design from the unseen world, wasn't it? A world which shows such utter contempt for this one! We, we in the flesh, hold just as much importance. Oh, we do not have all the answers or as much knowledge as our venerable spirit masters and ancestors, but we are just as worthy! How dare you see us as worthless against them? I would not wish to serve such monsters!"

He closed his eyes for a while and stood in silence. Then, speaking in a firm manner again, he said, "You have seen the Watchers, Su Ling."

"I have seen the way I and my colleagues have been tricked by them!" I shouted.

"You cannot possibly know what you are saying; if you were not one of us, you would be dead by now!" he answered. Still composed, he stood facing me, waiting for my next outburst.

"Do you think I care? Do you think I would prefer membership in Kou to having my loved ones returned to me? I hope you have protected yourself, Master Noih, from my own terrible thoughts and violations of the energy field in this room!"

"Naturally," he replied casually. "Before I came here, I prepared myself, as always, against any negativity. But unlike my old practice of adjusting my protective field to project back on my enemy, this time I have made sure that no harm comes to you. A long time ago I had the need to project my enemies' negative thoughts back towards them. It was a matter of survival. Since then I have gained much knowledge regarding ways to transform another's animosity; it is all done safely in the energy field, of course, rather than using like against like. That way we would have a never-ending circle of aggression, as we see within our country today."

My eyes almost bulged with anger at the hypocrisy of his remark. Before I could speak, he interjected, "You have forgotten much, Su Ling. The healing with Kou after Wu Fang returned to the spiritual realms should have taught you much. The merging with your unborn son, with the help of the Watchers, explained much to you." His words stirred a faint memory now, of sacred symbols and something called divinity.

"I see you are beginning to remember," he said to me softly. I would have none of it!

"These are just your tricks and the Watchers' tricks, Master Noih. You are all powerful enough to create a Doorway of Illusion; how many other illusions have you placed in our minds?"

He lowered his eyes, and everything was quiet in the room. I waited, and still he said nothing. "You have no answer for me, Master Noih?"

"I was giving you time to catch your breath; you are still quite frail. Sit!" At that moment, I became aware of how weak my legs were. They suddenly crumpled under me, so that I fell into a sitting position on the floor. *His doing,* was all I could think of. He sat down, cross-legged, on the floor opposite me. If I had had the energy to be surprised, I would have. Still, there was some fight left in me somewhere. I pondered.

"You have no need to remind me, Master, of how situations are brought about by our own choices – or so you say. You claim that a sacred contract may be made between some souls who wish to meet up again in the material world. Yet what is the point of this continual cycle of pain and suffering? While I have been lying here in the silence of this room, I have been analysing the belief which we all cling to. Whatever hidden knowledge there is left to learn, there is *no* justification for all this!"

"What, then, do you suggest is the real truth, Su Ling?"

"Oh, you are very clever, Master, always ready to outwit me with your words. There is no point to this belief of yours when over aeons of time; the same old, weary patterns are played out over and over again. Very little changes on the Earth plane if, as you say, things are seen more clearly from that other place in the Unseen World, for a wider benefit or purpose. I do not know of any explanation; I cannot envisage anything that would bring any kind of consolation to us here. Why would I wish to have any part of that belief?"

"So you feel sorrow and empathy for us poor wretches living at this level of existence, Su Ling?" I could not imagine anyone less like a poor wretch than Master Noih Chen; he knew exactly what he was doing! "Now that you have undergone this transformation, this clarity of thought regarding our very existence here, what do you intend to do with the rest of your life?" he said quietly. Silence again. I had not even begun to think about my future, but my mind wandered to the poor women struggling to get into the temple to give birth in the hope that their babes would be safer there.

"I may take my potions to the outlying villages and help the pregnant women in their labours," I murmured.

"That is not possible, Su Ling. You were never meant to do that; it is not part of your life plan."

I stared again into the master's eyes. "Then I shall leave the temple for good and live as a peasant once more." The matter was settled in my mind; there was nothing left for me to do.

"I see," he said, rising to his feet. "If you have any respect left for your colleagues, you may like to grant them one wish before you leave."

I thought of Wèi Wèi, Niang, Héshi, Ci, and Meirén. Then after a long pause, I replied, "What is it they wish of me?"

"Before you make your final decision, they have asked that you spend time contemplating on it before the small altar in the annexe, as you did before. I can escort you there now."

It was obvious that the master wished to be rid of me, and soon! Still, he caught me by surprise; I had not contemplated a journey so soon, as I still felt weak. Returning to the annexe would at least give me a little more time to rest. "Out of respect to them, I will go." I stood up, ready to follow him. Li Jing came back and, walking before his master, led the way. I followed them with little enthusiasm and encountered no-one on the way. It felt as if the whole temple had made me an outcast, but I did not care.

As we reached the small door to the annexe, Master Noih turned and said, "Li Jing will be waiting for you when you come out." With that, they both left. I entered the room and saw in front of me the small altar, this time without the white flowers which had greeted me before. I knelt down before the empty altar, not in prayer but with a clear mind. I found this most welcoming after the whirlwind of thoughts which had been going through my mind. Outside, I thought I could hear the wind blowing through the trees; my mind wandered back to my home village of Laopíe.

I remembered being out in the open washing clothes, working side by side with Lái. I could hear the sound of the wind then, and we would work on until Mother called us back.

Thinking of my sister brought a lump to my throat. I was anxious for her, especially after I saw what had become of her. "Oh Lái," I cried out. "Which one of us has the 'honour' now? You would not wish to be in my shoes now, and I am not sure whether I would wish to be in yours. What has brought us to this?"

As my thoughts turned to my childhood again, I could feel a stirring in the energy field. I knew what to expect this time – or I thought I did. As Wu Fang's spirit began to materialise, much of the joy had left me, yet the familiar heartache was there. What was that he was carrying in his arms? My son!

"You have my son, Wu Fang. Give him back to me!" The last word had barely left my lips when my little babe began to transform into a full-grown adult, looking very much like Wu Fang; they could have been brothers! I cried out in astonishment as Rènshi spoke. "My dear mother. We have known about these circumstances for a very long time; we are old friends." Faint memories of merging with him now stirred within me. "Wu Fang, my father figure, and I have also been together before, but not for so long as you and I, my dear. Aeons of time passed before we could make a joint agreement to return here to complete our souls' journey. We knew it would be hardest for you, but we would not – and, more importantly, you would not – let fear deter us. This moment was set for you to reach a higher spiritual goal, a position which you have earned over time here on Earth, and in the Unseen World. In order for you to attain that position and to grow and develop spiritually along with your fellow Kou members, a transformation deep within you had to take place. I offered myself as a sacrifice, along with Wu Fang, to bring about that change within your soul. Only such traumatic events could bring out an even greater strength from within you. That is why, as a babe – as your Rènshi – I had to touch the Earth plane for such a short while."

"But what if I had taken my own life and others along with me?" I shouted. "Perhaps you have both forgotten, or never knew, the madness from the pain that this brings; I never knew I could be so angry, so bitter at my fate! How do other poor wretches cope? They do not all belong to secret societies. Again I say to you what I have said to the master. What of those poor peasants already eking out a miserable existence; is that not enough for them to cope with? Beyond anger, there is despair! Where is the fire there to take them on to greater heights?"

"These are complex spiritual matters, my friend. There are the causes, and there are the effects. This is true of the individual or of the entire kingdom. Knowing you so well, Su Ling, we always knew you would come through this and live to serve others as before."

"Rènshi, I already served others before with my work in the birthing room delivering babes and my work with Kou!"

He answered quietly. "There is still more to do at an even deeper level. Many cannot cope with this, our kind of work. But you – you can, my friend."

"So I had to be destroyed first!" I cried. "You cannot fill the hole that is left inside me, Rènshi."

At this, Wu Fang spoke up in a warm and loving way. "My dear Su Ling, beyond your ancestors, beyond the masters and grand masters in the spirit realm, is a far greater source of power which encompasses both the masculine and feminine aspects. It is a divine mystery; we can only begin to understand it once back home in the Unseen World. Even then, all is not revealed immediately. We have spent much time together through the ages with many different personas, and we have been to both wonderful and fearful places. We knew that your sacrifice would be the loss of wonderment of the innocent child that you were. This sacrifice will allow you to develop into a woman with much spiritual knowledge. The extra fire you are feeling now will be needed in the future. You have undergone a great trauma; our hearts go out to you, but there are many who must benefit from your skills. It is your destiny and theirs."

"I am weary, Wu Fang; this is all too much for me," I whispered.

"You will find, Su Ling that all the anger and bitterness inside you will subside. All this has not killed your love and compassion for others. You will find it again and regain your balance, the balance of your Qi energy."

Then Rènshi spoke once more to me as his mother. "We do not underestimate how hard it will be at first for you, working in the birthing room having lost your own child. Remember that child as me, the old soul with another name which was given to me in the beginning. This will help you during the worst times. Remember this." I nodded my head wearily; aware that what they were saying was true. Much time had passed since we had prepared for this. The effect here in the material world was almost unbearable, but they were right; to serve others would be the only reason for staying. Even though they had faith in me, I did not know how I would summon the energy to carry on.

With a sorrowful good-bye, I watched Wu Fang and Rènshi disappear back into the Unseen World, knowing I would not see them for a long time. I sat in the silence for a while, collecting my thoughts. Then I rose and went out of the door to face Li Jing. "You will come with me back to your room, Su Ling; in the morning you can inform us of your decision, whether you will stay or go." I said nothing but followed him back along the passageways of the Temple of the Heavenly Bird.

CHAPTER 14

Testing Times

I WOKE THE NEXT MORNING after a long, deep sleep to the sound of a single bird's sorrowful song. After dressing and preparing myself for the day, I reached inside my pouch and examined my own broken Tóngshì. Meditating on its poor, broken body, I did not notice that Master Noih had slipped silently into the room. I looked up as I became aware of his presence. His eyes were fixed on the broken bird too!

"Hold the two parts together, Su Ling." For a moment I was puzzled, but I did as I was asked. "You have the power and compassion to heal your little bird because it means so much more to you than the material object."

Just as he spoke these words, I could feel my hands becoming warm. As I opened them, I saw that Tóngshì had become whole again, with no sign of the break. "This is *your* magic, Master," I replied a little stiffly.

He paused as usual before he spoke. "You know well enough that I could only help from a distance with your own healing gift; it was your higher will and your need which enabled you to do this. Some things are easier to heal than others. Now is the time to make your decision. Will you go or stay, Su Ling?"

"I think you know, Master that I will stay for my colleagues, for my husband, for my son, and to help others, though I can't imagine how I will manage to do that at this moment in time."

"Then it is done. Li Jing will escort you to the birthing room to work, however hard that may be. I have faith that you will overcome any obstacles you find within yourself. You will also resume your daily lessons with me as before, and of course Wèi Wèi will be there waiting. This evening you will return to the living quarters with your colleagues, who have graciously allowed you to return." With that, he left.

The walk to the birthing room seemed to me the longest I had ever taken. It was very busy that morning, with many patients in labour. The old women were hurrying from one woman to the next. They looked up as I entered and seemed relieved to see me – another pair of hands to lighten the load! The elder in charge came towards me. "The potions are almost gone, but there is no time for that now, they will have to do without. You are needed over here."

And so it was. As I was unable to bring some pain relief to my women patients on my first day back, I had to watch helplessly and instruct them best I could while they fought to bring their babes into the world. Each cry from the infants as they entered their new world was like a knife thrust into my heart, but my face and demeanour showed nothing.

As the last babe was born and things quietened a little, I went over to my table. Servants brought in fresh ingredients from the hillside: small insects and other creatures with which to prepare new potions. I was lost in my work for some time, and it was only a tug on my sleeve from the elder which reminded me of my next lesson with Master Noih.

I left the room and made my way along the well-worn passageway to his room. I was still feeling slightly detached from everything. However, the time spent with my potions had brought with it much-needed relief from the emotional turmoil of the birthing process, so I was feeling a little more prepared than I might have been.

I knocked softly on the door, and the familiar sound of Master's voice came from beyond it. "Come, Su Ling."

Wèi Wèi sat on the floor in her usual place before Master Noih, who appeared to be sitting on a low seat, slightly elevated from the ground. Beckoning me to sit down, he said, "I realise you must be tired today, so our task will be one of quiet contemplation and meditation, which will energise and uplift our souls." He took an ornate box from the floor beside him and placed it between us. Opening the lid, he pulled from it a large and very beautiful clear crystal quartz sphere on a wooden stand. Looking into it, I could see many things straight away, but the pictures moved so fast.

"Today is not for the purpose of scrying and recording many things. We must clear our minds and focus on one picture, which will appear soon."

We sat together and calmed our busy minds until Master spoke again. "Now you may open your eyes." As I looked into the facets of the crystal I saw a single rainbow, with all its colours gleaming in hues I had seen on the celestial level. "This is our focus. I will eliminate the candle and lanterns, and we will have no other light in the room but the rainbow."

Concentrating on one picture takes much discipline of the mind, but I knew that success came with 'relaxing' and not trying too hard. The rainbows colours had a deep impact on me; they did indeed both heal and energise me, and I heard many whispers of forgotten truths which I cannot divulge here. All too soon, Master called us back to the stark reality of the present. I could see how young, inexperienced pupils could wish to escape the day-to-day world in this way, but there were inherent dangers in doing so. If our souls chose to be here, they were here for a reason; keeping our feet on the ground was vital for our physical well-being.

As evening drew close, we ate a small meal together. Wèi Wèi and I were excused from eating in the large hall with the others. We left our classroom silently at first: I was the first to break the silence. "I have to apologise, Wèi Wèi, for any distress I have caused you and the others with my harsh words."

"No, Su Ling, we knew you only spoke them as you were consumed by grief. You spoke only of things which we had sometimes thought ourselves but never dared speak. Master Noih has explained the situation to us at a recent meeting of Kou. We have learned much from it, and we knew you had hidden strengths to survive your misfortune."

"Have I, Wèi Wèi? I am only just beginning!"

"You are over the initial decision whether to stay or go; that took a great deal of inner strength." We walked on again in silence until we reached the familiar doors of our living quarters.

Wèi Wèi opened them wide. I stood back a moment, hesitating. As I entered, I saw the rest of my colleagues standing facing the door, waiting for me. "I – can you forgive me?" I whispered.

With that, Niang stepped forward. "All of us, Su Ling, have shared with you the depth of your pain. We cannot pretend that your violent words did not hurt us a little, but we knew where they came from and why. Your fellow Kou members are determined to strive to emulate the spiritual courage you have shown, *are showing*, in your greatest time of need. You have a very special soul."

I gasped at the generosity being shown to me and knew at once how special my friends were to me. What shining spirits all Kou members were. I understood why they had been handpicked for the special work they performed! I was speechless for a moment. Despite my usual strict control over my feelings, the sacredness of the moment overwhelmed me, and I could not stop my tears from flowing. More tears! With that, my friends came forward and embraced me, and I knew that I should not underestimate the truly good things left in my life.

The months that followed were the hardest part of the spiritual journey; I could not have walked the path without the support of friends on both sides of the spiritual divide. I threw myself into my studies and into the creation of new potions, mixing and refining them until I was satisfied with the results. My work with Kou took on an added dimension. It was as if some of the old obstacles from the past had been removed and I was able to see some complex issues in a clearer way. This continued until one morning in the birthing room, when I was again approached by Master Fu Chang.

"The work I spoke to you of before, Su Ling, begins today. From today, you work only in the inner birthing room I introduced you to before." Seeing a flicker of alarm in my eyes, he continued, "You are to be given a special honour here; the patients you leave behind today will continue to benefit from your potions. You will be allowed a small anteroom which adjoins the birthing room to work in. There you will prepare potions for the patients in both rooms as an exceptional honour. Master Ma Sing has persuaded the governor's physicians to allow you to administer some of your potions to a small number of his household servants. The governor himself has followed your progress, but he would never wish to offend his older, loyal physicians, whom he holds in great esteem. Master Ma has had some difficulty in persuading them to allow you to work in this way; the greatest diplomacy was needed, as you may well imagine. Only Governor Choi's word and the promise of a few special favours to them made any of this possible. The work of Kou is behind all this, of course. You have been allowed this honour, but you are aware it is for a much more important purpose! Everything must move on, however slowly. Let us say that the ways of the physicians are rooted firmly in the past, and they need a little encouragement to try new ideas. However, never forget that they are eminent healers and must be respected at all times. Do not forget this, Su Ling! I have faith in your diplomacy.

"I will take you through to the small anteroom now. The ingredients for you to work with are already laid out and ready.

THE FLEDGLING

Each time you create a new batch of potions, a larger amount will be taken through to your old workplace, and a smaller amount will be kept in reserve for your new charges. For the first three days, you will work only in the anteroom. On the fourth, you will be allowed to work with patients under strict instruction from the old women and, ultimately, from the physicians. Your week will proceed as follows: you will spend three days working on potions and studying scrolls on human anatomy. Then there will be four days during which you help to deliver new babes into this life. Having experienced some of the practices first-hand, you know that this will be an additional challenge for you. You cannot afford to tread on any more toes! The whole future of this project depends on you, Su Ling. Only Kou know how important, on a wider scale, it is. Now follow me."

Just as he spoke these words, I noticed a young girl enter the room, reporting to the elder straight away. "This is your replacement, Su Ling. Now come!" I silently sent out my best wishes for the replacement and wondered how life in the temple would be for her. I would never know.

Walking through my new place of employment, out of the corner of my eye I noticed only patients observing me. All other eyes were firmly averted or on their charges. We went through to the small anteroom, which was splendid by any criteria. I noticed a larger window where the light shone through to ease my eyes when I was working with minute traces of ingredients. The utensils were of beautiful designs, but I knew that the potions themselves were worth far more. "I will leave you now, Su Ling."

"Thank you, Master. I am aware of the great responsibility

you have placed on me." As I bowed, Master Fu nodded to me as a fellow Kou member and left.

As I worked, my thoughts strayed to the new birthing room itself. I remembered from before two old women, and sometimes two physicians, attended to the favoured ones. Others had two birthing mothers and one physician. I could only imagine the numbers in attendance in Governor Choi's private residence!

There were nine places for patients to lie in their confinement; I felt that there was ample room for perhaps three or four more, according to the need. However, here it was deemed important for the physicians to have enough space to walk and talk in comfort around each patient. Each place had its own small, low table where trays of utensils were available for the physicians' own potions. There were alcoves in the walls where units housed bowls and such for the ablutions of each patient. There were fresh clothes and covers to lie on and for wrapping the infants in; these were brought in all the time as soiled articles were removed by servants. We were never allowed to care for the patients for very long in my old workplace, only to deliver them until servants came to take them to the other end of the room where the mothers and staff could hear their cries. Here things were so different. I had to put my former workplace firmly out of my mind and do my best for the patients there by creating the best possible healing potions for them. I sent out a final prayer for them as I began my work.

The first three days in my new surroundings were peaceful enough. No-one bothered me in my small room. Servants would come and go, bringing me the ingredients for my healing potions. I always acknowledged them, as a sign of respect, but they averted their eyes, unsure of how to respond to me. On my work table stood a small bell which I could ring to summon them. I kept its use to a minimum.

The scrolls on anatomy and Qi energy interested me, and I realised that much could be done to prevent illness in the physical body without resorting to healing potions. However, I knew that turmoil and emotional suffering in our lives can also result in disease; we could write the word as dis-ease and clearly understand the implications. Trying to understand this and lessen the long-term effects of anxiety seemed just as much a necessity as any potion or mixture. How easily words can sometimes come to us when we are trying to give advice to others! I pondered the problem of trying to help ourselves while in the depths of despair. I had come some way through a period of despair with the help and support of others and the wise words of my husband and son from the spirit world. That had been hard enough. Not everyone was able to believe in the laws of the universe as I did. I was reminded of the legacy that grief can leave behind and of how we can only diminish its effect by means of our attitude to our personal suffering.

As I worked I reminded myself of my position alongside the governor's physicians. I would have to be silent while longing to speak out about their patient care and their use of medication. I knew that I had much to learn too, and resolved to become even more detached from my work with the young mothers until I was known to the staff and trusted.

On the evening of the third day, I was reading in the social area. Wèi Wèi sat beside me, putting some finishing touches on a lacquered box. Niang came towards me, and I stopped reading, being interested in what she might have to say. I had come to see her in a completely new light, and she treated me very much as an equal. In fact, they all did; our work with Kou saw to that. It taught us all to see our lives in a different perspective. "Su Ling, how do you like your new surroundings?"

"So far I like them quite well, Niang. I have been working alone and studying the anatomy of the human body and Qi energy. I have mixed the ingredients in many different ways to produce my potions in the past, but I was thinking of trying something new," I said.

"Oh." She eyed me carefully. "Your potions have worked well for all concerned so far. Why try to change them?"

"Most often I will prepare them in exactly the same way, Niang, but I want to show the physicians that I can do more." I was surprised to see seriousness come into her manner as she looked deeply into my eyes. "This may not be the time to try out new things, Su Ling. I would wait until you are more established and accepted. This is a time for caution; study the scrolls, by all means."

I was a little taken aback to think that she thought me irresponsible and gently told her so. My new surroundings meant that I could work unhindered by others and achieve much more in a shorter time, leaving me a space to experiment with some new ideas. Niang nodded to me in respect and changed the subject of the conversation, but I could feel her curious gaze from time to time that week.

The next day was the first of my four days helping to deliver the new babes. I was used very much as a general dogsbody, fetching and carrying for the old women, whose attention was firmly on the physicians. This I did willingly, but I hoped in my heart that my chores would be short-lived, for I was very much used to taking a hands-on approach with the pregnant women, and I had been trusted by the servants I had just left behind. I knew that I had to bide my time until I was accepted. The physician whom I had displeased before pretended not to notice me and ignored me all day; this suited me very well! Determined to prove myself, I obeyed every other member of the staff. Discipline came easily to me. As long as there was a clear point to the discipline and something to aim for, I didn't mind. I could not envisage a lifetime of being a dogsbody now; I had changed. The following two days passed in much the same fashion, but the fourth and last day in the birthing room brought some relief. This was to be the day that Kou met together, and as before, no-one would notice my absence!

I brought back some clean bowls and placed them in the alcove nearest to one of the doors. This door did not lead to the larger birthing room but to another part of the temple. I had watched servants come and go and caught a glimpse of a passageway beyond. I glanced around and saw that no-one was watching me; this always seemed to be so when I was leaving for a meeting with Kou. It was as if the illusion began before we even got to the doorway. Once outside in this passageway, I found myself in a familiar place. It was the corridor that led alongside my old workplace. Walking along the corridors, I turned into the passageway where the others were waiting for me. Silently, we passed through the doorway, completely unnoticed by others.

Master Ma Sing and the Watchers began to introduce us to a more in-depth study of the planets and the stars. Master Noih had already taught us much about the constellations seen from our earthly viewpoint. This new lesson was in regard to what we could not see with the naked eye. However, during our trance meditations, many unseen things were revealed. There was much of the world that we were unaware of. To be given the opportunity to see the heavens in all their glory was a great privilege. Master Noih taught us how the stars and planets could influence our lives and how they could also be seen as signs of future happenings. The Watchers showed us the incredibly powerful energies at work and spoke of the greatest divine power of all. This they referred to in a whisper. Rènshi and Wu Fang had spoken of the divine before. I *felt* I understood him, yet I did not consciously know it.

While in the trance state we travelled through the heavens on and on, further and further, and began to see the invisible power in action! We saw places beyond places and stars which seemed to move and change; some exploded before our eyes. There were other planets occupied by creatures unlike the human form and then some which were similar to our own. These we saw as bodies of matter; others, we were told, inhabited the spiritual realm around their respective planets.

As my senses returned to the room, I felt a noticeable difference. The memory of what we had all seen was still firmly in my mind; it wasn't a hazy awareness, like the remnants of a dream. The memory of what we had witnessed was as clear and sharp as any unforgettable experience. All the members of Kou sensed this at once. There would be much to discuss.

Master Ma Sing stepped forward. "Today we have stretched our minds further than before. This was not possible before now; today you are all ready, and this is the time. Yet our experiences today are minor when compared to the experiences of our honourable friends the Watchers. It just gives you an idea of what their very presence has brought to us. Yes."

We sat for a while in silence, awed by what we had just witnessed and incredulous at the amount of knowledge the Watchers had gained! We felt very humbled. "Now before we leave, there is one more thing. As a group, and within the perimeters of your own experiences, there will be interesting issues coming up for you all regarding your spiritual development. These individual experiences will be scrutinised by the Watchers and your masters; they will all be linked to an overall development of Kou. All this will occur before we meet again. We will begin our closing sequence."

Returning to the everyday activity of the temple, we made our way to the large hall and waited in line to collect our last meal of the day. As was the custom, we ate mostly in silence, exchanging knowing looks across the room. We were becoming accustomed to the idea that we could read into each other's minds, if we wanted to. This practice was kept to a minimum and usually connected to our work. There were ways to close this mechanism off, for privacy's sake. We were all aware that in our highest states of awareness, *all* was known, but this higher state could not be attained all the time, as the physical body could not withstand it.

Walking back to our room, Wèi Wèi whispered to me, "I am concerned about the new development and what it means for us all." I could see how serious she was, but she seemed to be in a fog of confusion.

"Don't worry about that now, Wèi Wèi. Look, we're here." The moment we entered our room, we all began talking at once about the things we had seen. It was as if we were children again!

As we calmed down and began our discussion in earnest, Wèi Wèi sat in a world of her own for a while before she cheered up and joined in with the conversation. It was as well that we didn't ponder too long on any future developments; we had had more than enough to think about. Master Ma Sing had told us what to expect, and as far as I was concerned what would be would be! I caught Niang's glance from time to time, as if she were aware of something about me. I quickly put in place a mind barrier to prevent this from happening, as I was concerned about my privacy. I need not have worried because she just smiled and accepted this. Then a thought came into my mind concerning a lesson Master Noih had taught us. It was about seeing part of ourselves in another person: the mirror, they called it. We were not always aware that this was happening.

The discussion continued until Niang said, "We must retire for the night; we are a little late, and we need our sleep." As we rose and started to prepare for sleep, Meirén came across and touched my shoulder.

"We are all facing things together, Su Ling," she said with a warm smile.

"Yes, of course, Meirén." I didn't wish to analyse her words then. I began to feel tired.

The next day I woke again to the sound of birdsong; it was

dawn, and their messages of greeting to one other were heralding the coming of spring and a sense of rebirth. I felt restless and intuitively went into my inner self to try to discover why. I felt a ripple of disturbance and knew not to delve any further. I had been taught that decisions my soul had made were not always comfortable to acknowledge or experience before an appointed time. Creating a protective shield around myself, I stayed calm in the silence of the room. Most of the others were asleep; only Niang was awake, and she was deep in contemplation.

The next morning as we ate our first meal, the young male priests and Li Jing glanced across at us from time to time. Everyone seemed aware of something in the air, and there was a sense of anticipation for the days ahead.

As I set off for the birthing room later, I noticed two physicians in deep conversation outside the door. They did not notice me as I passed to go inside. That day there were only two young women in labour; one in particular seemed favoured by the old women who were fussing around her and seeing to her every need. This expectant mother, I was told, was Meja, a foreigner and a favourite concubine of the governor's inner circle. The young woman in the next place was a servant in the governor's household, and she served Meja exclusively. I did not ask how the servant herself came to be expecting a child at the same time or why she was allowed to lie next to her mistress. One of the old women motioned me across to the young servant, who seemed to be exchanging glances of great warmth and friendship with her mistress. *They are friends*, I thought. This was unheard of outside the confines of Kou, where all were acknowledged as equals and were just at different stages of their spiritual development. The old woman told me that one of her colleagues was ill, so I would have to forgo my day in the anteroom and help her. I did not mind this at all.

I sat silently beside the old woman who was giving instructions to the servant girl. After a while, I was allowed to administer a potion to relax the patient. I whispered a few words to her, as was my usual practice. At once I was sharply pulled aside by the now-familiar physician and given a strong reminder to stay silent. My old adversary seemed to have appeared from nowhere. He seemed more irritated than usual, and I could see why. He had not been chosen to minister to Meja, only to her servant! These things seemed to be important to some of the physicians I had observed; petty jealousies were the norm.

Both women were nearing the final stages of their labour. I began to feel sorry for the young servant; some of my caring feelings were beginning to return. I had to repress such feelings to survive after the death of my Wu Fang and Rènshi. Meja's delivery was much easier than her servant's; it was increasingly obvious that this poor soul's unborn child lay in the wrong position inside her stomach. Two of the old woman tried to turn the babe while I held the mother firmly but carefully; she was already enduring enough. Meja delivered her son safely into the world, with the physicians congratulating her and telling her how pleased Governor Choi would be to have another son. Meanwhile, our physician, to his credit, fought to save the servant and her child. She looked exhausted, but with one final push the child was born.

Meja, who had insisted on staying by her servant's side, called to her, "Shu Shi", which means 'belong to'. I could tell that the 'belonging' took on a far more spiritual meaning for Meja. She was becoming alarmed. Shu opened her eyes looking at her mistress, and I knew at once that she was a survivor. The poor child however, was not! Just like my Rènshi, it touched the earth for only a short time, and just like me, the servant was inconsolable. One old birthing mother spoke sharply to her to "Pull herself together." This brought wrath from the favoured concubine, who brought the old woman to her knees to beg forgiveness. The physicians immediately joined in the verbal onslaught, and I knew that it would be the last time the old woman would work in such favoured surroundings again.

I felt no sympathy for her, only for the bereft young woman. It seemed cruel that her mistress, who already seemed to have so much, was fortunate enough to keep her son.

"What, oh what, have I done?" she wailed. "I have tried to serve my mistress well; I must have been punished for something." As I fought back my own tears, I knew how wrong she was. Meja echoed my thoughts as she tried to comfort her servant. The loss in this case was for other reasons – reasons connected to the family genealogy, a weakness affecting some family members that were carried down through the generations.

I continued to care for Shu as best I could, but after a while Meja ushered all of us, including the physicians, away. Only such a favoured concubine could speak to a physician in such a manner. Something caught my eye as I was leaving Shu; it was an expression on Meja's face. The way she turned to the side and the look in her eyes mirrored that of Shu's expression a little earlier. I realised at once the likeness. They were from the same family: they were turned to greet my colleagues as they returned from their day's work.

The meal the next morning was taken in a similar atmosphere to the previous day. A slight apprehension was felt by all members of Kou, and only its members would be aware of this. "I think the next stage of my development has already started," I said.

Meirén looked across the table in my direction and waited. Before I could say anything, Wèi Wèi jumped in with, "Mine too, and there's more to come; mine is the very worst."

Niang shot a warning look towards Wèi Wèi, who instantly stopped speaking. The rest of the meal was taken in silence by everyone.

When I had finished, I headed straight for the anteroom. I glanced sideways at the places where Meja and Shu had lain; they had gone back to the rooms of Governor Choi's living quarters. My heart missed a beat when I thought of Shu and her child. I silently sent out a request to the Watchers to send some healing to her.

In the anteroom that day, everything was laid out as usual for me. I noticed that there were one or two extra scrolls on my bench. I opened them and allowed myself time to digest the contents before starting on a new batch of potions. I had been studying various scrolls on the human form; both of these seemed to be in regard to Qi energy. Near the end of the second scroll, I came across what looked like an old, worn piece of animal skin. As I pulled it out, I found that I was handling something very fragile indeed. I had never seen the like before, and I was anxious in case it should disintegrate before my eyes! Laying it back down onto the bench, I carefully moved it nearer to the light of the window. There were fading illustrations around the border of the script; they were only just visible. I couldn't imagine how it had come to be there. I imagined that one of the servants must have picked it up by mistake, but why was the manuscript not in scroll form like the others? I could see how such a small piece of material could easily be mislaid. It fascinated me, and I began to study it carefully.

The contents were very much concerned with my own work of healing. There were references to formulas I had never come across before to heal various ailments. This document before me, I concluded, must contain a rare piece of hidden knowledge. I decided to use my own initiative as well as my instinct to uncover the formula's true meaning. If this was what I thought it to be, it would help me to gain favour with the physicians. Perhaps they would take me more seriously!

As I studied each part of the old material and how it related to certain ingredients, I searched for hidden meanings. It seemed to suggest using certain herbs and insects I had never used before. I had knowledge of them, of course, but they would have to be fetched from another area further away from the compound, putting the servants in danger from raiding parties as they searched the hillside.

I meditated on this for a while before returning to study the formulas again. I came to the same conclusions. I wished with all my heart to do this; it felt like a breakthrough in the healing arts. But if the document was so old, why hadn't this been used before? Were the ingredients impossible to find? The instructions for the use of the potions seemed very precise. Perhaps others had tried before me but had failed to notice the hidden meanings. It was most curious. Then there was the question of the servants' safety. I decided that I would instruct them most carefully in just what was needed and I would ask for protection for them on their journey from the Spirit Masters. I was sure that the cause was a good one and that they would be well protected in their task. I rang my bell to summon them, and it wasn't long before two servants arrived. They seemed concerned when I told them that they would have to search further than they had done before but were relieved when I assured them that they would return home safely. I wrote down in my own hand the ingredients I was looking for, which could only be found in that far area. "I will need them today; they are to be prepared for use for the day after tomorrow."

A fleeting thought then crossed my mind: how did I know this? The servants hurried off, and I spent a little time ensuring that they would be fully protected in their task. I began preparing my usual familiar potions while I waited for their return.

They arrived back sooner than expected, both looking relieved and breathless as they told the story of their search on the hillside. "Everything was so easy for us, Su Ling. We found ourselves drawn to the exact spot for the ingredients you needed. There was no searching involved; it was as if unseen hands were guiding us there. As we began to gather the herbs and insects, we noticed a suspicious group of soldiers on horseback coming down the hill, but they passed by as if not even noticing we were there!"

"Good, I knew you would be safe. Go now." This seemed like a good omen, and I felt my actions were justified, my aim being a healing one. All was well.

Carefully following my own interpretation of the formula, I began to prepare what I believed to be my finest work yet: potions and ointments so powerful that they would be used by the governor's own physicians. I was a little perplexed at the thought that they would be confined at first to the governor's own household. I was sure that in time they would relent and make these wonderful potions available to all working in the temple, perhaps even in the villages. I realised then that my dreams were maybe a little too ambitious. Towards the end of the day, my new applications were nearly ready and would need to settle for just one more day. As if to prove that all was going to plan, the elder birthing mother called to me just as I was leaving. "The day after tomorrow, you are to be allowed to administer some of your own potions on one patient only. I am informing you now because I have work to do in Governor Choi's own private rooms tomorrow. Be guided by what the physicians instruct you to do. Go now!"

I wondered if this would prove to be my chance, but I was aware that my new potions could only be used in special circumstances. I would have to be patient.

I had one day to prepare myself mentally for what could be a splendid opportunity, though I could not neglect my usual potions. Working swiftly the next day, I was even more determined to finish my everyday tasks to give myself time to check my new formula against the instructions on the mysterious document. This time as I studied it, I thought I detected one or two more hidden meanings concerning the preparations of the ingredients. It was just like uncovering layers of instructions to reach the true definition of the work, which the author had hidden from prying eyes until the time was right for it to be revealed. Everything seemed to fall into place. I decided I had to take the responsibility alone; in fact, I felt compelled to! Master Noih and my work with Kou had taught me to trust my instincts. I made a few adjustments to the potions, and I felt sure that I was ready. The hours seemed to pass by slowly, and I couldn't wait for the next day to come. I would bide my time and wait for a suitable opportunity.

Keeping my own counsel in our living room that evening was not difficult to do, for I noticed that my colleagues were mostly quiet reading or contemplating. Only Niang studied me from time to time. I pretended not to notice.

The following morning, as we were eating our meal together, Wèi Wèi glanced up and whispered to me, "Today is special for you?" She spoke as if it were a question rather than a statement, as she usually did. I just shrugged my shoulders as if unaware of her meaning. Later, as I walked into the birthing room, I saw that there were already two physicians attending to the wife of one of the governor's scribes. I recognised her from some of the large official gatherings and had been informed about whom she belonged to. There were just two other beds occupied by women in the early stages of their confinement, with several birthing women scurrying around them. *What a waste of the other available spaces,* I thought. *Some of the women from my old birthing room could have occupied the other available places.* This, sadly, was never an option.

One of the physicians called me over to the woman who appeared to be the immediate priority. "This patient does not have long to go before she gives birth. However, all is not going quite as well with her as we would have hoped."

"We do not like the colour of her tongue or the look of her eyes," the other physician interjected.

The first spoke again with a slight look of disdain at me. "We have administered none of our usual potions and have been instructed to let you use your own on this patient, so let us see what you can do. We have been told about the clever Su Ling, so of course we thought you could work alone!"

My face must have shown the shock I felt then; how could they leave me to work alone? How could they leave the room when the poor woman was in some danger! I knew I had been tricked; they wanted to get rid of me, and I was angry that they thought so little of their patient. I knew they were hoping for something to go wrong and blame me, or for me to beg them to come back and rescue me.

I will show them, was my reasoning at the time. Comforting the woman as best I could, I glanced up at the old women fussing around the other two; they pretended not to notice. I hurried into the anteroom and picked up the new formula. My head felt as if it was buzzing, and I felt slightly dizzy as I hurried to her bedside. I felt sure that I had a miracle cure at my disposal for whatever was ailing my patient. Administering a little at a time to her, I prepared for an imminent birth. Suddenly I noticed a change in her! She showed an unnatural stillness, and her contractions seemed to have stopped. I desperately tried everything I had been trained to do to save both mother and child.

Realising that something had gone wrong, I looked around

and found that even the old birthing mothers had left the room. My head was fit to burst. I silently called out to Kou, "Help me, help me!" Suddenly a vision of the Watchers came into my mind, and I could hear their voices.

"Administer your usual orange and blue potions combined, quickly!" In a haze I ran into the room for my usual tried and tested potions; I mixed them together in a phial and hurried back to my patient. Tipping her head fully back, I poured some of the medicine down her throat. It had the effect of bringing her around, though she cried out in agony. I massaged her swollen stomach and shouted instructions to her at various intervals. With the greatest difficulty, she brought forth her babe into the world. Suddenly the birthing women appeared from nowhere to help with the babe. They also seemed to be aware which of my usual potions was needed to help the mother. One had fetched it for me, and in my state of panic I had hardly noticed! After careful nursing for the rest of the day, both mother and child were pronounced fit to survive.

The old woman said nothing much to me regarding this, and I knew that a full report on what had happened would go to the elder before leaving for the day, I took the miracle potion and threw it out of the window, letting the wind take it so that it could cause no more harm. Something told me to keep the old document to show the other members of Kou. I began to feel more like my old self again.

The next three days went by in the birthing room without any serious problems. I did as I was ordered, being allowed to use my potions only three times over the next three days. I felt that

I had contributed to the work which was carried out over that time, even though the physicians seemed to think that they were solely responsible for the care of the expectant mothers. In fact, our relations felt a little too cordial at times! I was waiting to be summoned before one sort of official or another and made to pay for my use of unapproved potions. By the third day, I took the atmosphere around me to be the calm before the storm. My own sense of failure, in spite of the fact that my patient and her babe had survived, only added to my feelings of worthlessness. Even after everything I had been taught, when I had been put to the test, I had failed!

My mood seemed to be matched by those of my female colleagues. During the early mornings and evenings of those three days, if someone had entered our room they would have been struck by the strange sense of melancholy pervading everywhere. I wondered if the same surrounded the male members of Kou. Yet it was precisely *because* of our own individual anxieties that we could not bring ourselves to ask how our fellow male colleagues had fared.

The next morning, and according to my rota, my work would be solely concentrated in the anteroom. As I prepared for the day, a knock came at the door. Niang opened it, and Li Jing informed her that there would be a meeting of Kou later that morning and we should adjust our workloads accordingly. Although no-one in the temple would notice our absence, they would certainly notice if certain tasks had not been carried out! Hiding the old manuscript in my pouch with Tóngshì, I left the room behind all the others.

Back in the birthing room there was the usual forced sense of cordiality. I walked straight to the anteroom and worked faster and harder than usual, so that all who would need the help of my potions would not be left wanting. When the time came, they would be available. As usual, people seemed to be looking the other way as I slipped out along the corridor to join my colleagues from Kou. We walked together with heavy hearts through the doorway and into the room which was invisible to others, as it existed in another dimension altogether. I expected the masters to immediately take charge of the proceedings, as it was their duty to hand out punishments in matters of discipline. Part of me knew that in Kou, things were looked upon in a different way, yet the old ways of our lessons in the outside world went deep. The terrible threats we had received as children against any perceived wrongdoing still formed a tight pattern inside us. There was a pause, and it was the Watchers who stepped forward that day, the same Watchers who had come to my rescue when had I cried out for help to save my two patients.

Shen prepared to speak first after carefully making eye contact with everyone in the room. "This has been a testing time for all of you. Every so often a testing of sorts takes place in regard to the very special work that we do here. You may be surprised to know that even you're Masters and teachers have recently faced situations where they were tested to the very limits of their knowledge. Now they have no need for such testing; they have risen above the obstacles which have been put before them and now await the next challenges they will face when they return home to the spirit world."

She paused for a moment to let the fact sink into our minds.

Of course, we could not imagine that the masters, who to us seemed to know everything, would ever need to be tested. We could not understand what momentous test would be set before them. Shen continued, "I know you are all wondering, so I will ask the question prominent in your minds. No, we do not need such testing programmes. For us, they would be a step backwards."

The Watchers changed positions. Jing continued, "There comes a time when the knowledge we have gained from the past, present, and future must be used as a teaching tool to bring about great changes in this world and others."

The vibrations in the room suddenly changed. There was a more relaxed and less anxious atmosphere, which made it easier to concentrate solely on Jing's words. "Each of you has bravely tried to fulfil the tasks which were put before you. All tried generously to help others by taking the initiative and responsibility for doing so upon yourselves. Your intentions, too, were to benefit the work of Kou, now and in the future. Even having learnt so much from us, you have succumbed to the human trait of feeling that unfairness has befallen you. Perhaps you even feel that the honour you have bestowed upon your tutors was not worthy of them?" A small number of pupils felt their faces redden at that remark, but just as quickly they regained their composure.

Shen stepped forward again. This time the Watchers spoke in unison, as one entity. Their voices became even more empathic towards the novices who sat before them. "There is not time to hear everyone's experiences, but we will hear three such stories today. We shall hear from Niang, Wèi Wèi, and Su Ling. Three of the boys can relate their tales at the next meeting; that will be all we will hear on the subject of the tests. By then you should have all understood the need for testing. Niang, please continue."

I could not believe that someone so knowing as Niang would have succumbed to a misinterpretation of her task. I suddenly felt very humbled and realised that all in the room felt empathy towards her.

Niang began. "I was taken by my teachers to a children's area and given the task of observing them very closely in order to pick out potential leaders for the future, children who would not be automatically chosen to lead just because they came from a family with low status. I was very pleased to be given this opportunity, though I was slightly awed by the responsibility. It soon became clear to me that I could also do a great service for Kou. After all, I reasoned, these same children could possibly become fine potential members of Kou, so that the work we do could continue on and on. So I watched the children at work very closely, especially during their break period, when I observed their play and even a little mischief at times. I picked out the best candidates for leaders, as I perceived them to be, and duly reported to the master tutor. Of course, no mention was made of our secret group. The master listened to my remarks very seriously and seemed to take everything I observed into account before speaking. It was at this point that I began to sense that a greater lesson for myself was about to be unfurled.

'Let us take your first candidate, Niang,' the master told me. 'This is a young boy who appeared to be showing all the signs of a great warrior. You observed him speaking loudly and forcibly, giving out orders to others. Even in his studies, he held himself erect as if he were very sure of his abilities. But if you had watched him a little more closely, you would have observed that he is in fact a great little actor who can put on a fine performance. The ones who speak most loudly are often the most insecure. The acts they put on, the personae of the warrior and clever pupil, are in fact very able performances to hide the truth of how they really feel about themselves. They do not just wear a mask; their whole demeanour covers up their fears. When another comes along and challenges such a child, he backs off and takes no action.'

Niang spoke softly to Kou. "That was my first error. The master tutor continued, then, to make his assessment of the next child chosen."

'And so we come to your second choice of leader, Niang. Your choice was a little girl this time. Tell me, have you ever known a female leader, apart from an empress?'

"Of course," Niang told us, "I was confusing some of my wider knowledge with the master tutor's own beliefs; I forgot for a while that I was dealing with a master who only inhabited the mundane world. I quickly made a great play of my stupidity, offering many apologies and humbling myself before him, although he was a man who I had not worked for before."

'Very well,' he said. 'Your fantasies may have gotten the better of you; I must ask them to send me a more intelligent creature next time. I am feeling benevolent today, so I will continue to teach you things you will remember.'

Niang looked up towards Shen and Jing. "As he made the remark about benevolence, I seemed to see a vision of you both, just for a moment." Returning to her recollections, she continued with her story.

'We will leave aside the fact that she is female and concentrate on her actions, Niang. This child is looked up to by the other children for some reason. You often see them following her and trying to copy what she does. However, we have noticed that she soon gets bored and moves here and there, looking for others to manipulate. This is a perfect example, Niang, of why females are not natural leaders!'

"Master looked very pleased with himself at this point," Niang murmured. "He came to my third choice then."

'Well, at least we have a young boy this time. Our candidate here is a natural organiser; he can't help himself. We have one or two occupations in mind that might suit him. The trouble is, he gets a little lost in whatever plan he is working on and leads his co-workers into total confusion. That, my dear, is why he lacks leadership abilities: he does not carry a plan through to the end.

'We come to your last choice! Again, I find it hard to understand why you made the same mistake twice by choosing a female! The child is, yes, always eager and needs to be part of a team. But she needs to be liked by all. Her view of her own worth should not be based on the opinions of others; it should come from within herself. The ideal candidate, as we see it, is an observer of everything. He needs to be cautious and helpful, listening to the opinions of others and not jumping in before carefully making his decision. Once that decision is made, he has to be brave and take responsibility, whatever the outcome. Leadership qualities often show up later as the child grows.'

"As this was something I felt I had been doing myself," Niang remarked, "I wondered why my masters had thought me capable of such a task, as I have so obviously failed." For the great Niang to speak such words was unheard of in our living quarters. I caught my breath and realised that in the invisible room, all such feelings are expressed.

The watchers in union sent a soothing vibration to Niang before they spoke. "When pupils confuse their tasks between two separate purposes, especially anything relating to Kou, things can become confusing. It can lead to a confusion of thoughts even when trying to do the right thing and taking personal responsibility, as you have all been taught. However, the greatest examples of our folly can become the dearest projects close to our hearts. If we understand the reasons why we err, then we can go on to produce triumphs. Kou members are hand-picked, first by spirit masters and then by your masters and us, though we speak to you as one entity for a moment. Your kind thoughts on new recruits for a future Kou group are not necessary. The reason will be explained at some point in the future." Niang bowed before the Watchers and her masters and said nothing.

Still joined as one, the Watchers beckoned to Wèi Wèi to begin her story. "I am overcome with this momentous opportunity," she said seriously, pausing for effect. "I was looking forward to being tested, and I had glimpses now and then of what it would involve. I was very calm regarding this because, you see, I was sure that I would triumph and that my training would not let me down. However, I was wrong." I glanced then at Wèi Wèi and respected her for her humility. She continued in her usual fashion. "My task involved two things. One concerned prophecy, which I felt I could be sure of. The other was not exactly new to me, but the importance of it certainly was!

"Two masters came to Master Noih's room and escorted me out to the temple gardens. I have never met or seen them before, and for some reason their names escape me now. It was a warm day, and I was led to the small pond that I had become familiar with, for I had seen visions in it before." This was something I had cause to remember myself very well; she was referring to the vision regarding my Wu Fang and Rènshi.

"Then one of the new masters spoke to me with an air of calm in his voice."

'You have taken responsibilities for many prophecies, Wèi Wèi. You have also been trained to not blurt out what you see or hear, for it can confuse the listener. I see you understand what I mean. This careful practice can take time, as your natural inclination is for everything to come out in a rush. Master Noih has tried to teach you discipline in regard to this.'

"I bowed to the master in recognition of the truth of his words," Wèi Wèi told the Watchers. "Then the other master began to address me." 'We would like you to tell us what you see in the pond today, Wèi Wèi. It can be anything, concerning any matter whatsoever. You may begin.'

"I prepared myself as usual and stared deeply into the pond. Things usually happen very quickly," Wèi Wèi said. "However, there seemed to be nothing emerging in my mind that day. It was most curious; I felt sure that something for Kou would have emerged because it seemed to be such an important test. There was nothing for me to interpret, as the only thing to emerge came out of the water, it was a small toad – a physical thing, not a vision at all. I was a little angry. Why had the spirit masters let me down at such an important moment? It was not my own fear that prevented this. I started with my apologies, and I felt that my failure would affect Kou in some unknown way. The masters raised their hands for me to stop, and I waited in silence for what seemed like an age.

"The first master spoke again. 'I asked you to tell us what you could see in the pond, Wèi Wèi; I believe I said on any matter whatsoever.'

"Yes, Master."

'Any *matter*. The word can be taken in two ways, can it not? Matter can represent a subject or a situation – and do not let us forget the 'world of matter', the material world, Wèi Wèi.'

"I gasped," said Wèi Wèi. "How could I overlook the importance of the toad, an animal living in this world of matter?

'Yes, I see things becoming clear to you now. You see, your thoughts were so focused on, shall we say higher things and showing us your accomplishments that they dulled the awareness within you. Your awareness and intuition need to be sharp for events happening on this physical level of existence. You must have heard of synchronicity and events that seem to happen at or around the same time. This shows you that everything is linked; everything flows together. Those who can pick up the clues can become aware of how everything is connected, both in the seen and the unseen worlds.

'Let us see what our little toad can tell us, Wèi Wèi,' the second master began to explain. 'As I understand it, beliefs surrounding this little fellow can vary quite considerably through different lands. So we concentrate, of course, on our own sacred beliefs and what the little water creature can mean in our lives, but we will also mention other various perceptions towards the toad. Some say he represents humidity and the dark side of nature and is evil and repulsive. Another perception of him is of residue, debris, and earthly matters; some say that he is a lowly but fertile creature. We will come back to this because we see him in the Yin principle and as a lunar animal. He represents to us the unattainable, longevity, wealth, profit making, and resurrection. As with all things, we look carefully for a balanced picture here. So we have the feminine principal, the Yin, and the lunar animal, which represents passivity. We can see how wealth and good fortune are pleasing to our minds and how many prefer to see signs in somewhat narrow but positive ways. We can also see the positive when studying what we perceive as negative interpretations. Resurrections occur, for instance, when there has been an ending or a destruction of some kind, hence the residue and debris of the past. The water itself here is a very potent symbol. The animal rises from the depths of what we can say here is the psyche. So there has been a synchronicity here of your own mind's perception at work with the manifestation of the symbol itself, which in this instance truly manifested in the physical realm!

"Master paused for a moment while I tried to take this in," said Wèi Wèi. "The importance of things which manifest in this world – it was as if I had seen them as secondary *to* and not working *with* the spiritual.

'So we have this duality of purpose,' murmured the second master. 'Do we only pick the aspects of this symbol which please us, and which we choose to believe? We look to our own existence here, our sacred beliefs, and we make our interpretation. I say *we* here meaning ourselves, your masters. We are willing to show you the way here. As the manifestation came through your will, we would see you as the feminine principle at work here. The belief that the toad represents wealth we see as signifying the wealth of knowledge which has come from your teachers. The debris and remains are those of your old ways of thinking; we would see these as dark thoughts or uninformed thoughts which have resulted in the resurrection of your soul to higher spiritual beliefs, to the satisfaction of our beloved ancestors.'

Wèi Wèi addressed the Watchers. "I have the greatest respect for the masters on that day who were my tutors for the test, and I have learned much. I felt humbled, and it was a reminder not to become complacent about my skills. However, they are unaware of the existence of Kou, and I feel there is more here for us all to see. I would like to know if I am correct."

"Yes," Shen and Jing said together. "We work together here looking at the wider aspects of belief systems, and we sometimes see similar themes, fear being one of them. Your particular task has brought a new understanding to you of what happens when we marry the spiritual world to the material world. These things have been spoken of before, but it takes a testing in action to really bring home to you what we have tried to teach in the past. Failure is simply failing to discover something new about our work or ourselves. It brings us a sense of balance. So the little amphibian came out from the depths to show you the way. Our perception in these circumstances is everything. As we think, we create; we bring something into being. That is why the balanced view is called for. All the beliefs spoken of by the two masters can come into play when we take the wider view. But when the masters chose to show themselves in a positive light, only mentioning you, Wèi Wèi, in a dark sense, no such balance of thought was shown. So here we will give you our interpretation as information for yourself and your colleagues.

"The feminine principle, often seen as the Earth plane, is necessary here to focus our minds on for this particular test. We do not ignore the masculine principle; it is just put to the side for a moment. We see the Earth plane as the divine mother who comes forward to show us a glimpse of a future Kou existence. Where we come from we see the past, future, and present as one; however, at this level, we recognise the differences. Our work will continue here, as the dark side of the mother implies. Dark here is in relation to the lunar principle and simply means the dark side of the moon. So we refer to those things which will be hidden until they illuminate our lives once more. She is often found when we are looking elsewhere for her. Wèi Wèi was following her usual pattern of focusing on her mind energy to bring forth pictures there whilst an ordinary, daily picture was materialising right in front of her. Our future lies in our extraordinary ability, which of course brings its own rewards when we educate and heal others as well as ourselves. We may feel as if there are not so many others who will want to listen or face certain aspects of life and death, and they make a definite decision not to do so. That is their right. The wonder is that any subtle hint we put out here and there is taken up in such a structured society as this. So we have the unforeseen, followed by illumination to some, and a refusal to hear subtle suggestions which are meant to inform and help. Our little creature that comes up into the light is not normally seen as a pretty sight and is only sometimes understood as an auspicious symbol of good luck and fortune. It cannot always be given to us; rather, it is something we give ourselves. The future of Kou lies in listening during our everyday lives and watching out for the unexpected, which often symbolises the 'as above so below' principle." After a short pause, the Watchers brought their attention to me.

"Now, Su Ling, let us have your story." I told my tale as best I could and tried not to leave out any detail. When I had finished I pulled out the mysterious document from my sleeve and laid it before the class. I was aware of Wèi Wèi's astonishment. I wondered if it was because my own failure could have resulted in someone's death.

"Yes, if only we had the magic elixir of life here, to make all well again and to put an end to suffering. If only." Shen and Jing were lost in their own private thoughts for a moment. "You see, Su Ling, this document, which is very ancient, comes from the temple archives and has been known of for centuries." My eyes opened wide in amazement at my own stupidity.

"Of course, this was always meant to be part of your test. There are healing techniques contained there which have been known of for a very long time. As the document stands, it is completely in order. However, the key lies in what is written between the words and is often open to misinterpretation. Especially vulnerable to misinterpretation are those who wish to prove their worth to others, not necessarily in an egotistical way but because they need to be accepted. The world is not yet ready for our particular kind of work, and the key to the ancient text is in linking the spirit to the emotions, believe it or not! They work closely together and are a force to be reckoned with. Where a soul decides to take on an illness in the human frame, for whatever reason, no newly found or ancient healing technique will work. There is much to be learned in regard to this. You, Su Ling, need to have enough respect for yourself and your own methods of communicating the skills you already have in place. You do not need to rely on the opinions of others to gain respect. We always respect our elders for their experience and wisdom. We do not have to look outside of ourselves for respect; we go within to obtain it, to understand it, and to accept it with humility. Your compassion is obvious; that has to be tempered with what you cannot do at the moment, however much you would like to be a miracle worker. We have to silently offer our healing thoughts for the higher good of the soul who is the patient; that may not mean a magical cure for them. We will return the valuable document to the archive. Thank you.

"All of you were given tests, not necessarily to win but rather for the sake of your wisdom and empathy. Through them you have all gained much experience." With that, the masters stepped forward and stood in line with the Watchers, and the closing sequence began.

CHAPTER 15

Joint Ownership

I LEARNED MUCH IN THE following two years. My training took me to many new places. I found that although the temple complex was a relatively small area, when observed closely it was a microcosm of the macrocosm: a mirror image of existence on a much wider scale. In the seemingly mundane activities of the day were clues to deeper and more meaningful things than I ever could have imagined. My observations were a closely guarded secret and only shown to my colleagues when I judged the time to be right. It continued to be important to see a balanced perspective in all things as I became aware of peoples' whispers in the background of temple life. Our training reminded us that listening closely to others should always be with a spiritual purpose in mind.

During those two years, a curious development took place. 'Curious' is a strange word to use when we think of the many varied wonders which I had experienced. The development – for that it what it was – took place over time in the large Central Hall, where the ceremony of She had been held all those years before, during a time of much change. Very rarely was the hall occupied by servants of the Temple of the Heavenly Bird; only priests generally used it. We became aware that one of the young priests who were members of Kou had been singled out for greater things by the elder priests of the temple. The elders had no knowledge of Kou, of course, but they would have been aware of something special about our young priest. His abilities, along with his secret training, lay in a specific kind of healing practice. He was indeed a great healer, but according to the ancient beliefs of the time, he held his gift back except when with his colleagues in Kou. The little talent that he did show was so impressive to the elder priests, that they chose him to train closely with them despite his young age. They could not have understood the magnitude of his gift in one so young. We knew him as Shaotie, a name given to him by a priest when he first entered the temple.

The situation developed over a period of time until an initiation ceremony was planned, coincidentally, on the anniversary of the day that the ceremony of She had been performed with all the other grand administrators present. We remembered assembling in the Great Hall and becoming aware of another area which was curtained off behind the three statues. Shaotie told us that the first half of the initiation ceremony would take place in the Great Hall and the second part would be behind the curtained-off area where only temple priests of a certain standing were allowed. Shaotie, of course, had to be seen to be overwhelmed by the honour being given to him, knowing that it would be of no comparison to his work with the Watchers.

"It will be interesting nevertheless" was all he would say. His dilemma lay in the fact that at some point he would have to be sworn to secrecy, and reporting back to us meant that he would have to break the oath he took. He had discussed the problem with Master Ma Sing, Master Noih, and Master Fu Chang together, as he was unable to see a way through it. To his relief, he was informed that he was to keep his oath of secrecy with the elder priests. The Watchers knew everything, and the three masters were aware of much that happened behind closed doors. They could foresee another dilemma for Shaotie after he had become initiated but kept their counsel at that time.

The time for the ceremony was fast approaching, and Kou assembled the day before to lend support to Shaotie. With direction from the Watchers, we sent our thoughts to the choices he would have to make and the things he would be asked to do. As this required bravery on his part, the strengthening of his spiritual self as well as his physical self was needed. As before, preparations during our collective meditative state meant that we were taken outside of the dimensions we normally inhabited. I remember being aware of a white mist this time and a gathering of the elders far below in a half-lit place. Shaotie rose up from the proceedings to where we stood. At this point, the strengthening took place, yet I remember nothing of it. When our senses returned to the room, we were all left in no doubt that the honour bestowed on him would be a challenging one.

I saw nothing of Shaotie for two weeks until the next meeting with Kou. On the actual day of his initiation ceremony, he was never far from our thoughts, and in the evening of that day we were strangely stirred by a foreboding. As we gathered in the social area of our living quarters, our thoughts continued to go out to him. Love poured out from each and every one of us during his time of need. He had been given the strength; now we were offering him our conscious support, and we were aware that the rest of our colleagues and teachers were doing the same in other areas of the temple.

By the time the next meeting of Kou arrived, we sensed that a compromise of sorts had taken place but were unclear of the details. We passed through the Doorway of Illusion just ahead of our male colleagues and sat patiently, trying not to stare at Shaotie. I did glance over to where he sat; his face looked very pale, and he looked tired. He did not seem to have the youthful vigour that we were accustomed to seeing. Master Ma Sing called the meeting to order, and we were informed of recent fighting on the border areas of our land, which had resulted in a change in the hierarchy of Governor Choi's army. His closest and most influential general had fallen in battle, resulting in a victory for his warriors but at great cost to our beloved governor and the rest of his troops. A new general was to be put in charge temporarily, and after a short period of mourning, a new general-in-chief would be appointed. "I tell you this now, my friends, because later on there will be repercussions from the tragic loss of a loyal servant. They will be divulged to you at the proper time; for now, our honourable friends Shen and Jing will take the rest of the meeting for today."

"So, as always," Shen said, "we have another interesting topic for our lesson today. It is one which we have all prepared for, even though we are not all consciously aware of what has befallen our colleague Shaotie."

A ripple of energy circulated the room, showing our empathy for him. "When one of us makes a sacred promise or takes an oath and is sworn to secrecy, it is important to our integrity that we keep to that promise and that oath. Because we have already done so regarding Kou and its secret work, it is very challenging to be put into a position where we are asked to do the same elsewhere. On the surface it seems an impossible task. Our loyalty to our illustrious emperor is well known and is perfectly in keeping with the sworn oaths we have taken here. Our emperor and dear Governor Choi may be unaware of our existence, but both are compatible, as we only wish for positive and spiritual outcome for those we serve."

Jing stepped forward. "We are not here today to divulge the details of the secret ceremony of the temple priests, and we would never ask Shaotie to do the same. His difficult task has been to please the temple priests on pain of death! He has sworn his loyalty to them while at the same time not breaking his oath to Kou or betraying any of our secrets. To be caught between two such forces is one of the hardest challenges one can face. To pull this off, Shaotie would have to word his affirmation very carefully indeed whilst others would watch and monitor him closely. Unfortunately, what we could not warn him of before his initiation was the totally unexpected turn of events on the day! The first part of the ceremony was held in front of all the priests of the temple, including our young trainee priests here. This took place in the Great Hall. The words that he was asked to repeat under oath were fortunately similar to our own: to honour our great ancestors in spirit, our emperor, and our governor, to keep the secrets of the ceremonies, and to give his life to that cause. This he will and can do, and it was not so much a challenge as he envisaged. However, he alone was then sent behind the curtained-off area for the final part of the ceremony, which was known only to those present there. Shaotie found himself in the presence of a relatively new chief priest to our Governor. His new position began some months ago. Little was known of Priest Duìmiàn at the time except that he was a brother of the governor's wife. He now holds the position of chief priest and has great power within the temple. His name means 'opposite'. He then appointed a deputy who was totally of his own choosing, Priest Fùzá. His name refers to a complex or complicated character. These, then, were the only priests present who knew the secret of the final part of the process. We will not ask Shaotie his feelings at the moment he stepped behind the curtain. Of course you would expect that I myself and Shen would be aware of them. His training stood him in good stead at that moment because at once, he sensed great danger!"

Jing stood back to allow Shen to speak again. My heart was beating faster, as I knew that part of my own being already knew the answer, yet my conscious mind had yet to fully understand. "Our friend the chief priest has somewhat misunderstood his role and has illusions of grandeur regarding himself. We told you that his name meant 'opposite'; he is just that. He is opposing our cause, including Governor Choi Yen-Shu himself!"

A gasp went up around the room as our unconscious fears

were realised. "Yes, he has a grand plan, my friends. He wishes that every newly initiated priest swear an oath of allegiance to him and him alone, making the previous oath taken in the large hall redundant! He, in his wildest imaginings, thinks that he can become more powerful than any grand administrator governor while feigning loyalty to him at the same time. His new initiates are made to follow him through personal threats to themselves and their families and a promise to teach them magical skills which, unbeknown to them, will only be used in support of the dark arts. The other priests, he thinks, cannot help but be sucked into his plan in time, thus causing the ruination of all the souls concerned.

"We have been watching him carefully, and only now have his preparations begun with Shaotie. You see, he, and other genuinely loyal elder priests of the temple, have recognised Shaotie's potential. Duìmiàn has certain knowledge of the esoteric principles, though not to our standard, of course: he is but a learner. If Shaotie had been a recruit who could have been manipulated, the danger would have been that his considerable skills as a healer could have been turned around by the chief priest to become a destructive force. In time, Shaotie's superior knowledge would be divulged to Duìmiàn and his deputy, causing the downfall of Governor Choi and a complete take-over of the Temple of the Heavenly Bird, which is the complete opposite of our cause here."

We could almost feel Shaotie's energy begin to drain at the very thought of the peril he had been made a part of. We took a moment, under the Watchers' direction, to send our own energy out to him to bolster his own. Shen spoke firmly. "This will never happen; Duìmiàn is no match for us, and he is not, as yet, aware of our existence. He is, though, a negative force to be reckoned with. Our future work lies in protecting our governor and the temple, and it can only be done from the inside with Shaotie as our representative of the Light of Spirit. It is an enormous task for him. At that ceremony, he had to put into place a blocking screen around his thoughts with all the might he could muster, and he was made to undergo a physical test of bravery amounting to some blood loss. We are so proud of our beloved pupil; he had the difficult task of appearing to swear loyalty to Duìmiàn while not allowing himself to become part of the priest's evil! This was one of the hardest trials that he and we, your teachers, have had to face. The only way the evil oath could be contained and transmuted to one of good intention was to act at an even higher dimension than our own, here in this room. You were all part of the strengthening process, as you will remember. The part you have consciously forgotten was during the moment when Shaotie made his oath of allegiance; we all took his true essence up to a sacred place which Duìmiàn will never know of, unless he changes. It was there that the darkness of the oath was transmuted. It could not have been done in the material world. Thus a compromise took place which is safe for Shaotie to bear.

"You will be wondering why we need Shaotie to tell us things about this dark plan that we could not have discovered ourselves. Because of the status we have reached as Watchers, the smallest contact with this dark energy reduces our power considerably. Taking Shaotie's essence to the sacred place left its mark on us! With a little work, this can be removed."

Looking around the room at the anxious faces of Kou, Shen said, "You need not worry or concern yourself with this; it will be done. We are only allowing Shaotie to be placed in this dangerous situation for a short time. He will not be battling with the dark forces year after year; his battle will last for three months only. It has been spoken of in the higher echelons of spirit, as the chief priest's soul is a dark one they have seen before many times and in many different guises. He has never been able to lift himself up into the region of light and of love. So this is to be the main thrust of our work for the next three months: the protection of the temple and all those souls within. It is a great responsibility."

After the meeting that evening, Niang gathered us all together in the social area. "We need to help Shaotie at specific times of the day. We often do this type of work during the evening time; it is during the day, however, that I feel some help must be sent his way. Duìmiàn, I know, will come to him in his dreams; a blockage of sorts has been set up in order to prevent this. The priest, through the Watchers' determination, will see this only as a shield that Shaotie has put in place to protect his healing power. He will of course try from time to time to penetrate the blockage, but he will not wish to spend too much time trying to get through: He will wish Shaotie's considerable healing power to remain intact in order to manipulate it for his own negative aims later. We are all very busy, of course, with our daily activities; just stopping what we are doing at any given time is not an option for us. That is why we need something to focus on, however briefly, which will represent a positive counterbalance to Duìmiàn and Fùzá. I suggest we meditate on this white candle. I will place it in the centre of the room. I am going to silently send out to you an image, a symbol of all that is sacred surrounding a vision of Shaotie, our colleague, who is in dire need of our support. When you all receive it into your thoughts, you will know what has to be done. Midmorning, midday, and mid afternoon, come the hour, we will briefly picture this vision. We will sense the times as they approach; no-one will forget to do so, and no others will be aware of what is happening."

And so it was. As we all meditated on the candle flame, a symbol appeared surrounding our friend Shaotie. We poured all the healing energy we could muster into that vision, and when it was over, the Watchers briefly appeared to us as if to confirm that all was well. Thus we sent our intentions three times daily and once in the evenings.

As my work continued in the birthing room, I was aware of a gradual lessening of the hostile feelings towards me from the others. I could not fully understand why this was, but I continued to do my best for my patients and even found new ways of preparing potions for them. It was a quiet time in contrast to the dangerous activity going on in the background.

During the first month of supporting Shaotie, one day when we all assembled together as Kou, Li Jing was allowed to tell the story of his experiences during his time of testing. Li Jing stood up and bowed to all present. It struck me how much humility he had gained and how much of the arrogance had left him. He began, "I was summoned at that time to the commandery to be with the governor's soldiers. I was a little surprised at this, being a scholar and servant rather than a fighter. I could present myself well in the practice of self-defence, but I had not been called on to use these skills very often. I was sent to the stables where the regiment's horses are kept. The soldier in charge there was certainly no master! He only gave me menial tasks to do: cleaning the horses' stalls, bringing them new hay, and fetching water. Apart from this being an act of humility; I could not see the sense of it. After working hard for some hours, I was amazed to see one of Governor Choi's generals walking around inspecting the horses! It never occurred to me that a general would enter such a place or that he would even have the need to.

'Ah, Li Jing, I have seen you many times, but not in such strange circumstances he said.'

I just bowed and said nothing; I was feeling a little embarrassed to be seen in that way, even after everything I have been taught during my lessons with Kou. I am ashamed to say that I still thought the work was a little beneath me. Suddenly, the general took up a bale of fresh hay and started to lay it down all over the floor of the stalls before leading several of his horses back into their places. I was ill at ease and did not know where to look."

'Do not concern yourself, Li Jing. I love each and every one of my horses. This will surprise you coming from such a high-ranking soldier, no?'

"Yes, General, I thought your mind would have been on more important matters," I said. 'More important matters, you think? Many have the same false impression, Li Jing. I know I am in a minority as far as looking after my troops and their horses are concerned. You see, like some emperors, I too came from a humble background. Unlike some of my high-ranking fellow soldiers, I feel very much at home in the stables caring for the horses. I have found that if you care for them, they will repay you a hundred times in battle. It is up to each soldier to discipline his horse and expect the animal to obey him at all times. When you have a rapport with your own personal animal, whether a horse or some other kind, it gets to know you and also your needs. Some amazing acts of bravery have been recorded of horses who have helped their masters at any cost, even to the end of their own lives, just like soldiers themselves. It is as if they know what you are thinking before you take any action at all. They will not run away; some humans could learn from them.'

"I looked at the general in amazement. I had never heard of this rapport with animals before. Oh, I have seen many fussing over their pet animals, but I never thought for a moment that such loyalty could be returned." 'You are thinking, Li Jing, that there are those who would see this as a weakness?'

"My face gave me away," said Li Jing quietly. 'When I am with my troops, Li Jing, none can accuse me of weakness. They have seen me fight and have witnessed my bravery. I expect nothing less from them, and as I have just stated, they too respond to me in the same way: they are all loyal to me. I am a disciplinarian, but I am fair. My men know this.'

"We worked together for a while. Suddenly General Huì stopped. 'Others have not always respected you as you would have wished, Li Jing. It is because of your manner, though I sense that you have made much progress in order to rectify this.'

"I replied that I had done my best, having very good teachers, and left it at that." 'Come, Li Jing, you are to spend the rest of the day doing some basic hand-to-hand combat with one of my men. I am very pleased with his progress too; we are hoping for greater things from him in the future.'

"With that, the general took me out to the parade ground, where many men were engaged in hand-to-hand combat training on foot, the most basic form of fighting. I was handed over to a rough-looking soldier who offered the greatest respect to his general but seemed off-hand with me!"

'I will go gently with you,' he said, smirking, and proceeded to take me through a basic form of combat. After I had fallen for about the tenth time, my anger knew no bounds! This common oaf was laughing and making a fool of me. How dare he, I thought. I got up and began to attack him with a simple form of martial arts which I was familiar with. He, of course, was also familiar with the move, but I was fighting on more of an even level with him. He stopped and ordered me to do the same. 'So, my angry, aloof friend, you can fight a little. However, your orders from General Huì were to be taught basic hand-to-hand combat. Do you usually disobey your superiors?'

"I knew my error immediately. I was so angry that a common oaf could humiliate me that I did not realise that changing the rules to suit myself would also lead me to break a direct order from the general. At once I bowed to my opponent and teacher and apologised for my lack of patience. With that, the soldier grinned, patted me on the back, and said, 'We will make a soldier of you yet.' The rest of the day meant undergoing many more falls, but these times were punctuated with several moves which put the soldier on alert. Each time this happened, he gave out a cry of amazement! Returning back to my room bruised and battered, I was thankful that I did not have to meet my opponent on the battlefield and grateful that even through my reluctance, I had made a new friend."

Li Jing sat down. We sat in silence with a degree of admiration for him, and also with some amusement. Shen then spoke. "It is a truism that sometimes the most valuable lessons are the hardest to conquer, Li Jing. There is nothing more to add; the story speaks for itself."

The days and weeks went by. Our support for our colleague did not waver. Outside time as we know it, in spheres which surround the physical world, Great Spirit armies gathered together to support us and an equal number of the dark forces were gathering to do battle with them in those unseen spheres. Events taking place in the Temple of the Heavenly Bird at that time were inexplicably linked to those spheres where consciousness wove in and out of time with a fluidic motion. Chief Priest Duìmiàn's work took him into darker and darker places, drawing in the dark forces closer and closer.

All through the second month, Shaotie's ordeal became more and more apparent. The Watchers were working as closely as they could with him in ways that we could never begin to imagine. Duìmiàn saw this pressure on Shaotie as proof that victory was nearly his. However, there were times when just as he thought Shaotie was broken and about to reveal the secrets of his power, the young priest seemed to recover and find more energy to withstand the onslaught. He did not understand why. Those moments, of course, were proof of Kou's intervention at certain times of the day and the hidden help that he was receiving from the masters and the armies of light working alongside the Watchers.

Halfway through the third month, when we were all feeling the pressure of sending out such powerful healing towards Shaotie, I sensed changes ahead. I was alone one day meditating, and when I opened my eyes I saw Niang standing there before me. Only then did I sense that she had been standing there patiently for some time. "I did not wish to disturb you, Su Ling, but I must take this moment to speak with you while we are alone."

Niang sat down next to me and paused for a while before speaking. I knew that this was a sign of careful reflection before she spoke. "As you know, Su Ling, Shaotie is nearing the time when his unfortunate situation must be brought to an end for the sake of the temple, our beloved governor, and all his subjects. It is actually an issue which goes much farther and wider than we can be told of in the here and now. You see some things that occur here have far-reaching effects that we are not yet equipped to fully comprehend."

This was a similar theme to one the Watchers had already spoken of, but now we were in the very midst of such an important issue. I nodded but sat quietly, because to say anything at that point would have been irrelevant.

"I have a task for you, Su Ling, which may prove quite dangerous." At once I felt a stirring deep inside me. "The masters have given me the responsibility of picking a member of our quarters to carry out this particular task." She looked deep into my eyes as if to read my thoughts. "I know you are thinking, 'why not pick my colleagues, Héshi and Ci?' They of course have been here longer than you, Su Ling, and they are capable of carrying out many important tasks, but some tasks are better suited to others. It is not that one particular adversary is on the same spiritual link as one of our members. It is more the case that one particular individual is more suited to counteracting something than another. Another young priest from Kou will also be given a task, one which we will never fully know of. It is not important that we know; we must concentrate on our own. I have given the matter much thought, and it is not a matter of favouritism or a punishment; it is just using the right person for the task at hand. Now we will allow you three days to prepare; you are excused from your work in the birthing room for the entire three days. The physicians and the elders have been told that you are needed elsewhere." I nodded silently again and centred myself while waiting for my orders.

"The task involves becoming a target yourself for Duìmiàn's dark magic – only temporarily, of course! But this involves putting yourself in the firing line, as it were, and this will not go unnoticed by the priest. Therefore you will momentarily be on the receiving end of Duìmiàn's wrath, but I cannot stress enough that you will be safe as long as you carry out your instructions to the letter. This is essential. All the temple priests will be celebrating soon the life of one of our forefathers, a great priest who has passed down much wisdom to those who came after him. The ceremony itself will be held in the Great Hall, and Duìmiàn, Fùzá, and other followers will emerge from behind the curtain on the podium to take control of the celebrations. No-one else will be invited, not even Governor Choi himself. He knows that this is a regular annual celebration for the priests themselves, and he keeps a respectful distance, hoping that it will bring great fortune to him and his family. Now, as Shaotie's ordeal is nearly over, I have to stress to you that the celebration itself will not be the final battle to rid us of the evil priest, but it will be just prior to it, a matter of days only. So your part here, Su Ling, is vital to the outcome of the final battle, as is the work of your colleagues. Many years ago, you witnessed the ceremony of She when we were honoured with the presence of our illustrious emperor at the time, Emperor Liu."

"I can never forget it," I murmured.

"You would have seen a beautiful crystal which Emperor Liu's chief priest, Mou, used in a positive sense in order to bring about a sense of unity amongst the governors of the provinces. The power was there to help, of course, but those involved at the time did not use it wisely, so the unity the emperor had hoped for did not come to fruition. There are crystals like the one Chief Priest Mou used which are also capable of withstanding a terrifying powerful surge of negative energy and absorbing it until a dark priest such as Duìmiàn comes along and releases it. Crystals can act as amplifiers of energy, as you are aware."

I knew then what was coming and just what would be asked of me. "You guess correctly, my dear. Duìmiàn has such a crystal and has been collecting the dark energy, invoking and directing it so that the crystal has absorbed it. His plan has been to use the ceremony to unleash its power onto all the unsuspecting priests of the temple. They will not be able to withstand its collective power and will absorb it into their souls as they are at their most vulnerable, during their sacred meditations." She paused for breath as the full impact of her own words and their meaning took effect on her.

"Please allow me, Niang, and correct me if I am wrong," I said. "Those temple priests who survive such an onslaught will be totally in Duìmiàn's power and will be ready to bring down our governor and the entire temple within days of the ceremony."

We sat in silence for a while, steadying and calming ourselves, before she spoke again. "Let us not forget, Su Ling that this can go far beyond the temple walls. This cannot be allowed to happen; it must never reach that stage. The Watchers have been secretly preparing a crystal of the purest and most sacred energy. It will not be let out of their sight until the time is right. This is where your own special plant from the temple garden comes into our plan. It has been nurtured well, even when you could not care for it during your time of grief. We have never stopped nurturing it, and now it has produced the most beautiful, delicate flowers. It was always meant to be part of our plan, for this was foreseen by some!

"Over the next two days you are to take three flowers from your plant and crush the seeds together with the petals. You will instinctively know which of your coloured potions will be needed to combine with the flowers and create a dark tincture. This will produce a shade almost black in colour. Only you will be able to distinguish the exact shade needed, for this colour will match Duìmiàn's crystal precisely. Your task will be to accept the sacred crystal which the Watchers will bring to you on the third day. They will show you how to prepare it in order that it can absorb the tincture and become a counterforce to the crystal which contains the dark forces. Your mixture of colours will only *appear* dark, remember. The colour comes from that which was rooted in love from potions made by your own hand, Su Ling, for the purposes of healing. This method of combining the mixture and the crystal will remain a secret. It will be between you and the Watchers. The young male priest from Kou will have his secret, and you will have yours. On the day of the ceremony of celebration, it will be your task to enter into the area where Duìmiàn keeps his dark crystal and exchange it with the crystal of light. This will be the most dangerous part. His crystal will be mounted on a precious stand; you will easily be able to identify it. However – and this is vital – you must not handle it with your bare hands! You will be given a wooden casket with protective markings engraved all around it. The Watchers will give you a secret sign which you will use to link in with them at the moment you first see it. Together, you will focus on a sacred power which will lift our crystal and its mount into the air, depositing it on top of the altar next to the dark crystal. At the same time, his crystal and mount will levitate into the casket in your hands. You will be surprised to learn that this will not be the most dangerous part of your task. By then you will have begun to feel the ill effects of just being in its presence. But it takes an evil mind to spur it into action, and it is at this point that the evil priest will know that something is wrong. You will have little time to escape before he sees you. I am sorry, my dear, but you will feel the force of his anger. He will not have much time himself, as the ceremony will be about to begin. He will shout to one of his underlings to deal with you, but we will be there to take you to safety. Duìmiàn and Fùzá will have no choice but to use the pure crystal in the ceremony, and only you will be harmed."

I gulped at the prospect. "My courage fails me a little, Niang"

"Understandably, Su Ling; you would be a fool if this were not so. It means that you have fully understood what is at stake here and the enormity of it. His anger will know no bounds after this, and that is when he will start to make mistakes.

"You will use this day as your first day of preparation my dear, and you will continue to work for as long as you wish until sleep overtakes you. I will take you now to the room reserved for you; everything you need will be there, including a place to sleep. You will continue to work hard all through tomorrow, and halfway through the day, the Watchers will arrive with the crystal. Follow their instructions with the greatest care."

Niang stood up and beckoned me to follow her. We travelled along short and unfamiliar passageways; it was not the way I had expected to see. I marvelled at the never ending complex of passageways and wondered why I had not noticed them before. There was a small, unobtrusive, plain door at the end of one corridor. Niang opened it, and we entered a larger and airier room than I would have imagined from the outer door. Inside were some strange pieces of equipment I had not seen before, together with all my familiar potions and ingredients. On a table stood several crystals which had been placed around my own precious plant, blossoming with six of its beautiful small flowers. In the corner of the room lay a brightly coloured bedroll and cover; some bowls had been placed against the opposite wall.

"Concentrate, Su Ling. Concentrate, and eliminate any doubts you have! You must work with clear intent and use your instinct well. My thoughts will be with you." With those parting words, she left. I went straight to my plant and put it in the centre of everything else, placing my Tóngshí beside it to keep it company and to show its significance.

Carefully picking three of the delicate flowers from my plant, I began my work, surrounded by a sense of calmness and warmth. I knew that I was far from alone. All through the rest of that day I continued to work, trying out different methods before I was willing to combine the ingredients with those from the plant. Now and then I stopped to take a little water and to centre myself so that my purpose was clear and uncluttered by irrational thoughts. Late into the night I worked, but my eyes began to feel heavy and unfocused. I knew sleep was essential then. I lay down and remembered nothing more.

The next morning, I woke early and refreshed and saw that everything in the room was in its place. I had made a few notes from the previous day, and instantly one or two new ideas came into my mind, as if I had been given them while sleeping. The second day flew by swiftly as I gained more and more insight into my task. There were one or two moments of surprise as I worked, proving again to me how we never stop learning. I noted each step of my investigations and by the evening of the second day I was drawing up my conclusions and intentions. There appeared at that time two clear methods to create the perfect shade to match that of Duìmiàn's crystal. However, I knew that I should not rush my decision. I stopped work late that evening, perplexed that two ways should emerge instead of the one clear one which I had expected. Feeling tested yet again, I decided to meditate before sleeping. All my intentions and affirmations before entering a state of meditation were focused on finding the right solution for the forces of light to win through.

I was aware of much movement during my trance state. Colours, patterns, and symbols came and went. I heard whispers as if from far away and saw strange landscapes and other forgotten things. Yet as I lay my head down to sleep, I was not consciously aware of the answer to my problem. On the third day, I prepared myself before the arrival of the Watchers. Walking over to my table of potions, I contemplated hard on what I should do. I had read my notes many times but decided to go over them again from the beginning, from the first rough jottings right through to my dual conclusions. As I read, I became aware that something was missing. I felt the faintest stirrings of panic but quickly composed myself, not allowing the doubts to take hold.

I instinctively gazed at the plant, forming in my mind a picture of my Wu Fang and Rènshi. The picture took on a luminescent quality as they both seemed to smile down on me to give me extra strength. To my surprise, they both nodded and winked at me as if everything were going to be alright. Then, suddenly, they were gone, and I knew. I knew without a shadow of a doubt that the delicateness of the plant with its petals would only suit one type of potion! I had been concentrating solely on the shade needed; forgetting that so much more was involved when using such a sacred plant. It had so many more qualities than the colour of its petals. The pure whiteness was a sign, a symbol of the significance of the *whole* plant. The essence of the plant had to be compatible with *how* I had prepared my potions and the precise nature of my thoughts as I worked with each preparation. I had believed that my intentions alone applied to everything as I worked, but there had been a difference, a fleeting feeling as I worked with one of the two preparations that I put down to tiredness. At any other time my instinct would have told me immediately of its significance. In the end, my instinct worked in a different way. It told me when to stop and sleep and it told me when to go back to my notes, and when to go back to the plant for help. At no point had I performed this task alone; there were always unseen friends nearby helping me!

I began work on combining the correct potion with the extracts from the plant. The colour they produced was striking, deep in hue and just right for the purpose. Yet I knew that it hid the most powerfully pure intentions.

The Watchers arrived on cue at midday, looking serene and smiling when they saw me. They carried with them the casket and placed it on the table before me. Using their mind-power, they slowly levitated the crystal above the casket. For a moment I was nearly overwhelmed by its beauty and its formidable power, and I could feel those from the world of spirit in the room with us. By bringing my own mind under control of my higher will, I was able to calmly watch the next step. Shen and Jing moved the levitated crystal through the air and across to the bowl filled with the potion, gently lowering it into the bowl where it was to absorb the tincture. Without any of us touching either crystal or liquid, the Watchers instructed me to work with them to instruct the crystal itself to absorb the entire colour which was so completely unfamiliar to it. This difficult and strange practice took some time and cannot be known to others in the material world. I have been sworn to secrecy; a sacred oath was made!

In due course the precious crystal had completely absorbed the colour, displaying its now unfamiliar hue. However, nothing could detract from its true purpose. I was then given the secret sign to link in with the Watchers at the exact moment I set eyes on Duìmiàn's powerful crystal.

A diagram of a secret passage in the temple leading directly into the curtained-off area of the main hall was produced, and the timing of the switch-over was set. "You have many watching over you, Su Ling," Shen said.

"Your pain will only be for a short while," added Jing. We three then bowed in respect to each other. When I looked up, the Watchers had vanished, leaving the room quiet and still once more. I picked up the diagram and the casket, which seemed to pulsate in my arms. At that moment Niang returned, and I followed her out of the room and along the passageway.

When we entered our living quarters, they were completely empty; my colleagues had not yet returned. At the back of the room where Niang sat, two screens had been placed to section off the area. Niang beckoned to me and pulled one of the screens to the side. There behind the two, a bedroll had been placed. There was also a cushion and a low table. She motioned to me to place the casket and the diagram on the table. "Here you will stay until tomorrow, Su Ling. You will meditate and then sleep; you must be completely silent in order to gather your strength for what lies ahead. The masters have put a mental blocking system in the minds of your colleagues. They will acknowledge your absence but will know nothing of tomorrow's plan until it is well underway. They can offer assistance when the time is right. I have been informed that the other young Kou priest Wèn Lù not Shaotie, has his instructions and is fully aware of the part he is to play. Any sound in the room from your colleagues when they return must be shut out by your meditation practice. There will be no communication between you at all. Tonight Héshi, Ci, and I will guard you as you sleep."

I awoke next morning while the others slept; only Niang, Héshi, and Ci were awake. I completed my ablutions and, nodding to my three guardians, sat in silence behind the screens. The crystal seemed to emanate a calming vibration through the walls of the casket that contrasted with the first powerful vibrations I experienced from it the first time. It was as if it could change its emanations at will, as it if were somehow alive! Meditating deeply, I was not even aware when my colleagues left for the day. Even Niang, Héshi, and Ci had left – each to play an important part in the day's happenings, I was sure.

I studied the diagram carefully again until I was very familiar with the route and could actually visualise the way. When the moment came, I sensed immediately that it was time to leave. Gathering up the casket and the diagram and holding my Tóngshì briefly, I set off along the new passageway. The huge responsibility that had been placed on my shoulders, instead of weighing me down, left me with a strange feeling of being outside of myself as I started to fulfil my instructions. I could see the nondescript door at the end of the corridor and began to hear the sounds of the priests gathering in the main hall. As was befitting of them, the sounds were only whispers but were magnified by the huge number of priests in attendance. All had been called, they believed, to honour their dead ancient priest. I stopped and waited for a while until I felt the moment had come for me to enter through the doorway which would take me straight into the curtained-off area of the stage. Then, holding on tightly to the casket, I gripped the long, thin handle and pushed the door open. At once my eyes took in the scene. I noted the intricate colours of the curtain across the stage; the same fabric had been draped over the altar, where many glowing candles surrounded an identical casket to the one I carried. However, there were very different markings around it that I did not wish to dwell on. I stepped forward and placed my casket next to Duìmiàn's. I opened his and relayed the secret sign to the Watchers at the very moment I saw the dark crystal. Despite almost being bowled over by its emanation, I hastily opened its rival, our own sacred crystal. I was aware of the Watchers in another dimension, and I knew that it was they who levitated both crystals into their opposite boxes. I grabbed my casket just as a cry went up from the back of the curtained-off stage! Events then happened very fast: I was hit by a wave of incredible pain, which was sent my way by the force of Duìmiàn and Fùzá's magic. At the same time, a pair of unseen hands pulled me out of the way while others took the casket with the dark crystal from my hands. It was then that I lost consciousness.

The other young Kou priest had carried out his task as instructed by pulling me out of the path of what would have been certain death. The Watchers, with other beings from the world of light, had dematerialised the casket and crystal into a very high and sacred plane in order to transmute its evil energy. That was their first task and it could only be performed by the few whose souls had been elevated to that place.

Meanwhile on the stage, Priest Duìmiàn had known at once what had taken place but not why or how. Soldiers were sent out in search of me, but there was no time for anything else; the sound of temple bells and chanting had begun in the main part of the hall. Duìmiàn knew that he had no option; he instructed Fùzá to continue with the plan. Both were unaware of the sacredness of the crystal they held as the curtains were drawn back. They carried the casket forward to another altar in the main hall. At first the crystal's energy lay dormant, awaiting the furore ahead. Duìmiàn's mind was in a swirling rage of panic; he tried desperately to think of a plan for seizing the only opportunity to capture the minds of all the priests of the temple and force them to go to the dark side at his bidding. He started to perform the ritual which was to honour the ancient priest who had become a legend in the temple. But his fear and his panic led him into making the biggest mistake of his life, one that countless others had made before him: an overestimation of his own power!

With all his might and negative magic, he silently called on the powers of darkness to give him strength. His own crystal would have magnified his evil intent many times over. Trying to contain such power in just a physical body was quite another matter. He began to speak in a low, manipulative voice that oozed calmness, attempting to mislead the priests into thinking that all was well. He began to tell his lies regarding Governor Choi Yen Shu. He tried to persuade the priests that madness had overtaken their beloved governor, who had now become a danger to the temple and its inhabitants. The calmness of the occasion suddenly changed as the priests became confused, not knowing who to trust! At that point the sacred crystal's power filled the hall and the hearts and minds of the priests, informing them just who to trust. Duìmiàn's wrath knew no bounds as he shrieked his instructions out to the ether to combat and destroy the sacred crystal and all that was sacred to the forces of Light. The people in the Temple of the Heavenly Bird had seen nothing like it; a great storm seemed to sweep through the corridors and rooms, and everyone was filled with fear. Between the two great planes of existence, and through many others in between, war raged between the forces of dark and light! The priests used their energy to join with the emanations from the pure crystal to fight Duìmiàn's darkness in the material world. Shaotie was freed from his invisible dark chains and could join his colleagues from Kou to take the fight to the spiritual plane while still playing his part in the hall with his fellow temple priests.

All this I witnessed as if in a dream, for I was unaware where I lay or what world I lay in. I could see in my mind great beings of such bright luminescence I could hardly make out their form. They all seemed to be riding white, shining horses. Some forms here and there seemed to resemble my fellow Kou members, and in the middle of the riders leading from the front rode Shen and Jing, who were bathed in breathtaking colours.

From the lower dark planes, a force of dark shadows rode up to meet them. There were great clashes of thunder, and I feared for the very essence of good souls coming into contact with them.

I was aware of a great fire burning within me; it was the pain combined with a deep fever that I was experiencing in my physical self. Then suddenly there was a deep, deep silence and a calmness which came over me! I was aware of Wu Fang holding one hand and Rènshi holding the other as I lay in my strange state. It was good to feel them close again, and I did not mind when they left me with their blessings this time; I knew I would see them again. Unbeknown to me, I was receiving some of the most powerful healing, even surmounting that from my fellow Kou members when I was beside myself with grief for Rènshi. I did not know if I would ever meet those healers from many planes of existence who took part in the healing of my whole self.

As I opened my eyes, I became aware of what had happened and the part my colleagues, masters, and Watchers played in my recovery. I gave my heartfelt appreciation aloud to them and the unknown healers so all could hear the depth of my gratitude. I did not know at that time that in spite of all the healing I had received, there were still parts of me that had been left damaged. I lay in the little annexe room next to the priests' hall and noticed the small altar bedecked with the white flowers that had come to mean so much to me. Surrounded by my colleagues, I noticed that Shaotie stood as his old peaceful self; he was beaming at me so that I knew that all was well.

"Duìmiàn, Fùzá?" I began.

"Their evil magic destroyed them, as is its nature," said Master Noih. "Governor Choi has been informed of Duìmiàn's plan and told that he was defeated by the sacred duty of the temple priests. That was all he wished to know; he knew something terrible had happened and was very afraid, as all his servants were. He knows nothing of the true cost of the fight or how far-reaching the battle went; we may never know ourselves. No doubt you were aware of some of the battle, Su Ling?"

"Yes, Master and it was my privilege to see my beloved Wu Fang and Rènshi briefly again."

"Yes, my dear. Such was your wish, and it was granted because like others, you put your life and soul in danger for the sake of others." He smiled. This was a rare moment indeed!

"May I ask just one more question, Master?"

"You are concerned, Su Ling, for the sacred crystal which was left in the hall. The moment Duìmiàn and Fùzá were destroyed, the dark shadows left the room. The sacred crystal's dark hue spilled out onto the altar, leaving its former brilliance shining out onto the priests in the hall. Shaotie advised that no-one should touch it and placed his own body in front of it so that none could witness the crystal vanishing from the room back to its proper home, a long way away from here. It appeared as if he had placed it back in the casket to be taken to the masters."

CHAPTER 16

Before and After

THE FOLLOWING WEEK, I WAS advised to carry out my duties at a slower pace. The physicians were informed, and it was decided that I was to be spared the work of delivering babies for seven days. Instead, I concentrated on my potions and on reading scrolls that detailed the vast amount of information on the human body which had been collected over the years by eminent physicians, some of which was questionable. I had to remind myself not to be too clever as I, myself, had much to learn.

The week went by smoothly enough. I was alone most days, and during the evenings I sat quietly with my colleagues, as this was expected of me. Their experiences, I learnt, had been a little different from mine. They had been exhausted from their fight at the spiritual level against the dark forces, but protected to a large degree by those highly evolved souls in front of them acting as a shield to those at the back. Their physical bodies in the temple were unharmed and remained in trance-like states. Their exhaustion was experienced mentally as they sent out an enormous current of power onto the spiritual planes. Our traumatic experience brought us even closer together, for only those who were there could fully understand.

A month or two passed by, and life in the temple took its normal course – or seemed to. At the third meeting of Kou after the war, we debated the finer points of what leads a soul into evil acts. We followed this with a meditation to calm our minds, something we all looked forward to. Often suitable music was used as a meditative tool to bring about a relaxed state. That day was a little different, as Shen and Jing began to hum a gentle piece of music that had not been written on the physical plane; where it had truly originated from was unknown. Their harmonies were perfection itself, and all in the room was still.

As a group we experienced being part of a great crowd who were watching and listening to an orchestra which, as it performed, sent glorious pastel colours into the air with each note. I was enjoying this exquisite performance with Kou when, suddenly, everything went dark! It was as if someone had blown out all the lamps in a large room. I felt completely alone and was not sure where I was. I felt a sudden coldness, which made me shiver, and then just as quickly I was back at the concert with my friends again! After the meditation, I felt sure that everyone would have been aware of what had happened; after all, what one felt, all felt. Yet no-one said a word. It was as if no-one else had been aware of what had taken place. Even the masters and the Watchers seemed oblivious and began informing us of the next Kou meeting. This was most perplexing, and I was confused. Thinking it may have been something that each one of us would experience as part of a lesson, I decided to wait before saying anything to the others.

My intuition and my awareness of the strange happening was quite another question. Sometimes for safety's sake, the blocking off of certain thoughts comes into play until a conscious mind is ready to accept them fully. I had learnt that much with the loss of my beloved Wu Fang and my little Rènshi. I concentrated hard on my chores, and when a nagging doubt came into my mind, I observed my colleagues a little more closely for any signs that they had experienced the same thing.

Nothing appeared unusual to me for several weeks afterwards, and as time went on I began to feel very settled, experiencing no more doubts or concerns. I thought that at some point in the future I would bring the matter up when Kou met, provided that it linked in with a project or lesson we were learning at the time.

At the end of one particularly long day in the birthing room, I didn't feel particularly hungry and had eaten very little. Leaving the hall alone, I walked back towards our living quarters. Master Ma Sing was coming towards me from the other direction and seemed to be studying me in a curious way. I stopped before him and bowed, saying, "Master." He acknowledged me with a nod of the head and was about to speak, but then he seemed to think better of it and carried on walking past me! Whatever our private thoughts regarding the masters, we knew better than to question their decisions or actions. It was simply unheard of. I reached the door to our quarters and was surprised to see Meirén already there. I had thought that everyone else was eating in the hall.

Meirén saw my surprise and said, "I left just before you, Su Ling, but you didn't notice; you seemed lost in thought and were toying with your food as if you had no appetite. Are you not well?"

Feeling strangely irritable at this remark, I just stared at her and replied, "Perfectly well, thank you." She gave me an odd glance sideways and continued with her studies. *What is the matter with everyone today?* I thought, and I sat down in the social area a little way away from her with my own silent thoughts.

After a while, the other girls returned; I could hear some chatter outside the door, which immediately stopped when they entered the room and saw me there. At any other time I would have wondered why, but I was glad of the quietness for some reason. Niang, Héshi, and Ci went to the top of the room as usual and began sewing on fine silk. Meirén nodded a greeting to them and returned to her work. Wéi Wéi sat down but shifted about restlessly for a while, which distracted me. I endeavoured to block her movements from my mind to begin to feel settled again. It only seemed a brief moment before the others began to prepare for the evening ritual of their ablutions and sleep. I looked up and saw that Wéi Wéi was looking at me and holding her head as if it ached. Ci crossed the room to give her some healing and calm her so she could sleep. Afterwards our usual occupation continued until the lamps were lowered and we all lay down for the night.

I can't remember exactly how it started, but sometime after that day, I began to feel impatient with those around me and preferred to withdraw into myself. I spoke with everyone and obeyed orders but began to feel that people were starting to treat me differently. This perception made me put up barriers, and I seemed to be forgetting some of the important lessons I had learned from the masters. It was about this time when I started to experience repetitive dreams of a dark nature. My dreams took me along dark corridors that twisted and turned, this way and that, until I thought I would never come to the end of them! All the time I could feel something drawing me closer to it: something that was waiting for me at the end. Then I would turn a corner, and in the distance I would see my Tóngshì. I would desperately reach out for it, calling to my little bird, but just as I was within reach of it, something pulled it further and further away from me, and a dark shape took its place! Then I would wake from my sleep shaking and calling out its name. This in turn would wake all my colleagues and disturb their sleep patterns; they started to become affected by my actions. I was confused and embarrassed by my apparent weakness, so I offered to sleep in another room. The same dream continued over several more nights.

On the last occasion, Meirén said to me in front of everyone, "I have only seen this happen once before. I feel that this should not be happening to any of us now, not at this stage of our journey. We must seek help from the masters."

Niang nodded knowingly, and Wéi Wéi, whom I seemed to have unsettled the most, murmured, "Must be stopped now, must be stopped now before it's too late."

My tiredness at work became apparent, and I was becoming more of a hindrance than a help in the birthing room. An emergency meeting of Kou was called. As we assembled in the passageway before the Doorway of Illusion, I suddenly felt a panic welling up inside me. I did not wish to go through the door! I struggled against it, but four of Kou's young priests held me firmly and took me through to the familiar room outside of time as we know it. Once we were inside, the Watchers ordered a meditation at once to calm the distorted energies in the room. I was aware that somehow I was causing this situation, but I did not understand how or why.

I was seated directly in front of the masters, with Shen and Jing on either side of them at opposite sides of the room. I couldn't remember seeing them stand so far apart before; it was most strange. I was surrounded very closely by my friends as I tried to calm and centre myself without much success. I had no wish to take part in the proceedings for some reason and was slow to understand what was happening in the room. The rest of Kou, I think, were humming a musical note which seemed vaguely familiar. Then I remembered nothing.

I opened my eyes to find that the masters were holding onto me firmly. "She is back with us." Shen's voice broke the silence as I looked around at my colleagues. Then Jing's voice echoed around the room, giving instructions to everyone.

Master Noih spoke firmly to me. "Su Ling, concentrate on my voice and listen! We have identified the problem, and it is very serious. We know that you have endured much suffering; most of us have, but sometimes when extraordinary things occur, we cannot be sure of every outcome. I speak of the evil Priest Duìmiàn and the incredible dark energy we fought off together. Sometimes there can be an imprint left behind deep in our very soul; in this instance, there is one in yours from Duimian's dark shadow."

"What is an imprint?" I whispered, not fully understanding his words – or not wishing to!

"Yes. There is not much there, but it is of such a nature that it could easily spread and destroy you. We thought our healing practices were thorough enough to spare you. We were wrong, which just goes to show you what we are up against. It can show itself in subtle ways at first until the mind of a person becomes affected and infected. Just as before, it must be rooted out." I tried to take in Master Noih's words but was beginning to feel weak and said so.

"There is no time to lose." Again I could hear Shen's voice, but it seemed to be further away.

Master Ma Sing gripped me firmly so that I would look into his eyes. "When you see the Watchers, run towards them!" he commanded. Then again there was a cold silence, with just darkness around me. I felt no energy within me to run anywhere. I could not see the Watchers; I could not see anything.

At first I thought I could hear a rustle of something to the left of me. Perhaps I had imagined it? Then slowly it came: an icy breath all over me, penetrating my body, right through to my bones. In the distance I could hear the muffled sounds of my Kou colleagues; they seemed far, far away. But something told me to listen hard to their muffled cries. I knew that wherever they were, they would be trying to help me. Yet the icy breath gripped me hard, and I was having trouble breathing! Whatever was there in the darkness was growing and seemed to be gaining strength from me somehow. I had the utmost difficulty not to panic. I tried desperately to remember lessons in closing myself off to protect myself, but the darkness seemed to have penetrated my mind already.

Out of the corner of my eye I suddenly saw the Watchers; they seemed out of focus, and I didn't know how I could run to them. Then came the movement: the desperate movement of my little Tóngshì, it was as if it were alive, fluttering and calling to me, "Run, run!"

I could not move my legs, but I found the strength to create an illusion of movement in my mind. I *willed* myself towards the Watchers, and as I did so I felt myself moving physically through the darkness towards them. The thing in the dark tried to gather more strength and pull me back, but once I was on the mental link with Shen and Jing, I began gaining ground! Just at the point of reaching them, there was an enormous explosion all around me. What was happening? I was afraid to look, but a moment later I had awoken and was safe in the confines of the room with all my colleagues. The masters were there watching me closely. They smiled suddenly, and I knew that the imprint had gone, but where were the Watchers?

Reading my mind, Master Noih answered my question. "They have gone to another dimension to recover. They put themselves in great danger to go into that place and save you. This they did; you are now completely free from Duìmiàn's influence. Your colleagues all helped and are now a little tired themselves."

"I know, Master. I was never in any doubt that they, all of you, were with me."

I reached for my prized possession, my Tóngshì, and sat quietly. All in the room were quiet. Each of us regarded our lives and the situations that had brought us together to experience such momentous and terrible things.

Master Ma Sing then spoke. "Today has shown us a very valuable lesson: even as we perform heroic acts on behalf of others, the dark energy can find a way in, just as it always has. It is we who should be alert to its influence. Simple negative human emotions – anger, jealousy, greed, and pride – are where it can begin; I could go on and on. We cannot eradicate emotions, and we have had many lessons on recognising the early warning signs as we feel negativity creep in. Today has proven if proof were needed, that it is often when we are giving of the best of ourselves that the danger can strike. Governor Choi Yen Shu was performing an act of kindness by appointing a relative of his wife-to-be as his chief priest. He and she would have had no idea of what actions he was setting in motion. From the first whisperings of Duìmiàn's appointment, your masters became aware of his treachery. The Watchers had foreseen this long ago, but the time was not right to disclose the problem. It was written that such a war would take place. Dark energy destroys; that is its function. So, ultimately, it destroys itself, until enough of its evil influence gathers over time to become an even greater threat. Throughout the world there will always be groups such as ours ready to hear the call to fight for the power of the light, a power so gigantic that we cannot envisage its mystery and complexity." After a long pause, the closing ceremony began.

During the days and weeks after my cleansing I felt distinctly different from before. I find it hard to adequately describe my feelings at the time and immediately after. There was certainly, I felt, an inner strength akin to my breathtaking hardness when I had lost my beloved Wu Fang and my Rènshi. This time, however, there was no bitterness; it was my own soul that I was in danger of losing, not my dear ones. Back then I did not care to live; I welcomed death. Now I understood the preciousness of life and the tasks I had been set – or perhaps set myself – to do.

CHAPTER 17

Farewell to a Great Warrior

MANY NEW BABES WERE DELIVERED that year to swell the numbers of souls already living and working in the temple and surrounding complex. As is nature's way, many of the elderly also left us and returned back to their spiritual home. In the pattern of life within the temple, many of our own brave soldiers continued to give their lives to protect their governor while in combat with their enemies on the border areas of our land. Just as Master Ma Sing had informed us, Governor Choi's own loyal general-in-chief, Fú Wù, fell in battle, providing a glorious victory for his warriors. There was much sadness throughout the Temple of the Heavenly Bird, not only among the soldiers of his army but among many others who had come to know him. Governor Choi appointed another general to the post as a temporary measure and then sank into a depressive state at the loss of such a loyal friend and servant.

A period of mourning was decreed to take place for one month, after which he would finally decide on a new general-in-chief.

After the official temple ceremony honouring the life of General Fú Wù and guiding him towards the spirit world, we in Kou held our own private ceremony for him. In our trance-like state, we saw him briefly smile contentedly at us. Through the Watchers, he spoke briefly of more turmoil coming again to the temple. As many had stated before him, he spoke of the inevitability of some patterns reoccurring, but he assured us that all would be played out to its conclusion and that the work of Kou was needed as much as ever. Each of us paid a silent homage to him, and then he left us.

Shen stepped forward, "We watch with interest the movements surrounding Governor Choi at this time. He has long had a successor to Fú Wù in mind for the post. Fú Wù himself had also favoured General Zuìjìn; they have both seen great potential in him. However, out of deference to his former general-in-chief, our governor will wait until the end of the period of mourning before finally making up his mind about appointing Zuìjìn. In the meantime, General Zì Qi will be put into the post temporarily. We see him as a different character altogether!

"When generals take their positions; albeit temporary ones, some are favoured with the gift of wisdom to temper the considerable power afforded them; others let power go to their heads. The latter is the direction we see Zì Qi heading. Having observed him closely in the past, we see him reverting to type. Seeing the distinguished General Zuìjìn as an adversary, Zì Qi wishes to seize the one opportunity in his life to destroy him and keep the 'crown' for himself. Zì Qi wants the role of general-in-chief permanently, and he wants it badly."

Jing took up the theme. "We as a group have already achieved many of our aims, and we can help here. It will not, I have to say, be as dangerous as our last venture. However, one man alone, given power, can strike at the very heart of our temple culture, alienating friends, if we allow it. We cannot approach our governor with this, just as was the case last time, so we keep our wits about us. As you can imagine, any first stirrings of unrest will come from the ranks of the soldiers, so different will the style of leadership be. Unrest breeds confusion and justification for carrying out their orders will be found in their thoughts in the form of, 'We are good soldiers carrying out the wishes of our general-in-chief.' For now, we are going to formulate a protective barrier around General Zuìjìn; we cannot use the same energy as before, so the protection will not be total. We rely on Zuìjìn's good sense and intuition to see Zì Qi's actions for what they are. For now the protection barrier is all we can put in place while we observe every little thing we see. Sometimes small things can be seen, like patterns or clues advising us which way the wind is blowing."

Our work that day could be said to be divided into that with which we were familiar and practices which were completely new to us. Our focus was towards the centre of the room, and we sat within a circle which was two rows deep. Following our instructions from the masters, we generated an image of a beautiful fountain of sparkling water which was pure as it fell downwards. There in the centre of the room, it rose and fell like the fountains in the courtyard of the Temple of the Heavenly Bird, but its beauty surpassed them all. So we began our work in earnest, working and weaving our intentions toward the protection of Zuìjìn. Our weariness that evening showed the amount of exertion needed to reach our objective.

Niang approached me before I lay down to sleep that night. "Su Ling, you have done well today, but we feel that because of your other recent exertions, it will be all we ask of you. Wèi Wèi will be asked to maintain a status quo here, keeping things moving in the right direction, and will take over a leading role along with some of our young priests."

"Yes, of course, Niang. I understand: each plays the part that they are most suited to. Then all the parts of the plan come together to make it work." Before closing my eyes, I studied Wèi Wèi's serious expression; then sleep overcame me.

During the week that followed, each of my colleagues kept the protective barrier around Zuìjìn very much in mind. As I was not to be included in this, I sharpened my powers of observation; everything around me I observed more closely than before. I decided to note down things which were of interest to me after I had prepared my potions and salves in the birthing room. It was also at about this time that I noticed that several of the physicians were continuing with a favoured pattern of treatment regardless of the differing needs of each patient. To them, if a course of treatment had worked on a patient from the governor's household and they had been congratulated, then it was good enough for all! I did not wish to be seen in a bad light again, but I wanted to help where I could by making slight alterations to my herbal potions to counteract some of the physicians' methods when I could see that harm was being caused: I had to think very carefully how to do this. There were some opportunities, as I was being given more responsibilities at that time. I had learned the hard way that there was much that the old physicians could teach me, but as the master had said, trying to change their attitude regarding some of the old, harmful ways would take time.

During the time our beloved Governor Choi spent quietly in mourning for an old friend, Zì Qi set about making his mark in his new role, endeavouring to change the way things had been done in the past by his predecessor. His approach to the soldiers under his command was to remain calm and give firm leadership in a way his governor would wish. He also offered flattering remarks to his troops so that they would be well disposed toward him. This was something General Fú Wù had never needed to do, as the relationship between him and his troops had been forged over time and was clearly understood. Zì Qi's persona would, in time, be in marked contrast once he had attained his goal, but for the time being he had to be careful. 'Softly softly catchee monkey' was his plan.

Those generals who had been close to and worked well with Fú Wù needed careful handling. They would not suspect anything necessarily, or so Zì thought; but if he were to ruin Zuìjìn's chance of taking over the cherished role, subtle doubts had to be placed in their minds. To this end he called another meeting of his top aides to discuss strategies in dealing with the enemies causing trouble along the borders.

One by one, the distinguished soldiers entered the room and took their places according to rank and service. Zì Qi observed each one closely. He knew many of these old fighters, and they knew him to a degree. Zì had long held ambitions to such lofty heights as becoming general-in-chief and had tried to curtail some of his negative traits in order to fool others. Some of his colleagues were more observant than others, and just as they would gauge an adversary's actions, they kept an open mind where Zì Qi was concerned. All, though, acknowledged him as a fine soldier general who obtained results on the field of battle.

"We meet today to discuss the recent border skirmishes and how our strategies in dealing with them have been working," he began. "I have noticed when fighting in those areas myself, that some of our past excellent tactics have not, how shall I say, always worked to our advantage in the way our beloved administrator would wish." Zì gave the impression that those very words had come from Governor Choi himself during discussions with Zì. He watched the puzzled looks on the faces of his men, who would not dare say anything at this point for fear of offending Choi Yen Shu, their leader. Zi went on to make some small but significant changes to Fú Wù's strategies. Then he swiftly changed the subject to past triumphs that they had all been part of. This subtle change of mood, if not completely endearing him to his men, was enough to unsettle some, who left thinking that perhaps there was a need for changes to the old ways if Governor Choi himself had taken an interest. The trust they had in General Fú Wù and the teamwork which had been built up over many years of fighting seemed to have been eroded a little. All there was left for men such as these to do was to obey orders. The rank-and-file soldiers had a habit of picking up a sense of unease from their leaders. So, too, the chief priest of the temple saw much and waited. Kou, in their role in the inner sanctuary of the place outside time, began making preparations while I observed changes in the atmosphere of the temple among its soldier guardians.

One morning I went into the Temple gardens to fetch a plant which was to be used in a balm to treat skin complaints being suffered by some of the governor's children. It was a chilly day, and I wrapped my cloak around me as I made my way to the area which was near to the door which led out into the second courtyard. To my surprise, it was open. A servant stood just outside, speaking to one of the soldiers. I kept my glance downward as I set about choosing the best of the plants. I could hear the soldier calling to the servant to collect something from the stables as he walked away. Then there was silence. I noticed out of the corner of my eye that the garden door had still been left open. Not sure what to do, I began to pull it to, so that it had the appearance of being closed. This, I thought, would save the servant a reprimand for being careless. As I did, other voices in the courtyard became noticeable, and I became aware of a conversation between two of our distinguished generals. "Zuìjìn, my friend, I hope things go well with you?"

"Yes, Zì Qi, and you?"

"Yes, I am taking my role very seriously, as you know. I am building up quite a rapport with my men; our teamwork is excellent, is it not? Tell me, have you spoken with Governor Choi recently?"

Zuìjìn thought this an odd question, especially as it had nothing to do with Zì. "Why do you ask?"

"Oh, no particular reason," Zì replied in a puzzled manner. "It's a little strange, is it not, that our governor did not promote you to general-in-chief immediately after General Fú Wù's funeral?"

There was silence for a while and I could just imagine Zuìjìn looking hard at the man who, after all, was his adversary. "You already know the answer to that, Zì Qi. It is out of respect for the former general-in-chief that another is not rushed into the permanent position. A period of mourning must be allowed!"

"Of course, of course, that is so. Calm yourself, my friend."

"I am perfectly calm," Zuìjìn replied with an edge to his voice.

With a false smile on his face, Zì continued, "I acknowledge that this is the usual way of things. I have often found it strange that in a battle situation when a general falls, the next in line automatically takes on the role, leading his men against the enemy."

Perhaps the enemy is nearer to hand, mused Zuìjìn. He knew that such a conversation would never take place in front of others: Zì was too clever for that. Instead of stating the obvious fact that even the new role of general played out on the battlefield would be seen as a temporary one until formally agreed, Zuìjìn growled, "So you doubt Governor Choi's wisdom in keeping to the proper protocol?"

"Oh no," Zì Qi said, laughing. "I would never doubt our beloved governor. I was just thinking aloud and wondering why a humble general like me was picked for such a prestigious role." I heard then only footsteps heading away from the garden wall and realised that Zì had already planted the first poisonous thought in Zuìjìn's mind. I had no doubt that he recognised Zì as his adversary. However, a thought which had once been shrugged off could return to cause a nagging doubt in his mind later.

The servant returned, looking quizzically at the door. Glancing at me, he spat out the words, "Be quick and leave!" I did not look at this silly creature but collected what I needed and made my way back to the birthing room.

Kou was to meet two days later, and I intended to bring the conversation I had overheard to the attention of everyone. That night as I lay waiting for sleep to overtake me, my thoughts were of people who can manipulate others for negative purposes. Even the strongest man can be vulnerable to this if the manipulator can discover his weakness. As I became drowsy, I also silently acknowledged how, in seemingly small and insignificant ways, we can all become manipulators.

Two days later, all the members of Kou were making their usual journey towards the Doorway of Illusion. I could feel a slight change in the vibration surrounding us: all seemed to sense confusion within the temple already. As we assembled in our room, we were to discover that within the short time that had passed since my observations in the garden, Zì Qi had made much progress towards his ultimate aim.

After our opening ceremony, the Watchers took up the day's subject for discussion. They were joined and spoke as one entity that day, as was often the custom. This did not always take place at the most dangerous times, which was puzzling to me because I thought the practice increased their power. "Su Ling has something to report to us. Speak, Su Ling."

I told everyone what had happened in the garden and the conversation I had overheard. I did not need to mention my conclusions, as these were already known. The Watchers continued, "General Zì Qi has been hard at work undermining the decades of loyalty and trust which have been built up under the leadership of General-in-Chief Fú Wù. Zì Qi's way with words, intimating a closer connection to Governor Choi whilst not actually uttering a lie, have left their mark. Generals and soldiers alike are aware of Governor Choi's grief over Fú Wù's passing, and no other military personnel have been sent for. All are wary of Zì Qi; not believing him to be trustworthy, but they dare not go against him in case he has managed to worm his way into our governor's affections while he is in a vulnerable frame of mind.

"The few subtle changes to military protocol instigated by Zì have actually been successful. In some ways, the general's strategies are very clever. However, he is too clever in the art of negative manipulation, and we cannot allow the sanctity of the temple and the whole complex to be ruined and weakened by his mania for power."

The Watchers motioned Master Ma Sing forward. The old man moved in his usual graceful manner, which belied the considerable strength and power at his disposal. "Zì has cultivated false friendships among some of Governor Choi's closest servants of very high standing. Some of the old clerics who have grown up alongside our beloved governor since his childhood have guarded their positions closely, and would do anything to please their old friend and leader. They are not all the most intelligent of men, and so they have been easy prey for our ambitious general. Another drop of poison has been firmly placed in the minds of several of these trusty, if somewhat dim, souls. They now find themselves facing a dilemma! Faking concern for his governor's welfare, Zì has let it be known that he fears for Choi Yen Shu's emotional and mental state since the terrible shock of the evil Priest Duìmiàn's takeover of the commandery and temple. The death of his most loyal general-in-chief, so soon after, caused him so much anxiety that he has barely been able to contain it. Such a consummate actor! Zì has professed over and over again how he would lay down his life for his eminent governor. However, he has made it known that an incident from General Zuìjìn's past has given him some concern that although he is the favourite, Zuìjìn is not the most suitable man for the post of general-in-chief. Indeed, he has implied that once in his post, General Zuìjìn could even work against the governor. The servants may be a little dim, but even they can see that Zì is grasping for the permanent post. What has put the favoured servants into a difficult situation is the decision to either inform the governor or to keep the nature of the incident regarding General Zuìjìn's past a secret."

So it began: the first real step to betrayal, through a web of deceit and lies. Zì spent a considerable amount of time weaving his web of lies with subtle, apparently humble words of fake concern for his governor. This led to two separate groups of servants within the higher echelons of power. The weaker, more naïve servants, anxious to protect themselves, felt that they should side with General Zì. The second group full of wiser souls, although perplexed and feeling uncertain of a way forward, were firmly in favour of Zuìjìn. They felt that General Zuìjìn had been picked as the favourite contender for the position of general-in-chief for good reason: he was firmly respected by many soldiers and servants alike. Zì was aware of this and formed a plan in his mind to turn this group away from his adversary. They would not necessarily trust him, but they may well trust a close friend of Zuìjìn's who could be manipulated to go against his old friend, however reluctantly. Zì began to put his plan into action.

Péngyou Tài had been a close friend of Zuìjìn's for many years. They had met as children and later served as new recruits in Governor Choi's army; they were two young men eager to serve and proved to be fierce in battle and loyal to their leader. To those observing them, it became apparent within the first year of their training that one of them had the potential for greater opportunities in the future if he remained alive long enough. He was, to their eyes, a much focused individual whose determination and careful way of weighing situations up before taking risks against the enemy illustrated his wisdom.

There were whispers about his potential among higher-ranking officers. Zuìjìn eventually came to the attention of Governor Choi Yen Shu, who had expected much of him because of the family he came from. Péngyou Tài had many qualities, and loyalty was always seen as one of them in Zuìjìn's eyes. They became close friends even when Zuìjìn was promoted and Péngyou remained a lowly foot soldier. Zuìjìn always sought his friend's company and vowed that if he was ever promoted again to a higher rank, he would try to keep Péngyou close to him. Péngyou fought like a tiger in battle, but he needed firm guidance to keep him alive to fight another day.

As was common with young warriors, they were inevitably attracted to young women. Drinking and molesting young servant girls at night was forbidden, though, and soldiers were generally kept busy, leaving little time for relaxation. However, Péngyou and a few others sought ways around this order, finding ways to create mischief among young women of low standing. His weakness and addiction for women was well known among the troops on the borders, some of whom found the fact highly amusing and wondered how he had not got caught while away from the commandery. Others saw his addiction to females as foolish and weak, recognising a worrying and dangerous trend if his mind was not entirely on the teamwork needed among the troops in battle! But loyalty always won the day, and none would betray their colleague – least of all Zuìjìn, who was only aware of some of Péngyou's activities. Nevertheless, he had warned his friend several times to be careful and leave the risk-taking to the battlefield.

The one thing that could have held back Zuìjìn's army career was his association with his foolish friend. A captain who had high hopes for Zuìjìn saw the problem and sought to put some distance between the friends. So Péngyou found himself transferred to one of the border control army units, where his recklessness emerged from time to time. Although they had gone their separate ways, the two childhood friends kept in touch through messages sent via merchants who brought their wares to sell in the courtyard.

Two years after their enforced separation, a merchant found Zuìjìn amidst the hustle and bustle of the commandery. After the customary bow, the merchant held out a piece of cloth with a roughly painted message on it. "I am told that this is most urgent,

Zuìjìn; I will be back in two hours if you wish me to deliver a reply."

Bowing again, he hurried off to the first courtyard to sell his wares. Zuìjìn tucked the cloth into his tunic and walked towards his private quarters to study it. The frown on his face deepened as he read the message and realised the extent of the difficult situation that Péngyou was placing him in. His friend had really crossed a line as far as he was concerned, and he felt torn between the help that Péngyou was seeking and doing what he knew to be right. His friend was expecting a reply that day; he had two hours to decide!

Péngyou Tái's weakness for village girls had led him into trouble with one girl's older brothers, who had caught him with her. There followed a fight in which two of Péngyou's friends joined. In the melee, the young woman was knocked to the ground; she hit her head against a stone and was killed outright. Her brothers immediately blamed Péngyou for her death, though in truth no-one was sure how it occurred. Their rage knew no bounds, more because they saw his actions as disrespectful to their family rather than because they were concerned with the poor girl's life. As the fight intensified, two of the brothers were slain. The third escaped to raise the alarm among the village elders. The villagers were not the enemy of the soldiers, and their outrage at what had happened was reported to the captain of Péngyou's unit.

Such situations occurred from time to time and were hushed up in one way or another. But the villagers' help and support were a key factor in helping the unit to secure the borders from enemy invaders. Some of the young men from the village effectively acted as agents for the army, keeping their eyes and ears open for any movement that would put the troops at risk. Their help was invaluable to Governor Choi's men, and they had no wish to do anything that might change that. The captain could not ignore the issue, and Péngyou was arrested and held before his fate was decided. Execution was the likely outcome. He was most fortunate: a border skirmish with the enemy delayed his fate.

The message brought to Zuìjìn was an urgent call for help. Time was of the essence; there seemed no sure way that anything could be done for the hapless Péngyou in time. Zuìjìn had his own position to consider as leader to a small but significant group of men. He had built up a good reputation among his troops as well as others; what could he possibly do?

Zuìjìn brooded on the problem for a while. He was angry with his friend, who hadn't learnt any lessons since they last met. Yet he knew that Péngyou's heart was in the right place even if his affections were often misplaced. Loyalty was put to the test. A vague memory stirred in Zuìjìn's mind. A small incident involving Péngyou five years or so previously came to mind. An elderly widow almost fell alighting from a carriage which had pulled up to the temple garden gate. Péngyou was on duty steadying the horses and leapt forward to save her as she began to fall. The old woman was the widow of one of Governor Choi's former chief advisers, a man highly thought of by the governor's family when he was alive. His widow, therefore, had not been neglected or turned out to fend for herself; it was understood that she was under the governor's protection. This was a small action by Péngyou, seen as an insignificant occurrence of a soldier's doing his duty.

Zuìjìn remembered the incident because he had praised his friend at the time to encourage him in his duties. The old woman had died since Péngyou's departure, but before her death she had mentioned the incident to the elders at court, asking them to tell the commander-in-chief at the time how pleased she had been at the soldier's courtesy. *Such a small incident would have soon been forgotten,* Zuìjìn thought, but perhaps the vaguest memory of it could be embellished to help Péngyou now.

Before the merchant's return, Zuìjìn had sought permission through his commander to send an army messenger asking for Péngyou's release to the main base to be interrogated over another matter before his punishment was served. Of course, Zuìjìn's commander knew this to be untrue, but Zuìjìn gave the story of Péngyou's gallantry in such a way to imply that he had actually saved the life of the widow of the governor's close friend! The interrogation tale would be far more believable to the unit captain. The commander was a little unsure, as he was aware of the close bond between Zuìjìn and Péngyou, but would not take the risk of causing even the merest ripple of unrest in the commandery or the temple. Gossips could turn an innocent act into far more!

That didn't solve the problem of having to appease the villagers who had been acting as agents for the army along the borders. People could be beaten into submission, but they would not make very effective agents under such conditions, and misinformation could bring the troops into more danger. It was decided by the unit captain to send for the family of the dead girl; he would need all his skills of diplomacy, if indeed he had any! Péngyou was to be dragged before the family on his knees and tell the truth as he saw it, however much the brother may protest. The family would be informed of the request for his interrogation from the main commandery, which would mean delaying his execution. The family members were expected to dismiss Péngyou's apology, but a hopeful outcome lay in the offerings to be given to the family in compensation for their suffering. The girl's life would not have been the primary concern; the family's honour was always the main issue. Zuìjìn's commander, being familiar with the local ways, was prepared to offer half of the family's compensation in the form of extra food for a one-year period and the other half in coins to be used as they wished. This was, of course, more than the poor people had ever seen in their lives, and there was no need for any compensation to be given. However, in view of the warring factions along the border areas, the agents' help had proved invaluable in the past.

The commander was angry. "All this trouble for a worthless soldier like Péngyou, Zuìjìn! I do not have the inclination to check with my superiors that all is in order in respect to our governor's old friends. But this association does not bid well for your reputation. I will decide what to do with Péngyou if he returns alive!"

So a message went out via an army courier, which would reach the border area far more quickly than a merchant on his travels. Fortunately for Péngyou, the courier arrived just in time. He reached the outpost the next evening; the hapless Péngyou was to be executed the following morning in front of the villagers as an example. The captain of the unit was angry at the show he would have to perform in front of the girl's family. Placating them went against the army way of doing things and was seen by him as a sign of weakness. He could not object, however, as the old widow Zuìjìn spoke of was close to the governor's family.

He reluctantly went through the process of dragging Péngyou in front of the family and explaining why there would be no swift execution was given. The eyes of the girl's father and brothers flashed with anger; only their greed when compensation was offered and accepted brought a grudging acceptance from them. Two men were chosen to escort the prisoner, securely tied up so that there could be no escape, and the trio set off for the governor's commandery.

Péngyou was indeed a very fortunate man. After a spell in solitary confinement, the commander decided that he was too much trouble to be part of his army and was thrown out. He was given the task of fetching and carrying for the temple gardeners, and the story of the old widow had to be taken on trust. Péngyou lost the honour bestowed on soldiers to the governor and was paid a pittance, barely enough to survive, but at least he was where Zuìjìn could keep an eye on him. The general didn't know, however, how his act of kindness and loyalty could backfire on him in years to come.

Zì's spies had been searching for information that would discredit the governor's favourite for the position of commander-in-chief. As Zuìjìn had been promoted through the ranks to a general, he had rescued Péngyou years later from his labours and requested that he become his aide even though he was no longer in the army.

Zì saw his chance. His opponent had a weakness: loyalty to an old friend, a friend who had a weakness for women to the point of foolishness. Servants of the governor who had turned their loyalty to Zì, believing his embellished story about Zuìjìn's lying to his superiors to protect a friend; were prepared to trick and betray that friend. They believed that Zuìjìn's decision years before made him as guilty as Péngyou by his association with him and therefore unfit to be commander-in-chief. Zì gave his orders, and the trap was set.

One of the servants approached Péngyou when he was alone in the office of his general. "We have a message, Péngyou, which needs your urgent attention. General Zuìjìn may be in some danger. A trusted servant who is close to Governor Choi is waiting in an inner courtyard of the temple with some information for you; hurry!"

Péngyou hesitated for a moment but, wishing to help his friend and master, followed the servant down narrow, unfamiliar passageways until they reached a small courtyard. At first he couldn't see clearly that to one side of the courtyard and behind some large pillars, sat one of Governor Choi's granddaughters with her guardian. As he stepped further forward, there were gasps all round as Péngyou and the two females set eyes on each other. "What is this?" were the only words Péngyou had time to utter before Zì's troops surrounded them.

One called out, "He is molesting our beloved governor's granddaughter." The old guardian, who was looking confused, was quickly ushered away and warned to keep her mouth shut. General Zì entered the courtyard, sneering at his opponent's friend. "Well, Péngyou, you do have a habit of getting yourself into trouble."

"You liar, you are a fiend!" Péngyou shouted as several soldiers held him roughly so that he could not attack General Zì.

"Oh, I know all about your past, my friend – or should I say General Zuìjìn's friend? Why should a soldier with a promising career risk all for the sake of worthless scum like you? Oh, your little weakness, shall we say, is well known through the complex; many cannot understand why you were never executed over the dishonour you brought to your unit all those years ago."

"I did not murder her; it was-" Péngyou never got a chance to continue.

"What do you think our governor would do if he knew of your general's lies to protect you? Do you think he would still be a favourite for the post of commander? And you! You will forfeit your life when he hears that you attempted to molest his beloved granddaughter. "

Péngyou's rage was only kept in check by swift body blows meted out by his captors; he was brought to his knees. "Of course I, being a generous man, the only one fit for the permanent post of general-in-chief can save you." A smile swept across Zì's face. "That is, if you are willing to do the right thing: to let it be known that your loyalties have switched to me. Even those undecided in the matter will know that Zuìjìn is not to be trusted if his closest friend turns against him."

With soft words, Zì continued. "I will let you live, and don't forget you could make a new start under my leadership. I would throw in a wife for you – of your own choosing, of course."

Péngyou was silent for a while. At the mention of a wife, his thoughts turned to a beautiful servant girl he had coveted for a while. His eyes filled with tears as he thought of Zuìjìn; he did not wish to betray his friend, but he did not wish to die at the hands of Zì's torturers either. The more Péngyou's thoughts turned to the woman, the more his judgement became clouded by longing for her. He could see why Zi was willing to destroy his friend's reputation. He realised that it would be too risky if just the possibility had crossed the governor's mind of Zì's involvement in his own foolish mistakes. All he could do was nod to Zi in his act of betrayal. Péngyou's heart was heavy and his conscience troubled him, but he was not prepared to die yet. When his thoughts turned to the young woman he weakened, trying to convince himself that at least his old friend Zuìjìn would have a place in the army, even if he *was* demoted.

There is a saying 'the walls have ears', and never could a saying apply more truly to the Temple of the Heavenly Bird. For Kou, as always, became aware of all that had occurred in the sorry saga between General Zuìjìn and General Zì Qi. They also knew the importance of a ring Governor Choi had given to Zuìjìn's father out of his respect for him and decided to act in a small way to help Zuìjìn in his distress. As is often the case, vulnerable people innocent of wrongdoing, can bring about a great change to a situation if they can find within themselves the courage to do so. This was later to prove true.

A few days after Péngyou's confrontation with Zì and his men, he was sent for by the crafty manipulator. The time had come for him to fulfil his promise. "Péngyou, there you are. Come walk with me in the courtyard; the weather is kind to us today!" The hapless Péngyou walked by Zì Qi's side with an entourage of soldiers following on behind. He felt sick to the stomach at what he was about to do. As expected, his old friend Zuìjìn was standing in the courtyard in deep conversation with an old friend of the governor. Zì approached them with a sly smile. Zuìjìn turned to see Péngyou standing side by side with Zì, and his surprise turned to an uneasy sense of doom as he watched his adversary pat the shoulder of his old friend. Looking into Péngyou's eyes, he could see that something was very wrong.

"Zuìjìn," Péngyou stammered, "I would not like there to be trouble between us."

Before he could go on, Zuìjìn interrupted him. "Why should there be trouble between old childhood friends? Your father knew my father; we have known each other for a very long time." He fixed Péngyou with his eyes, daring him not to betray him, for he could see that Zì had been up to something.

"Zuìjìn, we will always be friends. It's just that now I believe General Zì Qi would be more suited to the role of commander." Péngyou tried a light-hearted comment. "After all, General Zì has performed his duties in the post of temporary commander with honour. Governor Choi is most impressed with his contribution to our cause."

"He has told you so, has he, Péngyou?" Zuìjìn was not about to let his friend off the hook so easily. Zì Qi stopped his reluctant supporter from saying any more. "We will leave things as they are, Zuìjìn. Péngyou has said his piece. I am sure that you would not abandon your old friend. I wish you well." With that, his head held high in triumph, he nodded to his enemy and to the old servant, as was the custom. But there was no respect, only treachery in Zì's heart. The governor's servant was completely confused and just as surprised as Zuìjìn. He bowed and made his excuses to Zuìjìn, not knowing whether his governor should be informed. He decided to keep his own council for a while

Later that evening, Zuìjìn waited for Péngyou's return to his quarters. When he arrived, he did not waste any time. Entering Péngyou's room, he found his old friend gathering up his belongings and preparing to leave. "I believe you have something to tell me, Péngyou!"

Péngyou turned around, startled by his friend's sudden appearance. "I – I dare not, my friend. I am being blackmailed; I cannot say more."

"So your weakness has turned into treachery." Zuìjìn spoke bitterly. "I would never have believed it of you; even in the face of death I would not have believed it of you. Perhaps there was something else to turn you into a traitor – women or a woman. Am I right?"

Péngyou's face gave him away, and for the first time he felt the full depth of his weakness and realised that he would never be truly happy again, even with his new bride-to-be! All he could do was stammer, "I'm sorry, I'm sorry! Forgive me." He rushed from the room.

Zuìjìn felt bereft, and he finally knew the depths that Zì Qi would sink to. He could find out the exact details of the betrayal later; for now he had to think fast before the entire commandery and temple complex were weakened by Zì Qi's folly. Zuìjìn returned to his quarters knowing that he had to act quickly. He would have to risk all to fight Zì Qi; there could be only two outcomes, and he boiled with anger at the thought of his dishonest adversary. He entered a deep, contemplative state. He was a warrior primarily, but even he knew that there were forces far greater than the strongest warrior in the land. He wanted to seek advice from the right kind of force: a force of positivity! As he contemplated, a picture of his deceased parents came into his mind. His strong heart opened at the sight, and he felt a little vulnerable, just as he had been sometimes as a young boy. He didn't expect to see his mother standing beside his father because she had always been very much in the background, though Zuìjìn loved her dearly. To see them standing side by side with shining faces was wonderful to him! He was in awe and asked them if they could offer any help. As he mentally spoke, he bowed low in their honour. When he lifted his head it was as if he could hear their voices, though their lips did not seem to move.

"My son, we are most proud of you, but now you have to fight a greater battle, one you have never encountered before in the battlefields. There, men fight with honour; in this situation, there is none! There is only one option open to you: follow our guidance." Zuìjìn listened very carefully, willing to obey his parents even as they were in the spirit form. His father held out his hand to show Zuìjìn his sparkling topaz ring, a glittering jewel. Zuìjìn immediately recognised it. It was the same ring given to him by his mother on the death of his beloved father, who wished him to keep it safe. Zuìjìn had kept the ring in a safe place for a very long time; no-one knew of it.

"You know that ring was given to me by Governor Choi himself for services given. They don't matter now; his father and I were old friends. He told me that if ever I was in trouble, I should send the ring to him as a sign. He knew it was to be passed down to you."

"But father, will he remember it, and will he want to help me after Zì Qi poisons his mind against me?"

"Despite what you have heard about his mental state, we feel all will be well there. You have to give the ring to someone you know you can trust. Use your intuition, as you do on the battlefield. Truth is your armour now. Hold nothing back from the past now, including Péngyou's trouble on the border regions. Do not fight his treachery with the same! This is not hand-to-hand combat; things need to come out into the open. Go now with our blessings."

A light seemed to envelope Zuìjìn's parents, and then they were gone. He knew what he had to do! He went to the secret place in his quarters to retrieve the old silk box which held the treasured gift. He sent a silent prayer to his ancestors, and temporarily a vision of his parents came back into his mind. 'I will not dishonour you; I know what I have to do whatever the outcome, Father.'

CHAPTER 18

The Reckoning

ZUÌJÌN'S TRUSTED OLD FRIEND HAN was deep in thought that night regarding the desertion of Péngyou to Zuìjìn's opponent. Things had been so strange in the temple since the death of Commander Fú Wù, and he had listened to the stories of his governor's fragile mental state. He had always known Zuìjìn as an honest and honourable man, the favourite of Governor Choi. He felt that he had no choice but to wait until the governor had finished his period of mourning and observe how he appeared to his court.

The same night, as members of Kou slept, the Watchers entered our dream state, bringing an image of Zuìjìn's parents with them, and gave us instructions on how to help him. We were told to focus all our power onto the old ring that so much depended on. There was no time before our next meeting, and we had already observed closely the happenings inside and outside the temple.

Zuìjìn crept through the night towards the temple gardens in search of the servant Han's small dormitory. It was a dangerous move for him, as many guards patrolled the perimeter of the Temple of the Heavenly Bird. After a while, he came to the window of the room where Han slept. He faltered for a moment, not sure how to identify the sleeping figure he needed to make contact with. Then something strange happened: the box in his hand started to vibrate. Fearing that something was wrong, Zuìjìn opened it to find the topaz glowing! The phenomenon was caused by Kou's energy endeavouring to show him the way. Zuìjìn was momentarily stunned but held the box up to the open window, where its precious contents shone around a sleeping servant below the window to the right.

Zuìjìn had one serious obstacle: Han's sleeping neighbour. If he awoke and summoned help, all would be lost. Zuìjìn did not wish to startle Han, so he prayed again to his father while gazing at the topaz. He felt inclined to bring the ring a little closer to Han. On cue, Han seemed to stir quietly. He made no noise but stood up as if in a daze and turned to look out at the glowing ring. At the same moment, Zuìjìn beckoned to him to climb out into the garden. Han paused a moment but then obediently climbed out into the night air. Taking his arm, Zuìjìn led the old man away from the window so that they would not be heard.

Han gradually became more aware of where he was and was startled at seeing Zuìjìn. "Keep calm, my old friend. You know me, and you knew my father. This is his precious ring; given to our family by Governor Choi's father. It was to be used only in an emergency if his or my own life was in danger, and now my name has been dishonoured with a lie! It was to be sent to Governor Choi, who would know immediately that something was wrong." Zuìjìn looked straight into old Han's eyes, hoping to convey his truthfulness.

"There is much confusion at the moment, Zuìjìn. There have been whispers from Zì's followers that our beloved governor's mental health has deteriorated since Commander Fú Wù's death."

Zuìjìn's eyes were wide open now to the full extent of Zì's treachery, but still in the back of his mind was the nagging doubt that this could be true, in which case his plan of rescue would be in ruins. "Wait, Han; we only have his word for this. Zì has blackmailed Péngyou to turn against me; I thought he was my friend, but he has shown the depth of his weakness. My father and mother came to me in a dream; they feel that it is important that this ring reaches the governor safely, not just for my sake but for the sanctity of the whole temple and perhaps even Governor Choi's own life!" Together the pair gazed down at the topaz ring there in the darkness of the Temple gardens. With the influence of the Watchers standing with them unseen, they both knew that the ring must reach its destination.

Han returned the silk box to Zuìjìn, for he could not conceal it in his night attire. He took the ring, knowing full well the danger he was in, and climbed back onto his bedroll. But he would not sleep again that night; there was too much at stake!

Han rose some hours later. He meditated for a while with his companions, as was the custom. He needed a clear head and an inner strength if he was to fulfil his promise. He knew that the day had now dawned, which marked the end of Governor Choi's period of mourning, and no-one appeared sure of how their beloved governor would act. Such was the poisonous trail laid down by Zì Qi. There was the added problem of seeking an audience alone with the governor. He was quite used to being in attendance with others in Choi Yen Shù's personal quarters. Han decided that he could not formulate a perfect plan but had to act instinctively when the time was right.

Senior military figures, including Zì Qi, were among the servants summoned before their governor. All carefully watched him for signs of a disturbed mind but found only a thoughtful governor showing a peaceful disposition. Several in attendance were called to answer questions concerning the temple and any political changes that had occurred. After a while, Governor Choi's eyes rested on Han. "Come closer, my friend. Have you anything to report?"

Han slowly approached his master's grand chair, not sure how to continue. Then he noticed a silk scarf which had fallen onto the floor next to the chair. Immediately bending down to retrieve it, he whispered to the governor, "There is an emergency, Illustrious One; I need to speak with you alone urgently!"

Governor Choi seemed a little confused momentarily. To the onlooker it just seemed that the old servant was taking his time picking up something from the floor. Han straightened up and answered his governor's question, conducting himself in a calm manner as if nothing were amiss. "I am honoured and glad to see you again, Master. There have been a few changes, and you will be glad to know that my grandson Kèqi's wife has just given birth to twin boys."

The governor smiled, making much of the news. "You must tell me more; you must be very proud, Han. The rest of you leave me. I would like to hear more of Han's news!" Zì was irritated; he had hoped to speak with Governor Choi earlier. Now he would have to wait. *Never mind*, he thought. *All will come to me in good time.*

As the others left the room, the governor looked seriously at Han. "Has your grandson really produced twins?"

"Yes, Master. That is the only *good* news I have for you."

The leader's face darkened. "What is this, and what do you have there?"

Han produced the golden topaz ring, looking sideways for signs of recognition. Governor Choi's face gave little away, and he was silent for a moment. "I gave that ring to another old friend whom we both knew well."

"Yes, Master, and he passed it down to his son Zuìjìn; it is he who is now in trouble due to the treachery and poisonous lies of Zì Qi!"

The governor's eyes widened. "Continue."

Han then elaborated on the machinations of Zì during the period of mourning for Fú Wù. He left no stone unturned, telling the governor of the lies Zì had spread about him also.

"Master, even Zuìjìn was concerned for you at first, not knowing of the lies. But he found out later the full extent of Zì's dishonour to you and to the temple. I will lay my life on the line and say to you most humbly that I have looked into Zuìjìn's eyes and believe he is telling the truth."

THE FLEDGLING

Governor Choi stood up, his eyes ablaze with anger. "You do not need to convince me of his integrity; he is as his father was which is why I chose him to replace Fú Wù! I wish every soldier and servant in this complex to be present tomorrow morning in the second courtyard. That includes Zuìjìn and Zì. My own family will be present. This whole vile episode will be put to rest, and the ceremony appointing the new general-in-chief be carried out immediately afterwards. I want the destruction of the disloyal to be wiped out fully by the appointment of a brave new commander."

And so it was. The members of Kou knew exactly what was about to happen when they received the summons for the following day. Zì, however, had no idea that his day of reckoning was about to happen. All he could think was 'more delays'; he was impatient to begin telling his governor a pack of lies.

It was a fine, bright morning when Governor Choi's many loyal subjects gathered in the courtyard, waiting and wondering why their governor had called such an important meeting. They had been given no indication of a ceremony to entrust Zuìjìn to the role of commander-in-chief, but whispers regarding Choi Yen Shu's mental state had spread like wildfire throughout the complex.

Governor Choi entered, followed on the platform by his family, the heads of all the military, the chief priests, his counsellors, his friends, and his honoured servants. Servant Han, of course, had a place on the platform but stood in the background. Zuìjìn and Zì Qi stood uneasily side by side.

Choi Yen Shu did not take to his chair at first. He stood tall in his orange and yellow robe facing the crowd, looking intently across the courtyard at all assembled there. The air was electric with expectation during the silence. Then he spoke. "I hear there has been some concern about my mental state and my well-being," he called out forcibly. Those watching hardly dared breathe. "During my period of mourning, there has been treachery afoot here. I am of *very* sound mind, I can assure you, and if anyone here wishes to challenge that remark, they should speak now!"

As he made this remark he looked across the crowd and then turned to those on the platform. Zì Qi began to feel fear; it was unthinkable that his plan could go wrong now. He had planned to put the blame on Zuìjìn for spreading fake rumours about the governor's health. Hadn't he been very careful to only suggest things here and there into the right ears without actually saying that his concerns for the governor were true? He felt that he had put a very successful smoke screen around the whole issue. Yet what was this?

Governor Choi shouted an order to soldiers standing by to seize and bring forward Zì. The crowd gasped as he was thrown at the governor's feet. Kou watched calmly and unmoved, for they knew that his treachery had come full circle.

"You see before you a dishonourable and treacherous man, not content with the honour I bestowed on him giving him the post of temporary general-in-chief. No, he was greedy and jealous of Zuìjìn, the intended commander. If I had judged Zì right for the position, I would have chosen him! I have been proven right. Zuìjìn, who has been put into a dangerous position and betrayed by his own close ally, did not stoop to Zì's low tactics. You see how your governor has chosen wisely!"

The colour drained from Zì's face. The crowd bowed their heads in agreement with their governor's truthful words. Zì Qi knew that all was lost; he would not be allowed to speak.

"You see how one man, who is clever no doubt, can manipulate others into believing him with the drip, drip, drip of his poisonous words. He has used his gift negatively; he could have used it against our enemies together with his colleague Zuìjìn. No! He chose to use his gift to try to destroy me and, in time, the Temple of the Heavenly Bird! He will now be executed before you. Let this be a lesson to all!"

Zì was ordered to kneel at the front of the platform. For one moment Zuìjìn thought that he would be asked to perform the execution. Although he should have felt elated, as an honourable man he felt sadness at man's inhumanity to man. But he accepted it right and proper that the execution should take place; that was the way.

To his surprise, Governor Choi called to Péngyou. "You come here next to your new master. You were being blackmailed by this man, but an honourable death would have been better than betraying an innocent man. You! You will be his executioner." Péngyou shook as he drew his sword. He knew that he had to endeavour to keep his hands steady to behead Zì Qui in one swift action. He called out to his spirit ancestors, "I have betrayed my best friend." Thinking of Zuìjìn, he found enough anger within to overcome his fear and do the deed. He struck once, and it was done!

"Now go from my kingdom and do not return." The governor's words were also directed at Zì's other close allies, and they were sent out with nothing, not even horses. "No-one in my province will feed or offer shelter to these men; let the word go out!"

All were stunned at how close Zì had been to carrying out his plan. They watched as the remains of Zì were cleared from the platform and replaced by items of a ceremonial nature. "I have brought forward the time for the appointment of a new commander-in-chief to now – right now! After the stench of the betrayal of Zì and his followers, only a positive act can purify this complex." Governor Choi sat down, and the chief priest, the grand masters, and several military figures stepped forward.

A slightly dizzy Zuìjìn was told to step forward too. He was a disciplined soldier and composed himself without the help and influence of Kou. Sacred bells gently rang out; the air was filled with fragrance, and the full ceremony was played out, putting the true commander-in-chief in his rightful position. The rest of the crowd were awestruck at the spectacle.

"Behold my new General in Chief," Choi shouted and we all cheered. As Commander Zuìjìn knelt before him, the governor motioned to him to stand and signalled to his chief priest to come. He took the topaz ring from the priest's hands and placed it onto Zuìjìn's finger. "From now on to signal a new beginning, at every ceremonial occasion you will wear your father's ring. You have earned it." A new chapter had begun.

CHAPTER 19

Home

TIME PASSED, AND THE DAY-TO-DAY work in the Temple of the Heavenly Bird continued on in much the same way as before. We, as members of Kou, continued to support Governor Choi Yen Shu from the shadows. He was, as always, oblivious to our work and was able to continue in his role well into his old age.

At the end of one particularly testing day in the birthing room, I strolled back through the temple passageways and began to recognise a familiar feeling of unease stirring inside of me. I expected a new development; my emotions were a little too much in evidence for the issue to be a political one. Halfway through my journey, I could see Master Noih approaching from the other direction.

"Ah, Su Ling, I have been looking for you. I need to speak with you; this room is empty." He motioned me to a door nearby which I knew led to a small anteroom used sometimes by scribes of the temple. We entered, and I waited patiently to hear his news. He pulled out from his sleeve a small scroll and offered it to me. I did not question this and accepted it.

"You have in your hands a message from your eldest sister. It was delivered by a merchant who has only today had the opportunity to deliver it, so there has been a time delay. I will leave you to read it. As to your request *after* reading the message; the answer is yes again, and I will see you tomorrow regarding it."

He left me alone in the room staring down at the scroll, feeling uneasy about its contents. Of course, the master always knew ahead of time about certain events which inevitably proved to be just as he predicted. So mention of my 'future request' came as no surprise to me. I had yet to discover what the request would be! I unrolled the parchment and studied its message.

> *My dear sister,*
> *I hope with all my heart that you receive this message, as I fear it will be my last to you. I have been ill, and just writing this has been quite a considerable feat for me. I know my passing is close, and I need you to understand exactly how things have been here in the family.*
> *I have had to try to take the place of our dear mother since her passing. In addition to raising our little sister, Ha Chang, looking after the home, and feeding our father and brothers, I have also been expected to work long hours in the fields. I am sorry to have to tell you that I learnt the awful truth, even before our mother became ill, that I was also expected to fulfil her wifely duties of an intimate nature for*

Father. Ha Chang and our brothers became more aware of this situation after Mother's passing, but they have been too frightened to say anything to Father. Apart from considering taking my own life, I have found no way out of my private hell. If not for my concern for Ha Chang, I may not have cared much for my own life.

For some considerable time, I have managed to protect her from Father. As I became ill, I feared that all would be lost and that she would no longer be under my protection, but a saviour appeared in our village in the form of a young man who fell deeply in love with Ha Chang. He is unusually kind, and I could see the love developing in Ha Chang's heart. Father watched them and became increasingly angry at the new development. He felt that her place was with him and our brothers. One day when he was working in the fields, I crept out and, keeping out of sight, found my way to where the young man was at work.

"I have very little time, Chao. Please listen!" I explained my fears for Ha Chang, and his face darkened with deep sorrow and anger. I pleaded, "There is only one thing we can do: Ha Chang must go far away from here."

Chao agreed, and I promised to help them. And so with provisions that I had gathered for them, they prepared to leave secretly. The tears flowed as we parted. Ha Chang did not want to leave me to my fate, but I made her go. Of course, Father was enraged and beat me severely for allowing this to happen. I could not work for him for days, and they had to cope with my chores the best they could. It has brought me near to my passing, Su Ling, but I just wanted to reassure you that our little sister is safe. I send my blessings to you. I believe that one day we will meet in another place.

Your sister Lái

Tears fell down my cheeks, and I realised then why I had felt uneasy all those years before when Lái had come into the courtyard to bring Chuntian the news of our mother's passing. I had seen a great change in her then, but I did not want to give thought to what might have happened to her. She was not given the honour of working for Governor Choi as she was expected to. I wept long and hard, as I had for my Wu Fang and my Rènshi. Clutching my scroll and my little Tóngshì, I made my way back to our living quarters. My colleagues were very kind and sympathetic to me when I returned.

The following morning I was sent for. I was summoned to Master Noih's room, and I realised what my request to him would be. Master Noih told me that yes; a funeral for my sister had taken place in my village. Just as before; I was informed too late.

So again, the following day I found myself outside the main gates of the compound laying sweet flowers from the temple garden in front of the shrine where I had laid the same for my mother. Once more I lit a candle, this time for my poor Lái. I knew I would never return to pay homage to my father or brothers. My loved ones had all gone. On many nights my Mother and Lái came to me in my dreams, looking young again, and happiness shone out from them. Together we walked hand in hand through fields and gardens full of jasmine and sat beside rippling streams, talking and laughing. I woke in the morning longing to dream of them again. The dreams continued for a while until one night I knew I must bid them farewell and let them go on in peace.

One morning we all awoke together: Niang, Héshi, Ci, Meirén, Wèi Wèi, and I. We looked at each other in a calm but quizzical way. We had just completed our morning preparations when a knock came at the door. "Enter," Niang called out.

Li Jing stood in the doorway. "You are all excused from duties today. A meeting of Kou has been called; it will take most of the day. When you are ready, we will proceed." I thought Li Jing had a strange air about him, which told me that a change was about to take place.

We met our other colleagues in the passageway and passed through the Doorway of Illusion together. The Watchers were already there waiting for us. After the meeting had been opened in the usual fashion, we sat silently and expectantly, waiting for what was to come. Shen and Jing smiled down at us and merged together as one. The warmth and the love they exuded that day surpassed any they had offered us before. "Today we have some important news for you, my friends. We have encountered many dangers together working and supporting our governor, even though he has been unaware of this. Very soon he and his soldiers and servants must work to protect themselves, for we are moving on." Stunned, we sat and waited for them to continue while endeavouring to control ourselves and the energies around us.

"In a short while, we shall be leaving the temple to go back to our spiritual home together. We will not grow any older in this incarnation." Master Ma Sing sighed gratefully at this news. "Today will be spent preparing you all for the passing, which will be joyful, not painful. We all have three days left here after today, time to say your good-byes for now and leave kind words or gifts with those you are particularly fond of. People will be a little bemused, but you cannot tell them what is to happen, and you are not to concern yourself with how your absence will or will not be noticed. We will leave in three days' time from this room; we will assemble early in the day. But now we must prepare."

The sacred secrets of how we were prepared and what our instructions were will never be told. The next day in the birthing room, I considered deeply what items I would leave behind for old friends and colleagues. Many of the old physicians had either retired or passed on, leaving in charge slightly younger men who, while still following the old tried and trusted ways, had been a little more open to subtle suggestions to changes in their approach to medicine and to their patients! There was still a long way to go, so I thought of leaving some manuscripts for the head physician, hoping that he would at least consider some of my own conclusions. Then my thoughts moved to dear Tutor Chéng. I would try to find time the next day to see her in person, if circumstances permitted it. I decided to write specifically for her that night, and when I put pen to paper words flowed from my heart.

Dear Tutor Chéng,
We remember with warmth those who have affected our lives by their presence. Such people may

never come to know how they have touched the hearts and minds of those who have been in their care.

You, my dear tutor, are one such special soul, and your kindness will always be remembered.

I hope you will honour me by keeping this small gift, as I honour you.

From your ever-grateful pupil,
Su Ling

That night before sleep my eyes filled with tears again as I thought of those words. But this time they were not tears of sadness.

The following day I sought an audience with Master Noih and was given his blessing to take my gift to Tutor Chéng. A guard was appointed to take me out of the temple, and we crossed the second courtyard together. There were soldiers going about their duty in the commandery, and my mind went back to my Wu Fang standing in his armour ready to fight. Instead of an ache, I just felt a sense of satisfaction as we crossed towards the gate and entered into the first courtyard with its workhouses full of merchants and farmers engrossed in their trading. We came to the steps of the workhouse where Tutor Chéng spent her working day. My mind went back to the day I arrived as a child waiting at the bottom of the steps as Madam Shu came down to collect me. There would be no gift for her, though she had performed her duties adequately. I was just eager to see my Tutor Chéng once more before I left.

Tutor had been informed of my arrival, and as we climbed

the stairs and entered, my heart leapt as I saw her waiting for me with a radiant smile on her face. "Su Ling, my dear, my little star." She was of course much older then but just as beautiful as I remembered. Of course, *her* beauty shone from within.

"I have very little time, Su Ling. How can I help you?" With difficulty I tried to act in a calm manner, spinning a tale of being given instructions to meet someone in the courtyard outside. As I was passing, I said, I had thought of her and wondered if she would please accept a small gift from me. Her smile faltered for a moment as she studied me. She regained her composure and smiled, accepting my gift with gratitude. She stepped forward to hug me and whispered in my ear, "Blessings go with you, my child." Then she was gone. We made our way back down the steps and through the courtyards to the temple. This time I had a heavy heart.

That evening as we discussed our gifts in the communal area, we all realised that our closest friends were fellow members of Kou, so there would be no need for anymore gifts. But my thoughts strayed to the young girl who was my replacement in the large birthing room for the poorer women. I knew nothing about her; I didn't even know how or when she used the potions I had sent her. I decided that on the third and last day I would leave her my manuscripts on anatomy and herbs and their uses.

I collected my papers and entered the birthing room with all its hustle and bustle. There were old birthing mothers hurrying backwards and forwards as always. I made my way to the corner of the room where my bench stood beside the shelves of potions and small dead creatures. I saw her return ahead of me, so I stopped for a moment to watch her. She was carrying a new batch of herbs and plants, which she laid on the bench in front of her. She was studiously reading a small fragment of paper and looked concerned. I approached her, and she looked startled. "I am Su Ling, your predecessor; I used to work here in the corner."

"Oh, thank you for sending me your potions, Su Ling. I am Wèi Chéng, and I am trying to mix my own; I have had a little success."

Her voice trailed off; she obviously felt that she had a long way to go to produce effective potions. I could not tell her of the mystical side of making potions, so I just said, "Go about your work with love for your patients. Please accept these manuscripts as a gift; they will prove invaluable to you, Wèi Chéng."

Her eyes lit up at such a prize. She bowed low to me and said, "How can I ever thank you?"

"Just remember what I said: have compassion for your patients." I left the room feeling that my decision to leave my manuscripts with her was the right one.

The following morning was the momentous day. We all woke early, saying little to each other. After our morning ablutions, we sat in a circle in our social area. We held hands in the spirit of womanhood and began to meditate, as we had been instructed to do. As we came out of our meditative state, there was complete silence in the room. Eventually we heard a tap on the door. Surprisingly, Niang rose and opened the door to Li Jing standing on the threshold. Niang rarely opened the door unless it was a time of great importance. "The time has come; follow me," Li Jing half whispered. Silently, we filed out of our living quarters for the last time. I closed the doors and momentarily glanced at the plaque on the wall of the beautiful turquoise bird.

We followed Li Jing down passageways until we stood before the Doorway of Illusion once more. The masters and priests were already there waiting for us. Nobody said a word; we just stepped over the threshold together. There waiting for us were the Watchers, whose smiles held a particular poignancy that day. Seeing us all in our places, they merged once more, becoming as one. The warmth and shining emanating from them was spectacular, a sight to behold. They addressed us.

"My dear friends, before we cross over, there are one or two things to remember. First, we wish to thank you for working with us through some very difficult times; we are most honoured. You are not to concern yourself with others who may or may not notice your absence. Let the world worry about worldly matters; we have other work to do. Following our lead, we will all pass through into the spirit world together. Once through to the other side, each of you in turn will then go forward alone to be welcomed by those waiting to greet you." We all nodded and bowed to acknowledge our magnificent teachers. Silence ruled again, and there was a complete air of calm and readiness.

The Watchers turned around. There was a quickening of vibrations in the room, and the wall in front of us began to dematerialise. With The Watchers leading us, we stepped through into the spiritual realm from whence we came.

I was at first almost overcome by the brightness of the shining colours before me, and then through a haze there seemed to be a throng of people ready to welcome us home. One by one the masters went forward to be greeted, followed by Li Jing and the priests. Then Niang was the first woman to walk out. Each in turn, we stepped forward: I volunteered to be the last to go.

As I stepped forward holding on to my Tóngshì, I could see smiling faces everywhere clapping and welcoming me as if I had achieved some very special honour! As I walked along, some of the faces began to look familiar to me, but I couldn't quite place where I had seen them before. But there was no mistaking the small group at the end waiting to welcome me. Mother and Lái were waving, both looking younger and fit and incredibly happy. Standing next to them was my own Wu Fang and our dear Rènshi as a young man. I cannot even begin to describe the joyous reunion, for there are no words to match the experience. As time passed I knew that my own family and many others there had been with me forever. The *honour* was, and is, truly mine.

"And that is my story, my dear." We sat quietly on the bench in the garden listening to the rippling water and the birds calling to one another. There was a sweet smell of blossoms in the air. I closed my eyes, breathed in the perfume, and was lost in my own thoughts.

"There are so many questions I have Su Ling," she gracefully held up a hand to stop me. "Most of your answers can be found when you look within my child, but for now it is time to go back." We rose, and as she held my hands I could feel myself drifting backwards. I woke in the familiar surroundings of my bedroom with the sun pouring through the curtains. In the distance, I heard the familiar sound of a lone bird singing sweetly.

FINI

ABOUT THE AUTHOR

C K Osborne is retired, has a son and daughter, and lives with her husband in England. She has worked for a children's charity and the local government Youth Service.

Her interest in ancient mystery stories and spiritual themes led her into the practice of meditation. She was inspired to write 'The Fledgling' after receiving the drawing of a Chinese woman from a psychic artist.

Printed in Great Britain
by Amazon